Conspiracy of Silence

Other Suspense Novels by Martha Powers

Bleeding Heart
Sunflower
Death Angel

Romance Novels
(written as Martha Jean Powers or Jean Paxton)

The Kissing Bough
False Pretenses
The Runaway Heart
Double Masquerade
The Perfect Fiancée
The Grey Fox Wagers
Divided Loyalty
Gazebo Rendezvous
Proxy Bride

Conspiracy of Silence

A Novel

Martha Powers

Longboat Key, Florida

FIRST PAPERBACK EDITION 2015

This book is a work of fiction. Names, characters, places, and incidents either are the products of the author's imagination or are used fictitiously. Any resemblance to actual events or locales or persons, living or dead, is entirely coincidental.

ISBN: 978-1-60809-160-7

Published in the United States by Oceanview Publishing,
Longboat Key, Florida
www.oceanviewpub.com

2 4 6 8 10 9 7 5 3 1

PRINTED IN THE UNITED STATES OF AMERICA

To Matt Powers
Who has given us great pleasure and joy
and makes us proud to have him as our son

and

To Margaret Szczepaniak
Who has brought humor, compassion,
and happiness to our family

MIRROR IMAGE

Lights play across the surface of her face
She looks within, seeing only flat planes and
 deeply etched crevices
The years are there but she cannot define the moments
 when each line was carved
She thought she would recognize a turning point,
 a crisis, an epiphany
Baby roundness is gone
Where is her heritage, her past?
Her destiny lies hidden, shrouded in the shadows
Her need to know a deep ache
No answers here
Only more questions

—Jean Christy

Conspiracy of Silence

Prologue

Clare Prentice sat on the edge of the examination table, the blue hospital gown tied at her neck. Her fingers folded the edge of the gown in pleats where it lay across her thighs. She shivered as the air vent above her came on, and she pulled the gown closed where it gaped against her bare back.

Although she was in the office for her scheduled physical, she was also waiting to hear the results of the needle biopsy. Ever since she found the lump, all she could think about was the death of her mother two years earlier of breast cancer. She didn't know how much heredity played in the disease, but she had to admit that there was a leaden feeling in her stomach when she thought about it.

She twisted the engagement ring on her finger, trying to concentrate on happier thoughts, but fear crowded out any belief in the future. She was sorry she had insisted on coming alone after Doug had volunteered to come with her. Perhaps it was her need to feel in control that had made her refuse his support. In five months they would be married and then she would feel that he should be at her side, but for now she felt her medical problems were her own to solve.

She'd waited a year after her mother died before she accepted Doug's proposal. He'd been so patient, but now that she had agreed he wanted to move ahead so quickly that at times she balked. She had agreed to the big wedding even though she would have preferred something much more private. His mother had explained, since Clare had no family to provide for her, she and Doug's father wished to welcome her into the Kitridge clan in great style.

She wondered what her mother, Rose, would have thought of the lavish arrangements. Rose hadn't been pleased when she started dating Doug. She disapproved of the public lifestyle his family lived, and was clearly upset after Clare's picture appeared in the newspaper when she accompanied him to some society function. Clare hoped Rose, despite her grumbling, would be looking down on her with approval on her wedding day.

Footsteps sounded in the hall and Clare straightened up as the door opened. Dr. Paula Craig squinted over her bifocals as she bustled into the room.

"You look like the living dead." Dr. Craig dropped Clare's medical folder on the desk and settled on the stool. "I don't mean to make light of this, but I can see you've worked yourself into a real panic. I have all your tests here and you're fine. You're absolutely fine."

Clare didn't realize she was holding her breath until she heard the whistling sound of her exhale. "Are you sure?"

"What kind of a doctor do you think I am?" the older woman grinned as she brushed a hand across her close-cropped gray hair. "Of course I'm sure. I've looked over all the reports. Mammogram, ultrasound, breast MRI, and the needle biopsy. You have nothing to worry about."

Clare sagged, pressing her knees together to keep her legs from shaking. It took a moment before she could speak.

"You're right, Dr. Craig. I've been imagining the worst. I remember what mother went through and I was just plain scared."

"I suppose you couldn't help but think about Rose. She died so young. Fifty-seven. But in your case the news is all good." She reached out and patted Clare's knee. "You'll make a beautiful bride and if you keep up your healthy lifestyle you'll live to be a crabby old lady like me. When's the wedding?"

"In July." Clare could feel the joy beginning to seep back into her body as she thought about the possibility of a full life ahead with Doug.

"Five months. That's good. Before you get married I recommend you do a little research into your family history. It would be good to know if there are any medical issues in your background."

"That could be hard," Clare said, biting her lip. "My father died before I was three and I have no memory of him at all. Neither he nor my mother had any family that I know of."

"I don't mean your father and Rose, dear," Dr. Craig said. "You need to look into the medical history of your biological parents."

Chapter One

An hour after leaving the expressway for a series of two-lane asphalt highways, Clare Prentice drove through an opening in the trees above Grand Rapids, Minnesota. Accustomed to the bustling life of Chicago, she had been apprehensive about her arrival in such an isolated area. The picturesque view of the houses nestled along the shoreline and the businesses lining the edges of a park came as a pleasant surprise.

She drove slowly down the hill, pulling into a parking space in the center of the town. Her hands gripped the steering wheel as she stared through the windshield at her surroundings.

The park was a lovely rectangle facing the lake. A roped off section of water indicated the swimming area and on the sand was a tall wooden lifeguard platform with white slatted chairs, red and white buoys, and a Jet Ski anchored at the shoreline. Brick walkways crisscrossed the park. Benches, a fountain, and a small playground added to a sense of tranquility and peace.

The main street ran in a U-shape along three sides of the park. At the east end was the City Hall and the police station, combined in a venerable but well-kept building. Beds of red, white, and hot pink impatiens softened the otherwise austere exterior of the beige brick. Stores and office buildings faced the lake and at the west end of the park was the Grand Rapids Public Library.

Clare rolled down the car window, smiling at the sound of the children playing on the beach. The water looked inviting after her long drive. She'd considered flying but had decided to drive and enjoy the changing scenery as she drove north. When she left, it had been hot in Chicago, but the end of July was much more pleasant in northern Minnesota.

Nothing looked familiar.

Until that moment Clare hadn't realized how much she had counted on some sign of familiarity, a sense of déjà vu perhaps, which would indicate she had come home. She closed her eyes and focused on the rise and fall of her abdomen as she concentrated on her breathing. Her fingers loosened their grip on the steering wheel and the muscles across her back relaxed against the car seat.

And so it begins, she thought as she got out of the car and stared up at the library. The building was massive, towering over everything else. It was a square, three-story building with triangular front sections on each side. On the second floor, rounded window arches flanked each central section on the four sides. The reddish beige brick glowed warmly in the summer sun and the darker trim between floors and around the windows made each feature stand out distinctly. All in all, a most impressive building.

She brushed the travel wrinkles from her denim skirt as she walked through the park. The early afternoon sun pressed against the blue and white checked blouse. The breeze off the lake was welcome, cooling the sweat on her neck beneath the French braid. Every summer she swore she'd cut her hair, but somehow she put up with the inconvenience.

Doug had loved her long hair.

Her sandal caught on the rough surface of the brick sidewalk and she stumbled. She settled her purse strap more securely on her shoulder and glanced at her hand. Even though it had been two months since she'd broken her engagement, there was still a faint band of white around her finger. Perhaps as the mark faded, so would her misery.

Taking a deep breath, she straightened her shoulders and walked up the stone steps to the wide double doors.

Despite the old-fashioned look of the exterior, the inside was wholly modern. The interior walls had been replaced by glass partitions so that from the doorway, she could see into most of the rooms on the main floor. A wide stairway curved leisurely to the second floor. The loft area was open to view through spindled balustrades. Over the central foyer, mobiles of all shapes and sizes were suspended from the ceiling.

The soles of her sandals slapped softly as she crossed the cream-colored marble floor. A teenaged boy looked up expectantly from behind the information desk.

"I have an appointment with Mrs. Grabenbauer," Clare said.

The boy opened his mouth, but before he could speak, his eyes darted over Clare's shoulder. She turned to find a tall, white-haired woman bearing down on her.

"You must be Clare," the woman said, extending her hand. "One thirty. On the dot. I consider the courtesy of promptness a reflection of character. We should get along famously."

Since she knew Mrs. Grabenbauer was well into her seventies, Clare was surprised at the sprightly look of youth in the inquisitive blue eyes studying her. The woman's hand was softer than calfskin, the handshake firm and brief.

"Your directions left me with little chance to get lost. MapQuest couldn't have done any better."

There was a moment of silence as Mrs. Grabenbauer continued to eye her. Then as if satisfied, she turned on her heel and beckoned Clare to follow her toward the back of the library. They passed a row of offices until they came to a lounge area behind a glass-paneled door.

"Perhaps you'd like some iced tea while we chat a bit." Without waiting for an answer, Mrs. Grabenbauer pulled out a chair beside a small luncheon table. "Sit here and I'll get it."

Clare followed orders, grateful to have a moment to observe the woman who would be her landlady for the next few weeks. Although Clare was tall, Mrs. Grabenbauer towered over her. Six feet, was Clare's guess. Her figure was rather top heavy with wide shoulders, long arms, and a very full bosom. Despite her build, she moved with a stately grace, actions and gestures precise.

"Do you take lemon, sugar, or milk?"

"Just lemon," Clare said, reaching out for the glass of tea.

Mrs. Grabenbauer carried her own glass and a dish of lemon slices to the table. "Now tell me. How is my favorite niece Gail?"

"Since she's my best friend," Clare said, "I also know she's your only niece."

"Busted." Mrs. Grabenbauer let out a deep throaty chuckle. "I'm sorry my brother didn't have a dozen more like her. Bright, articulate, and full of fun."

"Despite Gail's working too many hours at the clinic, she still manages to out-party me on the weekends. I hope she told you that she's leaving next week for a vacation in Hawaii."

"Yes. We had a lovely talk on the phone." Mrs. Grabenbauer spoke briskly as if she'd decided it was time to end the social chitchat and get down to business. "I hadn't heard from her for a while and then she called to say she had a friend who needed a place to stay for a week or two and wanted to know if my guest cottage was empty. I'd had several offers this summer, but no one I felt comfortable renting to."

"I really appreciate your letting me take it on such short notice. Gail's pretty hard to resist when she gets an idea." Clare grinned. "I hope she didn't badger you on my behalf."

"Nothing I couldn't handle." The dry tone was in sharp contrast to the twinkle in her eyes. "She said you had gotten an interview with our local recluse Nate Hanssen. How did you manage that?"

"I work for a literary magazine in Chicago. Mr. Hanssen was the featured author at a fund-raiser for literacy that my editor attended. Apparently they hit it off and, even though he usually refuses to do interviews, he agreed to do this one."

"So that's why you've come to Grand Rapids?" she asked. "Somehow Gail made it sound more mysterious than that. I realize she has a tendency to be dramatic, but she said you'd explain everything when you got here."

For a moment Clare was silent, wondering what to say. She opened her mouth but no words came out. Taking a deep steadying breath, she tried again.

"I need your help to find out who I am." Clare could understand the surprise on Mrs. Grabenbauer's face because she was just as stunned by her own words. "I'm sorry for blurting that out. That's not what I intended to say."

Clare sat quietly as the older woman took a drink of her tea, studying her over the rim of the glass. She could feel the heat rise to her cheeks and knew that she was blushing. The awkward silence was broken when Mrs. Grabenbauer set her glass down with a sharp tap on the wooden table.

"First of all, Clare, I'd like it if you would call me Ruth. Since we will be neighbors for a while." She smiled at Clare's nod of acceptance. "Sometimes it is difficult to explain things and blurting them out, as you put it, is the best way. Since I now have an idea where we're heading perhaps you'd like to start at the beginning."

"My mother died two years ago." Try as she might, the emotions that she had experienced in the last several months surged. She swallowed several times and then she said, "Five months ago I discovered I was adopted."

Clare thought she had gotten used to the idea, but her throat closed and she was unable to continue. She took several sips of tea while she pulled herself together. Ruth leaned across the table and patted her arm.

"You had no idea?"

"None." Clare shook her head. "The doctor who told me thought I knew, since it had always been in my medical file. My mother, Rose, told the doctor when she first brought me to see her."

"Strange that your mother would tell the doctor and yet not tell you."

"Rose was thirty when I was born. I never questioned the fact that she loved me, but she was not a demonstrative sort of woman. Very private."

"But after she died, you must have had access to all her papers."

"Yes. There was the house and her will. Everything came to me. My name was on everything. Mother kept a very Spartan household. I used to tease her that we could be packed and out of town at a moment's notice." Clare laughed but it was not a humorous sound. "Now I begin to wonder if that wasn't partially true."

Although there was a question in Ruth's eyes, she didn't ask for an immediate explanation. "Birth certificate?"

Clare pushed her chair back and rose to her feet. She walked across to the window and looked out at the park. It was still hard to talk about something that hurt so badly.

"I had one. There were several notarized copies in her safety deposit box. It said I was her child. If she had adopted me legally in Chicago, the official birth certificate would show that she was the mother. When I began checking the details, I couldn't find verification for any of the information on it. The hospital listed had no record of my mother and none of my being born there. On the day listed as my birth date, three children were born. All three were boys."

"Well, that bites."

The slang term amused Clare and she turned back toward Ruth. She could read the empathy on the older woman's face, and smiled through a sheen of tears.

"You're damn right it does."

"Anger is good, my dear. As the shrinks say, 'it's all a process.' Oftentimes there's truth in the most banal of psychobabble. I'm assuming there were no adoption papers."

"None."

"Could you trace back through your mother's information?"

Clare shook her head. She paced to the sink and back again. She felt better moving around. Her emotions about what had happened in the last few months had been bottled up. It was strange how comfortable she felt speaking to Gail's aunt.

"My mother's name was Rose Prentice. The birth certificate listed her date of birth and said she was born in Park Ridge, Illinois. When I checked into that, I couldn't find any record for that date or name. It was as if neither my mother nor I existed."

"Extended family?"

"It's funny, but when you're a kid there's so much you don't question. It just is. We had no actual family in the Chicago area. I called your brother, 'Uncle Owen,' but I knew he wasn't a relative. Gail and her brothers were like cousins so I really never felt any lack of family."

"Your mother must have had friends you could talk to."

"Not really. My mother didn't socialize much. She went to PTA meetings and knew people at church and work, but there was no one you would consider a close friend. At the time it didn't seem strange. It's only now when I look back I begin to see how isolated she was."

"Marriage license?"

"I didn't find one. Since my father was dead, their anniversary was never celebrated so I really had no idea when or where she was married."

"When did your father die?"

"Mother said he died in a train accident when I was three. No details, just said he was dead." Clare could feel her mouth tighten at the words. "It wasn't that she made it seem like a secret. If she had, I might have been more curious. It was just a fact. Mother never talked about the past. When I asked her about her childhood, she said it was boring and changed the subject."

"Didn't that seem unusual?" Ruth asked.

"No. Mother wasn't very talkative."

"I know people like that," Ruth said, "and I've watched how my niece and her brothers interacted with their parents. A child gets a sense that a subject is off limits. It's one of those nonverbal signals that always intrigues me. I never had children so my knowledge comes solely from my observations."

"Gail said you were very perceptive."

"That's because I spoiled her. That's the joy of being an aunt. None of the annoyances of raising children. When they misbehave, you just pack up their bags and send them home. And if they grow up to be bright, articulate adults it's an added bonus in your life."

Ruth paused and stared across at Clare.

"Did it occur to you that you might be Rose's illegitimate

daughter and she just told the doctor you were adopted to cover her shame?"

Clare nodded. "Actually that was my original thought. It would have explained why she changed her name and said my father was dead. I asked the doctor about that possibility and she went through my mother's medical files. She had had a miscarriage, but had never had a live birth."

There was silence for a moment, and then Ruth asked, "So why have you come to Grand Rapids?"

"I think my adoptive mother might have lived here." Clare opened her purse and took out a picture in a small wooden frame. "This is a picture of my mother. I only have a few. She didn't like having her picture taken."

She set it on the table in front of Ruth.

"Gail said you were born and raised here in Grand Rapids. Does she look familiar at all?"

"I only lived here in Grand Rapids until my parents divorced. Then I moved to Duluth with my mother. My brother stayed here with my father. Except for occasional visits, I didn't come back here until after my husband died ten years ago."

Ruth picked up the frame and concentrated on the face of the woman in the picture. She pursed her lips, then sighed and shook her head.

"I don't believe I've ever seen her before. You think she was from Grand Rapids?"

"She might have gone to school here." Clare reached into the pocket of her denim skirt and brought out a plastic bag. "When I went through her jewelry box, I found this."

She opened the bag, placing a ring on the table in front of Ruth.

"It's a class ring from Grand Rapids Senior High School. At first I thought of Michigan, but when I did some research I found it was Grand Rapids, Minnesota."

Ruth picked up the gold ring with the gold Indian in profile, turning it from side to side to examine it.

"Nineteen sixty-two. My brother went to Grand Rapids, but he graduated five years earlier," she said.

"Gail's father? The judge?"

"Yes," Ruth said. "And in nineteen sixty-two, I was thirty, married for six years, and living in Duluth. Lordy where does the time go? So you think this was your mother's ring?"

Clare shook her head. "According to my mother's birth certificate, she would have been fifty-nine this year. She would have graduated in nineteen sixty-five or nineteen sixty-six. If the ring is hers, then she might be four years older. To me she always seemed old. To look at Rose you wouldn't be able to guess her age."

"So it could be hers." Ruth placed the ring on her finger. It was too large. "But at a guess I'd say it was a man's ring."

"Mother had large hands," Clare said, her voice defensive.

Ruth looked inside the band of the ring. "There are no initials or serial numbers to give a clue as to ownership. Without one or the other, we couldn't trace it through the manufacturer."

Clare sat down at the table again, staring in dismay at the ring in the palm of Ruth's hand. "It's the only clue I have."

Ruth placed the ring back in the plastic bag and handed it to Clare. She patted her hand.

"And a very good clue, it is. What if your father gave it to her? Do you have any information about him?"

Clare tightened her fingers around the ring. "No. His name, John Prentice, was on my birth certificate, but none of the information checked out." She sighed. "I spent endless hours on the Internet going through adoption Web sites. Finally one of the people I'd been corresponding with said that I might have been a black-market baby, and that was why none of the information was valid."

"What about your mother's maiden name? It would have been on your birth certificate."

"The name listed as my mother's maiden name was the same as her married name. Prentice."

"Did you try the hospital birth records in Grand Rapids?"

Clare nodded. "Yes. No records for either Rose Prentice or Clare Prentice. As far as the world is concerned, we never existed."

Silence filled the room. Clare could see that Ruth was as mystified as she had been for so many months. She rubbed the back of her neck as she felt a headache form. Ever since she'd discovered she was adopted she'd been searching for answers and she was exhausted, both mentally and physically.

"There's another clue to the fact your mother might have come from this area," Ruth said. "Did she give you that necklace?"

Clare automatically put her hand up to cup the pendant around her neck. Her fingers stroked the polished surface of the stone heart. "Yes. She gave me the necklace for my sixteenth birthday. How did you guess?"

"I'm almost positive that the stone is Binghamite. It's a form of quartz found only up here in the Iron Ranges. It's pretty rare to find any now that the mines are closed. Your stone is particularly lovely since it has so many detailed markings in gold and brown. There's even some green."

"It's my favorite piece of jewelry." Clare closed her fingers around it. "Rose said it belonged to her sister who had died."

"Well, it sounds like it's another piece of the puzzle. This will take some work to resolve." Ruth sat forward in her chair. "I'm glad you've come here. Libraries are the perfect places to do research."

"What do you have in mind?" Clare felt a glimmer of hope at the sparkle in the soft blue eyes of the older woman.

"Let's start with the class ring. It was either Rose's or was given to her by a graduate. We have the yearbooks for Grand Rapids and we'll start with nineteen sixty-two and see if we can find someone who looks like Rose. I realize it's a slim hope, but it's at least worth a try."

"And it's someplace new to start." Clare sighed. "I'm ready."

Ruth looked surprised. "We don't have to begin this minute. You've had a long drive up from Chicago. Don't you want to get settled in first?"

"No. I stopped last night in Wisconsin so that I could get here early. I've had lunch and I'd just as soon get started."

Ruth stood. "All right then. Come out to the study area and I'll get the yearbooks."

Clare followed the older woman out of the room. She liked the openness of the main floor of the library and smiled up at the mobiles swinging above the desk area.

"The high school art class studied and made mobiles this year and we offered to display them. It's been such a success that we're hoping to do it every year." Ruth tilted her head back. "There's something so enjoyable about watching the movement and trying to figure out how they created the balance."

Ruth pointed her to an alcove by the far wall, and then disappeared between the stacks of books. The rounded windows looked out on the park and some of the shops along the street where people walked in the late afternoon sunlight. Clare settled herself in one of the cushioned armchairs and stared outside. For the first time in many months, tension wasn't constricting every muscle in her body. Perhaps it was sharing with Ruth some of the feelings she had suppressed since learning about her adoption. She had talked frequently with Gail over the last few months, but there was something steadying about talking with the older woman that made her feel as if she finally might be able to get some answers.

It was totally disconcerting to wake up one morning to discover the life she had been living was a sham. It had shaken her badly not to know who she was and where she had come from. And made her angry.

The anger brought guilt. No matter the circumstances behind her adoption, she should have felt grateful to Rose for raising her. Although they weren't wealthy, Rose had sent her to excellent schools, and fed and clothed her. Perhaps she was not the most demonstrative of mothers, but she sat stolidly beside Clare's bed when she was sick, played games with her, celebrated all the holidays, and attended all the school functions. Although Rose wasn't social, she encouraged Clare to make friends. Rose had had many positive influences on her life, but Clare still blamed her for keeping such an important secret.

"Well, my dear," Ruth's voice broke into her reverie. "This ought to keep you busy."

Clare leaped up to take the stack of yearbooks from Ruth's arms and set them on the table.

"I've brought yearbooks from nineteen sixty-two to nineteen sixty-eight. Since we're not positive fifty-nine would be Rose's real age now, I figured we should at least start with the year of the class ring." She reached into the pocket of her dress and pulled out a magnifying glass, handing it to Clare. "This might help. Just take your time and don't get discouraged if you don't find any one who resembles her. People change. Different hairstyles, different clothes."

"What if I don't find anyone who looks like her, even a little?" Clare bit her lip, staring down at the books.

"There are other schools around Grand Rapids. She could have been living in Coleraine or Cass Lake, and dated a boy from Grand Rapids. All sorts of possibilities. Don't despair. It's two thirty now. I'll check on you shortly." With a bracing pat on Clare's shoulder, Ruth walked back to the front of the library.

Clare sat down in the chair. Her heart thudded noisily in her ears and she tightened her fingers around the black bone handle of the magnifying glass. For three months she had been searching and now when she had a real possibility of success, she was afraid that she would only find disappointment. Maybe some secrets weren't meant to be discovered. Tears clouded her vision and she blinked them away. Setting the magnifying glass on the table, she made a decision. She didn't have to do this. She had the right to change her mind. She didn't want to know; she wanted to go home.

As she reached for the strap of her purse, the white skin on her ring finger caught her eye. She had run away from her engagement and if she ran away again, where would she go? Where was home? Without knowing who she was, could she ever find her place in this world?

Her hand touched the topmost yearbook. Her fingers stroked

the suede-like cover, slightly gritty with dust. The title of the yearbook was *The Tomahawk*. She picked it up; surprised that it wasn't particularly heavy. She flipped to the back and checked the page count. One hundred sixty. She couldn't remember how large her own high school yearbook was.

Nineteen sixty-two. She thought back to her history classes and tried to remember anything she knew about that year. She'd just seen a biography about John Glenn whose birthday was in July. Forty-five years ago he'd orbited the Earth. The only other thing she could think of was that '62 was the year of the Cuban Missile Crisis. She was a big Kevin Costner fan, and had seen the movie *Thirteen Days* at least three times. She couldn't come up with any other events.

Clare opened the cover and began to flip through the pages, passing the pictures of the teachers and other sections until she came to the pictures of the students. Each of the seniors had his or her own fairly large picture, two to a page. There was a certain sameness to all of the students. The boys had short, slicked down hair, short sideburns, and faces turned either to the right or the left. They all looked neat and clean and, except for a few, uncomfortable. The girls looked fresh-faced with similar hairstyles and little makeup. Hair curled and usually parted on the side. There was an innocence to these girls from long ago that spoke of a different moral climate than Clare had grown up in.

After she'd made a brief survey of the pictures, taking in what she could of the group in general, she turned back to study each one. She skipped the boys entirely, focusing on the girls. She studied each face, checking eyebrows, teeth, and noses. When she had gone through each of the seniors without success, she picked up the magnifying glass and started on the smaller pictures.

It took forty-five minutes to get through the first yearbook.

Carefully, she placed it next to the original pile. She rubbed her eyes, trying not to think. Standing up, she walked across to the far wall where there was a water fountain. Her legs moved awkwardly, stiff from sitting almost motionless for so long. Her whole body ached. She would have to try to relax before she started on the next book. The water was refreshing and she returned to her chair, stretching several times before she sat down and reached for the next book on the stack.

Nineteen sixty-three. Fifteen years before she was born. She knew that was the year Pope John XXIII died and John F. Kennedy was assassinated, because Rose had worshipped both men and told Clare of the two events. She had always been convinced that there was some conspiracy that the two had died in the same year. Civil rights were being fought for in the South. Martin Luther King, Jr. delivered his "I Have a Dream" speech on the steps of the Lincoln Memorial in 1963. Beyond that she didn't know much about the year.

A half hour later she closed the cover with a sigh. Her eyes burned and her head throbbed. The faces had begun to blur after a while. Sometimes she thought she saw a resemblance in the smaller pictures of the underclassmen, but even with the magnifying glass she couldn't really be sure. Those she marked with a piece of paper so that she could find them again if necessary. She placed the book gently on top of the first one and quickly reached for the next yearbook before she could think better of it. An hour later she looked up as Ruth approached.

"By the look on your face, I can see it's not going so well," Ruth said as she sat down across from Clare. "You didn't think this would be easy, did you?"

The comment made Clare smile. "As a matter of fact, I did at one point, but that's long gone after . . ." She looked at her watch. "Almost three hours."

"I suspected you wouldn't get through the whole stack today. It's getting close to five. Why don't you start fresh tomorrow? I'm only staying another hour. When Gail told me you were coming today, I had already committed to a supper at one of the churches in town. It's always a lovely affair. Not knowing about your mission of discovery and the emotional toll it might have taken, I also made a reservation for you. Do you feel up to it? It would give you a chance to get some feel for life in Grand Rapids."

"I'd like that very much," Clare said. "And I don't mind waiting until you're ready to leave. I can do one more book before I lose my vision completely."

Ruth chuckled. "Gail said you were stubborn. I'll leave you to it. Come to the front when you're done."

She heaved herself to her feet and Clare reached for the next yearbook.

Nineteen sixty-six. Twelve years before she was born. She couldn't think of anything she knew about that year. She thought the Vietnam War was still going on, but she wasn't sure. This search, if it proved nothing else, proved that she should have paid more attention in her U.S. history classes.

Once more she opened the cover and began flipping through the pages. She was a third of the way through the senior class when she stopped, riveted by one of the pictures. Beneath dark hair and heavy dark eyebrows a young girl stared up from the page. The moment Clare saw the photograph she knew.

It was Rose, her adoptive mother.

Chapter Two

Rose Gundersen. That was her adoptive mother's name.

Gundersen not Prentice. Clare stared down at the picture, searching the face, trying to get used to the name. Gundersen. Gundersen. She repeated the name under her breath, rolling the syllables around in her mouth. Her heart beat strongly and her ears buzzed as if she were listening to an electric current. She didn't recognize the name, but was there any doubt that she had found Rose Prentice?

It was the eyebrows that had given her the first clue. She remembered, when she was a child, being fascinated by Rose's bushy eyebrows. Then as she got older, she wondered why her mother didn't have them trimmed. The girl in the picture was the norm for that age and time. Neither beautiful nor unattractive. She looked like most of the girls in the yearbook. The only difference that Clare could see was in the tilt of the head and the half-shuttered eyes that hinted at a sensuality that was surprising.

To Clare's eyes, Rose had seemed asexual. She had never done anything to enhance her looks. Clare had always thought that with a little makeup and her hair professionally cut, instead of braided and wound into a bun at the nape of her neck, Rose might have been a good-looking woman. Whenever Clare had suggested a new hairstyle or bought her a less-than-matronly dress, her mother would reject any attempt to "fancy" her up. It was as if she wanted to remain plain.

The second identifying clue was the mole on the left side of the girl's face, close to the hairline, just above her ear. Clare touched the picture, placing her finger on top of the mole. There was no question in Clare's mind that she had found Rose Prentice.

Once more she removed the framed picture from her purse. Holding it beside the yearbook photo, she could see traces of the girl reflected in the picture of her mother.

Although Clare realized she had just begun to plumb the mystery of her own identity, a jolt of excitement raced through her veins as she stared at the first piece of the puzzle. Her throat tightened and her eyes filmed, blurring her vision. Despite the tears, she could feel her mouth stretch in a smile.

Time stood still as she reveled in the disparate emotions that coursed through her body. Ever since she had learned of her lack of identity, she had been devoid of feeling, walled away behind a protective numbness that made her unable to feel anything except loss, anger, and a deep sense of betrayal.

Her fingers stroked across the page, and then, as if the tactile sensation had released her from a spell, she began to read the words beneath the picture.

Rose Gundersen
Still waters — Pin neat — Song bird

Predictions
She will marry soon.
She will win the Pillsbury Grand National
Recipe and Baking Contest.
She will become a famous singer.

Clare looked back at the picture trying to find some confirmation that this was the woman who had adopted her. Once more a wave of fury washed over her. So many lies and deceptions. She never knew that Rose could sing. It was a simple thing and yet it represented the total falsity of her life. It was apparent that singing was a major part of Rose Gundersen's life and yet Clare never knew that her mother was even musical. The only thing she had ever heard her sing was "Happy Birthday" and Rose had sung that grudgingly in a low monotone.

She shut the yearbook with an angry snap.

Tears streamed down her cheeks and she bent over to hide her anguish from anyone who might look her way. Her body vibrated with the hurt that spilled out along with her tears. The original heartache when she found out that she was adopted was nothing compared to the anguish she felt at this moment.

A gentle hand touched her shoulder. She sensed it was Ruth and was appalled that the woman should find her in such a state. She took a shuddering breath trying to stem the flow of tears. Ruth's hand moved back and forth across her back, offering comfort without intruding on her personal space. Calmness settled over Clare and after several minutes she was able to raise her head to give the older woman a weak smile.

She took the handkerchief that Ruth handed her, mopped her face, and blew her nose. Ruth removed her hand and once more sat down in the chair facing her. Back in control, Clare looked around, grateful that there was no one else close enough to witness her distress.

"It's a quiet time in the library," Ruth said. "Most patrons are home getting dinner ready. There's a meeting in the other room but that hasn't let out yet. I suspect once you've recovered you'll find you'll be ready for something to eat. Heavy emotions take a toll on the resources of the body. After a good cry I'm hungry enough to eat a horse, but of course I generally settle for a quart of mint chocolate chip ice cream."

Clare gave her a watery smile. "One of my favorites."

"I've got a gallon at the house that should get us both through the night."

Ruth sat at ease, not rushing Clare. Grateful for the chance to get over her emotional upheaval, she listened as the older woman talked a little bit about the library and how she'd spent her day. With a final sniff, Clare sat up and held out the open yearbook to Ruth.

"It's my mother. Rose Prentice is actually Rose Gundersen."

"Gundersen?" She cocked her head as if she was not sure of the pronunciation. When Clare nodded, she took the book and set it in her lap, staring down at the photo. "Rose Gundersen, indeed."

Wonder tinged her words and Clare smiled. "You probably didn't think I'd be able to find her. I know it's not the answer to my real questions, but at least it's a start. Maybe knowing her name I can work backward and find my biological parents."

Ruth looked across at Clare, studying her face before she looked back down at the yearbook. Her brows furrowed in concentration as she transferred her gaze back and forth. Her face was curiously blank of all expression and for a moment Clare wondered if she'd made a mistake.

"I'm sure it's her, Ruth. See how you can see the same eyebrows and the mole in Rose's later picture." She handed across the wood-framed photo.

"Don't panic, Clare. I believe you're absolutely right. This is definitely the woman you knew as Rose Prentice." She handed the frame back and closed the yearbook in her lap. Her long fingers stroked the raised green numerals on the cover. "Nineteen sixty-six. You were right that Rose would be fifty-nine this year. I'd say you've been stunningly productive for the short time you've been in town."

"Now that we know her name, I ought to be able to find out something about her and her family." In her eagerness Clare leaned forward in her chair. "Some of her people might still live here. I could contact them. Surely they'd agree to talk to me. And there might even be newspaper articles on the Gundersens that I could look up."

At Ruth's continued silence, she stopped talking and looked intently at the older woman.

"I know you're excited," Ruth said, "but I think you need to hold onto this discovery for a little while longer. You need to think about it before you do any more detecting."

Clare was taken aback by the cautionary tone in Ruth's voice. To her it had all seemed so simple. All she wanted to do was find out who she really was. She'd found her first clue and couldn't see any reason to wait to pursue the lead.

"What's there to think about?"

"There are always repercussions to one's actions. You've described an elaborate plan to give you and Rose a new identity. You need to think about the possibility that there might have been a good reason to keep your background a secret."

"I assume you're thinking that I'm illegitimate," Clare said. "That doesn't bother me."

"It might not bother you, child, but it might bother other people."

"You mean, my mother gave me away and might not want to be found?"

"Something like that. There could be other reasons. Complications that you know nothing about." Ruth reached across and patted Clare's hands, which were clenched together in her lap. "Trust me on this. You've been obsessed with this subject for months. Another day won't make any difference in the short run but could in the long run. Let's leave it for the moment. You can get settled in at the cottage and we'll go to the church supper and then you can come back to my place and we'll make a plan as to how to proceed. Does that sound reasonable?"

Clare gave a deep sigh. All of a sudden she realized that Ruth was right. She'd been living and breathing the anxiety of not knowing who she was and now that she'd found the first clue, she could feel all the energy that she'd been propping herself up with, draining out of her body. She leaned back in her chair, her body limp in reaction.

"Sorry. I think it all just hit me." She blinked her eyes to hold back another round of tears. "I've been running on adrenaline and now it's abandoned me."

"This has been a very rough time for you. You have no reason to apologize. You need to conserve some of your strength so that you can go at this with your mind clear and alert and with a definite plan of attack. I'm going to send you on ahead to the house so that you can get unpacked and rest a bit before dinner."

Still holding the yearbook, Ruth struggled to rise. Clare reached out to take the book.

"Let me hang on to this for a while," Ruth said. "I'm sure you're anxious to pour over it, but I need to follow procedures for taking reference books out of the library. I have things to do here at the library before I can go home. It'll go much faster if I don't have to worry about you. Us old broads have a good bit of stamina, but I have to admit I'd like to get out of here and have dinner. Besides, they always mutter if I work more than my allotted hours."

Reminded of the older woman's age, Clare felt embarrassed that she had been so focused on herself she had failed to consider Ruth.

"The mention of food has reminded me I haven't had anything since lunch. No wonder I'm hungry. Just give me directions and I'm out of here."

Still clutching the yearbook, Ruth walked Clare to the door. It had cooled off since she'd arrived in Grand Rapids. The sun was low in the sky and cast a reddish gold light over the scene. It was Clare's favorite time of night and she drank it in and could feel her body refreshing as she breathed in the oxygen-rich air.

"Just take this road around to the far side of the park and drive along the lake," Ruth said, pointing out at the street. "About a mile down you'll see a sign on the lakeside that says: HEART'S CONTENT. The number is 8378. You can't miss it. I put a key under the mat in front of the door of the guest cottage. It's five thirty now. Why don't you come over to the house around seven? Will that be enough time for you?"

"Sounds perfect."

With a wave of her hand, Clare started down the steps and walked to her car. She turned back as she unlocked the door, surprised to see Ruth still standing outside the door of the library watching her. Even at a distance, she could feel the intensity of the older woman's stare. With a final wave, she got in and started the car.

Pulling away from the curb, she drove past the library where

Ruth still held her vigilant pose. *She must think the city girl will get lost in the country*, Clare thought in amusement. She followed the road until it turned north, running along the edge of the lake. The road rose as it ran along a ridge above the houses that lined the lake. Private driveways turned off on either side of the asphalt. The houses were set well back, out of sight behind thick hedges and lilac and forsythia bushes.

She found it difficult to look for signs while she was enjoying the glimpses of the lake in the early evening light. Eventually she spotted the house number: 8378. A painted wooden sign swung between two carved posts. HEART'S CONTENT. A white picket fence separated the property from the road. Ruth's house looked surprisingly new. White aluminum siding and bright green shutters gave it a crisp appearance that blended well with the formal landscaping that surrounded the house. She turned into the driveway, pulling into the parking area beside the garage.

Directly ahead of her, flagstones led to a small cottage farther down the hill toward the lake. Trees and shrubbery blocked her view but the flowers along the path were so inviting she suspected no matter what she found in her week in Grand Rapids, she would enjoy her stay at Heart's Content.

Purse and computer bag on her shoulder, she pulled her travel duffel out of the trunk. Not knowing what she would need, she had brought an assortment of things, figuring she'd be ready for most contingencies no matter what the dress code in Grand Rapids.

The little cottage perched on a flat spot at the edge of Lost Lake. It was built of wooden clapboards, weathered to a silvery gray by many years in the harsh Minnesota winters. The only landscaping was a small patch of massed red impatiens on either side of the double steps up to the wrap-around porch. Setting the duffel down she reached under the braided mat for the key and unlocked the front door.

The door opened into the main room. The furniture was older, more of her mother's generation than her own. An overstuffed sofa and side chair were covered in a blue and gray plaid, faded but clean looking. The sofa faced a rough stone fireplace with a thick wooden mantel. A small television was perched on what looked to be an old cabinet-style phonograph player. Used to her own iPod, Clare smiled at the size of the musical oddity, wondering if it actually worked. A heavy mahogany rocker sat next to the fireplace. The back and seat cushions were upholstered in a cranberry-colored patterned material that might have seemed garish but was somehow welcoming.

On the right there was a counter with stools and behind that, along the wall, was a stove, dishwasher, and refrigerator all in an old-fashioned avocado green. A black microwave was the sole touch of modernity. The walls were wood paneled and the floors were hardwood with a few area rugs scattered around. On the left were two doors. One led to a bedroom and the other was open to show a fully appointed bathroom

Clare stared around the room and immediately felt at home. The place looked lived in. She would be comfortable here.

Sighing, she set her laptop computer on the counter along with her purse, and then crossed the room to the bedroom, smiling as she stood in the entrance. The bed was an old iron monstrosity with a patchwork quilt coverlet and a tumble of pillows. The lamp on the bedside table had a carved loon for the base and a tan woven lampshade. Loons dotted the green draperies that covered the window and there was a tall, weathered dresser on one side and a small closet on the other side.

Setting her duffel on the bed, she hung several items in the tiny closet, amused at the matching drapery, which served as a door. She set her shoes on the closet floor and put the rest of her clothes and toiletries in the dresser drawers. She smiled as she set her blue satin jewelry case on top of the dresser. It had belonged to Rose and she felt as if she were bringing it home.

Finished unpacking, she opened the draperies.

The lake shimmered in the reddish glow of the late afternoon light. At the edge was a small dock and beside that, pulled up on the shore, was an inverted wooden rowboat. The surface of the water was unruffled by any breeze, and the reflections of the trees and the clouds were clear as any mirror. Unlocking the window, she raised the sash, sniffing the fresh air as it filtered through the screen.

A noise in the other room brought her out of her reverie.

"Is someone there?" she called as she crossed the floor, back to the main room. At the sound of scratching, she moved to the back door that led to the lakeside of the porch. Opening the door she was confronted by a very large dog seated outside. Brown fur, slightly matted, puffed out around his body. His tail was thick, twitching back and forth across the porch floorboards. His big head was cocked to the side and she could swear he was studying her as if passing judgment.

"And just what do you think you're doing?" she asked.

He remained motionless, only watched as she approached. She held out her hand and when he made no aggressive move, stroked the top of his head, feeling the soft fur beneath the palm of her hand.

"Good boy. Or girl," she said. A slight breeze came through the open door, bringing with it the smell of wet fur and fish. "Whew. I think you could use a bath. I wonder who you belong to?"

Once more the dog cocked his head at the sound of her voice. As she gave him a final pat, Clare raised her head and took in the stark beauty of the lake and the homes nestled along the shoreline.

"It's quite a view, isn't it?" she asked the dog conversationally.

Flagstones led to the dock. She stepped around the dog and started down the path. With a long-suffering sigh at being disturbed from his rest, the dog lumbered to his feet and padded after her.

The dock was four feet square of bound-together logs, anchored solidly in place. There was a green plastic chair, tied by one leg with bright yellow nylon rope to a corner of the dock. She sat down in the chair and the dog sat beside her, his head resting against her knee. As she stared at her surroundings, she absently stroked the dog's head.

She thought about all she'd learned since she arrived in Grand

Rapids. She was somewhat stunned to find she'd actually discovered the identity of her adoptive mother. For five months she'd been searching and now she'd found a key piece of information. The question remained: how much more did she want to find out?

It had occurred to her as she drove toward Grand Rapids that a great deal of trouble had been taken to hide Rose's identity. She'd thought of various possibilities. Rose might have wanted a child so badly that she had somehow found a black-market baby to adopt. However, she had never seemed the kind of woman who wanted a child desperately. At her lowest point, Clare wondered if Rose might have kidnapped a child. Or did her real mother give her away?

"What do you think?"

She scratched the dog behind his ear. Her only answer was a thump of the tail on the dock and a wriggle of the hairy body. A metallic clink indicated he might be wearing a collar. Digging under the fur, she found a thin chain and turned it until she could read the tag attached. WALDO.

"Since I don't sense you're a stay-at-home dog by the smell of you, I think whoever named you has a sense of humor," she said. "Where's Waldo?"

Checking her watch, she decided it was time to get ready to go over to Ruth's. With a final scratch between the dog's ears, she pushed him away. One more glance at the lake, then she rose to her feet and walked up the flagstones to the cottage.

"Go on home, Waldo," she said firmly as she stepped onto the porch.

Without a backward glance, she went inside and closed the door. She washed quickly and put on fresh lipstick. With one more glance at her watch, she grabbed a corduroy jacket, suspecting it might be chilly when she returned. Leaving a light on in the living room, she put the house key in her pocket and went outside.

This time Waldo was sitting on the front porch as if he were waiting to escort her. Clare shook her head and followed as he slowly ambled up the flagstone path to Ruth's side porch. When she rang the bell, Waldo moved closer to her side, his body pressed against her leg.

"I see you've met our local freeloader," Ruth said as she opened the door and eyed the dog with disapproval.

"Is he yours?"

"Heavens no. He belongs to an artist friend of mine who lives around the far side of the lake.

"He scratched on the door as if he expected me to let him in."

"Usually he doesn't bother anyone in the cottage. He's somewhat shy of strangers. Especially women. However he seems to have taken to you." She leaned over and spoke directly to the dog. "I've told you before, you can't come in."

As if the dog understood, he flopped down on the porch, his head resting on his paws. Clare edged around him.

"I should warn you," Ruth said, opening the door wider and beckoning to Clare, "that my house is decorated in an unusual manner."

Clare halted in the doorway, dazzled by the display.

The living room appeared filled with roses. A sofa and several overstuffed chairs, upholstered in large cabbage roses, faced the wall of windows that overlooked the lake. A broad swath of floral material dipped and flounced above the sheer pink curtains and flowed down on either side to pool on the mauve carpet. On the coffee table and several smaller tables were bowls and vases filled with silk roses of every shade of pink. On either side of the fireplace were wicker baskets filled with balls of yarn and a few knitting needles. The basket handles were adorned with pink and red roses. Even the shades of the lamps had been adorned with pink and white flowers.

"Perhaps a bit too many flowers?" Ruth asked, eyeing Clare beneath one raised eyebrow. "A friend gave me a glue gun for Christmas the year my husband died and I moved back to Grand Rapids. It was a very long winter and I was very depressed. The snow was too deep to go out much so I was literally trapped with a sewing machine, several bolts of material, and a huge box of silk flowers."

Clare could feel her lips twitching with an effort to keep her voice neutral. "The flowers must have brightened the room in the bleakness of winter," she said.

Ruth let out a great whoop of laughter. "Well done, my dear. Very diplomatic. Just wait until you see the rest of the house."

The master bedroom was a riot of big cabbage roses. Roses adorned the comforter and the pillow shams. Even the bed skirt was a rose-patterned fabric to match the draperies at the window. The headboard was an intricately carved beige wood, which matched the bureau and the bedside tables. An old-fashioned dressing table was dressed in a filmy rose-colored skirt. Naturally the cushion on the chair was covered with the ever-present rose material. Looking up, Clare couldn't hold back a giggle as she saw that roses had been glued to the blades of the fan.

"It must have been a very long winter," she said.

Ruth laughed along with her. "Several years ago I thought about redoing the room to something less frenetic. Strangely enough, as bad as it is, I've gotten so that I'm rather fond of the appalling display."

"I will never look at a rose again without thinking of you," Clare said, kissing the older woman's cheek.

"Come along, you rude child, and we'll be off. If you wouldn't mind carrying the chicken salad, I'll lock up the house."

Ruth handed Clare a large covered bowl and then led the way out to the porch. Waldo was still firmly planted on the porch and Clare stepped over him as Ruth locked the front door.

"We're going out for a while, Waldo. Hope it won't be too much trouble to watch the place." His tail thumped for answer. "Would you mind driving, Clare? My eyes aren't the best at night."

They drove back to town, and following Ruth's directions, Clare found her way to the church. She pulled into the parking lot and gazed at the lovely building. It was an old-fashioned red brick building with white trim on the windows and a beautiful triple-paned window above the entrance. The bell tower was square with white shuttered openings. Double doors led off the parking lot.

A plump little woman with jet black hair stood in the entryway to the church hall to welcome them. “Hello, Ruth. I hope you’ve brought your famous chicken salad.”

“Yes I did, Bianca. How are you this evening?”

“Just fine, dear.” She gave her an air kiss then turned to greet Clare.

“This is my niece’s friend, Clare Prentice. She’s renting my cottage for a week or so. Clare, this is Bianca Egner, Pastor Egner’s sister.”

Bianca blinked her eyes in confusion as she turned to stare at Clare. “D . . . did you say this was your niece? Gail?”

“No. This is Gail’s friend. Clare.”

“Oh I’m sorry. I was just flustered that you were Gail and I didn’t recognize you.” Her hands flew up to smooth the hair off her forehead. “I’ve been so busy today, I barely know my own name. Come with me, Clare, and I’ll show you where to put that bowl.”

Bianca turned and led the way into the main hall. A long buffet table was set up in front of the kitchen doors. A long, white lace cloth and dishes of every size and shape covered the table. Bianca moved a few things and took the serving bowl from Clare and set it on the table.

It was a large square room with wood-paneled walls complemented by a golden marbled linoleum floor. There were tables set around the room, covered by tablecloths ranging in color from brown to orange to gold. Glass vases in the center of the table were filled with orange and yellow flowers.

“What lovely centerpieces,” Clare said.

“Bianca is the president of my garden club. She’s a wizard with flower arranging,” Ruth said.

“I have to admit it’s one of my few talents.”

Watching the older woman’s face flush with pleasure, Clare could see how delighted she was with the compliment. Although her hair was black without a strand of gray—thanks to modern chemicals—Clare guessed that Bianca was in her mid-fifties. Her skin was pale, almost pink in color, and her hands fluttered as if to emphasize her words. Looking around, she waved to a man across the room.

"I'd like you to meet my brother," Bianca said, taking Clare by the elbow and leading her and Ruth over to meet him.

Pastor Olli would have stood out in any room. He was tall with broad shoulders and a broad chest. He moved gracefully for a large man as he crossed toward them. He was older than Bianca, probably in his sixties. His cheeks were ruddy and he had bushy eyebrows above piercing hazel eyes. His most striking feature was his full head of white hair that had been styled in thick waves at his temples.

"Look at you, Miss Ruth. You look in the pink of health." His voice had a deep stirring timbre. In lieu of a hug, he placed his hands on her shoulders and shook her slightly then nodded to Clare. "Have you brought me a lovely new addition to my flock?"

"I'm Clare Prentice. I'm renting Ruth's cottage. She was kind enough to invite me to the supper."

"It's good of you to come. We always try to have a little celebration at the start of Tall Timber Days, Grand Rapids's annual event. I hope you'll join in all the festivities while you're here."

"I'm looking forward to it," Clare said.

"How long will you be staying in Grand Rapids?"

"A week or two. It's a combination of work and vacation. Lost Lake is beautiful and there seems to be lots to do in Grand Rapids. I gather from Ruth this weekend will be loaded with activities."

"Yes, the art show is on Saturday. My sister . . ." he turned to address Bianca, but she had moved away and was talking to some other women. "My sister will be showing some of her pastels. She's quite talented. It's always interesting that even in a small town, so many of the occupants have an artistic bent. I have none."

"I'm ashamed to admit my art talent is on a par with stick-figure drawing," Clare said. "Aside from roses, Ruth, can you paint or sculpt?"

"Knitting," the older woman said. "My mother used to say I came out of the womb with a pair of knitting needles in my hand. Must have been mighty uncomfortable for her."

Olli's hearty laughter rumbled from his chest. "You are a pistol, Ruth. I love that line. I've seen your work and your baby blankets are truly works of art."

"Thank you, Olli," she said. "And don't worry I'll be donating some to your Christmas bazaar."

Clare was conscious that Bianca had returned and was shifting from foot to foot beside Olli, waiting to break into the conversation. Although he seemed to be aware she was there, he didn't acknowledge her until she pulled on the sleeve of his jacket.

"I'm sorry to interrupt, Olli, but one of the ladies in the kitchen needs to have the pantry unlocked."

His mouth twitched in annoyance but he took a breath and smiled at Clare and Ruth. "Sorry, ladies. Duty calls. Make yourselves at home."

He swiveled around, brushing past Bianca as he strode toward the kitchen with his flustered sister trotting in his wake. Ruth smiled after them and led Clare to a table where she greeted several women. After introductions were made, she asked if Clare would like to go to the beverage area to get something to drink. Leaving Ruth chatting happily with her friends, Clare went to the far side of the room.

She was amused that the choices of drinks were cherry Kool-Aid and lemonade. She had just purchased two glasses of lemonade when her gaze was drawn to the doorway. Having seen his picture on his book jacket, she recognized Nathan Hanssen immediately.

In person Hanssen looked much less formidable than his publicity pictures. On the cover of his latest book, he had appeared handsomely literary in a conservative suit, hair brushed and styled, staring into the distance as if bored with the passing scene.

He was tall and lanky and his hair, collar length, was a tousled, streaky blond. His face was striking, sharp angles and planes. A carved, slightly beaky nose, strong chin, and high cheekbones gave him a faintly Native American look. What the publicity picture hadn't shown was the dark intensity of his blue eyes. Even across the room, she had the impression that little escaped his attention.

As if her scrutiny had drawn his attention, he looked up. For a moment they stared at each other. Embarrassed to be caught, Clare took a sip from her lemonade and tried to look nonchalant. Nathan raised his hand as if to signal her.

Chapter Three

Nathan Hanssen took a step forward, but a young girl appeared at his side and he turned his attention to her. He leaned down to speak to her. She pointed to a table near the back of the room, he took her hand and followed as she skipped across the floor. Clare assumed the young girl was his daughter Erika. She had the same lanky look as her father and her hair was similar to his except it was white blonde. They joined another couple and their daughter, a girl the same age as Erika.

Shrugging off the strangeness of the encounter, she carried the lemonade back to her table and joined in the conversation as the other ladies who were members of Ruth's garden club asked about her trip north and how she liked Grand Rapids. Eventually they got up and went through the buffet line.

Clare was surprised how hungry she was. She couldn't decide if it was the excitement of the day or the fact that so much of the food was different than what she was used to. Jell-O molds and casseroles. The conversation around them was lively and there was a lot of laughter in the hall. The chatter reminded Clare of several times she and her mother had been included at picnics with Gail's family in Chicago.

"Many years ago," Clare said to Ruth, "I went with your brother and the children to Belmont Harbor for a wonderful dinner on the rocks beside Lake Michigan. While we ate, we watched the boats going in and out of the harbor."

"Oh my, that takes me back," Ruth said, wiping her mouth

with a napkin. "One time when my husband and I visited Chicago, Owen took us there too. The summer night was beautiful and we had a little grill and Owen cooked brats and sauerkraut and beans. Must have been twenty-five years ago, but I can almost taste those brats."

Ruth was quiet after that, concentrating on the food at hand. Clare was content to eat her dinner. Occasionally her attention was drawn back to Hanssen.

"I see you recognized him," Ruth said.

"Yes. That's his daughter, Erika? How old is she?"

"Eleven. In some ways older than that and in others much younger. Would you like me to introduce you?"

"No, thank you. I'll call him tomorrow to make an appointment. I'm not up to being professional tonight." Clare looked toward his table and was startled to see him watching her. She quickly turned away.

"Yes, I noticed that too. He's been eyeing you for some time."

"He's probably wary of strangers. If I went over to introduce myself, he'd be annoyed that some media type was bothering him during dinner." Wanting to distract Ruth, she said, "Pastor Olli and his sister are quite charming. I've been watching them mingling with the crowd. They both have great rapport with the people here. Especially Olli."

"Olli has done wonders since he's been at the church. Unlike some of the ministers in the area, he's got a very active youth group. In the summer he runs a boys' camp for several weeks, which is very well attended."

"Does he run it by himself?" Clare asked.

"No, he brings in a faculty of young men and women, most of them from Duluth, who act as counselors and direct the activities. Olli lived in Minneapolis and Duluth for many years and made a great many contacts at the colleges there."

"You said it's a summer camp?"

"Yes. Olli and Bianca live on the other side of the lake. Actually their place is just beyond Hanssen's place. They have quite a bit of property. The land was originally owned by their parents who held on to it even after they moved to Minneapolis. Originally a summer cottage, eventually, as the Egner's became more affluent, they rebuilt it into a substantial all-season house. There's also a large guesthouse where the camp faculty live and a separate dining hall and boathouse."

"Was Olli's father a minister too?"

"Oh, no. Roy Egner, from what I can remember, would need a special invitation to set foot into the vestibule of heaven." Ruth leaned forward and lowered her voice. "He was a loudmouthed, overbearing man who browbeat his wife and children. He was a wheeler-dealer in banking and stocks and bonds. I never heard a good word said about him."

Clare was surprised at Ruth's vehemence. "That bad?"

"Probably worse." Ruth caught her breath. "I'm sorry, but the mere mention of the man's name raises my blood pressure. When I was younger I heard a good bit about him from my parents and then later Owen confirmed a lot of the stories. He bilked a lot of people out of money and property, foreclosing on people and scooping up their land."

"He's gone?"

"Yes. A lot of years ago and good riddance is all I can say." Ruth nodded her head with a quick jerk. "I guess that's why I'm so fond of Olli. He apparently found solace in the Lord and made something of himself. And he's always been so good to Bianca. In some ways she was the one who was most affected. She's very shy, but she's made a wonderful hostess and housekeeper for Olli. They're quite a team."

Clare looked across the room to where Olli and Bianca were talking to the women behind the buffet table. Bianca's hands fluttered as she talked to the women, touching them occasionally on the arm in a sweet, unobtrusive manner. It was as if when words failed her, she needed to give a touch of approval.

"Neither of them married?" Clare asked.

"Olli married in his twenties. I never knew his wife and I can't even remember her name. Word was she was a flashy city girl. That sounds pretty catty, but I'm just quoting my sources," Ruth said, grinning across at Clare. "I gather she didn't like Grand Rapids and was unhappy when they moved back here from Minneapolis. Bianca was in her teens and lived with them."

"That must have been hard for newlyweds. Did they divorce?"

"Yes. Owen said the wife just picked up and left. Olli had a tough time at first since he was the pastor and, of course, the congregation was wondering what had gone wrong. According to Owen, he broke the news during his service. Just said that like other couples they'd had trouble in their relationship and felt they couldn't continue their marriage. Never said anything bad about her, just said it was over."

"Must have been a blow to his ego." Clare watched as he leaned down to tell Bianca something. When she nodded, he patted her shoulder in thanks. "He's got a charming way about him that it's a surprise someone hasn't snagged him."

"Excuse me, Ruth. I haven't had a chance to talk to you tonight and I'm on my way out."

"You can't fool me, Ed Wiklander," Ruth said, beaming up at the man beside the table. "You've come for an introduction to my renter. I doubt if you ever miss a chance to meet a pretty girl."

The man didn't look the slightest bit uncomfortable with Ruth's comment.

"Guilty as charged," he said, then turned to Clare. "As you may have gathered, I'm Ed Wiklander, local connoisseur of feminine beauty."

Clare grinned and held out her hand. "Clare Prentice."

Ed's big hand engulfed hers and he eyed her thoroughly before he released his grip. He made no apology for his admiring glance and she found herself smiling back at him. A big, bearlike man, he had pale skin, freckles, and red hair. He stood out among the mainly fair-haired Scandinavian crowd. He appeared to be a little older than she was and was clearly interested in her.

"You live here in Grand Rapids?" she asked. She gave a slight tug on her hand, and, after a momentary hesitation, he released it.

"Yes. I work at the paper mill. You ought to come over and see the place. I'll give you a personal tour of the plant."

"They have tours everyday," Ruth added dryly. "If you want to go, Clare, I'd love to go with you. Haven't been for a while."

"You're mighty untrusting, Ruth," Ed said, his mouth wide in a grin. "You know I'd take good care of this young lady. I'm as harmless as a toothless otter."

Ruth snorted in amusement then patted his arm for reassurance. "You're a good man, Ed. I know you'd watch out for Clare."

"I hope Ruth is taking you to all the festivities this weekend. We've got a great parade and of course the bed races."

"Bed races? That sounds highly X-rated."

Ed laughed. "This is a family friendly town. It's mostly teenagers who are in it. They build beds out of all kinds of things and then dress up in costumes. They come flying down the long hill coming into town. The kids love it."

"I can imagine," Clare said. "We don't have a lot of bed races in Chicago. I think it must be the streets. Much too flat for a good race."

Ed smiled. "So you're up here from Chicago. What made you come here for a vacation?"

"Ruth's niece is my best friend. She's always told me how beautiful and restful it is in Grand Rapids. And from what I've seen so far I have to agree."

"So you're a friend of Gail. I used to see a lot of her when she'd come up for a week or two in the summer. How is she? Still single?"

"Not for long," Clare said. "She's going to Hawaii next week to make arrangements for one of those destination weddings. She's going to be married in the fall."

"That's great. Someone from Chicago?"

"You'll appreciate this," Ruth interjected. "She's marrying Tom, who is the principal of a grade school."

Ed threw back his head and laughed. Ruth turned to Clare to explain.

"Gail's finest achievement in elementary school was having cut school more times than anyone in her class. The child was incorrigible." Although Ruth shook her head in dismay, her eyes shone with pride. "How she ever managed to get through nurse's training is a mystery to me."

"I think it's because she found something she loved. And, of course, thanks to good background and breeding, she's extremely bright." Clare grinned, two fingers touching her forehead in salute to Ruth.

"Well, I can see your long day has taken toll of your senses. Time to go home."

Ed leaned over to help Ruth to her feet. While the older woman said her good-byes, Ed walked with Clare toward the hall doors. Clare glanced across to the table where Nathan Hanssen was sitting. He was staring at her and rose to his feet and started to leave the table when once more his daughter caught his attention. Clare turned away and followed Ed and Ruth. They stopped to thank Bianca who was waiting to bid farewell to the attendees.

The breeze had picked up and the night air felt cool against her cheeks. She glanced at her watch and realized it was only eight thirty. The sky was darkening as night closed in. Unlike Chicago, where the city lights blotted out the stars, Clare could see a blanket of stars overhead. Ed helped Ruth into the car then came around to Clare's side.

"It was nice meeting you, Clare," he said. "I hope I'll see you sometime over the weekend. I'm one of the parade organizers so I won't be free for much of the time, but I'll keep my eye out for you."

"I'll look for you too," Clare said, starting the car.

"Maybe you'd like to go for coffee sometime next week?" he asked as he leaned down to peer in the window. "Can I give you a call?"

"I'd like that." Clare smiled at the big man and his face reddened in pleasure.

Ed stepped back and waved as Clare backed out of the parking space. Ruth was quiet on the drive. Now that they were alone, the older woman had sunk into a silent reverie. She didn't speak until they arrived back at Heart's Content.

"Come in. I've got some wine or I can make some hot tea and

we can talk for a bit. Unless you'd rather wait until morning."

"No, a glass of wine sounds excellent. The dinner at the church perked me up. "She turned to Ruth. "Are you sure you're not too tired?"

"Not at all, my dear. I've been conserving my energy this evening."

She unlocked the door and led Clare into the kitchen, which was slightly less filled with flowers than the rest of the house. Getting a bottle of wine from the refrigerator, she handed it to Clare. She opened the cupboard beside the sink and took down two crystal wine glasses and pointed to the door in the corner.

"Gail said you liked New Zealand wines. I found a lovely one that I think you'll like. Villa Maria. Penny Gabel who owns the wine shop recommended the vineyard. We can sit outside on the screened porch so you can get the full benefit of the weather. In Minnesota days as beautiful as this are somewhat rare. I'll be right along with the rest."

Clare opened the screen door and stepped outside. She set the wine bottle on the glass-topped table. It wasn't fully dark and she was transfixed by the view. Being at the top of a hill rather than down at the edge like the cottage, gave her a full glimpse of most of Lost Lake. Used to the blistering hot July days in Chicago, she breathed in the cool air that carried a scent of roses from the garden.

"I never get tired of the view," Ruth said as she stepped out onto the porch.

"You must spend many hours out here. I know I would."

Clare took the glasses from the older woman and set them on the table. She opened the bottle and poured two glasses of wine and handed one to Ruth. Ruth raised her glass and touched the rim of Clare's.

"To your quest," Ruth said. "No matter what you discover, may it give you peace of mind."

At the intent gaze in the older woman's eyes, Clare felt a momentary chill. Refusing to give in to any sense of foreboding, she raised her glass in a return toast. "And to your hospitality."

"Umm. Very nice," Ruth said, picking up the bottle to check the label. "I'll have to get more of this." She waved to a chair. "Please, sit."

Clare drank some wine, letting the coolness fill her mouth and then slowly swallowed. She could feel the tension in her neck from the long day easing as she relaxed in the cushioned chair. Despite the excitement of her earlier discovery, she suspected she would sleep soundly tonight. Too many nights had been spent in tossing and turning as she tried to solve the mystery of her identity.

"How do you think I should proceed now that I've discovered Rose's real name?" Clare asked abruptly, breaking the silence that had surrounded them. "Do you think Rose has relatives still living here that I might ask? Do you know anyone named Gundersen?"

Clare was surprised that Ruth didn't answer immediately. There was a stillness about the older woman that made her uneasy. Her fingers tensed around the stem of the wineglass and carefully she set the glass on the table.

"You recognized the name Gundersen, didn't you?" Clare said, an accusatory note in her voice as she stared across the table. "Why didn't you tell me earlier?"

Ruth sighed. She turned her chair until she was facing Clare directly. Pursing her lips, she tapped them with two fingers as if gathering her thoughts.

"I'm sorry, Clare. I didn't mean to keep anything from you. I knew telling you before dinner wouldn't be appropriate. I wanted you to see and meet some of the people in town before you could make any prejudgments. You're right that I did recognize the name Gundersen. However, before I could talk to you, I needed to be sure that I was remembering the right Gundersens. So after you left the library, I began to check my facts."

An icy chill of anticipation ran through Clare's body as she suspected Ruth already knew her real identity. She would know her name, she would know about her family, and she might even learn why there was such a conspiracy of silence around her background.

"You knew my adoptive mother?" she asked, her hands clenched in the material of her skirt.

"No, I didn't know Rose," Ruth said. "We were four years apart and when you're a child that's a huge gap. By the time she was in school, I had already moved to Duluth. I recognized the name Gundersen, but I had to go back through the newspaper files to get the story straight. Rose Gundersen was your aunt. Your biological mother was Rose's sister Lily Gundersen Newton."

Clare's hand jerked and she raised it to her throat, grasping the necklace in her fingers. For a moment she could barely catch her breath.

"Rose said my heart necklace had belonged to her sister. She meant Lily Gundersen. All this time I've been wearing my mother's necklace and never knew it."

"That appears to be the case," Ruth said. "So in a way Rose left you clues to find the truth behind your identity."

"Does m . . . my m . . . mother still live here?" Clare whispered the words in a halting stammer. Her throat closed in fear of the answer.

Ruth's eyes glinted with tears as she shook her head. "No, Clare. Lily died twenty-five years ago."

Clare had always known that there was the possibility that her mother had died. Maybe even in childbirth. Although she had considered it, she had never really believed it. She had always hoped that her mother was alive and well, and that she would make a connection with her. A reunion of sorts. That dream crashed, leaving in it's wake a deep sorrow, an almost physical pain.

"She must have been very young when she died. How did it happen?"

Silence filled the screened porch. In the gathering darkness, the lines in the older woman's face appeared deeper than earlier in the day. Once again she touched her pursed lips with the fingers of her hand as if to hold back her words.

"Was she sick? An accident? Please, Ruth, I need to know. How did she die?" Clare asked again, her tone soft yet demanding.

"Your mother, Lily Newton, was murdered."

Chapter Four

"My mother was murdered?" Clare stared at Ruth as if she had lost her mind. "That can't be true."

"Forgive me for telling you in such an abrupt fashion, but I couldn't think of any other way. Now that you know who Rose was, it would be just a matter of a quick check before you found out yourself."

In the ensuing silence Clare fought a torrent of emotions. She had driven all the way to Minnesota in search of an identity and possibly a family and now all hope of such a happy conclusion was crushed. Worse than that, this new information made her feel as if she were in the middle of a nightmare.

"There must be some mistake."

"No, Clare." Ruth's tone was unyielding. "After you left the library, I looked it up in the newspaper archives. I've brought home a folder from the clippings file at the library for you to go through later, but it might be easier if I give you a brief summary. Would you prefer that?"

For an instant, Clare debated whether she wanted to know anything more. If she said no, she need not face the grim reality of her search. She could pretend that the trail she was following had led to nothing. The weakness was momentary; she knew she couldn't turn back now. In order to reclaim her life, she needed to find answers to her questions. Nodding, she sat up straighter in her chair.

"If you don't mind, I'd rather hear it from you."

She watched as Ruth took a fortifying drink of her wine, then settled back in her own chair. Her eyes were kind as she looked at Clare.

"I did not know your mother or your father nor did I live here at the time of her death, so I'm only able to tell you what I've managed to glean from a cursory look at the newspaper files."

Clare nodded, unable to trust her voice.

"Rose Gunderson was born in Grand Rapids. She was your mother's older sister. Eleven years older than Lily. Rose was living and working in Minneapolis, although she owned a house here. Lily and your father, Jimmy Newton, were living in Rose's house."

"Was I here too?"

"Yes. I didn't have time to do much research, but according to the newspaper accounts I'm assuming you were born in Grand Rapids since your parents had been living in Rose's place for four years. You were almost four years old when your mother died."

"No wonder I couldn't find any information prior to that time," Clare said.

"Lily and Jimmy had been married for four years. Your mother was working as a waitress at the Forest Lake restaurant. Your father worked for the Blandin Paper Company doing something in graphic design."

Ruth paused, staring at Clare, gauging her reaction and then, satisfied, she continued.

"Your mother died in 1982 during the Fourth of July weekend. Your parents and your Aunt Rose had gone to a dance that Saturday night at the Bovey City Hall. That's the next town over. There was some trouble at the dance. A fight. Your parents returned home with your aunt. At four o'clock on Sunday morning, your father called the chief of police and told him your mother was missing. A search was conducted, but it wasn't until morning that your mother's body was found on the lakeshore."

"My mother drowned?" Clare asked.

"No. Lily was shot."

The shock of the words jolted through her body. Murder was a big city crime. Murder didn't happen in small picturesque towns.

Most of all, murder didn't happen to people she knew. And yet, incredibly, her own mother had been killed. In her own mind she couldn't bring herself to use the word murder.

"I know it's a stunner, Clare. A lot to take in. I sat for a long time today after you left trying to decide how much to tell you without overloading you."

Clare took a shuddering breath, then reached for the wine and took a sip to combat the dryness in her mouth.

"It's dark," Ruth said. "Would you like to go inside?"

"Not unless you do. I'm enjoying the fresh air." She took another sip of wine, trying to take in what she had heard. It was so long ago that there was an unreality to the story as if she were listening to the plot of a book. She started at a sudden thought. "Twenty-five years ago. I was four when my mother died. Did the newspaper mention me? At least I would feel as if I really existed."

Ruth smiled cautiously. "You do in fact exist. Would you like to know your birth name?"

Clare had forgotten that her name might have been a total fabrication. She closed her eyes and took a deep breath. The word was barely audible when she replied, "Yes."

"Your name is Abigail Clare Newton."

"Abigail Clare Newton. Abigail Newton. Abigail Clare." She listened to the sound of the words as she spoke them aloud. "Wouldn't you think that I'd recognize my own name? I'm glad Rose kept at least one of the names. Clare. It doesn't sound so totally foreign. I don't feel like an Abigail."

"In the newspaper they mentioned that you were called Abby."

"Abby? It's weird but that sounds familiar. I must have some memory of being called by that name."

"You were four years old. Lodged in your brain there are probably remembrances that might come to the forefront now that you're looking into this. Would it help if I called you Abigail or Abby?" Ruth asked, curiosity in her tone.

"No! I've been Clare all these years. I don't know if I'll ever be Abigail, let alone Abby." Her voice was sharp and she fought against the anger that rose at this latest example of the falseness of her life. "Sorry for snapping at you."

"It's a lot to take in. I'm sure that you've spent five months feeling totally disoriented. It's as if you suddenly learned that there really were UFOs and that you were actually from another planet."

"That's exactly how it feels. I have no sense of place anymore." Clare sighed. "You better tell me the rest. I'd rather get it over with than have to hear it piecemeal."

"I'll keep it brief," Ruth said. "When your mother's body was found, your father was suspected of the murder. The chief of police asked if he had a gun. Jimmy admitted that he did, but when they went to the house the gun couldn't be found."

"Except for the usual fact that the spouse is always a suspect, was there any evidence against him?" Clare asked.

"There was evidence of a fire in the fireplace. Since it had been a particularly hot night, that was suspicious. When they sifted the ashes, they discovered a zipper and some buttons. The assumption was that he'd burned his bloody clothing."

Clare nodded. "You said there was a fight at the dance that night. Was Jimmy involved?"

"Yes. According to the newspapers there had been a lot of drinking outside of the hall where the dance was held. Jimmy got in a fight with another man and it took a number of people there to separate the two. The conventional wisdom was that Jimmy was jealous and angry over the attentions being paid to your mother by the other man."

"Did my father shoot my mother?"

"Yes."

The single syllable was uncompromising. Clare was grateful when Ruth paused, giving her a chance to absorb this latest shock. After several minutes she continued.

"When your father realized his arrest was imminent, he packed up a few things and disappeared. He left a note for the chief of police confessing to the murder. He said he couldn't bear the thought of going to prison and he couldn't imagine life without Lily."

"So he just abandoned me?" Clare interjected.

"No, dear." Ruth leaned forward so that Clare could see her expression clearly in the fading light. "Don't think that. He went on to say that you would always be safe with Lily's sister and you would not have to live with the stigma of a father who was a murderer."

"So he's somewhere out there alive and free? Some justice."

"In some respects I suppose you could say that justice prevailed. The final news article was almost eight months after your mother died."

When Ruth didn't speak immediately, the muscles in Clare's stomach began to tighten as if she expected a blow. It was a moment or two before the older woman continued.

"Two men had been walking beside the railroad tracks in Prairie du Chien, Wisconsin when they saw a man jump in front of a freight train. One witness said he had committed suicide while the other claimed he might have been trying to beat the train and lost his footing. The man was identified as Jimmy Newton, your father. The case was closed."

In the silence that followed, Clare stared down at the lake. The moon had risen and the surface glowed whitely in the circle of darkened trees that surrounded it. Here and there lights shone in the houses, but the lake itself appeared iced over and she shivered at the deep chill that invaded her bones. It occurred to her that Ruth must be feeling the change in temperature too.

"I think it's time to go inside," Clare said. "There's a hint of dampness in the air and I don't want you to catch cold." Reaching out a hand, she helped the older woman to her feet. "You take your glass and I'll bring the rest."

It was strange how comfortable Clare felt around Ruth, as if she'd known her for much longer than half a day. Ruth made a pot of tea. They settled down in the rose-decorated living room. The hot tea brought welcome warmth to Clare's body.

"I hope this hasn't all been too much for you. You came here with such high hopes and I hated to dash them." Ruth's expression was troubled. "I'm a firm believer that ultimately the truth cannot hurt you. It can bring you pain, heartache, and sadness but it cannot destroy the person you are. It can bring you understanding of whom and what you are."

"Right now, I'm not sure I agree with you. Maybe after I've had time to absorb this I will." Clare took a deep breath. "You're right that I came here with certain expectations. I remember as a child when I was angry because of something Rose did or, more probably, what she wouldn't let me do, I would imagine that I'd been kidnapped by Gypsies and my rich parents would claim me someday."

Ruth chuckled, a warm throaty sound. "I had the same thought, but I was always a misplaced princess. And had the firm belief that when I became queen I would make everyone very sorry they hadn't been nicer to me."

For the first time since they returned to the house, Clare could feel her mouth widen in a grin. "You see all those wonderful TV shows where a child is put up for adoption and the birth mother searches for years to find the child. There's a tearful reunion and the adopted child has the benefit of two loving families."

"Reality is usually harsher."

"I didn't really think it would be like that. When I was having trouble getting any information I realized that my birth family might not be thrilled to have me turn up after all these years. All I had hoped for was to be able to fill in a background. To not feel so lost."

"And now," Ruth said, "you feel even more lost?"

"Exactly. Angry. Confused."

"I'll admit it's overwhelming. You'll need to take some time to get used to the whole thing. Try to think of it as a process of rebirth. You can't rush that in real life and I don't think you should rush into this now. I've brought you some clippings to look at but you'll need time to absorb the information. Besides, you'll have questions and those will lead to other things."

"I don't even know where to start." Clare heard the childish whine in her tone. She straightened in her chair, refusing to let the situation dominate her but at a loss how to get beyond the sense of helplessness that surrounded her.

"Work is always the way to ground yourself." Ruth's voice was brisk. "You mentioned earlier that you had come here to interview Nathan Hanssen."

"That was the plan. I really never expected to tell anyone my real reason for being here. When I told my editor at the magazine that I was coming to Grand Rapids, she said the most famous natives were Judy Garland who was born here and Hanssen who was currently living here. When she mentioned arranging an interview I jumped at it. I like his work, but, more importantly, it gave me a legitimate excuse for being here."

"Excellent," Ruth said. "This is a small town and people will be curious about you. It will explain why you've come up to Minnesota. And you'll be free to ask questions and dig into the history of the town."

"You think people will be upset if they find out who I am?"

Ruth shrugged her shoulders. "I don't really know. From what I've read, it was a sensational case at the time and many of the people involved still live in town. They might not want their youthful indiscretions brought up again." After a slight hesitation she continued, "Have you talked to Nathan Hanssen before?"

"No. My editor made the arrangements."

"Strangely enough, you already have a connection with Nate although you would have had no way to know this. Nate's father was the chief of police at the time of your mother's death."

"You're kidding."

"No, it's true. Thatcher Hanssen was the chief of police here for many years until he retired."

"What a bizarre coincidence. I've come all this way to interview someone whose father was involved in the investigation of my mother's death." Clare shook her head, trying to clear away some of her confusion. "I'm still not sure how deeply I want to delve into this but if I do, do you think Thatcher Hanssen would talk to me?"

Ruth sighed. "Unfortunately, Thatcher died three years ago. He was a very fine man. Honest and well liked. A real loss to us all."

"So many dead ends." She smiled at the unintended pun. "I have so many questions and it would help to talk to people who actually knew my parents. Rose never talked about her family and rarely mentioned my father. Now I'm beginning to wonder if she was ever married."

"No pictures of her husband?"

"None. She said all the early photographs had been lost in a fire. I suppose it doesn't matter since Jimmy Newton was my father and there are probably pictures of him in the newspaper accounts."

"Yes. He looks grim in all the pictures, but you would expect that under the circumstances. As far as I could tell he was a tall, heavyset man with a thick head of red hair and a beard."

Clare touched her own chestnut hair, understanding where she got the red highlights that glowed in the sunlight. "You didn't know him?"

"No, I had already moved away. According to the newspaper, Jimmy was born and raised in Minneapolis. He'd only been living in Grand Rapids for seven years before your mother died."

"Do you know how old she was?"

"Lily was twenty-three."

"I'm twenty-nine." Clare swallowed around the lump in her throat. "I've been alive six years longer than my mother and I'm only twenty-nine."

"I can hear the sadness in your voice and I can't say I blame you. All you can do is to try and let it go. Maybe time will change the perspective. Would you like to see your mother's picture?"

"No."

The word burst from her lips and she covered her mouth, appalled at her reaction to the question. Her heart beat loudly in her ears and she concentrated on her breathing until she was able to look across at the older woman.

"I'm not ready to meet her yet." Clare's voice shook. "It's all too much."

"You poor child," Ruth said. "This has been a very long day for you. I'm sure your emotions are in an uproar. This is much too much to take in."

Ruth pushed to her feet and reached across to take Clare by her hand. She stood up, staggering slightly as a wave of exhaustion washed over her body. Ruth steadied her and she drew in an energizing breath of air.

"You're definitely right that I'm done for the moment. I didn't realize how tired I was."

Ruth put an arm around her shoulders and walked her toward the door. Feeling chilled, Clare slipped on her corduroy jacket and zipped it up to her neck. Ruth reached for a thick envelope on the hall table and handed it to Clare.

"Don't rush this, dear. My phone number at the library is on the front of the envelope. Sleep in tomorrow. Call Nathan Hanssen and set up the interview. I've put some groceries in the refrigerator that should get you through the day. I suspect you might want to just get acclimated. I don't want to be an overbearing landlady, but I'm right here if you need me."

"Thank you for everything, Ruth. I don't mean to be ungracious, but I do need a bit of time to get used to things." She hugged the older woman. "I'll give you a call tomorrow after I've had a good rest."

Ruth opened the door. She jumped back when she saw Waldo lying at the edge of the porch, his snout on top of his folded paws. He raised his head and his tail thumped against the floor, then he sighed heavily as he lumbered to his feet.

"I think he must be waiting to walk you home," Ruth said.

"I've had less courteous dates," Clare said, leaning over to pat his head. "However, I have to admit they smelled better."

"It's Eau de Northern Pike."

Clare giggled. "I better not let my escort wait any longer. Good night."

Clare followed the soft padding of the dog as he led her along the flagstones down to the cottage. The light she'd left on was a welcome beacon. The dark surrounded her and the soft breeze off the lake caressed her cheeks. The fresh air revived her slightly, but her body hummed with the aftermath of her emotional day. When they got to the porch, Waldo led her around toward the lake.

Rounding the corner she came face to face with a dark figure seated in one of the wicker chairs on the porch. She gasped in fear as a man rose to confront her.

Chapter Five

Clare opened her mouth to scream as the man loomed out of the darkness on the porch and came toward her. Waldo pushed her aside as he hurled himself forward, tail thrashing wildly.

"Oof," the man said. "Down, you idiot dog."

In a split second Clare realized that there was nothing to fear as Waldo nuzzled the man who was trying to ward off the enthusiastic gyrations of the dog.

"Sit," the man snapped.

Obediently Waldo flopped his rear on the deck, gazing up while his body continued to wriggle in pleasure. The man reached out and stroked the dog behind the ears until he was calmer.

"I'm sorry for frightening you. I'm Waldo's sometime owner. I spotted him sitting on the dock with you earlier in the evening and I came over to make sure he wasn't being a nuisance."

Clare held the envelope of newspaper clippings tight against her chest as her breathing steadied. "He's been acting as my escort since I'm new to the area."

"I gathered that someone was renting the place when I saw the lights on."

"I'm Clare Prentice. I'm a friend of Ruth's niece Gail."

The man was silent for a moment but finally his deep voice came out of the darkness. "I'm Jake. Nice to meet you."

He made no attempt to offer his hand, just continued to stroke the dog's head.

"Ruth said you were an artist?"

"Yes. I'm right across the lake." He pointed vaguely to the far side. "Well, Waldo and I will be heading home. Just shoo him off if he bothers you."

Without waiting for a response, Jake walked down the steps toward the lake. Waldo turned his head toward Clare, gave a low woofing sound, and followed his owner along the path. In the moonlight, she caught a glimpse of a thin man in a flannel shirt and blue jeans. She couldn't see his face but his white hair and slow pace indicated that he was older than his voice had sounded. Although she was watching intently, the man and the dog seemed to melt into the dark blur of trees along the shoreline.

How strange, Clare thought. She had to admit that she'd been frightened when she first found Jake on the porch. If it hadn't been for the dog, she would have run back to Ruth's. She'd have to ask Ruth about the artist. He hadn't seemed particularly friendly, although he hadn't been menacing either. Reaching into the pocket of her jacket, she pulled out the house key and unlocked the door.

She relocked the door and placed the envelope on the table beside the sofa. In the bedroom, she hung up her jacket in the closet, and then opened the dresser, grateful that she'd finished unpacking before she went to Ruth's. She pulled out a red and blue silk nightgown with a bright red mandarin robe. Although she was never flamboyant in her clothing style, she thought of her lingerie as her "inner tramp." She could feel the tiredness creeping into her body, as she washed quickly and changed into her nightgown and robe.

Barefoot, she went out to the kitchen and opened the refrigerator. She was reminded again of Ruth's thoughtfulness. She had bought orange juice, milk, eggs, and bread. There was a plastic bag with sliced ham and Swiss cheese. On the counter was a box of cereal, several apples, and two bananas. A box of lemon-flavored tea bags was beside the stove and a bright blue kettle was set on the burner. Best of all was a plate of cookies on the counter.

Opening several cupboards, she eventually found some blue mugs and filled one with water. She placed it inside the microwave and set the timer. When the bell dinged, she set the cup on a plate, dunked one of the tea bags, and added several cookies. Grabbing some paper towels for a napkin, she padded across to the sofa and set her things down on the table. She sighed gratefully as she curled up in the corner of the couch and reached for the mug of tea.

The moist lemony scent rose to fill her senses. She held the cup in the palms of her hands, closed her eyes, and breathed deeply. As if an echo to her feeling of contentment, she heard the call of a loon on the lake. For the first time in three months she felt at peace.

The emotional turmoil she had been through faded into the background and she took a careful sip of the hot tea. So many times she'd cried herself to sleep, but she suspected that tonight she would sleep soundly, free of nightmares.

She ate the cookies — oatmeal raisin — her favorite, and drank the tea, letting the warmth flow through her body. Her fingers stroked across the surface of the manila envelope. This was what she had been searching for. This was her identity.

Now that she knew part of the story, she needed to decide how much more she wanted to know. Could she look at these clippings and be satisfied? Obviously she couldn't go through them tonight. She was far too tired. Tomorrow would be plenty of time.

She took her dishes back to the kitchen, turned out the lights in the main room, and returned to the bedroom. She removed her robe and lay it across the end of the bed. Pulling back the coverlet, she turned down the sheet and searched through all the decorative pillows until she unearthed a down pillow. She sat down gingerly, testing to see if the iron bed frame squeaked. As expected it let out several rusty groans, but once she was settled, she found the mattress delightfully firm. Turning out the light, she lay back and closed her eyes.

Twenty minutes later, she turned on the light and sat up.

Throwing back the covers, she got to her feet and padded out to the living room. She glared down at the envelope on the table. She'd tried to put it out of her mind but she knew if she didn't open it she wouldn't get any sleep. Picking it up, she returned to the bedroom. She fluffed up her pillow and put it against the metal headboard. Climbing back into bed she sat with her back against the pillow and her legs crossed. She smoothed out the covers, placing the envelope on the comforter.

Much as she said she wasn't ready, Clare wanted to see what her mother looked like. There had to be some pictures in the envelope. Her fingers shook as she opened the clasp and she prayed that she wouldn't find a sensationalized photo of her mother's death. With the top undone, she poured the contents onto the comforter.

On the top was a newspaper with a picture of her mother under the headline: GRISLY MURDER IN GRAND RAPIDS.

The picture was not a formal photograph. With the lake in the background, it looked as if it was taken at a picnic. Lily was sitting down and the way the picture had been cropped indicated that other people were sitting on either side of her.

The old newspaper had a yellowish cast and Lily's features were slightly blurred. Her face was slender with high cheekbones and she stared into the camera with wide, serious eyes. Because the picture was black and white, Clare couldn't tell what color her eyes were. The one thing that was clear was her blonde hair that, even on the grainy newsprint, glowed as it curled around her shoulders. Sculptured eyebrows and an aristocratic nose added to the picture of a very pretty young woman.

Perhaps she had been expecting a mirror image of her own face but, if so, she was disappointed. Staring down she could see very little resemblance. The woman in the photograph looked something like Rose, but she did not see much of herself.

Looking up, she stared into the mirror above the dresser across from the bed. She held up the newspaper so that she could look back and forth from the photo to the mirror. Perhaps there was a similarity in the eyes and the eyebrows but her own chin was much firmer and line of her nose was softer. She stared at her mouth, then her ears and her hair. Except for the color, their hair seemed to be the same thickness and have the same sheen.

She'd have to look for a picture of her father to see if she favored his side of the family.

The faded photograph blurred as tears filled her eyes. She tipped her head back against the pillow and let the silent tears flow unchecked. The rising emotion caught her unexpectedly. It took her a moment to realize why she was crying.

She hadn't recognized Lily.

Clare had always been convinced that when she found her mother she would feel an instant connection. She had been adopted at four years old. Four was old enough to have memories. It had occurred to her that her mother might be dead, but that didn't matter. Seeing her mother in person or finding a picture of her would bring back the memories and she would remember bits and pieces of her early life.

Nothing. Looking at the photograph, Clare felt no recognition, no rush of memories.

She had been running on adrenaline and this final blow seemed to drain the last bit of energy from her body. She wiped her eyes and blew her nose. Without looking through the rest of the pile, she slid the papers back into the envelope. She set the envelope on the bedside table and once more turned out the light. Plumping her pillow, she lay down on her back, pulling the covers up to her chin. Her head was propped up just enough so that she could see the lake beyond the window. Moonlight shone on the far side of the lake and she could hear the occasional forlorn sound of the loons. Lulled by fresh air, night sounds, and the knowledge that she actually had a real identity, she slipped into an exhausted sleep.

Clare lay motionless in bed, listening to the morning chirping and felt the heat of a shaft of sunlight on her hand. She opened her eyes a slit, took in the light at the window and wondered what time it was. Turning her head slightly until she could see the clock on the bedside table, she noted with surprise that it was almost ten o'clock. She couldn't remember when she'd slept so long. And so peacefully.

She heard a scratching sound at the front door and threw back the covers. She put on her robe as she walked into the main room. As she opened the front door, Waldo's tail beat a happy rhythm on the floorboards. Leaning over she patted his head. His fur was slightly wet, but this time he smelled of shampoo not dead fish.

"Much better," she said. She picked up the newspaper that was tucked under the bristled doormat. "I suppose it's all right if you come in today."

She motioned the dog forward, but he huffed as if in disapproval and sauntered along the porch until he disappeared around the corner of the house.

"Well, thanks for stopping by," Clare said.

She breathed in the fresh air. She could feel the heavy warmth in the August air and suspected it would be quite hot without the breeze off the lake. Perfect day for shorts she thought as she went back inside.

Opening the newspaper she found a note from Ruth. It wished her a happy Wednesday and asked if she'd like to go to the art show on Saturday. After a long shower to get two days of road dust out of her system, she made breakfast and slowly read the paper.

Used to the *Chicago Tribune*, she enjoyed reading the smaller *Herald-Review*. Lots of local news to give her a flavor of the town. There was a write-up on the Tall Timber Days that were being celebrated on the weekend. The art show on Saturday was only one of the scheduled activities. There were also the parade and the bed races that Ed Wiklander mentioned. She would have to make a point to check them out. Sunday was the farm and tractor exhibits and a lumberjack show. Apparently she'd come at an excellent time.

After breakfast she cleaned up the cottage, and then called Ruth to tell her she'd finally awakened.

"That's exactly what you needed, Clare," Ruth said. "I could see in your face how exhausting the last several months have been. Nothing like sleep to get you back to feeling like problems aren't monumental. Besides last night's information overload was a lot to take in."

At the apologetic tone in Ruth's voice, Clare was quick to reply. "There wasn't any other way to get the information. If I'd had to read all the clippings to get the main points of the story, I'd have gone nuts. I'm going to spend the day looking through the files you left me."

"Excellent. I'm going to a film discussion over in Coleraine with a friend tonight. Will you be all right on your own?"

"Yes. By the way, I really enjoyed the church supper last night and the goodies in the cottage. I managed to eat only half of the cookies, although I was tempted to eat them all. I'm going into town later to pick up some other things and thought you might join me for dinner tomorrow night. Then I can let you know how I'm progressing."

"That would be lovely although you don't have to cook. We can just as easily go out to dinner."

"Nonsense," Clare said. "It'll be easier to talk here."

"All right then. " Ruth's voice was brisk. "I'm usually done at the library by six."

"Then I'll see you around seven tomorrow."

"Lovely. Enjoy your day and take it all slowly." On that note of caution Ruth ended the call.

Deciding she'd better call Nathan Hanssen to set up a time for her interview, she dug in the dresser for her notebook and set it on the counter while she searched for her notes on Hanssen. After a quick scan, she reached for the phone and dialed the number on the top sheet of paper.

"Hanssen's," a gruff voice answered after the second ring.

"Nathan Hanssen, please." Clare said.

"This is Nate. Who's calling?"

"I'm Clare Prentice from *Illinois Literary*. My editor, Ann Taylor, said she had made arrangements with you for an interview."

In the silence that followed, Clare tensed, wondering if he was going to refuse the earlier request. "She said if you couldn't remember your agreement to give her a call."

She heard an audible sigh at the other end of the phone.

"How is Ann?"

"She's fine. She just got back from Italy. Said she ate her way through Tuscany and may have to go to detox after all the wine she drank."

"Sounds like she had a good time." A hint of warmth crept into his voice. "What was your name again?"

"Clare. Clare Prentice. I've just arrived in Grand Rapids and would be able to do your interview whenever it's convenient for you."

The warmth disappeared as he said, "I have a particularly busy week. A couple of deadlines and various other things that need to get done. I'm not sure how much time I could give you."

As the silence on the other end was extended, Clare took a chance. "Ann said if you attempted to weasel out of this I was to remind you that she could do an exposé on your behavior the night she met you at the adult literacy event in Chicago."

A harsh laugh was the only answer.

"I don't need a lot of time," Clare continued. "What I'd like to do is a preliminary visit to get acquainted and, then after I've done some more research, I'd appreciate another slightly longer session to talk with you."

"Since I wouldn't want anything unflattering written about me I guess I'll have to agree. Ten o'clock, Thursday morning."

He didn't ask if it was convenient, just issued the order. She'd been looking forward to meeting Hanssen, but now she wondered if rudeness was an integral part of his character.

"Thank you. I'll be there." Not wanting to give him the satisfaction of hanging up, she immediately ended the call.

Standing beside the phone she could feel the heat rising to her cheeks. She took a deep breath and blew it out. It wasn't a good sign that she already disliked the man. She had to do the interview and she hated the thought that her own emotions might get in the way. She'd heard Hanssen was a semi-recluse as far as the media was concerned. Despite Ann's assurances that he would cooperate with the interview, she wasn't convinced after her phone call.

* * *

Nate Hanssen lunged for the receiver before the answering machine could pick it up.

"Hold please," he said.

On the couch beside the telephone, his daughter jumped at the sudden motion beside her and he glared as she reached up to take the earbuds out of her ears. From three feet away, he could hear the music blaring from her iPod.

"I thought you were getting ready. We're supposed to pick up Cindy in ten minutes," he said as he jerked his thumb in the direction of the second floor. "And turn that down, Erika. It's too loud if you can't hear the phone beside you. You'll be deaf by the time you're fifteen."

"Oh, Dad," she grumbled getting up off the leather couch.

"Get your stuff together. Don't just stare into space while your eardrums are permanently damaged."

"Whatever," she said as she started toward the stairs.

"And don't say that."

He sighed as he dropped down on the spot his daughter had just vacated and put the phone to his ear.

"Nate, here."

"Hi. It's Ann Taylor. I was just reliving my childhood listening to you. My father was convinced the loud music in my room would cause me brain damage."

"I'm beginning to sound just like my old man. I'll never tell Erika, but he was always yelling about my music." He pressed the phone tighter to his ear. "You're fading a little."

"Sorry I'm in the car. I'm out in California working on a cover story for *Illinois Literary*. Stuck in a traffic jam so I'm returning all my calls."

"I heard you just got back from Italy."

"Ah," she sighed. "Clare must have made it up to Minnesota. I just looked at the map the other day and I was amazed to find out how far north you were. Must be lovely in the winter."

"If you're a polar bear. And yes, to answer your question, your reporter arrived and called a little while ago." He paused then continued. "How come I have no recollection of ever agreeing to do this interview?"

"You were probably drunk."

"No good. Why have you dumped this woman on my doorstep?"

"She was coming up there anyway so I thought if you did agree to talk to her it would be—helpful." Ann's deep throaty laugh came clearly through the phone. "Tell me you didn't chew her up into little pieces."

Nate felt his annoyance at the situation easing. He pictured Ann with her long legs stretched out as she waited for the traffic jam to clear.

"I'll admit I snarled at her but I would think she'd expect that from a famous literary figure. She must not have known my reputation because she's coming to see me tomorrow. And what did you mean that it would be helpful?"

"Clare needed to get away. A couple of years ago, she quit work to take care of her mother who was dying of cancer. I'd just gotten her back to work after a year at home when something else came up. She asked for time off to look into her family history. I was stunned to learn she was going to Grand Rapids. Knowing you were there I told her you'd agreed to do an interview."

Nate snorted in disgust. "She sounds just like one of those pasty faced female reporters who are good hearted souls and write three-hanky stories."

"Surprisingly enough she's an excellent writer. And you won't find her pasty faced. Treat her gently. She just had a disastrous breakup with her boyfriend—a couple of months before the wedding."

"Bloody hell, Ann! You're not matchmaking, are you?"

A choking sound came through the phone. "Oh Lord, no. I never even thought about it. Unless of course you're interested. She's very attractive, although a bit on the serious side."

"I'm not interested." His tone was hard. "In fact the more I hear about her the more convinced I am that doing this interview is a bad idea. Good to her mother, serious but attractive. You might as well have said she has a great personality. The next thing I know she'll be swooning on my doorstep."

"You wish." Nate heard a long horn beep before Ann's voice came back on. "If you're nice to her and she likes you, she might tell you why she's really coming to Grand Rapids. It's pretty damn interesting if I do say so."

"You've always had a nose for a good story, so I'll see if I can coax it out of her."

"Thanks, Nate. I really appreciate this." Ann's voice had lost the bantering tone. "I like Clare and I'm concerned about her. Keep an eye on her."

Surprised at her request, he nodded then spoke aloud. "It sounds like you're worried. Grand Rapids is a small town. She couldn't be in a safer place. You make it sound like she's walking into deadly peril."

"Wait until you hear her story," Ann said. "You may find it totally intriguing."

Clare returned from a brisk walk along the shore road. She felt less annoyed over her phone call with Hanssen. She already knew his dislike of reporters so she should have been prepared for his response. Inside the cottage she gulped down a glass of cold water. Filling her glass again, she stepped out on the back porch. She half expected Waldo to be waiting for her, but he must be off on his daily wanderings. Alone, she stood at the railing and let the breeze off the lake cool her. In the late morning there wasn't much activity on Lost Lake. Several fishermen were trolling along the shoreline, but aside from that the scene was peaceful. One more look and she decided it was time to get to work. She retrieved the envelope of clippings from the bedroom and spread the contents across the counter.

The articles had been placed in chronological order. The newspaper with the picture of her mother was dated the day after the murder. She read through it slowly. It only confirmed what Ruth had told her last night. Her father, Jimmy Newton, had called the police chief to report Lily was missing and her body was found later that morning. She had been shot three times. There were not many details but there was a picture of Thatcher Hanssen, Nathan's father.

Thatcher was a bull-chested man with a grim expression. He refused to say much about Lily's death except for the usual: "they were considering everything before jumping to conclusions." The only thing reported that was of interest was that during the dance Jimmy Newton got into an altercation with a man named "Big Red" Wiklander. According to the witnesses, the fight started because Jimmy was jealous of Big Red's advances toward Lily.

Big Red must be the father of Ed Wiklander who had been at the church supper, Clare thought. What a small world. She had gotten the impression that Ed was a bit of a womanizer. It remained to be seen if much of Ed's approach was serious. If his father was anything like Ed, that might be a formula for trouble.

Looking back through the article, she checked the ages of her parents. Lily was twenty-three and Jimmy was almost twenty years older. She supposed it was reasonable that he might have been jealous of younger men hitting on his wife.

According to Thatcher Hanssen, Lily had not been shot on the lakeshore. She had been killed somewhere else and her body placed beside the lake. Chief Hanssen described it as "lying peacefully on a soft patch of grass." Her clothing had been neatly arranged and her hands had been crossed over her chest.

The murder weapon was never found. It was a .25-caliber handgun, a baby Browning, like the one owned by Jimmy Newton.

Clare read through several other articles that rehashed much of the story. As the investigation progressed, the stories tended to be far less sympathetic of Jimmy Newton. Although it was never stated, the clear indication was that he was the prime suspect in Lily's murder. The only direct hint was when it was reported that, during a search of the house, Newton "claimed" his gun was missing.

In one clipping there was a small picture of the house. Clare felt a slight jolt of familiarity as she stared down at the grainy photo. Bushes and trees shrouded the screened porch, giving it an overgrown, deserted look. Did she recognize it? She couldn't really tell. She'd have to find the house and see if that would shake up her memories.

She scanned the pictures taken at the funeral but saw only one picture of her father, head down, as he followed the crowd into the church. In all the clippings there were really only two pictures of her father that gave her any sense of what he really looked like.

The first showed a picture of her parents that was taken at some sort of fair. Lily was leaning against Jimmy who had his arm around her, smiling and happy. She didn't know how tall her mother was but her father was at least six or eight inches taller. While Lily was slender, similar to Clare's own build, her father was heavily built, not fat but well muscled. His beard was neatly trimmed and his hair was slicked down as he stared straight ahead into the camera.

The second picture was a headshot on the front page of the newspaper. Carrying the newspaper, she went back to the bedroom and held it up as she had done with her mother's picture so that she could look back and forth from her face in the mirror to the picture. His eyes were dark under bushy eyebrows. His features were unremarkable. His cheeks were full, made more so by the beard. In the photo his beard appeared lighter than his hair or his eyebrows.

It was almost painful to look at the picture. Since she hadn't looked like her mother, she had hoped she would find a striking resemblance to her father. It wasn't there. This second disappointment was stronger than the first. She felt as if she belonged to no one.

Worse yet, she didn't recognize her father either. The harder she tried to find some memory of him, the more it hurt. Why couldn't she remember? She didn't cry this time. It was almost as if the pain went too deep to be eased by tears. She closed her eyes for a moment and concentrated on her breathing. Feeling the tension in her body diminish, she returned to the kitchen and placed the picture back on the stack.

Several more clippings indicated that an arrest was imminent.

Then three weeks after the murder, Chief Hanssen announced that Jimmy Newton had disappeared. Jimmy had left a note saying that he had committed the murder out of anger and couldn't bear the thought of going to prison. He was leaving Minnesota and beginning a new life somewhere else. He hoped that somehow he could make amends for his actions by living a life of service to others.

It wasn't until the end of the article that Clare was mentioned. Chief Hanssen reported that also in the letter Jimmy had mentioned that his daughter would be living with his sister-in-law in another state. She would be well cared for and he hoped she would not have to live under the shadow of his crime.

Tears filled Clare's eyes and she hiccupped a muffled cry. She'd read the other articles as if she were reading a fiction story. She didn't feel as if she knew either Lily or Jimmy. Now hearing again that her father had tried to protect her by sending her away with his sister-in-law made her conscious of him as a flesh and blood person.

He didn't sound like a murderer.

She got off the stool and walked around the room. Her neck was stiff from bending over the counter and her eyes burned from reading the fine print.

There was nothing in the paper to indicate her father was a bad person. Someone mentioned that he had a quick temper but all the other comments had been favorable. The priest at the church and his boss at the paper mill where he worked, his neighbors. Everyone seemed to like him. Said he was a trusted worker, faithful husband, and loving father. Could he have ruined his life and taken another in one moment of anger?

Clare decided she needed a break. She wrote down several things that she would need at the grocery store and then scooped up her purse and headed into town. Now that she knew her way around a little she could enjoy the scenery. As she drove, she passed several tailings piles. Ruth had told her they were the leftover rock piles from the open pit iron mines. They were jokingly referred to as Minnesota mountains. She was fascinated by the red color and, despite their barren quality, was amazed at the occasional trees that had taken root on the rocky surface.

The water that filled the pits below the rock hills was a beautiful greenish blue, the glassy surface broken by an occasional fish rising to the surface. She had read somewhere that birds dropped fish they'd caught into the water and that was the beginning of the fish population in these abandoned quarries.

Ruth had given her a hand-drawn map of the downtown area that had pointed out Gordy's, the grocery store. She found it without difficulty. Smaller than the Jewel stores she was used to in Chicago, she found it far more accessible. She didn't need much. She'd decided to make her favorite sweet and sour ramen salad along with some ham slices. She spotted half a coconut cake that looked positively sinful so she decided to splurge.

Mentally going over the staples she'd need, she turned the corner into the next aisle and slammed into a grocery cart coming out. The stranger gasped at the contact and her purse dropped, knocking a glass jar of applesauce off the bottom shelf. The jar broke, scattering its contents on the wood floor.

"Oh, I'm so sorry," Clare said. "Are you hurt?"

"No. I'm fine."

"I wasn't looking where I was going."

The older woman seemed totally flustered by the incident. She stared at Clare, bending over the shopping cart as if she needed the support.

"Are you sure, you're all right?" Clare asked, coming around to help pick up the purse items scattered on the floor.

"Be careful of the glass." The woman grabbed her purse and began to stuff things back inside.

"I think we have everything." Clare handed her a comb and a lipstick, eyeing the floor to see if they'd missed anything else. "Well I certainly made a mess here. I'd better go get someone to clean this up before someone slips."

"I can do that. I'm done with my shopping," the other woman said. "Why don't you wait here, Abby?"

Leaving her grocery basket in the aisle, the woman walked quickly toward the front of the store. Clare pushed her cart to the side so that shoppers could get past without wheeling through the glass and applesauce.

"Clean up on aisle six," came a woman's voice over the PA system.

Clare relaxed as she waited for the woman to return. After several minutes a stock boy arrived with a mop and began to clean up the mess. Curiously the woman didn't return. Clare moved her grocery cart along the aisle and waited a few more minutes. It finally dawned on her that the woman had left the store without her groceries.

How weird, Clare thought. Could the woman have been so upset about the accident? Shrugging, she finished shopping for the last items on her list and checked out. It was only as she was putting the groceries in the car that she wondered if she had done something to offend the woman. Reviewing the conversation, she almost dropped the carton of milk.

The woman had called her Abby.

Chapter Six

A total stranger had called her Abby. She hadn't imagined that. The woman had said, "Why don't you wait here, Abby." How could she have known her real name? No one but Ruth knew her name was Abigail Clare Newton. Abby.

Putting the milk in the car, she returned the cart to the store and drove slowly back to the cottage. When she got inside, she reached for the phone and called Ruth. She hadn't noticed the time. It was six o'clock and Ruth had already left the library. She rang Ruth at home but there was no answer. She didn't leave a message; she'd ask her about it tomorrow when they were having dinner.

Her mind kept going over the curious scene in the grocery store as she put away the things she'd bought. If for some reason the woman recognized her as Abby Newton that might explain the shocked expression on her face after the clash of carts. But the real question was, how anyone would recognize her, since the last time anyone had seen Abby, she was four years old.

After looking at the pictures of her mother and Rose she knew she didn't look like either of them. In the pictures of her father that she had seen, she didn't think she looked much like him. As far as she could tell the only possible answer was that Rose had stayed in contact with someone in Grand Rapids.

So many questions.

If only she'd been more alert when the woman had called her by name. Flustered that she'd caused the accident, Clare's mind had been concentrated on the broken glass and the mess on the floor. She wasn't sure if she would even recognize the woman again.

Reaching into her purse, she pulled out a bottle of aspirin. Her head had begun to throb and she could feel her neck stiffen with returning tension. In the early days, after discovering her life was a total fabrication and beginning her research, she had begun having headaches. She had the feeling she should remember something, but her memories were totally missing before the age of four.

Had the trauma of being separated from her parents been enough of a psychological jolt to erase her memories?

She wished she had recognized something about Grand Rapids when she arrived. The only tingle she'd gotten was when she had seen the photo of Rose's house where she'd been living with her parents. Even that was only a slight sense of familiarity. Nothing concrete.

To relax, she watched the news, and then cooked some soup for dinner. Afterward she made up the ramen salad and prepared the ham slices for dinner with Ruth so that she only needed to put them into the oven. She made a pitcher of tea and set it on the counter to cool. Finished with her preparations for the next day, she sat on the couch and went back to reading the last of the newspaper clippings.

Although there was a constant rehashing of the main facts in the case, there didn't appear to be anything new that surfaced. The next major article was when Chief Thatcher announced that Jimmy Newton was dead. The clipping was dated March 5, 1983. Eight months after Lily's murder.

Two men had been crossing a bridge above the railroad tracks late at night near Prairie Du Chien, Wisconsin. It had snowed heavily and their car had gotten stuck in a snow bank and they were heading into town to find a tow truck. They were almost at the far end of the bridge when they stopped to watch an approaching freight train. Just before it reached the bridge, they saw the figure of a man jump in front of the train. They raced across the bridge and ran down the hill to the tracks to check on him. He was dead. One man stayed behind with the body and the other went for help.

The witnesses differed in their story. One thought the man had slipped on the snow and ice, while the other said he was convinced the man had jumped in front of the train.

Although the body was badly mangled they were able to identify him by certain items on his person, according to the newspaper account. Chief Thatcher said the items were a gold chain and a wallet that held several thousand dollars. Apparently Jimmy Newton had cleaned out his bank account.

The remainder of the articles held little of interest. Newton's body was brought back to Grand Rapids and buried in Itasca Cemetery. The newspaper pointed out that he was interred at the far end of the cemetery, not near Lily's grave. No reason, other than jealousy, was ever put forth as to why Jimmy had killed Lily. The case was officially closed.

Clare sighed as she read the last of the clippings. Despite all that she had learned, she didn't have answers to some of the important questions. Why had Rose gone to so much trouble to keep Clare's identity a secret? Was it only to keep her from discovering the scandal of the murder? But more important to Clare was the fact that she had no clue as to what her mother and father were really like. She had read all the accounts but still couldn't see them as flesh and blood. For that she would have to talk to people who knew them.

How could she even bring up the subject of the murder? If she told them she was Abby Newton, they would probably agree to talk to her. The drawback was that once they realized who she was, she wasn't sure she'd get objective answers to her questions.

She opened the refrigerator and poured a glass of white wine. Taking the rest of the oatmeal raisin cookies she went out to the porch and sat down in one of the rattan chairs. She sipped the wine and ate the cookies as she breathed in the fresh air.

The answer was simple. She was a reporter, here on assignment. All she needed to do was state that, aside from interviewing

Nate Hanssen, she was also doing research on the murder. It had happened twenty-five years ago, which was some sort of landmark. She would then have an excuse for interviewing anyone who might have information about the murder. It wasn't like researching a murder mystery. She knew that answer. But if she were ever to find real peace with her background, she needed to find the answer to one question. Why did Jimmy Newton kill her mother?

Standing in the shadow of trees, he watched as she went through the newspaper clippings. He wished he could get closer to get a better look at her face and see her expression. With the illumination spilling out from the living room, he couldn't risk it. He'd have to wait until she went into the bedroom where there was less chance of discovery. He couldn't see with any clarity the headlines and photos she was studying, but he already knew what she was looking at.

Except for an accident, he might never have known.

He'd been at the library when the young woman was there. If he hadn't been so busy helping clean up at the meeting, he might have had a face-to-face confrontation with her. When he arrived, he'd seen her sitting in the alcove, but had paid little attention to her other than to note she was very attractive.

As he was carrying the coffee pot to the lounge to empty it, Ruth Grabenbauer came out of the file room. She was so engrossed in the folder she was carrying that she bumped into him. He'd reached out to steady her and several newspaper clippings fell to the floor. He set the coffee pot down and picked the clippings up, surprised when he glanced at them.

"Looking up an old mystery?" he'd asked.

"No, we just had a request for some information," she'd replied.

Before he could continue, she closed the folder and hurried away. Returning to the meeting, he'd heard that the young woman in the alcove was renting Ruth's cottage. There was much speculation as to why she'd come to Grand Rapids for a vacation. He'd wondered as he finished cleaning up whether there was any connection between the renter and the clipping file.

Why was anyone interested in the Newton murder? Why after all this time?

No matter why she'd come to Grand Rapids it couldn't be good if she was digging around in areas that had been closed and finished years ago. It was too dangerous. Too dangerous for the town and too dangerous for the snoop.

Thursday morning, Clare woke up close to eight, stretching slowly as she breathed in the fresh air coming through the open bedroom window. Used to living in the city, she reveled in the sound of birds as a substitution for horn honks and screeching brakes. It looked like it would be a beautiful day. She'd read in the paper that it would be hot, but hopefully there'd be a breeze.

After a shower, she dressed in a soft chambray skirt and a short-sleeved white blouse with an embroidered floral pattern across the back. Casually professional, she thought as she hooked gold hoops in her ears. She brushed her hair into a loose ponytail, low against the back of her neck. Lipstick and a brush of powder completed the look.

The newspaper was at the front door, but there was no sign of Waldo. For breakfast, she had cereal and tea and read the paper, enjoying the luxury of not having to rush off to work. Eventually she pulled out her notebook and took a quick run through her notes on Nathan Hanssen.

Hanssen was thirty-seven, a single father raising an eleven-year-old girl. Thirteen years earlier, he had exploded on the literary scene with a novel that combined an ancient civilization and a modern day archeologist into a highly marketable thriller. It was an instant bestseller and was made into a blockbuster movie a year later. Not only did it bring financial success, but also the reviews lauded him as a fine writer with a promising future.

The twenty-five year old author was a favorite on talk shows and at book signings, but at the height of his popularity tragedy struck. His high school sweetheart, whom he had married at twenty-one, died a year after the first book came out when their daughter was two years old. Clare had only found a few news stories on Mrs. Hanssen's death. They were on vacation in New York City and Rebecca had drowned in the East River.

At the time of his wife's death, Hanssen had been teaching at Case Western Reserve in Cleveland, Ohio. A year later he moved back to Minnesota with his daughter and virtually dropped out of sight. Four years later he published another book. It did not achieve the same commercial success as his first, but the critics were almost effusive in their praise. Two more books followed and his latest book was short-listed for several awards and eventually won the Pulitzer Prize.

She eyed his publicity photo again. He didn't look as arrogant as he'd sounded on the telephone. On the other hand, he didn't look as intensely intriguing as he had at the church supper. She could only hope the meeting would go well.

Clare scanned the rest of her notes then closed her notebook and went out to the car. She was looking forward to meeting Hanssen, yet she felt some lingering annoyance over his abruptness on the phone.

Hanssen's house was halfway around Lost Lake at the opposite end from Grand Rapids. It was a much more heavily forested area with fewer houses dotting the shoreline. Clare was tempted to stop several times as she passed the mountains of red rock. She marked one place in particular when she saw a gravel road cutting across the highway that led to some abandoned buildings and a ragged trail that led to one of the flooded pits.

No time now, she thought as she glanced at her watch. She was determined to be at Hanssen's house by ten o'clock sharp. No need to give the man any excuse to cancel, Clare thought as she drove down the gravel driveway leading to the house. When the trees opened up, the first thing that caught her eye was the mass of red geraniums on either side of a stone walk that led around the right side of the house to a deck overlooking the lake. She parked the car on the far side of the garage and walked back toward the screened porch that led into the main part of the house.

The house itself was made of large, multicolored fieldstones. Wood beams were visible as support and decoration, which gave the place a solid rustic look. Myriad red, white, and yellow flowers lined the edges of the screened porch. A rectangular wooden plaque hung above the door. The background was bright blue. In the center was a red circle flanked by two crescents facing out, one a white moon sliver and the other black. As folk art it was striking and had a familiarity about it that made her think she had seen something similar before.

Tucking her leather notebook under her arm, she rang the doorbell.

She could hear the chime inside the house, but it was a minute or two before the inside door opened and Erika came out. Up close, Clare felt as if she were watching a pixie flitting across the screened porch. Dressed in denim shorts and a pink tank top, the willowy youngster danced across the floor, her flip-flops making soft slapping sounds on the wooden boards.

"Are you the magazine lady?" she asked, staring at Clare through the screen door.

"Yes, I'm Clare Prentice. And you?"

"I'm Erika. Erika Hanssen." The girl cocked her head and her white blonde hair spilled across her shoulder. "We don't have a lot of visitors."

I'm pleased to meet you." Clare smiled, surprised when the girl didn't respond. If anything, her expression seemed to harden. "I have an appointment with your father."

"I know. That's why he's been so grouchy all morning." She stared at Clare accusingly. "He doesn't like reporters."

Clare sighed. So far it was an inauspicious start to the interview. "May I come in?"

The girl remained motionless as if she were thinking over the request. A sound from inside the house caught her attention and after a quick glance over her shoulder, Erika reached for the door handle. Before she could open it, Hanssen appeared.

"Well done, Miss Prentice. Right on time," Hanssen said.

Looking at him, Clare had that same feeling of breathlessness that she'd experienced at the church supper. He peered intently at her and his eyes widened in surprise.

"You're Clare Prentice?"

"Guilty as charged," she said, feeling suddenly awkward.

"I saw you at the church last night." He remained motionless as if he still couldn't believe it. Then with a shake he stepped out onto the porch. "Don't just stand there, Erika. Let the poor woman in out of the heat."

Erika let out a harrumphing sound of annoyance and pulled the door open. Clare stepped inside, grateful to be out of the sun. As the door closed behind her, it let out a prolonged squeak and she felt a shiver run through her body. The sound made her knees weak and she clenched her fingers around the notebook under her arm. Beckoning her to follow him, Hanssen turned toward the house.

Still feeling unsteady, Clare followed, walking cautiously on trembling legs. Erika skipped around her and disappeared. As Clare put her hand out to grasp the doorframe in a fight to control her body, she spotted the decorative bell that hung beside the door.

The cast-iron bell was an oval shape with a slight flare at the bottom below the floral carvings along the midsection. It hung by a ring from a metal post driven into the wood beside the door. Above the post was a slender angel with delicately engraved wings.

Hanssen turned and noticed her scrutiny of the bell. "The bell was originally on the front door of the house and I kept it after we renovated the place. It's got a lovely sound."

He pulled on the black braided twine attached to the bell and a low gong resonated in the morning air. The sound seemed to reverberate inside Clare's entire body. The bell's tone intensified her unsteadiness. Her knees buckled. Waves of blackness washed over her. Strong hands grabbed her before she could fall to the ground.

"I've got you." Hanssen's deep voice came from a distance and she fought to remain conscious. "Erika!"

Clare relaxed against Hanssen's arm, feeling dizzy and slightly nauseous. She closed her eyes and listened as he barked out orders.

"Get a wet washcloth and some ice. Bring them to the family room." With his mouth close to her ear, he asked, "Can you walk?"

She nodded her head, immediately regretting the movement as her vision blurred. Half carrying her, he led her along the hallway toward the back of the house. She felt the cool leather against the back of her legs as he set her down on the sofa. A wet cloth was pressed against her neck and she jumped at the cold sensation.

"What's wrong with her?" Erika asked.

"We'll have to wait to find out," Hanssen replied.

Clare felt the heat rise in her cheeks as she listened to the voices. She was feeling better but was now too embarrassed to open her eyes. Knowing she'd have to eventually, she covered her eyes with her hand, and peered through a slit in her lids.

Nathan Hanssen was kneeling beside the couch, a washcloth in his hand. His expression of concern was in sharp contrast to Erika's look of annoyance.

"Maybe she's faking it," the girl said.

"Why would she do that?"

"To weasel her way inside the house."

Nathan laughed, "She was invited inside, remember? She probably didn't eat breakfast."

Unable to stand having them talk over her, Clare dropped her hand to her lap and opened her eyes.

"I am so sorry," she said. "I feel impossibly stupid."

Relief was evident on Nathan's face as he smiled at her. If Clare weren't already dizzy, his smile might have sent her into a maidenly swoon. Nathan Hanssen was incredibly handsome when he turned on the charm.

"Are you all right?" he asked.

Clare moved to a more upright position and nodded. "I don't know what it was." As she said the words a picture flashed into her mind. "For some reason when I heard the sound of the angel bell I thought I was going to faint. I don't know if it was the tone . . ."

"It's the curse," Erika interrupted.

"Oh please, Erika. Don't start that nonsense." Nathan's voice was sharp.

"It is, Dad. We put the bell there to ward off any danger from the curse."

"Try to be nice to Miss Prentice while I get us some brandy. All the best romantic comedies recommend brandy, so who am I to go against tradition."

Shooting a warning glare at Erika, he left the room. The girl made a face at his back then returned her attention to Clare.

"Is it an ancient curse?" Clare asked, anxious to fix her mind on something other than her current dizziness.

With a careful glance to be sure her father had really left the room, Erika bounced down beside Clare and leaned toward her, her own face alight with excitement. It was clear that she was enjoying every bit of Clare's discomfort.

"When the house was being rebuilt, I found that plaque to hang outside the screen door. Dad liked it too but said it was a pagan symbol. A witchy thing."

"Wicca?" Clare asked.

"That's it. He wasn't sure if it was good luck or not to hang it over the door. But I really liked it and I talked him into it." She cast her father a gloating expression as he came back into the room.

"I'm sure Miss Prentice would rather hear about something else," he said.

"It's all right. I'm interested in her story."

"Well, take a sip of this. I don't know what caused your sinking spell, but I'm sure this will help."

He handed her a small crystal snifter. She sniffed tentatively then raised it to her lips to take a small swallow. It was a very fine brandy, she thought, as she rolled it over her tongue and let the warmth slide down her throat. Cautiously she took another sip and could feel the heat spread throughout her body.

Erika tapped her foot against the floor, watching Clare much like a robin eyeing a worm. Setting the glass on the table beside the couch, Clare nodded to the girl.

"So the sign above the door is a Wiccan symbol?"

"Dad thinks it is." Erika cast a disparaging glance at her father who was sitting on the ottoman beside the couch. "I looked it up at the library and it's also a symbol of the three phases of the moon. A waxing crescent, a full moon, and the waning crescent."

"It's an ancient symbol used in pagan and nonpagan cultures." Hanssen's deep voice was nonjudgmental. "You see it in many decorative objects. Sometimes it's three spirals or it could be intertwined crescents. In Wicca it's the symbol for the Triple Goddess."

"Strangely enough, I know about that," Clare said. "Maiden, mother, and crone. I thought there was something familiar about the sign but I just couldn't place it. I can even quote a passage from Robert Graves's *The White Goddess.*

> The New Moon is the white goddess of birth and growth;
> The Full Moon, the red goddess of love and battle;
> The Old Moon, the black goddess of death and divination.

That explains the paint colors on the plaque over your front door."

"Very good," Hanssen said. "Not many people would have caught that. You must be well read."

He smiled across at her as if she were a particularly apt pupil. Erika tapped her foot again, annoyed at the talk between the adults.

"Rose, my m . . . mother, used to call me a changeling when I misbehaved." Clare stumbled over the word, but recovered and spoke directly to Erika, wanting to include her in the conversation. "I have a birthmark on my shoulder. It resembles three intertwined circles. My mother told me it was a witch's symbol that marked me as someone who could be bad. She said it was put there to remind me that I would have to try very hard to be a good person."

"It sounds like your mother was a bad person," Erika said, folding her arms across her chest.

"Not bad. Just rather stern."

Clare flushed. Her dizzy spell must have rattled her tongue loose since she couldn't remember when she had mentioned this personal fact to anyone but her friend Gail. She'd never even told her ex-fiancé. With a quick glance across at Hanssen, she could see in his expression that he was assessing her comments. Wanting to deflect his attention, she turned to Erika.

"So the sign is to ward off any bad luck to the house?" she asked.

"No. Not the plaque." Erika lowered her voice to a more conspiratorial tone. "That was for good luck. The bell was to ward off the curse."

"Erika." There was a warning note in Hanssen's voice.

"Oh, Dad. She's a reporter. She's bound to dig it up anyway." The girl shrugged her shoulders, then flipped her hair away from her face. "The bell was on the front door of the old house and I saved it when they started to tear it down."

"We didn't tear it down," Nathan explained. "The house belonged to my father. I pretty well gutted it after he died and I decided to move in here with Erika."

Clare looked around the room for the first time and was surprised at the modern simplicity. The room was entirely open, part kitchen, dining space, and family room, surrounded by floor-to-ceiling windows that looked out onto a deck and the lake. The furniture was wood and leather with a luxurious area rug in warm browns, reds, and green.

"I'll show you around when you feel up to it."

"Not until I've told her about the bell," Erika said.

Her voice held a bit of a whine as if she wasn't used to being interrupted. In fact it was apparent to Clare that Erika was very used to having her father's total attention and didn't relish Clare's presence as a distraction.

"I'd like to hear about the bell," Clare said.

Erika wriggled on the couch, like an excited puppy. "I took the bell down when they hauled the old door away. When Dad complained about the sign over the porch door, I told him we should move the bell to the door into the house. That way if the murderer had cursed the place, the evil spirits would be trapped on the screened porch between the sign and the bell."

"The murderer?" Clare asked, amused how the young girl was relishing the drama of the storytelling.

"Yes, there was a murder right in this house. How weird is that?" Erika leaned toward Clare until her face was only a foot away. "A man shot his wife to death and then dumped her body in the lake. And it all happened right here in this house. Maybe in this very room."

In an instant Clare understood why the sound of the bell had jogged her memory. This was the house where she had lived with her parents until she was four years old. This was the house where her father had killed her mother.

Chapter Seven

"James Newton killed his wife in this house?" Clare asked.

"You've obviously done your research since you know about our famous murder case," Nate said.

"This was the house the Newtons lived in," Erika said. "James Newton shot his wife, Lily, to death and then dragged her body outside and threw it in the lake."

In an instant Clare realized that it was the sound of the bell that had triggered her fainting spell. She hadn't recognized the house because of the renovations. It was the squeak of the screen door that had jogged her memory and then when she heard the ring of the bell, the connection was made. As she tried to force the return of the memories, she could feel the waves of blackness creep over her again.

"That's enough, Erika," Hanssen snapped as he got up and came toward Clare. He recognized her distress instantly. "Breathe deeply, Miss Prentice. Don't even consider fainting."

"Oh, Dad, it's just like an old ghost story. She's acting like a sissy."

Erika jumped to her feet and plopped down on the abandoned ottoman as Hanssen took her place on the couch. He reached across and grabbed the brandy glass.

"Take another sip," he said as he held it to her lips.

Clare covered his hand with her own and took a quick swallow. The liquor burned her tongue. She sucked in her breath and she started to cough. The coughing cleared her head and her vision steadied. She realized she was still holding his hand and she snatched her fingers away.

"Good lord, I'm swooning like a Victorian debutante," she said. "I can't tell you how sorry I am, Mr. Hanssen."

"For starters, you can call me Nate. If I'm going to keep reviving you, I think we might consider ourselves on friendly terms."

The warmth in his blue eyes took any sting out of his words. Clare ignored Erika's snort of disgust. "You and Erika can call me Clare. And please don't look so concerned. I'm really much better now."

"Why don't we go out to the deck. I think the fresh air will be good for you. Would you like some more brandy?"

"No! I try not to get drunk before noon."

Nate grinned. "Then how about some iced tea?"

"That would be fine."

Clare was aware of the stormy expression on Erika's face as Nate held out his hand to help her up. She smiled at the girl to diffuse the situation but sensed that it was a lost cause.

"Can you get out the tea, Erika?" Nate asked.

Without replying, the girl pushed herself off the ottoman and stomped toward the kitchen. Nate opened the French doors that led out to the deck.

"Please, make yourself comfortable," he said. Nate brushed off the cushion on the chaise lounge, waiting until she sat down. "Put your feet up and breathe in some fresh air. I've got a couple of things to do and then Erika and I will join you."

Nate watched her as she settled back against the cushions and closed her eyes. Her cheeks were still pale, but her breathing was more even than it had been before. It had frightened him when her skin whitened and she appeared ready to pass out again. Wait until he told Ann Taylor that her reporter had indeed fainted on his doorstep.

Now that she was resting, he felt it was safe to leave her. He returned to the house, closing the door quietly behind him. He turned left into the kitchen spotting Erika in the family room sitting cross-legged on the couch. If he hadn't been angry, he might have laughed at her look of innocence. A ball of yarn lay beside her and her head was bent as she concentrated on the knitting in her hands.

Crossing the room to stand in front of her, he remained silent until she looked up at him. "Aren't you the industrious little worker," he said. "Weren't you supposed to be getting the iced tea ready?"

Her tongue stuck out as she negotiated the end of a row and then turned the piece around. "I just remembered that I hadn't finished my knitting project for class tomorrow."

"Just remembered?" Knowing that sarcasm would be wasted on her, he abandoned that line of questioning. "What's going on here, Erika? Why are you being so rude to Miss Prentice?"

"I'm not being rude."

At least she had the grace to blush, Nate thought as he eyed his daughter. How much she'd changed in the last year. He suspected that her hormones were in high gear but didn't know what to do about it. Her mood swings in the past month would rival the ups and downs of the roller coasters at any theme park. He'd almost been tempted to call his mother in Florida for help, however he wasn't that desperate yet.

"It started before she even got inside the house. When I came out to the porch, you'd left her standing in the hot sun and you were glaring at her as if she was an unwelcome visitor."

"You didn't want her here," Erika said.

"Whether I wanted her here or not has nothing to do with your behavior. That would be for me to deal with. Not you."

"Whatever."

"You know how I hate that word. Now put your knitting away and come help me. We'll talk about this later."

With a put-upon air, she sighed. She stuck her knitting needles into the ball of yarn and grudgingly got off the couch. Nate had always wondered what it looked like when someone flounced, and now he had an actual example of it as she headed for the kitchen. He followed in her wake trying to hide his amusement.

"She seems a nice enough woman, Erika." He picked up a tray leaning against the back of the bar and put it on the countertop. "Why don't you like her?"

"I don't know why she's come all this way just for an interview. She could have done it on the phone." She set two glasses on the tray. "And then she gets all fluttery at the mere mention of the murder."

"Maybe she forgot to eat breakfast and standing in the sun so long made her lightheaded," he countered.

"It's not that hot out. I think she's covering up something. She's going to take notes and you're going to be mad again."

"I'm sure she's going to take notes. She's a reporter." At Erika's snort, he chuckled. "Speaking of notes. What happened to her notebook? Check around for it, would you?"

With another long-suffering sigh, Erika inspected the family room, and then headed down the hall. Nate got a lemon out of the refrigerator and took a quick look out on the patio. Clare was still on the chaise and he wondered if she'd fallen asleep. Her head was turned away and her hair in the ponytail glinted in the sunlight. Despite her pallor and the fragile look about her, he'd been struck by the beauty of her green eyes and reddish hair.

He'd noticed her last night the moment he walked into the church hall. During the evening, he'd made several attempts to approach her. Either she'd been talking to people or Erika was vying for his attention. There was something about her he found extremely appealing and hoped that his rudeness on the phone hadn't put her off.

"I found the notebook," Erika said, returning to the kitchen. "She must have dropped it on the porch."

"Excellent. You can give it back to her when we go back outside. It'll give you an opening to make your apology."

"Oh, Dad."

"Don't 'oh, Dad' me. Even if you don't like someone, you need to be polite." Although Erika's face darkened as if she wanted to comment, she apparently thought better of it. "Would you get the sugar bowl out and fill it?"

She nodded and opened the cupboard beside the sink. In surprise he noted that she didn't need to stretch to reach anymore. He hadn't realized how much she'd grown in the last year. Both he and Rebecca had been tall and he could see that Erika would be too. He'd been so involved in her emotional changes of late that he'd failed to notice how much her body had changed. He had a tendency to think of her as a child, but looking at her objectively he saw that she was beginning to lose the straight-bodied look and gain some actual curves.

Thank God she looks more like Rebecca, he thought. Her skin was clear and her features were well shaped. She wore her hair long and it fell straight and full, a streaky almost white blonde. When she wasn't sulking, as she was now, she had an incredible smile. As he looked at her, it struck him that she was going to be a beautiful young woman. *And how unprepared I am to handle that*, he thought.

"All set?" he asked as she put the sugar bowl onto the tray. Looking out the window, he could see that Clare was finally stirring.

Hearing the French door opening, Clare rose to her feet. Relieved that she knew what had caused her fainting spell, she breathed in the fresh air, letting it clear the last of the fuzziness from her brain. The peaceful scene did much to calm her, and she was able to face Nate and Erika with some equanimity.

"You look as if you're feeling better," he said, as he set a tray on the glass-topped table. "You actually have some color in your cheeks."

"I'm fully recovered," Clare said as she crossed to the table.

"Here," Erika said, thrusting Clare's notebook toward her. "I found this on the floor."

"Thank you, Erika. I forgot all about it." She smiled at the girl as she took the notebook and set it on the table. "It seems like I've totally bungled this interview. Hardly professional to faint on your doorstep."

"I find it disarming to say the least." Nate pointed to a pitcher of tea and two glasses on the tray, beside a dish of lemon slices and a sugar bowl. "Please help yourself. I'll join you, but Erika has a project to finish before her knitting class."

He nudged the girl who stood awkwardly beside him.

"It was very nice meeting you, Miss Prentice," she said. "I'm sorry if my story about the murder upset you."

She spoke as if she'd rehearsed the words and Clare couldn't help smiling at the lack of contrition in her voice.

"I quite enjoyed learning about the bell and the moon symbols over the door. I hope I'll see you again."

"Me too."

Erika looked up at her father, nodded curtly then retraced her steps into the house and closed the French doors. Clare braced for a slammed door and apparently so did Nate because he sighed when it closed gently.

"The next thing we will hear is music blasting in her room. Eleven is a very difficult age," he said. "She's usually not quite so . . ."

"Territorial?" Clare suggested.

Nate laughed although there was little humor in the sound. "That's the word I was looking for. It's just been in the last year I've noticed this."

"Erika's growing up and you've been a twosome for a long time now. It's only natural."

Clare poured tea into the glasses, adding lemon to hers. She walked across to the stone wall edging the flagstone patio that ran along the entire back of the house. The house was set at the top of a sharp rise, sloping up from the lakeshore. The lawn was mowed down to the dock so the view of the lake was unobstructed. Despite that, the house felt secluded since it was bounded on either side by thick woods. The deck was in shadow and comfortable despite the heat from the late morning sun.

"It's beautiful here and totally peaceful. I almost fell asleep just looking at the lake," she said.

"I think it's one of the best views in Grand Rapids. I prefer being above the lake rather than down at the water's edge."

Nate added lemon and sugar to his tea as Clare came back to

join him. She sat down in one of the metal deck chairs beside the table. He took another chair, swinging it around so they were both facing the lake. Music emanated from the house, loud enough to be heard outside but not too intrusive.

Nate grinned, raising his glass in salute toward the house. "Erika's mother died when she was two. I had pretty much been an absent father. My first book was out and there was a lot of publicity on the movie. It was a pretty heady time."

"I can imagine. *Field of Reeds* was a wonderful book. There's always been a lot of interest in Egyptology and your book tapped into that perfectly. The movie didn't do it justice."

Nate turned his head and stared at her as if assessing whether she was making a joke. His tight mouth indicated his annoyance.

"It was never intended as a thriller. It was designed as a scholarly comparison of cultures and an in-depth analysis of the *Book of the Dead*."

"I actually trembled at the muscular build of Harry, your—can I say—hero?" Clare fluttered her eyelashes as she grinned at Nate.

"God Almighty, can you imagine anyone in his or her right mind casting that ex-wrestler in the part. As you know the character's name was Horus, which means distant one. He was seventy-four and an astronomer, for God's sake."

Seeing his fingers tighten around the iced tea glass, Clare realized that he found little humor in her comment. "I'm sorry, Nate, I shouldn't have kidded you about it. It must be incredibly difficult to see your work mangled."

"You'd think I'd be used to it by now. Especially since it was the success of the movie that enabled me to quit my job and stay home with Erika after Rebecca died." Once more he turned to study her, his eyes narrow and less than friendly. "I forgot you were doing an interview."

Clare took a long swallow of her iced tea and then set the glass on the table. She could understand his quandary. She felt they had made some sort of weird connection and now he was worried that if he spoke freely to her, what he told her would appear in the magazine article. She knew from talking to her editor that Nate had little faith in the media and knew there was only one way to convince him she could be trusted.

"Before we go any further, I need to tell you something. Please hear me out before you jump to any conclusions."

"Now you've got me curious." Nate turned his chair so that he was facing her more directly. Although his tone was light, his eyes studied her with an unsmiling intensity. "Don't tell me you also work for the *National Enquirer.*"

She tried to smile around the lump in her throat. She was still in such an emotional turmoil that it was a leap of faith for her to confide in this man whom she had just met. When she arrived at the house, she had been convinced that she would thoroughly dislike him. Yet in such a short time she found she was totally comfortable in his presence. Maybe having read his books and researched his background it was like meeting an old friend.

"My name is not Clare Prentice." She raised her chin as the muscles in his jaw rippled in anger. "My name is Abigail Clare Newton."

The widening of his eyes indicated that he recognized the name.

"I am the daughter of the woman who Erika says was murdered in your house."

"That's just not possible."

Clare pleated the material of her skirt across her knees. Even as a child she'd done it, if she were nervous or tense. The steady motion of her fingers was soothing.

"It's true. I just recently discovered that I was adopted and eventually came here to find my birth parents. I'm staying in Ruth Grabenbauer's cottage closer in to town. She was the one who discovered my real name."

"I don't know what to say." Nate reached across and covered her hands with one of his. "No wonder you almost passed out. I gather you had no idea that this was the house you lived in."

"No. I'd seen a picture before it was renovated but when I arrived it looked so different. It was only when the screen door squeaked and I saw the angel that I felt peculiar. However when Erika talked about the murder then I connected the dots."

"I'm so very sorry." His blue eyes held steady on her face and he tightened his grip on her hands. "I'm sure Erika will feel dreadful when she knows she upset you."

"Please don't tell her," Clare said. "I'd rather no one in Grand Rapids knew. I'm hoping to find out about my parents and if people know who I am, I'm afraid they won't feel free to tell me the truth. All anyone will think is that I'm here to do an interview with you and to do some research on a long-ago murder."

"Yes, I can see the sense in that."

He squeezed her hands as if to reassure her, then released his clasp. Strangely Clare felt bereft at the loss of physical contact. To cover her awkwardness, she reached for her tea and took several swallows. Nate sat quietly beside her, not seeming in any need to rush her. She closed her eyes and leaned back in her chair. The breeze off the lake filled her senses with the smells and sounds of summer.

A calm settled over her and she began to tell Nate about the last five months and her trip to Grand Rapids. Occasionally he asked a question, but for the most part he just let her talk. When she finished with her arrival at the house, he smiled across at her.

"Quite a journey of discovery you've had. I'm sorry this part was so rocky."

"There was no way you could have known. I had no clue I'd lived here."

"How much do you know about the murder?" he asked.

"I've read the clipping file that Ruth brought home from the library. I think I have a pretty good idea of the broad strokes of the case."

"Then you know that my father was the Chief of Police at the time?"

"Yes. Ruth told me he died several years ago."

"A heart attack. He was eighty. He's badly missed."

"At a guess, the protagonist in *Guardian of the Scales* was modeled after your father."

"Yes. Much of what he was is in that book. Much of what I'd like to be."

"It was a wonderful book. No doubt as to why it won the Pulitzer."

"It's ironic considering the fact that the theme of the book was how fame is the ultimate corruptor." His laugh was harsh. "Sometime I'll tell you how my early brush with fame and fortune impacted my life. My father warned me. He was the one who got me interested in Egyptology and the idea of the *Book of the Dead*. He felt that not only did it teach how to get over the obstacles in the afterlife, but also it made you search for ways to live your life in balance while you were alive."

"I'm sorry I never met him. It sounds as if I'd have liked him."

"Most people did, despite the fact he was chief of police. He was a fair man. He didn't talk often about the murder, but it was definitely on his mind. He kept the case files in his office and went through them frequently, especially toward the end of his life."

His eyes widened as he stared at her.

"What is it?"

"You're Abby," he said as if discovering the fact for the first time.

Clare nodded. "I gather that's what I was called."

"What an idiot I am," he said, slapping his forehead with the palm of his hand. "I don't know why I didn't put it together immediately. My father left something for you. I forgot about it until just now. Wait here."

He leaped to his feet and hurried into the house, leaving the door open in his eagerness. Clare sank against the back of the chair, her chest tight as she tried to imagine what Nate's father could have left for her. She could feel the tension in her muscles and opened her clenched fists, laying them palms down on her lap as she focused on her breathing. No point in anticipating anything, she thought. She closed her eyes, resting her head against the back of the chair. It seemed a long time until Nate returned.

Placing a small cardboard box on the table beside her, Nate returned to his seat. He was holding a plastic bag, but she couldn't see what was inside.

"After my father died, I found these things in his office. The box had a note on it that said it was to be given to Abby Newton if she asked for it. I had no way of knowing how to contact you and, quite frankly, I'd really forgotten all about it. When we rehabbed the house, most of Dad's things were put in storage. Even after you told me who you were, I didn't immediately connect you with Abby."

Clare stared at the box but she made no attempt to touch it. So much had happened since she arrived at the house that she was totally bewildered.

"It's mine to take?" she asked.

"Yes, of course. I don't know what's in it, but it definitely was to be given to you."

"Would you think I was terribly rude if I didn't open it?"

"Not at all. I realize this has all come as a shock, and I want you to know that I have no intention of intruding on something like this that can be very personal." Nate reached out and patted the back of her hand. "Take it when you leave and open it at your leisure."

"Thank you for understanding," Clare said. "I tend to be a private sort of person and I don't know what's inside or how it will affect me."

"You don't have to apologize. I'm just glad that the box finally got to its rightful owner. " He lifted the plastic bag in his lap. "I do know what's in this however. After Jimmy Newton died, his effects were sent to my father since he was the chief of police."

"Items that were found with his body?" she asked, feeling chilled by the thought.

"Yes. This is Jimmy's wallet and the gold chain he was wearing at the time of his death. Because of the amount of money in the wallet it was kept in my father's safe. After he died, I found the bag and a note that said to give it to Jimmy Newton's heir. I knew he had a daughter, but I had no idea how to contact you. Now that you're here, as next of kin it is yours to keep."

He extended the bag to her and, after a momentary hesitation, she grasped it with shaking fingers. She placed it in her lap, unwilling to open the bag and touch the objects inside.

"I'm sure this is a lot to process, but once you have a chance to catch your breath it will all seem less overwhelming."

"Did you talk to your father about the m . . . murder?"

"Yes. At the end of his life he used to spend a great deal of time going over some of his case files and this one he seemed to be more personally involved with. Your father had been a friend of his and he also knew your mother. I knew them too."

"You actually knew them?" Clare's hands tightened around the plastic bag and she leaned toward him in her eagerness. "What were they like?"

"The murder took place in July nineteen eighty-two. I would have been twelve since my birthday is in August. At that age I didn't pay much attention to adults. Your father occasionally stopped by or I'd see your parents at church. I remember your mother was a very pretty woman. She was shorter than you and had beautiful blonde hair. Strangely I can remember her voice. She looked sort of fragile so it was a surprise that her voice was strong and very precise when she spoke."

"Did she seem like a nice woman?"

Nate's eyes were focused straight ahead as if he were trying to picture her. "I don't really know. I do recall that people at church liked your parents. After services in the summertime, people generally stood around and talked. All I can say is that they both appeared to be popular."

"I'm sorry to ask so many questions, but you're the first person I've talked to who knew them personally."

"I'm happy to tell you what I can. Your father was a big man. He was Scandinavian, built like those skiers you see in the old Olympic films. Big in the shoulders and the chest. He was tall, although when you're a kid everyone seems tall. He had reddish brown hair. I remember that because so many of the Swedes in town were blonde, including your mother. He had a beard too. Very neat not bushy." Nate shook his head. "I wish I could think of something more definite."

"You said he was a friend of your father's. Did he say anything about my father and the murder?"

Nate turned to look at her. His forehead was furrowed and his eyebrows bunched together. He hesitated for a full minute before he spoke.

"I got the impression that he liked Jimmy Newton very much. As I said, they were friends. Fished together. I remember how upset he was all through the investigation and when your father disappeared, he seemed almost relieved. At the time I thought it was because he didn't want to be the one to arrest him."

Once more Nate paused as if debating if he should continue.

"Please," Clare said, "I'd really like to hear anything your father said at the time."

"I was home the night Dad got the telephone call about Jimmy Newton's death. He was in his office and I couldn't hear what was said. After the call was over, he slammed the phone down. He was usually a mild-mannered man but I could hear him cursing like I'd never heard before. My mother went into the office and I stood outside just listening. Dad told mother that Jimmy Newton had committed suicide. He kept asking why he would do a damn fool thing like that. Mother kept trying to calm him down, but he was furious."

Nate ran his fingers up through his hair.

"He said, 'Why couldn't he trust me to get to the bottom of this?' "

Chapter Eight

"What did your father mean? Get to the bottom of what?" Clare's voice was too loud and she forced it to a more level tone. "Was he saying he didn't think Jimmy killed my mother?"

"I probably shouldn't have told you that because it will only raise more questions in your mind. Don't get your hopes up. What he said didn't make any sense. According to anyone you asked, Jimmy Newton killed Lily."

"Then what did your father mean?" Clare asked.

"I don't honestly know." Nate shrugged. "I didn't hear any more of the conversation because my father saw me in the doorway and sent me to bed." Nate grimaced as he continued. "At the time, it was something I heard but it didn't mean much to a kid. It was only in later years when I found him going through the case files that I asked him about it. At first he said he didn't remember."

"Was he having trouble with his memory?"

"No. It was his usual excuse. He had never liked talking about his cases. So I asked him what he thought about Jimmy Newton. He said he was a good friend and a very fine man. I asked if he knew why Jimmy had killed his wife. He said he never believed Jimmy was a murderer."

"From everything I've read, there was never any question that Jimmy was guilty," Clare said.

"I said the same thing to Dad and he agreed. Your father signed a full confession to the crime. What little forensic evidence they had at the time all pointed to your father. No one, even my father, registered any doubt that Jimmy Newton killed Lily. Dad said it was just a gut feeling because the Jimmy he knew wasn't a murderer. Personally I always thought it was wishful thinking on Dad's part."

In the aftermath of Nate's comments, Clare could only shake her head in bewilderment. What did any of it mean?

"Ever since I discovered I was adopted, there has been one stunning revelation after another. Every time I think I'm beginning to find the real story, something happens to turn it all inside out again. At this point I don't know what to believe."

Clare pressed her fingers against her temples rubbing the sides of her head. She had another headache building and knew she needed to get back to the cottage and lie down. Nate stood up as if he too realized she needed to get away.

"That's enough for now, Clare." He picked up the box and her notebook from the table. "You look as if one more piece of information will have you fainting away again. I'll walk you to the car and when you feel better and have sorted some of this out, you're always welcome to come back and talk about it."

"Thank you for being so understanding." Clare shoved the plastic bag into her purse and followed him back through the house.

"It's been a very long morning. And I haven't even gotten to the interview."

"Don't worry about it. We'll be seeing each other very soon. I was going to the art show in town on Saturday. Would you like to go? It would be a nice change of pace for you."

Clare smiled. "Ruth already asked me to go with her so I'll probably see you there."

"Then before someone else asks, how would you like to go to the Farm Exhibit on Sunday. You haven't lived until you've seen a long line of antique tractors and sat in the latest models."

"Now you've really tempted me. How could a girl refuse such an invitation? What time is this fantastic display?"

"Let's say I pick you up around two."

"Excellent. I'm at Heart's Content cottage."

"I know just where that is. I didn't realize that was Ruth's place." He opened the screen door and the squeak of the hinges sent a shiver through Clare's body. "I'll see if a bit of oil won't fix that door. I hate to think of you flinching every time I open the door for you. It's not good for a man's ego."

Clare was able to laugh now that she knew the source of her distress. He opened the passenger-side door and put the box and her leather notebook on the front seat. Then he walked around to the driver's side and stood at the open door while she settled herself and put on her seat belt.

"I apologize for being rude on the phone yesterday. As you may have gathered I don't have a lot of trust in the media. In this case I think we'll get along just fine. In fact, I'm looking forward to seeing you again and, if I can, I'd like to help you to fill in some of the missing background of your early life."

Clare tilted her head to look up at Nate. His face was in shadow and she didn't know him well enough to verify his sincerity.

"Background for a book?" The moment she said the words she regretted it. "I'm sorry, Nate. I'm not usually so caustic. Your problem is with the media and my problem is that, ever since discovering my life was a sham, I can't take anything at face value."

"I can understand that. Don't give it a thought. Erika and I will be going to the art show Saturday afternoon. If I see you there I'll treat you to some of the coldest beer in the county. And the best hot dogs."

"Now you're talking my language. I'm not sure the dogs can compete with the Chicago brats I was raised on, but the cold beer sounds great." She reached in her purse and pulled out a business card. "I can't remember the phone number at the cottage. But this has my cell phone number. I think I need a day or two before we do the interview."

Nate took it and slipped it into his shirt pocket. "We'll talk again about it on Sunday." He stepped away from the car as Clare closed the door.

She started the car, took one last look at the house and smiled at Nate as she drove down the driveway to the main road. Back at the cottage, she parked the car and took the box into the house. It was just after noon but it felt as if she'd been gone for a full day. Dropping everything on the sofa in the living room, she opened the back door and stepped out onto the porch. She brushed off the cushion on the wicker chaise lounge and sat down. Kicking off her sandals, she swung her feet up and laid back.

Lost Lake glowed in the noonday sun. Although it was hot, a slight breeze felt like silken brush strokes across her skin. On the far side of the lake, a fisherman cast along the shore, the silent rhythm soothing. As Clare relaxed she felt as if her bones were melting and closed her eyes, letting the tension seep from her body.

She came awake slowly, reveling in the sense of peace that filled her. The lake shimmered in the heat of the day. She didn't know what time it was. The sun was closer to the horizon but she was far too comfortable to look at her watch. It was hard to believe that she had fallen asleep since she had slept so fully the night before. She stretched her legs and wriggled her toes. She was grateful that she'd been in the shade most of the time or she might have gotten a sunburn.

The familiar swish of tail against floorboards alerted her to the fact that her furry guardian had returned. Looking toward the sound, she spotted Waldo lying beside the chaise. Amazed to realize his arrival hadn't woken her, she grinned at the dog.

"You must think I'm a total slacker," she said.

Waldo clambered to his feet with the slight clink of tag against chain. He rested his head in her lap and she stroked the silky fur between his ears. A soft snuff and wagging tail were indications of his appreciation.

"What have you gotten into this time?" Clare asked as she lifted her hand to her nose. "The usual fish, I see." She sniffed again. "Ah, with a hint of rosemary and mint. Rolling in someone's garden? It's a good combination but not guaranteed to overcome the fish smell."

A sharp whistle cut the air and Waldo cocked his head, tail wagging more vigorously. At the second whistle, he rose to his feet and sauntered down the walk, angling toward the shore line. Clare watched his unhurried pace until he disappeared among the trees.

She stretched, then swung her legs over the side and slipped on her sandals. When she looked at her watch, she was stunned. Three fifteen. She'd been sleeping for three hours.

Luckily she didn't have much to do before Ruth arrived for dinner. Getting up she looked at the furniture on the porch. She hoped it wouldn't be too buggy because she wanted to eat outside as long as the weather was nice. She'd found napkins and a checkered cloth to cover the wicker table and she just needed to wipe off the cushions of the two pull up chairs. Ruth wasn't due until seven so she had plenty of time to get ready.

Back inside she spotted the things she'd dropped on the sofa when she came in after her meeting with Nate. Since she'd missed lunch she took a yogurt out of the refrigerator and poured herself a glass of iced tea. She ate the yogurt standing behind the couch, staring down at the cardboard box and the plastic bag in her purse. Throwing the empty container in the trash, she sat down on the couch. She took a long drink of the tea, gaze steady on the box, then, with a shake of her head, she reached for the plastic bag.

According to Nate these were the items used to identify her father after the train accident. She poured the contents of the bag onto the table. A brown leather wallet and a gold chain.

The chain was a simple rope style. The spring catch was broken and if there had been anything on the chain it had been lost in the accident. The chain wasn't delicate; the rope looked strong and appropriately masculine.

The wallet was shaped by its contents, the leather mottled with watermarks, sweat, and age. It was a simple folded style, bulging with the amount of bills inside. Opening it carefully, Clare stared down at the driver's license in the ID window. The picture was small but clear. Jimmy Newton's hair and eyebrows were a light reddish brown while his beard was closer in color to Clare's. His eyebrows were drawn down over his eyes, giving his face a somber expression.

Clare's first thought was that he didn't look like a murderer.

He looked totally normal. Someone you'd see on the street any day of the week. Obviously she couldn't make any judgments based on his looks. After all, Ted Bundy hadn't looked like a serial killer either.

The details on the license showed Jimmy's height at five eleven and his weight as one hundred eighty pounds. Hair: red. Eyes: brown. His birthday was February 19, 1940. Calculating quickly she realized he would have been sixty-seven if he'd lived. He was forty-two when he died.

Looking at the picture she felt little emotion for the man who was her father. She didn't know him and had no memories to give her a sense of personal loss.

In the five card slots on the left side there was a library card, a claim ticket for shoe repair, and a health identification card from the Blandin Paper Company. The divided currency well was filled with paper money. Taking it out, she set it on the coffee table.

Except for a few, all the bills were new one hundreds, although the top edges were slightly curled as if they had gotten wet. She counted the bills twice. There was two thousand, eight hundred fifty-six dollars. She supposed he had taken the money to help him get far away from Grand Rapids and start a new life.

Putting the money back in the wallet, she placed it and the gold chain back in the plastic bag. She didn't know what to do with the bag. She didn't like the idea of having so much money in the house. Standing up, she searched the room for a safe place to keep it. Above the kitchen cupboard, various decorative items had been stored. One was a box about the size of a shoebox. Pulling the step stool from the corner, she climbed up and reached for the box.

She dusted it off with a towel as she brought it back to the table. The wood appeared to be cherry with brass hinges and a brass latch on the front. On the top was a picture of a loon made of painted inlaid woods. The box itself was nicked and scratched and the brass hinges and latch were tarnished with age. Opening the lid, she found that the plastic bag fit easily inside.

Once it was back above the cupboard, Clare turned her attention to the cardboard box. She didn't think she wanted to open it when Ruth was due for dinner in such a short time. Since her morning meeting with Nate, her emotions had been in a constant state of upheaval. It was hard to keep a psychological balance through her search for identity. She suspected the contents of the box might be upsetting and she decided whatever was in it could wait until the next day.

She put the box on the shelf in the bedroom closet, closing the curtain to hide it from sight. Getting out cleaning supplies, she washed the table and chairs then looked through the cupboards until she found dishes and other things she needed for the dinner.

When she'd completed the arrangements, she had time for a brisk walk along the lake road. The activity was just what she'd needed. Walking along, she enjoyed the beauty of the lake as seen through the trees and between houses and yet her mind was free to go back over all she'd learned since she'd arrived in Grand Rapids. After a good workout, she returned to the cottage for a long shower.

She dressed in blue and white floral Capri pants and a simple white blouse. After she blew her hair dry, she twisted it up into a pseudo-French roll and clipped it with a large wooden barrette. She brushed on lip gloss and returned to the bedroom. Unzipping her blue satin jewelry case, she rummaged inside until she found a pair of chandelier earrings set with blue cat's-eye stones and a matching bracelet. Although she would have preferred to go barefoot, she put on her soft leather sandals.

Clare had just put the ham slices in the oven when Ruth arrived. She was wearing a flowered cotton dress that did little to diminish the size of her ample figure. She was holding another plate of cookies.

"If you keep this up, Ruth, I'll have to walk back to Chicago." Clare laughed as she kissed the older woman's cheek. Setting the cookies on the counter, she held up a bottle of wine.

"Make it a tall one. There must be a full moon coming because the library was filled with lunatics today."

Clare poured two glasses of wine and handed one to Ruth. "I

sprayed the porch with some bug repellant about an hour ago in hopes that the mosquitoes would leave us alone."

"I hope you realize that you're speaking of our state bird. *Aedes communis*—the common mosquito."

Picking up her wine glass, Clare led the way out to the porch. "I meant no disrespect," she said with a grin. "I just happen to be one of those people who hates those little bloodsuckers."

Ruth sat down and raised her glass in salute before she took a sip. "Now that's the kind of gentle sting I like."

"Me too."

"As to our Minnesota bloodsuckers I'll share some facts with you that might make you look on them more kindly. Male mosquitoes don't bite. Only the females. They require protein for egg development but they live on nectar and fruit juice so they need the protein in blood in order to lay the eggs."

"So you're telling me that I shouldn't mind the bites because it's just a motherhood thing? Truly, Ruth, female support is one thing, but it doesn't lead me to a love of the little beasts," Clare said.

"They really are quite fascinating. They've been around since the Jurassic Age. If you saw the movie *Jurassic Park* you saw what a vital part they played in preserving the DNA of the prehistoric animals. A long movie, but scientifically interesting."

"How come you know so much about mosquitoes?"

Ruth smiled and took another sip of wine. "One of the benefits of working in the library is that you have so much research material at your fingertips. Plenty to read on those days when all you do is give directions to the restrooms."

"Besides, I suspect everyone in Minnesota wants to find out what to do about mosquitoes."

Ruth shook her head. "Tourists mostly. We who live here find them a necessary evil and try to ignore them. There's really no getting rid of them. One female can lay one to three hundred eggs at a time. Since she lives up to a hundred days, a single female could lay three thousand eggs in her life span."

Clare brushed at her arms. "That makes my skin crawl."

The timer on the oven beeped. Excusing herself Clare went in and set the ham slices on plates and added sweet potatoes. She carried the plates outside and then returned for the ramen salad. Dishing it up into wooden salad bowls she added slivered almonds that she had browned earlier. For a while the talk between them was general, but eventually Ruth asked about Clare's day. The older woman listened intently as Clare described her discoveries.

"So it was the squeak of the door and the angel doorbell that brought back some of your memories?"

"Not enough unfortunately," Clare said. "I can't really understand why I can't remember anything concrete before I was four. The pictures of my parents don't trigger any reactions. Only things about the house have nudged at my subconscious."

"I've read about people who have something like situational amnesia. Something has happened—an accident or some tragedy—and their mind has blocked the entire incident from their memory. It's as if it never happened." Ruth finished the last of her salad. "I think it's God's way of protecting us from deep pain."

"Do you think I saw my mother murdered?"

"It's possible I suppose. It seems more likely that your memory lapse was due to the sudden separation from your parents. Just imagine what a trauma that would be to a child."

Clare poured them each another glass of wine and they drank in silence, watching as the light changed over the lake in the setting sun.

"How did you like Nathan Hanssen?" Ruth asked.

"He was incredibly kind." Clare felt the heat rise to her cheeks. "Our phone call had been rather bristly so I was not prepared to like him."

"By the look on your face, I'd say it was quite the contrary."

Clare tried to ignore the twinkle in Ruth's eyes but her mouth widened in a grin. "I have to admit I liked him very much. He invited me to the Farm Exhibit on Sunday."

"Ah men. Always trying to seduce women through the viewing of man toys."

"Really, Ruth." Clare tried to look arch but ended up giggling.

"I think it would be good for you to get to know Nate. He's had some rough times in his life and he has a quick mind and might be able to help with your search."

"I know his wife drowned, but I don't have many details on that. According to my notes, it was after her death that he went into his reclusive state."

"The town grapevine had it that the marriage was on rocky ground. Nate had been dating her so long that it was more or less expected that they'd marry. From what I could gather, Rebecca Hanssen was basically a small-town girl with no ambition other than to be a wife and mother. No question that they loved each other, but no one thought it was a good match."

"What a shame. Erika could use a mother."

"So the fair-haired child was there. What did you think of her?"

Clare hesitated, unsure how to put her opinion into words.

"She's not exactly spoiled," she finally said. "It's more a case of a bright child who knows how to push all the buttons to make her father react."

"Very good. And much kinder words than most people would have used to describe the girl."

"I can imagine. It's an interesting dynamic between the two. They've been together so long that Erika knows her father's emotional moods. She knows how to keep his attention." Clare pursed her mouth in dismay. "As you might have sensed, she saw me as a rival."

Ruth nodded in agreement. "Yes, that would figure. I saw something similar quite recently when Erika and Nate were at the library. He got to talking to the mother of one of Erika's classmates, a divorced woman, when suddenly Erika knocked over one of the rolling carts. I just happened to be looking in that direction and realized the girl had done it deliberately to get her father's attention."

"I suspect they're in for a rough patch. Even knowing him so little, I sense he'll eventually see the problem and try to correct it.

It's logical that Erika should almost feel like a surrogate wife since they've been each other's companion for so long."

"And when the hormones start bubbling up, Erika will need the strong support of a father not a friend."

"Doesn't he have any family here?"

"No. His parents were living in Florida when his father died. His mother's still there. Nate's an only child and there are no aunts, uncles, or cousins around." Ruth smiled across at Clare. "You see. You have more in common than you knew."

To get Ruth off the subject, Clare said, "I almost forgot the dessert."

She hurried inside and set the water to boil for tea while she cut two pieces of the coconut cake. She got out lemon and sugar and tea and set them on a tray. When the water was ready, she carried the tray outside. At the first taste of the cake, she was reminded of the incident at the grocery store.

"I almost forgot to tell you what happened yesterday. It's got me somewhat freaked out."

While Ruth ate her dessert, Clare told her about the woman in the grocery store. When she finished, the older woman looked puzzled.

"Are you sure she called you Abby?"

"Absolutely. It came out as naturally as if she'd always known me." Clare set her empty plate on the tray. "Since I don't look much like either my father or my mother or Rose, I thought she might have seen a picture of me sometime after I'd grown up."

"Could Rose have been in contact with someone in Grand Rapids all these years?" Ruth asked.

"I suppose it's possible. I wasn't aware of anyone. At one point I was sort of into stamp collecting and Rose saved me some stamps. States other than Illinois but none that I can remember. I was far more interested in the stamps from other countries."

"Were there a lot of those?"

Clare squinted her eyes as she tried to remember. "There were quite a few. Mostly from Europe, but one or two from China. The

Chinese stamps fascinated me. When I asked who sent them, Rose said they were from her best friend from high school."

"Then it's possible that she did keep in contact with someone. And if so, she might have sent pictures of you as you were growing up."

"Now all I have to do is find someone who went to school with Rose and lived in China." Clare's voice held a hint of sarcasm in it. "I wonder if it was the woman in the grocery store."

"It's curious that she left the store without talking to you again. Why would she avoid you?"

"That's just one more thing I don't know. It worries me that someone knows who I am though. I'd hoped to keep my identity secret."

"It doesn't sound like this woman is going to spread it around since she didn't have the courtesy to introduce herself." Ruth waved her hand in dismissal. "Just go along as before unless someone challenges you. For all anyone knows you're Clare Prentice, here to do a story on Nate and an update on the famous murder."

"My whole life has been based on some sort of deception. I hate lying to anyone here."

"Other than holding back your real identity, your cover story is the truth." Ruth set her empty cup down with a soft clink. "My that was a wonderful dinner. I especially loved the cake. A perfect end to the day."

"I'm so glad you could come tonight. It's wonderful to have someone to talk over all this with. My head's whirling with each new fact and discovery."

"You're welcome to tell me anything," Ruth said.

"Thank you," Clare said, feeling slightly guilty.

Although she felt at ease talking to the older woman, she hadn't shared the fact that Nate had given her the plastic bag and the box. It was something she wasn't ready to talk about since her own feelings were so ambivalent.

"What's your plan for tomorrow?" Ruth asked.

"I want to go to city hall and look up whatever records I can find on my parents. Once I have some actual facts I can begin to build a picture of what my life was like."

"Good girl. You may not find the answer that you're looking for on why your father killed your mother, but at least you'll have a sense of time and place."

A sense of time and place. Clare ran the words over in her mind after Ruth left. Perhaps that was what she was seeking. She cleaned up the kitchen and got ready for bed, pointedly avoiding looking at the closed drape across the closet. Tomorrow she'd open the box. She needed the safety of sunlight around her in order to delve into any more family secrets.

She read for a while in bed. The air felt heavy with humidity but there was still a good breeze through the open window. Turning off the light, she lay relaxed, listening to the sound of the loons on the lake, as she drifted away.

The explosion woke her. She sat up in the darkened room, shaking from the sound in her head. A flash of light blinded her and she screamed.

Chapter Nine

Another flash of light blinded Clare and the explosion that followed brought her fully awake. It was only then that she realized that it was thunder and lightning. She turned on the light and, seeing the open window, she threw back the sheet and hurried across the room to close it. The floor was wet beneath her bare feet.

Taking a towel from the bathroom, she wiped off the windowsill and the dresser, then the floor. She hung the wet towel over the shower rail and returned to the bedroom. The clock on the bedside table read four o'clock. She didn't think it had been raining long since there wasn't that much water on the floor. Chilled and shaking, she climbed back into bed.

She bunched the pillows up behind her and pulled the sheet and a blanket up to her chin. Her heart was still pounding in her ears and she tried to slow her breathing to a more even pace. When she closed her eyes, quick bursts of pictures, like a broken series of films, played inside her head.

It was the old dream.

When she was a child, Clare had been plagued by a dream that turned into a nightmare when she was stressed or upset. As she got older, the dream had only come occasionally and had stopped altogether until she discovered that she was adopted. Then it returned. At the time she put it down to stress, but now she wondered.

It was always variations of the same dream. In this one she was running. Lost in the woods. It was raining. Just a slow misting spray and then it turned into a steady downpour. Lightning flashed all around her. She was holding something in her hand, trying to protect it from the rain. She saw an old wooden boat. A pirate appeared in front of her with a knife in his teeth. Suddenly she tripped and fell. There was blood on her nightgown and thunder crashed all around her.

Then she woke up.

Huddled under the blankets, Clare could still hear the thunder but now it was farther away. Her breathing wasn't so labored and she could feel her heart beat slowing to a more normal rhythm. With the light on in the bedroom, she felt safe. The fear engendered by the dream was fading, however, in its place was a vague uneasiness.

This time the dream had started with the squeak of the screen door.

It was the sound she had heard at Nate's house. The sound that had first triggered her fainting spell. Had the dream actually happened? Was she just reliving something that had really occurred in her own house twenty-five years ago?

So many questions. An occasional answer, all leading to more questions.

The dream was probably a combination of things. Maybe it revolved around her being taken away from her parents at the age of four. Maybe she had morphed the whole trauma into being kidnapped by pirates and trying to return to her home in the woods. She probably would never know the true meaning of the dream. It would eventually fade away again, to return, she supposed, when she was upset.

The storm had passed and now the thunder was a low rumble, well spaced from the occasional flashes of lightning. Warm and drowsy after her scare, she snuggled deeper in the covers and reached up to turn out the bedside lamp. She watched the flickering glow outside the window, her eyes heavy-lidded as sleep approached.

The last thing she saw was the angel doorbell at Nate's house.

Although this time the angel was on the front door of an older version of the house. The house she had been living in at the time of the murder.

Clare came awake slowly. It was eight thirty. The cottage felt stuffy with the windows closed. She padded across to the window and frowned as she stared out at the gloomy day. It looked like the storm of the night might still have some rain to deliver. The sky was overcast and the water in the lake was a gray, leaden color. It suited Clare's mood.

She had slept fitfully after wakening in the night. Each time she dozed she would find herself inside another dream, one more unsettling than the last. It wasn't the recurring dream. Just a series of nightmares where she was being chased or she was chasing someone.

After her shower, she felt considerably better. She put on white cotton slacks and a blue and white striped jersey. She carried her sandals to the living room, dropping them by the back door. The paper was at the front door and she flipped through it while she had breakfast. A small town newspaper felt so much more personal than the Chicago papers she was used to. She was almost finished when she heard the scrape at the back door. Opening it she found Waldo, tongue lolling out the side of his mouth and tail fluttering in greeting.

"Good morning to you too," she said. "How about a stroll to the dock?"

Refilling her mug with hot tea, she slipped on her sandals and went out to the porch, stopping to pat the dog. He followed her as she walked down to the dock and sat beside her with his head on her knee.

"Your owner must have to bathe you every night." She stroked his head, feeling the silken fur under her fingers. "Was it Jack? No, Jake, I think."

She stared across the lake, wondering which house was his. It was a long way to the opposite side, and unless the man was using binoculars she wondered how he'd spotted Waldo with her on the dock. Of course, with Waldo's habits, the man probably spent all his time searching for him.

Drinking her tea, she tried to plan her day. Despite the fact she wasn't sure she wanted to know what was inside the box, she knew she had to open it. Even out of sight, behind the curtained doorway of the closet, it was on her mind. She might as well do it when she went back up to the cottage. Then she could get on with her day doing research at the courthouse.

"Well, my friend, it's time for me to get to work." She nudged Waldo's head and he reluctantly moved so she could stand up. "There must be a shoreline full of dead fish for you to roll in. You might rethink your day. Find that patch of mint and spend a little more time in that."

Walking back to the cottage, Waldo padded after her, leaving her at the steps to the porch. She cleaned up the breakfast dishes and then reluctantly returned to the bedroom. Pulling back the closet drapery, she took the box from the shelf. Back in the living room, she sat down on the sofa.

The box was about a foot square, sealed with packing tape. An envelope was taped to the top. On the front of the envelope the name of Thatcher Hanssen was written in a bold cursive. Underneath his name in smaller letters it said: Hold for Abby.

She pried off the envelope, slit the flap with her thumbnail and drew out a handwritten note.

Thatcher,

I tried to deliver the box Jimmy Newton left behind for Abby, but Rose refused to accept it. She doesn't want the child living in the shadows of the past. She doesn't want her to know anything about her background until she is older. Please keep this until Abby comes to get it.

Yours,
Owen

It took a moment before she could take in the real import of the letter. Nate's father apparently knew she was living with Rose.

And Owen had to be Judge Owen Shannon, Ruth's brother and her best friend Gail's father. The man she knew as Uncle Owen had known her identity all along. Had he somehow arranged everything? Was he the one who had provided the fake birth certificates for both Rose and her "adopted" daughter? She wondered how many other people had known who she was and where she was.

She dropped the letter on the coffee table where it lay, face up. Over and over she reread the sentences. She couldn't bear to think about Rose's refusal to take the box. Without knowing what was in it, she couldn't make a judgment. Clare didn't know what she would have done in a similar case.

Her overriding emotion was anger. It was just another example of the conspiracy of silence that surrounded her whole life. She could understand that Rose wanted to protect her while she was a child, but when had she planned to tell her? Clare had been twenty-six when Rose died. She had known she was dying because she had a very aggressive form of breast cancer. Clare had quit her job to be able to help care for her.

Yet Rose never said a word.

In the last days of Rose's life, Clare never sensed that there was anything her mother wanted to say to her. Never any indication that there was unfinished business between them. It had to have been a conscious decision on Rose's part not to tell her about the adoption. Did she assume that it would never surface?

Rose must have forgotten that she'd told Dr. Craig about the adoption when she became their family doctor. Except for the coincidence of the breast biopsy, that one fact might never have come to light.

Furious at the deception, Clare couldn't remain still while her emotions were in such upheaval. She got up, pacing the living room, front door to back door, side to side. She wanted to throw something as the anger built inside her. She felt like a child, crying out that the world wasn't fair.

The phone rang in the midst of her turmoil.

For a moment she felt disoriented and stared blankly at the

cell phone beside her purse. The second ring brought her back to reality and the third ring broke through her immobility and she crossed the room to answer it.

"Hi, it's Nate. I was worried and I just wanted to check on you. Are you fully recovered from your discoveries of yesterday?"

Clare opened her mouth but the only sound to come out was a slight choking laugh at the coincidence of this call and her latest find.

"Hello, Clare?" came Nate's deep voice. "Are you there?"

"Yes," she managed to get out. She coughed to clear her throat and then continued. "I'm here."

"I don't like how you sound. Is everything all right?"

"No." As soon as the word was out she wanted to snatch it back. "Sorry. It's one of those days. I'm really fine."

"Is it the box? After you left, I wondered if I should have waited before giving it to you. You already had a great deal to absorb."

"You must be psychic." She shook her head at the connection they'd made in such a short time. "I haven't even opened the box. I just finished reading the letter that was taped on top. It seems your father and Ruth's brother knew who and where I was all these years."

Silence. Then he said, "If you're upset by the letter I don't think you should open the box when you're all alone. Erika's gone to the library for her knitting class. I'm just on my way out and can be there in ten minutes."

"You don't have to come, Nate. I'm really okay."

"Well you don't sound it. Besides you're not supposed to argue with the man you're trying to interview."

Before she could comment, he disconnected. She stared at the phone in her hand torn between anger and another unidentifiable emotion, then flipped it closed and put it inside her purse. For some reason she felt a sense of relief that he was coming. It made no sense since she barely knew the man. Walking to the bedroom, she checked the mirror, annoyed that it should matter how she looked. She brushed her hair, pulled it back, and caught it in a claw barrette. Picking up her lipstick, she made a face at herself in the mirror and put it back down on the dresser. This wasn't a date, after all.

Ten minutes later she heard a car drive into the parking area above the cottage. A car door closed and she heard footsteps coming down the path. She opened the door and smiled as Nate climbed the steps to the porch. A contrast in styles, he wore a button-down blue oxford cloth shirt tucked neatly into leather belted khaki shorts, no socks, and scuffed boat shoes. He removed his sunglasses as he approached, sharp blue eyes steady as he studied her face.

"Do I pass muster?" she asked as she led the way into the cottage.

"Your face is flushed, but you look good." He stopped inside the doorway and looked around. "Nice place. Looks homey." He spotted the box on the coffee table and turned to face her. "What was in the letter that upset you?"

Clare went over to the table and picked up the letter. She handed it to him and then watched as he read it. She didn't know if he would understand.

"Did you know Ruth's brother, Judge Shannon?" she asked.

"Only slightly, although I did know that he and my father were great friends. The judge lived in Minneapolis for many years after he moved from Grand Rapids. He came back here frequently in the summer to do some fishing. Then he moved to Chicago, and I don't recall seeing him again."

"Rose and I saw him all the time. We were as much a part of the Shannon family as if we were actually related. The judge's daughter Gail is still my best friend. And it stuns me that he knew all along that my whole life was a lie."

"You see it as a betrayal," Nate said, surprising her with his perception. "But it doesn't have to be that. It's obvious from the letter that Rose didn't want you to know about your past and he was respecting her wishes. I think everyone was trying to work in your best interests, to protect you."

"I don't feel protected." She heard the petulant tone in her voice. "I'm sorry, Nate, for dumping on you. I sound like a woman with raging PMS."

"I've had many a date like that," he said.

His humor brought her back to a more balanced emotional level. "I appreciate your putting up with me. You never could have guessed what you were getting into when you agreed to an interview."

"I'm at my worst around the press, so this is a pleasant reminder that the whole world doesn't revolve around me and my reclusive state. Besides, after yesterday, I was concerned about you. I wasn't sure I'd done the right thing giving you the box and your father's effects. When I called you seemed distressed over the letter and I thought it might help to talk to someone."

"It was your timing that threw me. I'd just opened the letter and was furious with Rose, Judge Owen, and anyone else I could think of." She took the letter and put it on the counter, then reached out and patted his arm. "Although it wasn't necessary, I do appreciate your coming."

"I don't mean to intrude in your personal life. I can stand outside while you open it."

"You could press your nose to the window and watch from a distance. Is that the idea?" Her mouth widened in a grin as she caught the twinkle in his eye.

"That did sound rather pathetic. Okay, I'll admit it. I'm curious as hell."

"Now we're getting at the truth. I'm actually happy to have you here. I had worked myself into a state when you called. It's surprising how much better I feel just talking about it." She made a face. "And why are we standing in the middle of the room. Come on outside and we'll take a look at the mystery box."

She picked up the cardboard box and opened the back door, leading the way out to the porch. Although it had started out as a gloomy day, the sun had broken through and the lake was bathed in sunlight. She sniffed the air, grateful for the breeze since she had noted the thermometer beside the door was close to ninety. Setting the box on the wicker table, she pointed Nate to a chair and took the other one.

Nate reached in his pocket for a small knife, opened it and, after Clare nodded permission, used it to cut the sealing tape on the box. Clare folded back the flaps. Inside was a round red satin case. She caught her breath in surprise, unprepared for the wave of emotion that washed over her. She reached inside and took out the jewelry case and put it in her lap. Her fingers stroked the delicate embroidery.

"You look as if you've seen a ghost," Nate said, leaning toward her in concern. "Do you recognize it?"

"Yes. It's identical to the one on the top of the dresser in the bedroom," she said. Her voice shook slightly and she smiled to let him know that she was all right. "Except this one is red. The one I have is blue. It belonged to Rose. I think this one belonged to Lily."

"Since they were sisters it makes perfect sense that they would have matching things. Perhaps they got them as Christmas presents. Or bought them when they were together. In any case, it's beautiful."

"I must have seen it as a child. I'd always loved Rose's, but I remember thinking it would be prettier in red."

She unzipped the case and folded back the top. Inside was a small matching drawstring bag and a thick envelope. She put the envelope on the table. Pulling out the satin bag, she returned the jewelry case to the cardboard box. She untied the satin cords at the neck of the bag and emptied the contents onto the surface of the table. There was a ring, a teething ring, and a string of pearls.

"It must be my mother's wedding ring," she exclaimed as she picked up the ring. It was a simple platinum band about a quarter of an inch wide. "There's a date inside. Can you read it?"

She thrust the ring at Nate, who rocked it back and forth in the sunlight. "It says: 4/2/78. April second, nineteen seventy-eight," he said, handing it back.

Automatically she slid it onto her ring finger. It jammed at the knuckle. "She must have had small hands."

She held her hand up, ring wedged at the knuckle. Her right hand cupped the left and she stroked the ring with her thumb. If she hoped to feel some vibration she was disappointed. However, she did feel a sense of comfort knowing one more piece of the puzzle. She now knew her parents wedding date. That at least was something.

Slowly she withdrew the ring and put it back on the table. Next she picked up the teething ring. It was a circle of grayish white bone with a flat silver bell. On one side of the bell was a crown and the words: OLD KING COLE. Despite the dark tarnish on the other side of the bell, she could make out the initials ACN.

"My full name is Abigail Clare Newton."

"I prefer Clare," Nate said. "It's an old fashioned kind of name. You must have been a voracious little thing. Look at the teeth marks on the bell."

Clare smiled as she examined the dents on the surface. The circle of bone was smooth to the touch as she turned it in her hand. She set it on the table beside the ring and picked up the string of pearls. Pulling them through her fingers, she admired the soft rose color and the high luster of the strand. She raised them to her mouth and rubbed the pearls across her front teeth.

"What are you doing?" Nate asked.

"I wanted to know if they were real or imitation."

"And that tells you?"

Clare chuckled. "Actually it does. Imitation pearls are highly polished to give them a shine. When you rub them across your teeth they feel smooth. Natural pearls or cultured pearls will feel gritty because of the nacre that forms them. It's a sort of crystal substance. I think that's what makes the texture rough."

"How on earth do you know that?"

"My ex-fiancé was going to buy me some pearls so we went to a jeweler and he gave us a quick lesson." Clare slid the pearls back and forth between her fingers. "It was fascinating. Some foreign object gets inside the oyster and, to protect itself, the oyster secretes a substance called nacre around the irritant. Year after year and layer after layer until it's totally encased."

"No wonder they're so expensive. And what is your opinion on these pearls?"

"Definitely not imitation."

She handed him the strand and, with a sheepish laugh, he raised them to his mouth. Cautiously he rubbed them against his teeth, his forehead puckered in concentration. His eyes widened.

"You really can feel the grit. So these are natural pearls?"

"Natural or cultured. The only difference is that with a cultured pearl someone actually inserts something into the oyster to begin the process."

"With this kind of information, I'll be a hit at the next cocktail party I go to." He reached in his pocket and brought out a handkerchief. Carefully he wiped the pearls and handed them back to Clare. "Assuming these were your mother's, you will have something beautiful to wear to remind you of her."

Clare stared down at the pearls in her hand. They felt warm as if they retained the body heat of the wearer. She didn't recall ever seeing them before, but Nate was right that they would be a lovely reminder of her mother. Gently she placed them on the table.

"How strange that I was dreading opening this box. In my own mind, I felt like Pandora releasing all the evils of mankind. You can see how self-absorbed I've become."

She picked up the ring, the pearls, and the teething ring and put them back into the drawstring bag. She put the bag back inside the jewelry case then turned her attention to the envelope. She opened the flap and was excited to find a packet of photographs. Carefully she took them out, holding the stack in her hand. The top one was a formal picture of a baby, lying on her stomach on a blanket, wearing what looked like a christening dress. She turned it over. Written on the back was a date.

"Nineteen seventy-eight. I was born in December. My parents were married in April so I was born nine months later. It must be me," Clare said, fingers shaking as she turned the picture so that Nate could see it. "I'm not positive, because I've never seen any of my baby pictures."

"What fine, plump cheeks you had," he said, his tone teasing. "You've lost that chipmunk look. Even as an infant you had fantastic eyes. Now they're a striking green. It was the first thing I noticed about you."

Heat rose to her cheeks and she looked sideways at Nate not sure how to take his compliment.

"You don't have to look so surprised," he said. "You must have felt the connection when we met. I think we were both set to dislike each other so it was strange how quickly we seemed to get along. Don't tell me you didn't notice."

Clare studied his face, wondering what it was about him that made her trust him so completely. "I know I feel totally comfortable talking to you. It's as if we're old friends."

"That'll do for a start." His mouth twisted into a grin. "We'll save this discussion for another time. Right now I'd like to look at the rest of the pictures."

Clare dealt the pictures onto the table as if they were cards. There were a dozen or more of them. Several were of Lily holding the baby Clare. Some pictures were of Clare alone. Two of the pictures showed Clare sitting on her father's lap. Another showed Jimmy holding her while she was playing with his bearded face.

"You know my father," she said. "And this one is Rose, Lily's sister, the woman who raised me. It's strange seeing her so young."

"She looks very serious. How much age difference was there between them?"

"Almost twelve years."

Clare turned each of the pictures over, but aside from the christening picture, the only other picture to have a date was a single picture of her parents. Her father was wearing a dark blue suit, white shirt, and a blue, black, and white striped tie. He had a small white carnation on his lapel. Her mother's dress was white, a square-necked embroidered bodice above a soft full skirt.

"This says nineteen seventy-eight too. I wonder if it's their wedding picture."

Nate pointed. "Look at her neck, Clare."

Clare peered closer and saw that her mother was wearing a string of pearls. Suddenly the emotion she had been missing, welled up inside her. Having the picture in her hand gave a reality to the jewelry she'd been holding just moments before. As her vision blurred, she blinked rapidly trying to keep from crying. She dropped the picture on the table and covered her mouth as tears ran down her cheeks.

Strong arms encircled her and she rested her forehead on Nate's chest as he leaned toward her. He patted her awkwardly, seeming to be in no hurry for her to get control of her emotions. After a minute or two, Clare's tears eased. He released her as if he realized her storm of emotion was over. Without a word he handed her the handkerchief he'd used to wipe off the pearls.

"I'm so sorry," Clare said as she brushed away her tears. "Ever since I met you, I've done nothing but embarrass myself."

Nate laughed, a great full-bodied sound. When she looked at him, curious as to his reaction, he began to laugh harder. Eventually he stopped, his face flushed in amusement.

"I'm sorry to laugh, but I talked to your boss on Tuesday . . ."

"You talked to Ann?" Clare interrupted. "Were you trying to get out of the interview?"

"Yes," he admitted sheepishly. "During our conversation, she was describing how nice you were and I made several facetious comments and ended by saying you'd probably be swooning on my doorstep."

Clare's lips quivered with the effort to hold back a smile. "I can't decide if I should be insulted or amused."

"Stick with amused," he said. "As soon as I met you any reason that I had for wanting to escape the interview flew out of my head. Now I'm jumping at any excuse to see you."

Unprepared for the warmth of his words and the look in his eyes, Clare tried to keep her comments impersonal. "I'm glad you came over this morning."

Nate's eyes glinted with a mischievous light as he sat back in his chair. He opened his mouth to make a comment, then shook his head as if he'd thought better of it. "So what got to you just now?"

"It's like all of a sudden, Lily became a real person. Up until now she's just been a picture in the newspaper."

"That's a good thing. I think it's because you're coming to terms with your real identity."

"How strange. After twenty-nine years to find your background is totally different than you imagined it." After a final swipe of her eyes, Clare stuffed the handkerchief in her pocket. "I don't feel different exactly. Maybe freer is the word I'm looking for. I never felt as if I fit in. As if I was somehow different from the other children I played and went to school with."

Nate picked up the picture of Rose, studying it closely. "What was your childhood like?"

Clare looked out over the lake, thinking back. "I can't say I had an unhappy childhood. I assume it was like everyone else's. Lots of good times and occasional bad times. Rose was very strict. I had the feeling that I never came up to her expectations. When I got into dating she reminded me constantly about the difference between good girls and bad girls."

"Rose was trying to mold you into the child she wanted you to be."

"Don't get me wrong. She was never unloving or abusive. I don't think she knew how to express her emotions. She was uncomfortable with hugging or any display of affection. Luckily we saw a lot of Judge Shannon's family. They were a funny, noisy, and passionate family. Gail's mother was very dramatic. Sweeping us up into a huge embrace for no reason at all except that she loved having us all underfoot."

"Sounds like my mother. Strong, opinionated, and very passionate." Nate chuckled. "Erika and I always look forward to her visits and then are totally exhausted by the time she returns to Florida."

"Too bad she's so far away. I would have thought she'd want to be here after your father died. Close to you."

Nate laughed, pulling at his ear sheepishly. “Actually she and my dad moved down there in order to get away from me.”

“And Erika?”

“Especially Erika.”

“But why?” At his hesitation, she immediately held up her hand to stop his reply. “Wait. It’s really none of my business.”

“What kind of a reporter are you?” he asked, his mouth turning up in a grin. “You’re supposed to ask probing questions.”

“You’re talking to a reporter who’s just been pouring out her life history.”

His expression sobered as he stared across at her. “In part that’s why I’d like to tell you. We seem to have breached the unwritten rule of don’t get personally involved. You mentioned that you felt so much freer once you began to discover who you really were. I’d like to feel that too. I’ve never found anyone I thought I could trust. At least until now.”

“I feel honored,” she said. “And I swear that nothing will go into my magazine article that you don’t approve of.”

She held up her hand as if taking an oath. He waved it away. He pushed his chair back and got up, pacing across the porch and back.

“I don’t know how much you got from your research, but I’ll assume nothing of real importance except the usual statistics. I grew up here in Grand Rapids. Being the son of the chief of police meant I was constantly under scrutiny. I wanted to live in a big city where I could be anonymous. After high school, I went to Case Western Reserve in Cleveland. It was the big time compared to Grand Rapids.”

Clare sat quietly listening as he paced back and forth. In part it was like he was talking to himself as well as her, trying to explain his motivations.

“I’d been dating Rebecca all through high school. She was shy and nurturing and encouraged everything I did. Her folks had a farm, and after high school she stayed home helping them work it. Her brother was a couple years younger and he helped out too. When I graduated from college, we married and moved to Cleveland. I was going on for a master's and had a part-time teaching assistant job. It was exciting being in the city and I thought Rebecca would enjoy it all as much as I did."

"She didn't?"

Nate shook his head. "No. She'd never been outside of Minnesota, and she missed her parents and her brother. Max and his wife Susie moved to Bemidji, but when Rebecca was in Minnesota she could see them frequently. She didn't like living in the city and she was never comfortable with the academic crowd. I was busy, and she didn't have anything to do. I suggested she take classes, but she said she hated school. Finally, she got a job working at a day care center."

Clare could almost sense what was coming. Even to her mind it seemed a marriage doomed from the start.

"It wasn't long before she wanted to have a baby. After three years of marriage, I didn't know if the marriage was worth saving. I may sound like a real bastard, but Rebecca bored me. She hadn't grown any since high school. Aside from live theater, she wasn't interested in books, history, politics, or travel. The only thing she wanted was to be a mother."

"I can understand that," Clare said.

"You can?"

"Yes. I've known girls like Rebecca. All they ever want out of life is marriage and a baby. Some of them will settle for the baby. It's the need for unconditional love that a baby gives. I don't know if that's true, but it makes some sense. When you're young you don't think about the long-term consequences."

Nate nodded as if he understood. He stopped pacing and leaned against the porch railing, arms folded across his chest.

"Along with everything else, I'd been working on my first book. I know now that Rebecca must have felt totally alone. When I sold the book, she gave me what I took to be an ultimatum. She looked at the contract and said: 'You've got your baby. Now I want mine.' Erika was born a year later."

"Was she thrilled?"

"Yes. There was a glow to her that had been missing for

several years. The baby might have saved us if I hadn't been such an arrogant prick. *Field of Reeds* was not only a literary success but also a huge commercial success. I was just twenty-six, and loved every one of the reviews. I was the darling of talk shows and thrived on the excitement of the book signings."

"I can see that. Rebecca was right. She was busy with her baby and you had yours. I've interviewed enough authors to realize in general they're a pain in the butt. And the more acclaimed they are, the more inflated their ego and their sense of entitlement."

Nate shifted slightly as if uncomfortable with the assessment. "I was all of that and more. Fame is a corrupting force. Suddenly people are listening eagerly to your every word as if you know more than you did before the book was published. People want to be around you. A tight circle of friends. From those people you get no criticism, so you tend to cut yourself off from the real friends who might be inclined to tell you off."

He went back to pacing. "After Erika was born, the marriage went downhill. Rebecca was depressed and took the baby back to Minnesota as often as I'd let her. And to my eternal damnation, I was glad when she was gone. From my lofty position in the literary world, Rebecca was provincial and unsupportive. I drifted into a stupid affair with my publicist. A friend of hers was kind enough to let Rebecca know about that."

"Somebody always seems to feel it's their responsibility. I know you feel guilty, as I'm sure Rebecca was devastated."

"She was." He bit the words off as if it pained him to think about it again. "I talked to her about it. I told her that it was only a fling, not a relationship. She said she was at fault because she'd been so busy with the baby. At that moment I wanted to shake her, because I knew it was all my fault. I felt grateful that she could love me no matter what I'd done. I vowed to make it up to her."

Clare could hear the pain in his voice. He was brutally honest about his own culpability and in truth she knew he was to blame for much of it. Granted the marriage had been a mismatch, but it sounded as if Rebecca wasn't the most stable person.

"Her parents died that year. Rebecca was grief stricken. She and Erika stayed with her brother in Bemidji for a month then came back to Cleveland. She was deeply depressed. I got her some counseling and it seemed to help a bit. For our sixth anniversary I thought a vacation might help. The one thing Rebecca liked was the theater. My parents agreed to watch Erika for a weekend while we went to New York. I got tickets to some plays. It was going to be a second honeymoon."

Nate cleared his throat several times before he could continue.

"At the urging of my publisher, I agreed to do an afternoon talk show and speak at a luncheon. Rebecca didn't want to go to the lunch. She said she'd rather shop. So once again she was alone. She was cheerful at dinner that last night. I put it down to the fact we were going home. We went to bed early because we had a flight the next morning. The phone woke me at midnight. It was the police. They asked me to come to the hospital. Rebecca's body had been found in the East River."

Chapter Ten

"She was in the river? What happened to her?" Clare asked.

"The police said she was found near the United Nations area. They said there was no evidence of foul play. It was assumed she either fell or jumped into the river, although no one knew why she was even in the area. They were wavering between suicide and accident."

Nate shook his head as if he still found it difficult to believe.

"The thought that Erika would one day see the death certificate made me determined to prevent a finding of suicide. When they asked if she'd been depressed, I said absolutely not. I said she was excited about going home to our daughter. Even the doorman said she'd seemed cheerful when she went out around ten thirty. She had a room key in her pocket and her wallet so they were able to track me down at the hotel. After a full investigation, her death was ruled an accident."

"I'm so sorry, Nate. It must have been a dreadful time." Clare wanted to reach out to him but didn't think it would be appropriate. She could see the guilt in his bowed head as if he feared it would be visible if he raised it. "How old was Erika?"

"About two and a half. Rebecca had been her caretaker. I barely knew her, let alone how to be her father. My parents stayed for a while after the funeral, but then they returned to Grand Rapids. Alone in Cleveland, I left Erika most days with a babysitter and drank a good bit of the time. Although everyone was very understanding in the beginning, it wasn't long before my teaching assistant's job was no longer available. My life was falling apart and I decided to come back to Minnesota."

He stopped talking and sat down sideways on the railing, looking out over the lake. Clare didn't know how long he'd been speaking. She had been so fascinated by the recital that the time didn't seem to matter. His honesty was impressive. He made no excuses for himself, just stating the facts and his shortcomings as they had happened. It was interesting to note that his body was less tense than when he had started talking.

"Before you continue, would you like something cold to drink?"

He didn't turn back, just spoke over his shoulder. "That would be great. Some ice water, please."

Inside, she got down a flowered metal tray and glasses. Filling a glass pitcher with ice, she added water and set it on the tray. Nate was still standing with his back to the door, but he seemed to sense her presence and walked over to open the door. Clare set the tray on the table and poured two glasses of water. She handed one to Nate.

He drank the whole glass and then poured a refill. "I'm parched. I'm not used to talking for any length of time. And you were muttering about telling your life story. I've been babbling on for ages."

"Like me, you've had a lot bottled up inside. My guess is you'll feel better for getting some of it out." Picking up her glass of water, she returned to her chair. She took a long sip and then asked, "How long has Rebecca been gone?"

He thought for a minute. "It's almost nine years. Hard to believe but Erika is eleven now."

"You've done a fine job raising her."

Nate let out a harsh laugh that had very little humor in it.

"That's actually what I started out to tell you. Remember I said that my parents moved to Florida to get away from us?" Clare nodded. "When I came back to Grand Rapids, I assumed my parents would be delighted to help out. My father was retired and mother adored Erika. I suggested that I leave her with them during the day and then pick her up at bedtime."

Clare's mouth widened in a grin. From what little he had told her about his mother, she suspected that suggestion wouldn't go down well. Nate took another drink of his water, smiling at her over the rim of the glass.

"You guessed it. She said, 'This child is yours and you damn well better pull yourself together and figure out how to raise her.' "

"I do like your mother. That's probably the only thing that would have caught your attention. So they moved to Florida to force your hand?"

"Actually, not right away. She wanted to make sure I would figure it out before starving Erika or botching the whole job." His mouth curved into a soft smile and he appeared to be thinking back to that time. "I, of course, was furious. I felt like the star-crossed father cast out in the winter storm, clutching a baby to my manly breast."

"Nice visual," Clare said. "I hope you had a scarf wrapped around you like Little Eva."

"I can see I'm going to get little sympathy from you," he said, dropping down into his chair. "Back at the house I'd rented, I sulked until Erika started to cry. Luckily Mother had packed a basket of kid-friendly food and other necessities. I wasn't totally inept, but I sure wasn't happy."

"How long did it take for you to fall in love with Erika?"

"About a week," he grinned sheepishly. "Thank God, Mother stopped by, 'when she happened to be in the neighborhood,' to drop off food and to show me how to give Erika a bath and other assorted things. By the end of two weeks, I was less terrified of making a mistake. I was exhausted both mentally and physically. When Erika slept, I slept."

"Just like a new mother."

"It was quite a time." He chuckled. "I learned you can't put on a diaper when you're angry. All those damn sticky tabs get stuck on the wrong areas and then you pick the baby up and it falls off. I must have gone through four boxes of diapers in the first two days."

"Well you can certainly be proud of your accomplishment. Erika is a lovely child. Your mother was right to force you to step up."

"She's told me that many times. That fall she knew everything was going to work out well. The first cold snap and she and Dad bolted for sunny climes. I took Erika to Florida that first Christmas, but they stayed down until May. By the time they returned, I was a full-time father and back to writing."

"Well done, Nate. It's really a remarkable story. Thank you for sharing it with me."

They sat in silence for a while. Drinking water and enjoying each other's company. Nate raised his arms over his head, stretching his body.

"I have to admit I haven't felt this relaxed in ages," he said.

"What's that old saying? Confession is good for the soul?"

"Speaking of souls reminds me that my body hasn't had any food for a while. Would you like to go out to lunch?"

"I would. But don't you have things to do? Erika?"

"Erika's with a friend so I don't have anything to do all afternoon. Uh-oh. Excuse me. I've got a call." He reached in his pocket for his cell phone. "It's Erika," he said as he flipped the phone open. "What's up?"

Clare put the glasses and the pitcher back on the tray, as Nate listened to his daughter. She added the cardboard box with the jewelry case inside. Wanting to give him some privacy, she took the tray back into the house. She had just finished putting the glasses in the dishwasher when Nate came inside.

"I spoke too soon. Erika and her friend Cindy have been at a knitting class at the library. She's been invited to spend the night at Cindy's house. I need to pick them up because they want to go swimming and Erika needs to pack her things so I can drop them at Cindy's next-door neighbor whose mother will take them to the pool." He snapped the phone closed. "The social schedule of an eleven-year-old is very complicated during summer vacation. It's hard for me to keep up."

"Wait until she starts dating, if you think it's bad now."

Nate groaned. "I don't want to go there. The good news is that now I'm free for dinner. Any chance you want to go to one of Grand Rapids's finest dining spots?"

"I've got some research to do at city hall, but I'm free after that."

Nate headed for the front door. "I'll pick you up at seven thirty if that's good for you."

"See you then," Clare said as she closed the door behind him.

Taking the cardboard box into the bedroom, she checked the closet and pulled out a white eyelet shirtdress. Holding it up, she examined it for wrinkles and decided it was neither too formal nor too casual. Looking in the mirror, she noted the flushed cheeks and chided herself for being so pleased about spending the evening with Nate. She hung the dress back in the closet and gathered her notebook for her trip to City Hall.

She parked the car and walked across the park to the stone steps leading into City Hall. After consulting with the security guard, she was directed to a room at the end of the hall. Inside was a long counter with stools and several writing areas along the wall. Other than a young woman seated at one of the desks behind the counter and another man looking through a pile of file folders, the room was empty. The clerk rose and came across to the counter. Clare glanced at her name tag.

"Hi, Taffy. I called yesterday and asked where I could get copies of birth certificates and marriage licenses. I have a list."

Clare opened her notebook and withdrew a paper with the names and dates she had written down.

"That will help a lot," Taffy said. She walked away, glancing down at the paper in her hand.

"I'll be right here." Clare pulled out a stool and sat down as the clerk moved away. Opening her notebook again, she looked over her notes to see if there was anything else she needed to do.

She became aware of the hushed conversation between the young clerk and the man at the other desk. From his surreptitious glances it was apparent that she was the topic of their conversation. When Taffy went into the adjoining room, the man closed the files, put them in his briefcase and then stood up. Straightening his suit jacket, he crossed to the counter, flipped up a section, and came toward her.

"Taffy said to tell you that it will take her a few minutes before she can locate the files and make the copies you need."

"Thank you," Clare said.

"She said you're a reporter. She saw your press credentials," he said by way of explanation. "Are you up from the cities?"

"No. Chicago."

"Long way to come for a story, isn't it?" When she didn't answer immediately, his face reddened. "Sorry for seeming to be so inquisitive. I should be welcoming you to Grand Rapids. I'm Bruce Young."

"Clare Prentice," she said giving his hand a firm shake. "I'm here to interview Nathan Hanssen."

His eyebrows raised. "Nate doesn't do a lot of interviews."

"So I gathered. My editor knows him so that gives me a bit of an edge."

Bruce was in his late forties or early fifties. His navy blue suit was expensive, cut to fit his tall muscular body. He was a good-looking man with well-cut features set off by his tan. She suspected he was a golfer because his right hand was much darker than his left and there was a line of white on his forehead that suggested a golf cap. His body was fit and, except for his receding hairline, he might have been taken for a much younger man.

"Taffy said you're checking into the Newtons."

"Yes." For a moment Clare debated not giving in to his curiosity, but decided that would only serve to increase the mystery around her sudden appearance in Grand Rapids. "When I was doing my research on Grand Rapids, I came across the story of the murder. My editor thought it might be a good human-interest piece."

"I can't imagine many people would be interested in it. It was a long time ago," Bruce said.

"Twenty-five years. Sort of an update of an historic event in a small town. People love that sort of thing," she said. "Have you lived a long time in Grand Rapids?"

"Born and raised," he said with pride. "Except for college and law school down in the cities, I've been here for fifty years."

Just then Taffy returned with a stack of papers. Clare paid for the copies, thanked the clerk, and then turned back to Bruce.

"I don't usually run around picking up men, but I'd really like to talk to you about Grand Rapids." She shoved the copies into her notebook. "Unless you're in a hurry."

"Actually I was just going to take a break for lunch," he said.

"Great. I just realized I haven't had lunch yet. Is there someplace close where we could sit and talk?"

"Miller's Place is just across the street. They have great soups and sandwiches. I'll show you the way. And if Willi's there I'll introduce you. For a reporter she'd be a good contact because she knows everyone in town."

Clare followed him out the door and, talking casually, they crossed the park to a small storefront café. Inside it was pleasantly cool and very welcoming with yellow and white check tablecloths and white painted tables and chairs.

"Let me buy and then I won't feel guilty for taking time out of your day," she said.

The waitress arrived before he could refuse and Clare ordered a BLT and some iced tea. Bruce ordered the same. She smiled warmly across the table, grateful to have the opportunity to interview him.

"What kind of law do you practice, Mr. Young?"

"Please call me Bruce," he said. "I mostly deal with real estate. There's been a lot of interest in Lost Lake in the last few years as the baby boomers start to retire. A lot of them have come up here over the years to fish and boat. Property around the lake had been selling well until the last couple of years when the prices got a little out of hand and the bottom dropped out of the market."

"That's true in a lot of places. Chicago has had a rough couple of years. It's been a crisis time for sellers who've bought a second place and now can't get rid of the old house. I can see why someone would want to retire here. It's a lovely little town."

"You're not looking for a place, by any chance?"

Laughing, Clare shook her head. "No. I'm just here for a short time and then back to Chicago."

"Staying at the motel?"

"No. I'm renting a place from Ruth Grabenbauer."

"I thought I saw some lights on in the cottage and wondered if she'd found a renter. My house is just another half mile down the road from Ruth's."

"Then you probably know everything about the area. I was at Nate Hanssen's yesterday and discovered that it's the house the Newtons were living in at the time of the murder. Since you're in real estate, you might know the answer to one of my questions. How did Nate end up owning the house?"

For a moment Bruce's gaze sharpened, and she sensed he was gauging the advisability of talking to a reporter.

"I'm just looking for background information at this point, Bruce. Nothing I'd hold you to or quote you on."

He shrugged. "You can find all this information in the public records but I can save you a little time. The house originally belonged to Lily Newton's sister, Rose Gundersen."

"Was it the Gundersen family home?"

"Yes. Rose was ten or twelve years older than Lily. Lily came as a surprise. Her mother was almost fifty when she was born. Her father in his sixties. They both died before they updated their wills, so everything went to Rose. Near as I can tell it didn't make any difference between the sisters. They both lived in the house and appeared to be on good terms with each other."

"You knew them?"

"Yes. Lily was just two years younger than I was. We went to school together and dated for a year until she met James Newton. She never looked at anyone again. She was only nineteen or so when they married."

"I gather he was a lot older than she was."

"He was in his forties. He had a good job at Blandin. Something in graphic design. Lily was waitressing at the Forest Lake restaurant. He quite literally swept her off her feet. Before anyone even knew they were an item, they were married." Bruce shook his head. "I sound like an old gossip, wandering so far off topic."

"I don't mind. It's all pretty interesting. Were you at the dance in Bovey the night before the murder?"

After a slight hesitation, he nodded. "It was the Fourth of July. We were having a fun time until the very end. When the fight started, it pretty much broke up the evening."

"What was the fight about?"

"I don't really know. Everything was fine one minute and then the next thing you know there were punches flying everywhere. After that everyone bailed out. I'd gone stag so I just piled into the car and drove home."

The waitress arrived with their sandwiches and Clare waited until they'd each had a chance to eat a little before she continued her questioning.

"I really appreciate all the info, Bruce. I've just read some of the articles in the newspaper, but talking to someone who was here at the time really helps to flesh out the story."

"I'm glad I can be of some help."

"So Rose Gundersen owned the house. Were all three of them living in the house after Lily married?"

"No. Rose was working in Minneapolis. She rented the house to the newlyweds and occasionally came to Grand Rapids for a weekend. The Newtons had a daughter. Abby. She was three or four when her mother was killed."

Clare tried to keep any emotion out of her expression. It was strange having Bruce talking about her parents and herself in such a dispassionate tone.

"In the newspaper it said that Abby went to live with Rose Gundersen. In Minneapolis?"

"I don't think so. They both just disappeared. I suppose Rose was desperate to protect the child. She had never married and so she was free to pick up and start a new life someplace else. In any event, Rose gave a power of attorney to Judge Shannon, your landlady's brother, in order to sell the house here and the one in Minneapolis. Nate's father bought the lake house."

"Nate's father was the chief of police at the time, wasn't he?"

"Yes." Bruce wiped his mouth with his napkin and took a drink of his tea. "Thatcher had it appraised by the bank and several realtors and paid full market price for it. It was all aboveboard."

"I didn't mean to imply there was anything wrong with the deal," Clare said. "I was just trying to get my facts straight."

"You'd never recognize it now. After Thatcher died, Nate practically gutted the place." Bruce shook his head in disapproval. "It's a little too modern for my taste."

Clare ate her sandwich in silence as she tried to digest all the new information. "His daughter said that the murder took place in the house."

"Don't believe a word of it," Bruce snapped. "That child just loves to dramatize everything. There was never any evidence at all to indicate that anything untoward had taken place in that house. Not a scintilla of proof."

After his outburst, Bruce relaxed and they finished their lunch as he told her about the activities in Grand Rapids during Tall Timber Days.

"Make sure you catch the lumberjack show on Sunday. The boys are really talented with an ax and there are plenty of laughs."

"I'll make a point of seeing it," Clare said. "Thank you so much for all your help today."

"My pleasure." He reached in his pocket for a leather card case and handed her one of his cards. "In case you need any other information, don't hesitate to call."

After shaking hands, Clare headed for her car, anxious to get back to her research. At the house she spread out the papers on the counter and, pulling up a stool, she looked with amazement at her own birth certificate. She knew from talking to other adoptees that an amended birth certificate issued after an adoption would reflect her birth date, her new name, and show Rose as her mother and Thomas Prentice as her father. Her name was listed as Abigail Clare Newton, and Lily and James Newton were recorded as her parents.

Rose never legally adopted her.

Clare wished that Ruth's brother was still alive. Uncle Owen seemed to be involved in every aspect of the mystery. Did Owen arrange for the fake birth certificates? She knew judges had certain powers and many connections so it was not unlikely that he had set everything in motion. He was in Chicago at the time of the murder and Rose may have gone to him for help. With him gone, she would probably never know the reasons behind the deception.

As she stared at the certificate she realized one more inconsistency. Her other birth certificate showed her birthday as December 2, 1978. Her actual birthday was October 21, 1978.

Why had that been changed?

Looking at her parents' marriage license she thought she might have a clue. Clare had been born seven months after their wedding. Lily must have been pregnant when she married.

After what Bruce had said, the sudden marriage made sense. If Lily had been pregnant there would have been a need for speed. In the seventies there was still a stigma to babies born less than nine months after the wedding. And what struck Clare as consistent with Rose's strict moral code was changing the date. She could imagine the rationale that with the new date, Clare was not a child conceived out of wedlock.

With a sigh, Clare put the new documents inside her notebook and set it on the counter. She moved her laptop over to give herself a little more space. She was compiling a substantial amount of notes. Each new fact changed the picture she'd been forming in her mind. It was still a puzzle, but now the search for identity was less painful and was beginning to be a mental challenge to fill in the gaps.

Checking the clock, she headed for the bathroom and stood under the shower for a long time, letting the water wash away the tensions of the last few days. She took her time getting ready for her dinner with Nate. The white eyelet shirtdress and white sandals showed off her summer tan. Although the day had been hot, the breeze had picked up and was streaming through the open windows in the cottage. She decided it would be cool enough to wear her hair loose around her shoulders instead of tied back.

The cardboard box she'd gotten from Nate was still on top of the dresser. She reached inside and removed her mother's satin case, smiling as she set it beside the one that had been Rose's. There was no doubt that except for the color difference, the two cases were identical.

For a moment she debated wearing her mother's pearls, but decided she needed more color. Rummaging in her own jewelry, she chose a malachite pendant on a gold chain and matching earrings. Then she opened the dresser drawer and pulled out a soft pashmina wrap in case the evening turned cool. She'd bought it originally for Rose the Christmas she'd started chemotherapy. With her hair gone, Rose needed something lovely to look at and the wrap was like a security blanket in the days ahead.

A glance at her watch showed she still had another half hour before Nate was due. She looked around the bedroom, then realized she'd left her purse in the kitchen. Setting the wrap on the counter, she reached inside for her cell phone, wallet, lipstick, and the house key and transferred them to a small white knit shoulder bag.

Going back into the bedroom, she picked up the handkerchief Nate had given her during her bout of crying that morning. She'd washed it but hadn't found an iron in the cottage. Ready at last, she started out of the room, then turned back to pick up the empty cardboard box to put in the trash. She automatically looked inside.

In the bottom of the box was a small, white envelope.

Chapter Eleven

Clare stared down at the envelope in the cardboard box.

Fingers shaking, she picked it up, holding it gingerly by one corner. She examined the box thoroughly, but it was empty. Setting it on the floor in the kitchen, she sat down on one of the wooden stools and contemplated the letter in her hand.

The envelope was three by four inches, the size of a note card. The color was beige and the stock was of good quality. There was no address on the envelope. No writing at all.

With her thumb she pried up the flap of the envelope.

Inside was a folded sheet of notepaper. Pulling it out, she opened it. The handwriting was a strong masculine script and her gaze automatically dropped to the signature. Stunned, she sucked in her breath and the letter shook violently until she could steady her hand and read the words.

Abby,

I'm sorry I had to send you away. I just wanted to make sure you would be safe and cared for. No matter what you hear, nothing that happened was your fault. Please know that your mother and I were so happy when you were born and loved you completely. You have always been our angel. You brought sunshine and laughter into the house. I'm sorry that I have to go away too, but I love you more than I can tell you and I will keep you in my heart forever.

Your Father

The initials JN were scrawled at the bottom of the page. Clare stared down at the letter, reading the words over and over. Knowing the reason that Jimmy Newton had to leave Grand Rapids, she was surprised by the sweetness of the letter. In her mind she couldn't connect the loving words to the murderous actions of the man. He made no mention of his sorrow over the death of her mother. Or his guilt. He made no excuses at all.

"Why did you do it?" she said.

At first she didn't even realize that she had spoken aloud. Her voice was just a whisper, almost as if the thought had merely passed through her mind. It was the question she wanted answered more than anything else.

"Clare?"

She had been so engrossed in her own thoughts that she let out a quickly muffled screech at the sound of Nate's voice outside. Placing the note inside the envelope, she shoved it in her purse and hurried to the front door to let him in.

"Was that a scream? I didn't mean to frighten you."

"I'm sorry. I was just in another world and didn't hear your car." Not wanting to talk about her latest discovery, she picked up her wrap and walked over to the door and snapped on the outside light. "I'm all ready to go."

He looked surprised at their abrupt departure but stepped back outside, waiting as she checked to be sure the door was locked before leading the way up the path to the car.

"I somehow thought a famous author would be driving a flashy sports car."

Nate laughed. "I actually did have a sports car until Erika was three. It was a little blue beamer convertible. A real babe magnet. However, I had a hell of a time getting Erika in and out of the car seat and eventually gave it up for the RAV4," Nate said, as he held the door open for her. "I thought we'd go to the Cedars at Sawmill Inn. They've got great steaks, and, if you like fish, you can't beat their walleyed pike."

"That sounds perfect. I liked the look of the place when I drove past it and I've been looking forward to going there."

* * *

Once settled in the restaurant, Clare looked around, pleased at the ski lodge ambiance and the stone fireplace on the far wall.

"Good choice," she said. "The room has a wonderful warm feeling and I suspect in the winter with a fire roaring, there must be a capacity crowd."

"The local folklore has it that many babies have been conceived in the winter after dinner at the Cedars," Nate said.

"Thankfully it's summer but I'll keep it in mind."

"That probably ruins my chances of getting lucky tonight."

Clare could feel the heat rising to her cheeks. "Behave yourself or I'll mention your womanizing reputation in my interview."

Nate laughed, unruffled by her comment. Their drinks arrived and he waited to see if she liked the wine before asking her how her day was. He watched her as she talked about finding her birth certificate and her parents' marriage license. Listening to the emotion in her voice he wondered what it would be like to discover that your whole life was a lie. He could imagine anger and a sense of betrayal being the predominant feelings.

"Do you think whoever chose December second as your birthday picked it at random or could there be some significance to the date?" he asked.

With her thumb, Clare wiped the condensation off the side of her wine glass. "I haven't found anything yet. It wasn't either of my parent's birthday or Rose's. It may be another one of those things I'll never find out."

A shadow of sadness crept into her expression and, wanting to offer comfort, Nate reached across the table to take her hand. She looked startled at the contact and, for a moment, he thought she was going to pull away.

"I was going to be married last weekend. A week ago tomorrow," she blurted out.

Her fingers tightened on his hand and she shook her head in chagrin as he sought for some sort of response.

"Why is it I feel compelled to tell you my life's story?" she said.

"Probably for the same reason I told you mine."

Nate smiled across at her. Although she held his hand tightly, he could see the tension easing in the rest of her body. He was dazzled by the green of her eyes and the trusting way she looked at him.

"Did you postpone the wedding when you found out about the adoption?"

"In part. Doug was a lawyer. Having a wife who didn't know her family background presented a problem for a man wanting to pursue a career in politics. His family was wealthy and well established socially in Chicago. As his mother was happy to point out, it would be unfortunate if, after the marriage, it turned out that my family had a scandalous side." Clare's laugh was harsh. "Wouldn't she love to hear my history now?"

"What did Doug think?"

"He thought we should put our wedding plans on hold until I could look into my family history. Instead the wedding was canceled."

Nate was surprised that she didn't seem as upset as she had been over other things she'd discovered in her search for her identity.

"Doug canceled it? What kind of idiot were you marrying?" Nate released her hand, surprised at how angry he was. He downed the last of his Scotch and signaled the waitress for another round. "Sorry, Clare, for my rudeness. Perhaps he was the same kind of jerk I was when I was screwing up my marriage."

Clare chuckled.

"Thanks for your defense, but I was the one who canceled the wedding. I did it originally in anger. Now I realize that my subconscious was just recognizing the fact that I shouldn't marry Doug."

"Were you madly in love with him?"

Nate tried to keep his tone slightly humorous, but he was anxious to know the answer to the question. Clare tipped her head to the side. Her eyes were focused on a spot over his shoulder. Her mouth was unsmiling, her lower lip caught up in her teeth. Finally she shook her head.

"It's funny, but I never asked myself that question. Now that I think about it, I don't think I was. I was flattered by his attention and proud of him. He was fun to be with and interesting to talk to. But to answer your question, no, I don't think I was madly in love with him."

"Had you dated long?"

"Almost three years. Rose never approved. In retrospect I can understand her concerns. When she moved to Chicago with me, her whole purpose was to make sure no one ever discovered my family background. She was angry when my soccer team was going to the state finals. The newspaper wanted to profile all of the girls and Rose wouldn't let them run my picture."

"And now you're dating a man who would be taking you to political dinners and fund-raisers and your picture would be appearing in the society section of the newspaper and the Chicago magazines."

"Exactly. Besides if Doug went into politics full time, the newspapers were bound to dig around until they discovered what I'm just finding out now. It makes sense why Rose would try to discourage the relationship. She would have been much happier if I'd dated a plumber or an advertising exec."

Clare finished her wine just as the waitress returned with another round of drinks. Nate took a long sip of his before he spoke.

"Last weekend must have been a rough time for you."

Clare shook her head. "I left Chicago last Friday and went up to Lake Geneva, Wisconsin. I'd gone there quite a few times with Gail and her family and stayed at the French Country Inn. Lake, pool, and wonderful balconies. Totally relaxing. I needed to get away and thought this would be the perfect start to my Minnesota trip."

"I figured you didn't get that tan in downtown Chicago. That was a smarter idea than staying at home and staring at the walls."

"Lots of walking and swimming and thinking. The latter was interesting. I realized the canceled wedding didn't devastate me. When I went back over our relationship, I could see that we didn't have a lot in common in the areas I thought were important. We had fun together, but when I really looked into the future I didn't see us aging well together. He didn't like to be around children, didn't like plays, didn't read much, and we didn't talk much. When we went out on dates, we were always with other people, rarely ever just the two of us."

"I recall when my marriage to Rebecca was falling apart, we did the same thing. We'd go out with either her friends or mine."

"In our way Doug and I were as wrong together as it sounds like you and Rebecca were."

"Then you made the right decision to cancel the wedding." Nate sighed. "If I'd been so self-aware I might never have gotten married."

"In your case, your bonus was Erika."

Before he could comment, the waitress arrived with their dinners and the serious discussions were suspended. He was pleased that she liked the walleyed pike and for a while they talked about food and restaurants that he knew from his travels to Chicago. Toward the end of the meal, he brought the conversation back to Erika.

"I realize Erika was rude to you yesterday. I'd like to apologize for her."

"There's no need," Clare said. "Eleven is a tough age for a girl. So many changes and so many feelings she doesn't understand. Believe it or not she'll grow out of it."

"Soon?"

"Ten years should do it."

"Now that was cruel." When Clare laughed, her smile was like sunshine, warming him. It made him uneasy at how quickly he'd been drawn to her. What was it about her that made her so appealing?

"It's probably a little frightening if she thinks some woman might replace her in your life. She needs to be busy to take her focus off of you."

"I haven't been conscious of it until lately. I signed her up for everything I thought she'd be interested in and some she wasn't.

She's taking clogging and knitting lessons and there's a creative writing class she's signed up for through the school."

"What's clogging?" Clare's eyebrows were drawn down over her eyes. "Does that have anything to do with blocked pipes?"

"Ah, you city girls. It's like tap dancing except the taps aren't tight to the sole of the shoe. They're loose and make a jingling sound when they tap. I think it's related to Irish dancing except the music is usually bluegrass or, these days, country."

"I can imagine she'd have a lot of fun doing it. In Chicago there were a lot of Irish dancers and I think it gave the girls more confidence when they hit puberty. Dancers move well and that helps when you're going through that awkward stage."

"Several of the girls in Erika's class took it up and then when we went to the Showboat several years ago they had an exhibition and she was hooked."

"Showboat?"

"I forgot you're new in town and haven't even tasted the cultural and musical delights of Grand Rapids."

He signaled to the waitress that she could clear the table. He ordered coffee but Clare preferred tea. When it arrived, he sat back feeling totally relaxed.

"I hope you're ready for some geography and history," he said.

"If you're paying for dinner, I guess I'll be forced to listen."

"The source of the Mississippi River is west of Grand Rapids at Lake Itasca. It flows right through town. Long ago the only communication some of the towns along the river had was the arrival of the riverboats. With paddlewheel churning the water and the whistle blowing for miles upstream, they'd pull into shore and announce that there'd be a show in the evening."

"I remember hearing about those boats along the Ohio river too. It must have been an exciting time in those days."

"About fifty years ago, someone had the bright idea to resurrect a riverboat and put on a show right here in Grand Rapids. It was going to be a special celebration, but it was so successful that it became an annual tradition. It's called the Mississippi Melodie

Showboat. There's an amphitheater along the shore and the riverboat pulls in along the edge where there's a stage."

"What a treat," Clare said. "Do they have shows all year round?"

"No, just for a couple weeks in the summer. Unfortunately last week was the last, but I'll take you out to the amphitheater and you'll be able to get a good idea of what it would be like."

"I'd like that. So I missed my chance to see real live clogging."

"Professionally done, that's true. Although that was just one small part of the show. The showboat really recreated the feeling of the old vaudeville-type shows. Big cast and elaborate period costumes. Lots of singing and dancing and the old slapstick broad comedy routines."

"Does Erika want to dance on the showboat?"

"The girls in her class are part of a performing team. They go to nursing homes and churches and carnivals and do shows."

"Oh I'd like to see them dance. You've got me thoroughly intrigued."

"I think you'll have to stay in town longer than you planned because there are plenty of things to see in Grand Rapids."

Clare was startled by the expression on Nate's face. His gaze was steady as he examined her. She wasn't prepared for her own reactions and considered a change to a less serious subject. Opening her purse she reached inside and pulled out his handkerchief.

"I thought you'd like this back," she said, passing it across to him. "If I'm going to play the weeping, fainting ingénue, I should start carrying one of my own."

He held it in his hand for a moment and then slipped it into his jacket pocket. "And I decided that I better have a spare on hand just in case I run into another damsel in distress."

"I hear there's a rash of them heading to Grand Rapids."

When she'd gotten the handkerchief out, she'd seen the letter she'd jammed in her purse before she left the house. Taking it out, she handed it to him.

"I didn't find this until just before you came. That's why I was a little abrupt before dinner. I had only just read it and I didn't want to bring it up until I'd had a chance to think about it. It was in the bottom of the cardboard box. It's a letter to me from Jimmy Newton."

Carefully Nate removed the note and read it.

"It's a very nice note. If he left it with the jewelry case you can see that his last thoughts were about you. That has to be some consolation."

"It is. Comforting, but there's still so much that I don't understand. It's apparent that Jimmy and Rose planned everything after the death of my mother. He must have decided right from the beginning that he was going to escape."

Nate pulled at his earlobe, mouth pinched in thought. "I agree. He must have sensed that his guilt would be uncovered immediately so he had to work fast."

"Ruth's brother Owen seems to have been included in much of the planning. He was the one who arranged the sale of Rose's houses and for the fake birth certificates. I can't imagine that he would have helped Jimmy escape, but he certainly facilitated my new life in Chicago."

Nate nodded. "It does look that way. I agree that Jimmy escaped on his own. Owen had too much at stake to risk helping him. I didn't know him, but from everyone who's spoken of him, Owen was one of the most honest people around. Unfortunately we'll never know what his part in this whole scenario was."

Nate paid the check and they left the restaurant. It had turned chilly outside. Clare shivered and unfolded her wrap. Nate reached for it and draped it over her shoulders.

"Is that going to be warm enough?"

"You might know literature, Mr. Hanssen, but it's obvious you know nothing of haute couture." Clare's tone was arch as she flung the material across one shoulder. "A million Himalayan goats have shed their fleece so that I and other fashion-conscious women might ward off chills and look exotically beautiful."

"I'll buy the beautiful part but what is this stuff?"

Clare laughed. "It's called pashmina. I think it means wool."

"No, wool is cheap. With a name like pashmina, it's bound to be pretty pricey." He put an arm around her shoulder and led her to the car. "I better get you home before the Minnesota goats catch wind of a foreigner in town."

Back at the cottage, Nate walked side by side with Clare down the flagstone path, holding her hand. She'd left a light on inside the cottage and the overhead porch light enabled her to unlock the door. He followed her in, bumping into her back as she halted on the threshold.

"What's up?" he asked.

"Someone's been in here."

Chapter Twelve

"Someone was in the cottage while we were at dinner," Clare said. She could feel the goose bumps on her skin as she looked around the room.

"Are you sure?" Nate asked.

"Yes. I know how I left the papers on the counter. They've been moved."

"Stay here," Nate said.

He crossed the room to the bedroom and bathroom. Clare watched him moving from room to room.

"There's no one here now," he said. "Are you sure there was someone here?"

"Yes. Just before you came to pick me up tonight I'd been at the counter looking through my research files. My laptop was on the coffee table in the living room and I brought it over here earlier in the day. That's been moved too."

"Would you know if anything was taken?"

"I can't believe anyone would take my notes. However if someone looked through this pile, they would find my birth certificate and the other papers I got at the courthouse."

"That doesn't mean that they will know who you are, if that's what you're afraid of. You're a reporter doing a story on the murder case so it would be logical you'd have all sorts of documents and notes."

His reasonable tone penetrated her panic. She took a deep breath and tried to think more calmly.

"The only things of any value are in the bedroom."

Setting her purse and wrap on the table beside the sofa she went into the bedroom. She was still feeling shaky and was grateful that Nate followed her. She walked across to the dresser where the satin jewelry cases were side by side. Opening the blue one she looked through her jewelry and found the few things that she'd brought still there. Inside the red one were the pearls and the wedding ring. Then she picked up the letter that Owen had taped to the top of the cardboard box.

"Whoever was here read this letter."

"How can you tell?"

Clare held the envelope in her left hand, backside facing up and the flap opening pointed to the right.

"The note is facing the wrong way." She held it out so that she could see as she extracted it. "In grade school when we first learned how to write letters my teacher, Mrs. Zenda, was a stickler for etiquette. She told us that with a single page this size, you inserted the bottom first with the note facing toward the back of the envelope."

Once more she demonstrated how it should have been placed in the envelope.

"The theory is that when it's extracted, the person doesn't need to turn it to read the contents. It's funny how things like that make an impression on a child. I've always done it that way even though I realize now it's really not that important."

"You were upset when you showed it to me today. Are you sure you didn't put it back the wrong way?"

"I don't think so. It's a long ingrained habit." She put the envelope back in the jewelry case, then turned to face Nate whose expression was concerned. "Whoever read the letter has to realize the only reason I would have this note is because I am Abby."

"How would anyone get in? Did you lock the back door before we left?"

"I'm sure I did." She walked out to the living room and crossed to the back door. Opening it, she stepped outside and tried the doorknob. "It's unlocked."

She came back inside, locking the door behind her. She rubbed her forehead, thinking back to her actions after she came back from City Hall and before Nate arrived.

"I didn't go out on the porch after I came back from town. I took a shower and dressed and then read my father's letter."

"How about after I left this morning? Did you go back outside?"

Clare shook her head. "No, I cleaned up everything while you were talking to Erika. I gathered up my notebook and left for City Hall."

"Do you remember locking the back door?"

Clare closed her eyes trying to visualize those last few minutes. She opened her eyes and stared across at Nate. "No. I don't think I locked it."

"If someone was here they got lucky finding the door unlocked. You'll remember to lock up from now on. It isn't Chicago, but there are still criminals in any town. Do you think it might have been Ruth just checking on the place?"

"No. I can't picture her snooping around." Clare shivered. "I don't like the fact someone was in here."

"Me neither. On the face of it, it looks like whoever was here wanted to find out about you. Otherwise it's strange that someone would break in and not take anything." When Clare opened her mouth to argue, Nate put up a hand to forestall her. "I'm not saying it didn't happen. If you think someone was here, then I can accept that."

"Thanks, Nate." She sighed. "I'm just a little bit spooked."

"Would you like me to stay for a while? Or I could sleep over since Erika's gone for the night."

He wiggled his eyebrows for emphasis and Clare laughed feeling her mood lighten.

"I detect a slightly leering tone so I think I'll be well advised to say no."

"The question is, do you feel comfortable here?"

She thought about it for a moment and realized that after the initial feeling of disquiet, she didn't feel frightened. Nothing was taken and she had no sense of menace in the intrusion.

"I feel fine. I'll lock up tight and get a good night's sleep. I think I've been running on a lot of adrenaline and maybe that makes me liable to paranoia."

"You've got my number on your cell phone. Don't hesitate to call me if you feel any concern at all."

"I will. And thanks for a very nice evening."

She opened the front door and stood aside for him. He put his hand on her shoulder and leaned over, kissing her lightly on the mouth. She knew if she made the slightest move he would stay the night. Much as she was tempted, she merely smiled up at him.

"I'll look for you tomorrow at the bed races," he said.

With a salute of his hand, he walked across the porch and up the path to his car. She closed the door and locked it. She turned to face the room and tried to think about the possibility that someone could still be outside watching her. Taking the cell phone from her purse, she set it on the bedside table. She took her time getting ready for bed and read until she was sleepy. Knowing it was important for her to regain confidence in the safety of the cottage, she finally turned off the lights.

For a time she listened to the noises outside and the creaking sounds in the house itself. Eventually the far off sound of the loons lulled her into sleep.

"Wow, this is quite an event," Clare said, following the crowd of people walking toward the park. "Looks like half of Minnesota has come out for the art show."

"The weather cooperated too," Ruth said, cutting between the sawhorses set up to funnel people across the street from the parking lot. "There's always a big turnout since in the North August means summer is coming to an end."

"Now that's a depressing thought," Clare said as she took Ruth's arm to help her over the curb. "The park is perfect for this. With all the trees, even as hot as it is, there's plenty of shade."

They wandered along the line of artists' booths, stopping occasionally to look more closely at someone's work. Clare was drawn to the bigger paintings, especially the local landscapes.

"I have no idea where I'd hang that one," she said, pointing to an oil painting that was six feet square. "It's lovely, but it would take up a whole wall in my place."

"I think that's what they refer to as a sofa-size painting," Ruth chuckled.

Clare moved back into the stream of traffic and bumped into a solid body. Looking up, she smiled as she recognized Ed Wiklander.

"I'm sorry, Ed. I wasn't looking where I was going. How are you this morning?"

Expecting a warm greeting she was surprised that he didn't return her smile.

"I'm fine, thank you."

"Afternoon, Ed," Ruth said, joining them. "Are you coming or going?"

"Just leaving."

"Excuse me while I catch a friend," Ruth said as she darted across the path to another booth.

"Any artist in particular you'd recommend?" Clare asked.

"I'm not much of an expert."

Ed fidgeted as if anxious to get away. Curious, Clare came right to the point.

"Did I offend you somehow the other night?"

He flushed, turning his head away for a moment before he turned back to stare down at her.

"I heard you're a reporter. Is that true?"

"Sort of. I work for a literary magazine in Chicago. I'm here to interview Nathan Hanssen."

"You're also looking into the Newton murder?"

"Yes, my editor wants to do a story on it. A human-interest story about small-town crime."

"No one in town wants the subject brought up again." Ed's voice was harsh. "It was a long time ago and better left forgotten."

"I'm sorry you feel that way, Ed. The article will run in Chicago, so I don't think anyone here will even see it. I was actually hoping I might interview you in order to get your take on the story."

"Not a chance," he practically spit out the words.

"I didn't mean to upset you. I'm not planning to sensationalize anything. I . . ."

"Take some advice, Clare," Ed interrupted. "Leave it alone. Do your interview and stop digging into something that's best left alone."

With an abrupt nod of his head, he brushed by her. Clare turned, watching his angry figure disappear in the crowd.

"What was that all about?" Ruth asked coming back to stand beside her.

Clare smiled grimly. "Apparently the news that I'm a reporter and doing a story on the Newton murder has gotten out. Ed was just warning me to stop digging into it. When I asked if I could interview him, he almost snapped my head off."

"My, my." Ruth looked thoughtful. She pulled Clare out of the movement of foot traffic. "It makes sense though. Ed adored his father, who died five years ago. If you remember in the article, Big Red and Jimmy had the fight the night of the murder. I'm sure Ed doesn't want that brought up again."

"What an idiot I am. I forgot all about it. I just saw it as an opportunity to interview someone who was around at the time of the murder. Ed's older than I, so I thought he might have had some impressions about what went on at the time. Or at least he'd have heard his parents talking."

"He probably did and that's why he doesn't want it brought up again. His father was a married man and yet he was flirting with Lily Newton."

Clare sighed. "I have to remember that other people may be more emotionally invested in this case than I am. I'm still at the stage where it's like reading a murder mystery. I don't feel an emotional impact. If I could remember my life back then, maybe I'd be passionate about it too."

"It'll come in good time." Ruth patted her arm.

"So much for trying to keep my identity a secret."

"You look worried, but I don't think it's a problem that people know that you're a reporter."

"If that's all they know." Clare led Ruth across to one of the picnic tables near the concession stands. She bought two bottles of water and they sat down in the shade. "I haven't had a chance to talk to you since our dinner on Thursday. So much has happened."

Between sips of water, Clare told Ruth about her father's wallet and chain. Then she told her about Judge Shannon's note to Thatcher and Nate coming to the cottage while she opened the box and found the photos and the jewelry box.

"I wish I could tell you what Owen's part in all this was. I suppose he could have arranged all the paperwork, but it still surprises me that he didn't push Rose to tell you about your identity. He was the most honest of men," Ruth said. "The only thing I can think of is that my brother thought he would live forever and there was plenty of time to tell you."

"It was such a sad time when he died. I know it took Gail a long time to recover and I'm not sure her brothers ever did."

"Yes." Ruth shook her head. "I had been widowed for two years when he had his heart attack. Fifty-nine is much too young. And worse yet, I wasn't able to attend the funeral. I'd broken my leg and the doctor wouldn't let me travel."

"I loved your brother dearly, Ruth. He always made Rose and me feel like family."

They sat quietly for several minutes, both caught up in their memories. Finally Ruth stirred.

"Enough sad memories. Let's get back to your search for identity," Ruth said. "So with the help of the pictures and the date in the wedding ring, you were able to find your parents marriage license?"

"And my birth certificate," Clare said. "It's strange how a simple piece of paper could give me the feeling that I really do exist." Clare took a long swallow of the cold water. "And I went out to dinner with Nate last night."

"So you've definitely been holding out on me. I sensed the night of the church supper that he was interested, although the devil child was keeping him from coming over to meet you. Don't just sit there. Give me all the details. Hopefully there will be some salacious ones."

"Sorry to disappoint you but it was a fairly chaste evening."

"Ah well, there's always next time."

"Really, Ruth." Clare could feel a blush rise to her cheeks. Looking across at the twinkling eyes of the older woman she found herself laughing. "Yes, it was a good evening and, yes, there appears to be some kind of connection between us."

"Lovely. I won't even pry anymore. I'll just trust you'll keep me informed." She finished her drink and looked down at her watch. "For the moment we have to cut away from your social updates for something much more exciting. The bed races are about to start."

Clare stood up. "One question before we go. Did you stop by the cottage last night?"

"No. I was too tired when I got home and, although your car was in the lot, there was only one light on so I thought you'd gone to bed early. Why?"

"Someone was in the cottage while I was at dinner with Nate."

Ruth's eyes widened in shock. "A break-in?"

"No. I think I left the back door unlocked."

"Are you sure?"

"Yes. The papers on the counter had been gone through and other things in the bedroom had been touched. Nothing was taken, but someone clearly knows who I am."

"Was Nate with you when you came back from dinner?"

"Yes. He thinks it was someone who was curious as to who I am."

"Maybe so, but the mere fact whoever it was entered without permission is troublesome. I don't like that at all, Clare."

"I don't either. I'll just have to be more careful when I leave the house."

"If it was curiosity I don't see that they will come back, but I still don't like the fact it happened. Do you feel threatened at all?"

Clare thought about it for a moment, then shook her head. "No. Since it wasn't robbery, I can't imagine any reason for anyone to break in. Perhaps he or she came to see me and walked in when they found the door open. I suppose I'll never know."

"Let's hope so."

"Enough of this. We don't want to be late for the bed races," Clare said.

Ruth led the way in a quick sprint, cutting through the park over to the main highway on the far side. They came through the crowd and walked along the street until there was a shout from one of the spectators. One of the women from the church supper was waving to Ruth.

"You remember meeting Maya Peterson," Ruth said, as she led her over to the lovely white-haired lady, sitting on one of the wooden benches beside the parade route. "She's been saving us seats."

"Thank you, Maya," Clare said. "I've been looking forward to this ever since I heard about the races."

"They'll be coming down that hill." Maya pointed to the long hill on the right. "It's always great fun."

Looking up at the top of the hill, Clare could see an old, metal bed frame with a mattress was poised on the crest. A young girl in footed pajamas with a stuffed teddy bear was holding onto the headboard. Three boys similarly attired were standing behind the bed ready to push. Beside them was another bed, made out of plywood, shaped to resemble a spaceship. A costumed alien was on the bed. A horn sounded and the racers pushed the beds, which came flying down the hill. The spaceship was well in the lead until one of the wheels hit a bump and the headboard came loose. The spaceship screeched to a halt and the alien rolled against the footboard causing the entire bed to collapse.

The crowd applauded and whistled their enjoyment as the iron bed frame crossed the finish line. Several other races were run. One of Clare's favorite entrants was an old-fashioned porcelain bathtub, which came to a disastrous end when it veered off course and crashed into a telephone pole. Apparently the pajamaed first team made the best time as it was declared the winner.

"See what you've been missing in Chicago," Maya said as the crowd began to disperse.

"What fun," Clare said. "I can't decide who had more laughs. The people watching or those involved in the race."

Ruth led her back to the art show. She was amazed at the quality and variety of the displays. Although she much preferred the paintings, she really admired the bronze figures and some of the intricate pottery pieces.

"Waldo's owner is one of the people exhibiting. His name is Jake Jorgenson. He's a friend of mine and I'd like you to meet him."

"I forgot to mention that I met him the first night I was here," Clare said. "He came over to make sure Waldo wasn't bothering me."

"Jake is a wonderful artist. I think you'll like his work." Ruth pointed along the row of canvas tents to one at the end of the line. "It's a good spot for him. Right before the turn to the food concessions."

As they approached Jorgenson's booth, Clare was impressed by the landscapes hanging on the canvas walls. Lake and woods were the subjects of all the pictures. The detail was meticulous but it was the use of light that she liked best. The warm reddish tones of early evening brought a glow to the paintings that she found delightful.

Ruth had hung back as Clare looked at the paintings, letting her view each one undisturbed. As she approached the middle of the booth, she spotted a man seated in a canvas director's chair at the back of the tent. His head was bent over a book in his lap and she suspected he was asleep.

He reminded Clare of pictures of Ichabod Crane. Long legs, awkwardly bent, sticking out from beige shorts. A rumpled cotton jacket and shirt hung on his thin, almost gaunt body. She could see he had a sharp-edged chin but the rest of his face was in shadow.

His hair was full and white, cut shaggily around his neck. Clare smiled as Ruth came up behind her.

"What kind of salesman sleeps on the job," Ruth said, just loud enough to wake him.

He raised his head slowly, his eyes blinking as he stared up at Clare. It took him a moment to focus and then he lurched forward. He rose so quickly that he knocked over his chair. Muttering under his breath, he picked it up and set it back in place.

"Sorry for being so clumsy. I'm stiff from sitting so long." He came forward, brushing at the creases in his jacket sheepishly as he leaned over to kiss Ruth on the cheek. "And, yes, I was asleep."

"It's hot in the sun," Ruth said, then nodded at Clare. "I gather you've already met my renter, Jake."

"I'm not sure you'd recognize me since it was so dark. I'm Clare Prentice. Waldo's friend."

She held out her hand and after a slight hesitation he gave her a quick handshake. Looking at his weather-beaten face, she suspected that he was older than she'd first suspected. Deep lines cut across his forehead and alongside his nose and mouth. His ears jutted out away from his head, freckled and leathery from too many years under the sun. He moved like an old man, yet his brown eyes had a youthful twinkle as he stared at her.

"You're much prettier in the light of day," he said.

"Careful, Clare, the man has a silver tongue and a soft spot for the ladies," Ruth said, turning back to Jake. "Clare's come up from Chicago to do an interview with Nate Hanssen. She's also doing research on the Newton murder."

Jake's eyebrows raised and he gave Clare a sharp look of inspection. "That was a long time ago. Twenty years ago at least."

"Actually it's twenty-five years. I'm thinking of doing an anniversary piece. Trying to talk to people who might have known the Newton's. Was Jimmy a contemporary of yours? He would have been sixty-seven if he was alive today."

"Thanks for the compliment, but I'm seventy-three so even if I'd lived here I probably wouldn't have known him." He brushed his hair back with a heavily sun-spotted hand. "I've only been living in Grand Rapids for three years. Came here when I retired."

"What did you do before you retired?" she asked.

"I was a graphic designer in Duluth. Used to come here to fish and eventually bought an old cabin on the lake. It's beautiful country and there's plenty for me to paint," he said, waving his hand at the pictures on the walls of the booth.

"Where is the hound from hell?" Ruth asked. "I half expected Waldo to be here. "

Jake chuckled. "My plan was to bring him. First thing this morning, my neighbor Barbara Peck asked if she could take him on a picnic with her grandchildren. It seems my dog has a busier social calendar than I do." He pulled at his earlobe as he looked sideways at Clare. "How are you enjoying the art show?"

"Very much. Although it can't compare for excitement with the bed races."

"Poor girl lives in Chicago, and has never had the opportunity to see them before," Ruth said.

"Culturally deprived obviously," Jake said. "Minnesota is considered a trendsetter in most things."

Ruth snorted in amusement. "Look around, Clare. I told you Jake was highly talented."

Clare had to agree as she looked more carefully at the paintings. The brushstrokes were precise and the colors were so true to life that they almost looked like photographs. She moved around the tent impressed at the display, stopping occasionally to peer more closely. She was aware that Jake was watching her reactions, but she didn't really know what to say to indicate her pleasure.

She got to the last one and turned back. Ruth had been standing at the side but shifted slightly and Clare caught a glimpse of a small picture she'd missed the first time around. There was something about the picture that drew her forward until she was standing in front of it.

It was a dark, brooding study of an old boathouse seen through the mist of a rainstorm.

Something about the picture caught her attention and held her in place. She could feel her heart beating strongly as she stared at the painting. Her gaze swept back and forth across the canvas and she could feel a tingling in her hands. It was as if she were looking at the picture through the wrong end of a telescope. What was it about the picture that frightened her?

Her vision blurred and for a moment she thought she might faint.

Chapter Thirteen

"Clare." Jake's voice close to her ear brought her back to her senses. "Are you all right?"

Embarrassed by her momentary faintness, Clare stepped back and took a deep breath.

"For some reason I'm feeling a little shaky," she said.

She turned to face Jake. He was watching her intently, his eyes shadowed and his mouth pulled into a frown.

"It could be the heat." Jake said. "It's usually not this hot for the show. This year it's pretty brutal. Would you like to sit for a minute?"

"I think I'm all right now. I was a little dizzy. Almost as if I was having a reaction to the picture."

She knew her explanation was weak, but she didn't know how else to express the feelings she had when she looked at it.

"Come look at this one," he said, turning her toward another canvas on the far side of the booth. "I think you'll like this one better. I was fishing in the evening in a little bay off Lost Lake. The light was perfect. There was no breeze and the loons were just beginning to call across the water. Everything was still except for right against the shoreline where you can almost see the ripple of the water as a muskie swam just beneath the surface."

He pointed to a spot on the canvas and Clare narrowed her eyes to get a closer look. Whether it was the storytelling tone of his voice or the skill of his painting, she could swear she saw the water move. She looked at him and smiled.

"It's a beautiful painting."

"Thank you."

"There's Jake," came a shout from in front of the booth. Erika Hanssen stood in front of the opening, her hands on her hips. "Have you sold lots of pictures today?"

"That's a rude question, Erika," Nate said as he pulled on his daughter's pigtail. "Don't encourage her, Jake. This child needs to learn some manners."

Erika ran up to Jake and gave him a hug, asking a series of rapid-fire questions about Waldo. Nate smiled across at Clare as he said hello to Ruth.

"I came to steal your renter," he said. "I promised her beer and hot dogs if I ran into her. Want to join us?"

"I'll walk over with you. I told Jake I'd pick up something for the two of us and come back to keep him company," Ruth said.

Clare turned to say good-bye to Jake and caught him staring at her, his expression pained. He was holding on to one of the metal support poles, and she walked over to him.

"Now it's my turn to ask if you're all right," she said softly.

"Thanks for asking. I've got a pinched nerve in my back. Every once in a while it gives me fits. Gettin' old is all about maintenance. Patch. Patch. Patch."

"I'm starving."

Erika's whine effectively broke the group up. With a wave, Clare said good-bye to Jake.

While Nate bought the hot dogs, she and Erika scouted out a table in the shade. It was close to one in the afternoon and the sun pressed down heavily. Erika seemed a little more friendly than she had the first time, chattering happily about the parade that Clare had missed.

"You should have seen the high school drill team. They were the best," she said. "The uniforms are so cool. I think I'd like to be on the team when I get to high school. I love marching. My friend Cindy and I are practicing doing flags."

"Carrying them?" Clare asked.

"No. Waving them. It's like rhythmic gymnastics. With those

streamers. I'd much prefer to do that, but they don't have teams here in Grand Rapids. The flag teams are cooler than cool."

She held her arms out, waving them enthusiastically, nearly knocking the hot dogs out of her father's hands as he arrived at the table.

"Sorry, Dad. I was showing Clare about the flag teams. Oh, there's Cindy. I'll be right back."

She darted across to another table where her friend was eating with her family. There was much chatting and gesturing between the two girls. They made the perfect foil for each other. Erika was willowy and blonde while Cindy was shorter and more compactly built with cropped black hair. Looking at the girl's parents, she recognized Bruce Young, the man she had lured out to lunch after meeting him in the courthouse. She waved as he looked up and acknowledged her.

"You know Bruce?" Nate said.

"He was at the courthouse when I got my birth certificate. I interviewed him briefly."

While they ate, she told him about her run in with Ed Wiklander.

"Ed's a bit of a hot head," Nate said. "He'll get over it. He might even consider doing an interview once he's had a chance to think about it. He wouldn't want his father shown in a bad light so he might want to put his two cents in."

Erika returned and the subject was dropped.

"Can Cindy come and spend the night?"

Nate groaned. "We'll talk about it when we get home. You know how I hate overnights. You girls just sit up and talk and watch videos, and I never get any sleep."

When Clare smiled at Nate's tone, Erika glared at her.

"That's what my mother used to say when I wanted an overnight but she usually gave in." Clare tried to make amends but she suspected it was too late.

As they walked back to Jake's booth, Nate asked Erika if she wanted to go to the farm show the next day.

"It's so lame," she said, her mouth set in a pout. "Just tools and tractors and farm animals. Can I go to the movies if Cindy's mom can drive one way?"

"Sure. I'll call and see if that would work," Nate said. He turned to Clare. "After I drop the girls off, I'll come pick you up for the show."

"Would it be easier if I met you there?" Clare ignored Erika's dragging feet and slumped shoulders at the news that Clare would be going with Nate.

"No, then we'd be juggling cars and besides I know the best place to park so you don't have to walk miles." He grinned. "Don't wear sandals. It gets a bit mucky around the animals."

"Good thought. Give me a call when you're leaving and I'll be ready."

When they arrived back at Jake's booth, Nate and Erika said good-bye. Jake didn't seem particularly talkative and eventually Ruth announced it was time to leave.

Clare took one more look around at the paintings and realized that the picture that had bothered her was no longer hanging on the wall. She would have liked to have one more look at it to see if it was the picture that had bothered her. She had had the same kind of reaction when she'd seen the angel bell at Nate's. Was there something about the picture that had struck her as familiar? She was just about to ask Jake about it when a customer wanted to purchase one of the larger landscapes.

The rest of the day was spent at the Judy Garland museum. They toured the restored home where Judy lived for her first five years. Since she moved to California in 1926, the house was a time capsule of the 1920's style. Clare thoroughly enjoyed the museum, which showcased some of the Wizard of Oz memorabilia. The most interesting was the carriage that Judy rode in on her way to see the wizard.

When Clare noticed that Ruth was getting tired, she suggested a quick dinner out and then home.

Even Clare was tired by the time she got back to the cottage. There was a message on the answering machine from Bianca, inviting her to have lunch with her and Pastor Olli on Monday. She watched TV for a while and then went to bed.

She found the note in the morning.

It had been slipped under the backdoor sometime during the night or in the early morning. It was a plain white envelope containing a single piece of white paper folded in three. The message was written in block letters.

GO BACK TO CHICAGO. POKING YOUR NOSE INTO PAST HISTORY CAN BE VERY DANGEROUS.

A shiver ran down her spine as she read the note. She crumpled it in her hand and threw it into the wastebasket by the sink. She paced the floor trying to rid herself of the feeling of being watched. She suspected the person who wrote the note was the same person who had come into the cottage when she wasn't there. It took time, but eventually her fear was replaced by anger.

Walking back to the kitchen she took the note out of the wastebasket. Laying it on the counter she smoothed out most of the wrinkles. Staring down at the note, she couldn't guess whether it was written by a man or a woman. She had the right to find out her family history no matter if it upset the entire town. She wasn't going to be scared away by such melodramatic tactics.

She drove to Pastor Olli's church for the morning service. After the service, she looked around for Bianca. The woman gave her directions to their house on the lake and suggested that Clare come the next day at noon.

Back at the cottage she changed into cotton slacks and a red sleeveless blouse. Mindful of Nate's comment, she wore sneakers instead of sandals.

"You're in for a rare treat, Clare," Nate said as they drove into the fairgrounds. "I can't decide which would be more exciting for you the plowing demonstration or the log stripping."

"You can laugh at me if you like, but I know I'm going to enjoy it all. I've been to county fairs in Illinois and love learning about old-fashioned farming techniques. You're just jaded living here full time."

Walking along with the crowd, Clare noticed how many people nodded and waved to Nate. It was clear that he wasn't a city boy living in a rural community. He was definitely well entrenched in the town, comfortable with the people.

Although there was good cloud cover, the day was hot. The tractor display was in the open and, after wandering up and down the aisles of both antique and modern machines, Clare was ready for some shade. When Nate stopped at a long line of engine parts, she said she'd like to go check the baked goods in the exhibit tent. They agreed to meet in an hour and a half at the beer tent.

"Make sure you get a *lefse*," he said. "You'll like it."

Clare wasn't sure what a *lefse* was but inside the tent she found the display easily enough since the exhibit had the largest group. A young girl in a Norwegian costume stood behind a long table while an older man worked the griddle. She mixed up some batter, all the time explaining the process.

"A *lefse* is a thin pancake made of potato, cream, and flour," she said. She demonstrated rolling out the pancakes and then handing them over to the man who set them on the griddle. They reminded Clare of tortillas but the smell was more doughy.

"Would you like one with lingonberries or cinnamon and sugar?" the girl asked as she set one on a paper plate.

"I better try the cinnamon."

Clare paid for the treat and then taking the paper plate, blew on the rolled pancake until it was cooler. She took a bite as she strolled along, stopping occasionally at a display that interested her. Finished with the *lefse*, she put her plate in the trash and licked the last of the sugar from her fingers.

Standing in front of a tableful of homemade jams and jellies, she picked out several she thought Ruth would enjoy. She carried them over to the cash register. As the woman behind the table turned, Clare froze. It was the woman in the grocery store who had called her Abby.

"You know me, don't you?" Clare blurted out.

The older woman hesitated for a moment, then nodded her

head. "I know who you are, but I don't really know you. You're Abby."

"Yes," said Clare. Her mouth was dry and she swallowed several times. "Did you know Rose?"

"We went to school together. She was my best friend." The woman's voice was practically a whisper. "I'm Margee Robinson."

Clare smiled in relief. It was a name she recognized from the past. "Rose talked about you. You were the one who sent the China stamps."

"Yes. I lived there for many years. I taught school."

For a moment there was silence as each of them eyed the other. Clare guessed that Margee was in her late fifties, the same age that Rose would be if she were alive. She was short and very petite with beautifully styled blonde hair. Her celery-colored linen dress was understatedly expensive. In her younger days she must have been very striking.

Clare's heart beat excitedly at the realization that she had actually found someone who knew Rose and maybe even knew her parents.

"Can we talk?"

Margee looked around at the crowd of people milling around the tent. She lowered her voice further. "Since you're here in Grand Rapids, I gather you know some of your history."

"I know about my mother and the murder." Clare raised her chin defensively. "I'd like to know more."

"I can't talk now. The murder's not a popular subject in town, but there's something I think you should know. Can I speak to you someplace later?"

Clare looked at her watch. "I'm meeting a friend in front of the beer tent in forty minutes and then we're going to the lumberjack show."

"I'll see you at the show. Beside the log rolling pool," she said, then in a louder voice. "I think you'll like the rhubarb and raspberry jam. It's not too sour. And the apple is always good. That will be five dollars for the two."

Margee reached across the table and took the jam jars and put them into a paper bag. Surprised at the abruptness, Clare reached in her purse for her wallet just as someone bumped into her shoulder.

She turned to face Pastor Olli who was walking with Bianca and Ed Wiklander. Olli patted her arm.

"Sorry, Clare, I didn't mean to mow you down," he said. "We were so busy chatting I wasn't watching where I was going."

"No problem. It's good to see you again." Clare nodded to the others. "You too, Bianca and Ed."

"Hope you're enjoying the farm show," Olli said.

"I am. I just had my first cinnamon *lefse*. If I stay here too long I won't be able to fit in my car. Who knew the food in Minnesota was so good?"

"That's our secret," Bianca said. "Next time you'll have to try the *lefse* with the lingonberries. That's my favorite."

Clare pulled out a five dollar bill and passed it across to Margee. The woman's face was blank of expression as she accepted the bill. She handed Clare the paper bag, then moved off to straighten the display of jars on the table.

"Are you here with Ruth?" Olli asked.

"No, I think I wore her out at the art fair yesterday. She decided to stay home today. Nate Hanssen brought me."

"I heard he'd agreed to an interview. Mostly he doesn't cotton to the media, but for a pretty girl like you I can see he'd want to make an exception," Olli said. "Nice of him to bring you over to this event. He's quite a catch, you know."

"Hush, Olli, you'll embarrass the girl."

Bianca grabbed her brother's arm and pulled him along, muttering at him under her breath. Ed Wiklander stayed behind. As Clare started to walk away, he blocked her path.

"I want to apologize, Clare," he said. His round cheeks were red and he shifted awkwardly. "I don't know why I was so riled up yesterday. When I got home I realized I was out of line. You're a reporter doing your job. You've every right to look into our little murder."

Although she bristled at his calling it "our little murder,"

Clare decided he was being sincere. "No need to apologize, Ed. You were just speaking your mind."

He shrugged in relief. "I got to thinking about it and I thought it might be better if I talked to you. Sometimes the newspaper accounts aren't totally accurate. I'd be happy to speak to you if you had any questions. Maybe meet for drinks?"

"That would be nice," Clare said. "I'm still doing some research, but when I'm ready I'd be pleased if we could sit down and talk. Why don't I give you a call?"

Ed gave her his business card and she tucked it into her purse. He walked along with her, pointing out some of the exhibits he thought would interest her. As they came to the shooting range, Clare jumped at the sound of the gunfire.

"That's something you might want to know," Ed said. "Every year at Thanksgiving time there's a turkey shoot. Nowadays it's pretty lame. People shoot at a cut out of a turkey, not the real thing. The crackpots who make such a ruckus over hunting, called the old version animal cruelty." He paused mid-rant." At any rate, back before the murder, Jimmy Newton won the contest three years in a row."

"So he was familiar with firearms."

"According to my dad, Jimmy could shoot farther and straighter than most guys could see. And Big Red was no slouch either." Ed grinned. "My dad used to win the turkey most years until Newton came to town. Most guys can shoot pretty well with practice, but Jimmy's shots were always right on the money. Dad said, you couldn't give him a target he couldn't hit dead center."

Ed came to an abrupt halt and the tips of his ears reddened. Clare suspected that it must have dawned on him that his comments might be inappropriate considering the fact Jimmy Newton had confessed to murdering his wife. After a few more stuttered sentences, Ed disappeared into the crowd and Clare went in search of Nate.

She was a little early for the meeting so she stopped and watched a teenage girl leading two goats around a small track. Twin boys were sitting in a red wooden cart that was hitched to the goats. A man who was probably the father held a video camera and followed them around as the mother waved her hands to direct the children's attention to the camera.

She watched several more rides then checked the time and headed for the food tent. Nate was outside watching for her.

"You were right. I did like the *lefse.* Hope you got one."

"I did. After I tore myself away from the spark plug display. I ran into Jake Jorgensen and we both had one. Didn't you see him? He walked right past you while you were talking to Pastor Olli. Jake was heading for the pies and cakes with a determined look in his eyes. I saw Ed Wiklander over there too."

"He apologized to me for being rude."

"Good. That's just like Ed. He goes off half-cocked and then comes to his senses when he cools down. I think he's a good guy although I suspect he's being nice so you'll go out with him."

"Jealous?" she asked, grinning up at him.

"Yes." His reply startled them both. "Don't give me that wide-eyed look. You must have noticed that I'm spending more and more time with you. I don't want to rush you, but I think we have some kind of good connection."

Clare found it difficult to respond in a crowd of people, pushing past them. They were clearly blocking the doorway, but she couldn't find the energy to move. As if he'd read her mind, Nate put his arm around her and pulled her over to the side of the tent where they stood face-to-face.

"Well?" he asked. "Am I wrong?"

"No," she mumbled under her breath. "I feel the electricity too, but I'm not sure what it means. I'm in a highly confused state and I've just ended a serious relationship. I don't trust my emotions at this point."

"I'll accept that. This is hardly the time or place for a serious discussion, but I'd like you to think about it. Life is precious when you find someone you like to be with. We've both made mistakes so we need to take it slow. But not too slow."

He grinned down at her, squeezing her shoulder although she sensed he would have liked to hug her.

"Let's get a beer," he said. "Then we'll hit the lumberjack show."

While they drank a cold beer, she told him about the woman in the grocery store calling her Abby and how she had found her again.

"She was my adoptive mother's best friend. She recognized me so I think she must have been in contact with Rose over the years. She must have seen pictures to know what I looked like."

"That's fantastic, Clare. She might be able to answer some of your questions. What's her name? Maybe I know her."

"Her name is Margee Robinson." Nate shook his head at the mention of the woman's name. "You'll get a chance to meet her since she's going to catch up with us after the lumberjack show."

They finished their beers quickly and walked over to the bleachers that were set up across from a stage and a plastic swimming pool where the log rolling contest would be held. The show was a real crowd pleaser. Lumberjacks competed in log splitting, log sawing, and pole climbing. Clare was amazed at how quickly they could climb with the long spikes on their boots. There was a lot of good humored ribbing between the contestants and the crowd cheered wildly for each winner. The log rolling was the highlight of the show.

Dividing the audience in half, each side had a champion to cheer for. Clare's side was the cheering section for the lumberjack in the red plaid shirt and red suspenders. She and Nate yelled and whistled along with the rest of the crowd as their man tried to catapult his opponent in the green suspenders into the waist-deep water. At the end of four rolls, it was tied two and two. The cheering was thunderous for the final bout. Much to Clare's delight, red suspenders was the winner.

She had been so caught up in the show that she forgot to keep an eye out for Margee. As the crowd began to thin, she scanned the pool area but didn't see her. Looking around, Clare couldn't see her anywhere.

"I wonder where she is?" she said, searching the last of the stragglers.

"Are you sure she said she'd meet you here?"

"Yes. She said beside the lumberjack pool."

They waited for twenty minutes but by that time the workers were finished cleaning up the area and there was no one else in the stands.

"I don't think she's coming, Clare." Nate squeezed her hand as he realized her disappointment. "Maybe she couldn't get away."

"Maybe," Clare said. "She seemed so nervous just talking to me. I wonder if she ever intended to meet me."

"Let's go back to the baking tent and see if she's there."

There was no one at the table with the jams and jellies. Nate asked several women at the adjoining booths but they were all volunteers and didn't know who'd been at the other tables. Even mentioning the name Margee elicited no recognition. Close to tears, Clare let Nate convince her that it was time to go home. He asked if she wanted to stop somewhere for dinner, but she said she'd rather go home. Back at the cottage she apologized for being so depressed.

"I had such high hopes about talking to Margee," she said.

"Get out the phone book and we'll see if she's listed," Nate said.

After searching around in the cabinets, they finally found a phone book. Clare thumbed through the pages until she came to the right section.

"No Margee Robinson. In fact, no Robinsons at all."

"You're sure that's the name?"

"Yes," Clare snapped. "I'm sorry. I was so counting on this."

"It has to be a huge letdown. Don't worry about it tonight. Talk to Ruth tomorrow and see if she has any ideas how to find the mystery woman."

Putting his arms around her, he kissed her on the forehead then held her against his chest and patted her back as if she were Erika. Clare giggled and he grinned down at her.

"I'm out of practice in the role of lover," he said. "What have you got going tomorrow?"

"I'm having lunch with Bianca and her brother."

"If Ruth doesn't recognize Margee, then ask Bianca. Despite her sweet fluttery ways, she knows most of the gossip in town. In fact, I'd guess she started a third of it," he said. "By the way, do you want to come for dinner tomorrow?"

"Only if I can cook. You've fed me enough. Besides I make a really great chicken and artichoke heart casserole. And since I'm in Minnesota and want to follow the local customs, I'll make a Jell-O mold."

Chuckling at her joke, he kissed her chastely and left.

Clare took a shower and read for a while. She spent some time looking at her notes, but her heart wasn't in it. When she got hungry she heated up some soup. It had begun to rain, which added to her feeling of depression. She watched some news and then, after a cup of hot tea, went to bed.

The clap of thunder woke her. With the windows closed, the room was hot and stuffy. The flash of light was so bright it blinded her and the darkness that followed was without relief. A flat black with no lighter shades to give definition to objects around her. A flash of lightning illuminated everything in the room, then plunged it into darkness. She seemed to be in the very center of the storm. Clare threw back the covers and scurried across to the window. Thunder rumbled all around her and she could feel the vibrations along the floorboards against her bare feet.

She huddled at the edge, behind the draperies, transfixed by the fury of the storm playing out beyond the window. Like an army on the move, the storm advanced across the lake. Lightning silhouetted the trees at the shoreline as rain sheeted off the eaves of the cottage. Beyond the trees there was nothing but blinding white. The far shore of the lake was invisible. Bands of rain whipped across the open area leading to the dock. After one particularly explosive crash of thunder the pounding of the rain eased. She stayed beside the window watching the streaks of lightning spread across the night sky.

Another flash of lightning and she saw a man standing at the edge of the trees. It was only for an instant and then the darkness descended.

Heart pounding, she waited, her eyes fastened to the spot where she'd seen the figure. Nothing but black. A distant boom of thunder and then a flash of light.

Someone was outside in the rain.

Chapter Fourteen

Clare clung to the side of the window and waited for the next flash of light. Her eyes burned as she stared at the tree line. It came again and the man was still there.

Unmoving. Unrecognizable. A dark figure standing motionless. It looked like someone in a hooded coat. A thin oval of light where the face should be. Too far away to tell if it was a man or woman.

Another flash and he was gone. She searched back and forth in the open space between the house and the dock. In the next flash, she spotted him, catching the wet glint on a slicker. He was closer to the cottage.

She pulled away from the window, terrified that he could see her watching him. She covered her mouth to hold back a scream. Had she locked the back door? More light and he was gone. Where was he? She couldn't stand the waiting and ran out of the bedroom and across the living room to the back door. She touched the lock, reassured that the door was bolted shut. Fumbling in the dark, she reached for the light switch and flipped on the outside porch light.

The backyard leading down to the dock was lit and as she searched the areas along the trees she could see no one. She sagged in relief.

Suddenly she remembered another time, another place. She was on a screened porch. Her fingertips pressed the screening as she watched a storm outside. She was just a child. A tall man stood beside her, his hand lightly touching her shoulder. She felt safe. She didn't know if it was real or only wishful thinking but she sensed that the man was her father.

Thunder crashed in the distance and she blinked her eyes back in the present.

Outside the rain was slowing. It rolled off the roof, puddling and splashing beside the porch. The windows were steaming and hard to see through but as she stared outside she could see that whoever had been outside was gone.

She left the outside light on and went back to bed. She lay on her back for a long time, wondering if there really had been anyone outside. Waking up in the midst of the storm she might have still been caught up in a dream. The scene on the screened porch had surely been part of a dream. She listened to the steady rhythm of the rain and eventually turned over and fell asleep.

The morning was hot and muggy. The air was so thick that it looked as if there was a slight mist rising off the surface of the lake. She still was uncertain about what she had seen in the night. She had been upset when she went to bed, disappointed that she hadn't been able to talk to Rose's friend. Maybe that had triggered some sort of waking nightmare.

She called Ruth at the library and told her about finding the woman from the grocery store. She described her, but Ruth didn't recognize the description. After straightening up the cottage, she drove into town to run errands. She stopped at Gordy's to get what she'd need for dinner at Nate's. By the time she finished putting the groceries away, she had to hurry to get ready for lunch. She drove around the lake, passed Nate's place and, following Bianca's directions, found the entrance to the Egner's place.

Bianca met her at the front door of the beautiful old stone house. Clare looked around the large foyer, admiring the glass cases on either side that were filled with porcelain figurines. One case held birds of every size and shape, the vibrant colors of the feathers in sharp contrast to the case on the other wall. Here most of the figures were in soft muted colors of white, grays, and soft blues. Lladros predominated but there were other artists represented that she didn't recognize.

"It's a breathtaking collection, Bianca."

"I'm glad you like it. My mother started me collecting. Other people have added such beautiful pieces over the years. Most of the birds were given to Olli, and I thought they should have a place of their own."

"Ah, here you are, Clare. Right on time." Olli's voice boomed in the high-ceilinged hall as he strode forward to shake her hand. "Come along and we'll see if we can give you some more good Minnesota food."

With a hand at her back, he steered her toward the dining room across the hall. The furniture was old but clearly expensive. The cherry table gleamed beneath a crystal chandelier. He pulled out a chair for her while Bianca bustled off to the kitchen.

"I can only stay for a lunch and then you and Bianca can have a good chat. I run a summer camp down by the lake and we've just completed our season. Several of the counselors have stayed behind to clean up the place and get it ready for winter."

He talked a little bit about the activities at the camp and Clare could see how enthused he was about how well it had gone. He was especially proud of the fact that this year they had opened up the camp to some inner-city boys from Duluth.

"One of my first postings was in Duluth, so I've stayed close to many people there. The youth minister and I arranged for eight boys to come to the camp for free."

"I'll bet it was a big change for them after living in the city," Clare said.

"At first they were very tentative. Everything was new to them. Sleeping in tents, building fires, and learning to canoe." Olli's mouth stretched in a smile. "It was a few days before they began to feel comfortable. By the end of two weeks, they were as adept as the other boys."

Bianca came back into the dining room carrying a large tray. Clare was surprised when Olli remained in his chair, watching passively as Bianca struggled to set it on the buffet.

"I hope you'll like our simple meal," Bianca said as she set a plate in front of Olli and then another in front of Clare. "More often than not we have soup. It's too hot for that this time of year so we usually have a fruit salad at lunch. The raspberries and blueberries are locally grown. This has been a good year for both."

She kept up a stream of chatter as she circled the table, setting down plates and water glasses as she went.

"This is sunflower bread. It's one of my specialties." She set a plate of sliced bread in front of Olli. "And this is local clover honey. You may not have had it before in the comb. Some people don't like the wax with the honey."

"I remember having it when I was very little." Clare eyed the wooden square with a piece of honeycomb in the middle. "It's messy but a wonderful treat. My mother, Rose, would let me lick the frame when it was almost empty."

"Childhood memories are lovely," Bianca chirped.

"Grace, Bianca."

At Olli's words, Bianca fell silent and took her chair. He extended his hands to Bianca and then Clare and bowed his white head.

"Thank you, Lord, for the bounty of your table and for sending us a charming guest to share it with. Amen."

Bianca and Clare repeated the Amen.

Olli dominated the conversation during lunch, talking about his postings in both Minneapolis and Duluth before he returned to Grand Rapids. He spoke directly to Clare, ignoring Bianca. When Clare responded to a question, she tried to include Bianca in the discussion. She needn't have bothered because the woman kept one eye on her plate and one eye on Olli trying to anticipate his needs.

"You're a very lucky man to have a devoted sister to help in your work," Clare said.

For a moment, Olli looked startled as if he hadn't thought of that. He tipped his head to the side as he looked down the table at his sister.

"You know, Clare, I probably don't praise her enough, but

it's only through her housekeeping and hostessing that I'm able to get so much done."

Bianca's face turned red and she dropped her gaze to her plate.

"Watching the two of you the other night at the dinner, I couldn't help but notice how attentive you both were to the people there." Clare smiled at Bianca. "And your centerpieces were lovely."

"Bianca has been with me ever since I graduated from deLaSalle High School in Minneapolis. I knew I had a calling then and she's followed me everywhere since that time. A true handmaiden of the Lord."

Although Clare considered his tone patronizing, she could see that Bianca was overwhelmed by his praise. Her face glowed and she sat more erect.

"Oh, Olli, you know it's been my pleasure."

"Well, ladies, this has been charming," Olli said, wiping his mouth with his napkin. "I know you won't mind if I slip off and leave you to some girl talk."

Clare managed a weak smile as she shook his hand. "I'm just delighted that you invited me to lunch. I know you're a busy man."

"Never too busy to spend time with two lovely ladies."

Clare half expected him to make a courtly bow, but he contented himself with a nod of the head as he left the room. With her brother gone, Bianca gave Clare her full attention.

"Would you like another slice of lemon cake?"

"No more cake, thanks. Everything was delicious."

"Tea?"

"Yes, please." Clare reached for the pitcher. "I can get it. Would you like some?"

Bianca seemed flustered that Clare was waiting on her. She started to shake her head, then nodded. Clare filled the glasses and added lemon to hers.

"Ed Wiklander mentioned that you're doing an article on the murder," Bianca said.

"Yes. I haven't started it yet. I'm just doing research at this point." She looked at Bianca questioningly." Were you here at the time of the murder?"

Bianca picked up her napkin ring, passing it back and forth between her hands.

"Yes. Olli and I were living in Minneapolis at the time. We came home to Grand Rapids for the weekend. Saturday was the Fourth of July."

"Did you know Lily Gundersen?"

"Not really. She was seven or eight years younger than I. She was well known around town because she was a waitress at the Forest Lake restaurant. That was a very popular spot back then."

"I gather from her picture she was very pretty."

"Yes, she was." Bianca's mouth tightened. "I imagine that was hard on her sister who was rather plain."

"Did you know Rose?"

"Yes, we were closer in age. Once we got out of school, we hung out in the same crowd. Rose was very active in the youth group up until she moved to Minneapolis. Unlike her sister."

"I suppose being married made a difference," Clare said. "She would want to spend more time with her husband."

"You knew Lily was pregnant when she got married?"

"Yes." Clare took a sip of tea to cover her agitation. It was difficult not to react to Bianca's innuendoes.

"I don't mean to speak ill of the dead, but there was some talk that the baby might not be Jimmy's."

Clare set her tea down carefully. Her fingers felt numb and she didn't trust herself to hold the glass. "All the newspaper accounts said they had a happy marriage."

"People always say that sort of thing. Jimmy Newton was almost twenty years older than Lily. He lived in Minneapolis, and met Lily one summer when he came up fishing. They married the following spring. Lily was young and vivacious. She liked the attention of men." Bianca sighed. "Before they were married, Jimmy was still traveling back and forth between Grand Rapids and Minneapolis, so he didn't see her every weekend."

Bianca spread her hands out as if that explained everything. Clare clenched her hands under the table. Her palm itched to smack Bianca for her gossipy insinuations. Although she might pity the fact that the woman was under the domination of her brother, she hated the sly way she suggested that Lily was at best fun loving, and at worst promiscuous.

Her quest for information was a two-edged sword. Although she wanted information about her parents, she was finding some of it hurtful. She supposed she should have expected that. A person is not murdered by someone who loves them. All sorts of negative emotions build until there is an explosion and violence.

Clare stayed for another half hour, letting Bianca talk about what a circus it had been at the time of the murder. There wasn't anything new, just a rehash of the articles she'd read. Having had enough, she changed the subject and asked after Bianca's garden. After a tour of the new plantings, Clare was able to get away.

She spent the rest of the afternoon preparing the dinner and then carefully carried everything to the car. After several trips back and forth, she locked up the house and drove over to Nate's. He apparently had been watching for her because he came to the door before she was out of the car.

"You smell wonderful," he said as he opened the car door. "Just like chicken."

"Be careful when you get the tray out of the backseat. It's hot."

"You look pretty hot yourself."

He leaned over and kissed her on the mouth just as Erika came through the front door. The girl scowled at Clare, coming over to stand beside her father.

"Hi, Erika. I hope you'll like the dinner."

She might not have responded if Nate hadn't nudged her.

"I'm sure I will," she said, her voice a monotone.

"I've got the hot tray," Nate said. "Can you help Clare with the rest, Erika?"

Instead of a comment, she nodded and went to the passenger side and reached in for the basket Clare had set on the floor of the car. Clare caught the flash of anger on Nate's face and shook her head to indicate it was nothing.

"That's good, Erika," she said. "I can get the rest."

Once the food was inside, Erika disappeared.

"I'm ready for a drink," Nate said. "I hope my daughter's behavior doesn't send you running?"

Clare laughed. "I'm taking it as a compliment that she sees me as a threat. Even so, I'd like a tall cold white wine."

Nate poured her wine and himself a Scotch while she put the casserole in the oven to keep it warm. He pulled out a stool for her beside the counter and brought out cheese and crackers. He leaned against the counter and asked her how the lunch had gone. Clare told him what Bianca had told her about her mother.

"Do you believe it?" he asked. "And if you do, does it make any difference?"

"When I was growing up Rose used to harp on the fact that I had to act like a lady. She wouldn't let me date until I was a junior in high school. Oh, I could go out with a bunch of kids, but never alone with a boy." Clare sipped her wine. "She told me that men weren't to be trusted and that I had to be particularly careful because I was morally weak."

"That's an awful thing to lay on a kid. I suppose that was when she told you about being a changeling. By the way, I keep meaning to ask to see that mark on your shoulder."

He leered across the counter at her.

"Never before dinner," Clare said. "Keep your mind on a higher plane. I used to be self-conscious about it until I was in high school. A friend of mine was rebelling and went all satanic. She saw the mark when we were changing for gym and she thought it was the coolest thing going. She thought I'd gotten a tattoo."

"That would certainly change your perspective. Instead of wearing a devil mark of shame, you were now just a rebellious teenager."

"I hadn't thought about it that way, but I suspect you're right." Clare laughed. "It's so easy to look back and see things differently. I can't believe all of what Bianca said about Lily. From

Jimmy Newton's letter and the pictures, I'm convinced he was desperately in love with Lily."

"In love enough that he would have married her if she were carrying someone else's child?"

Clare shook her head. Getting off the stool, she paced across the kitchen floor. "I don't know. Maybe. Would you?"

"In those days an out of wedlock baby was a disgrace. I think if I loved someone enough I'd want to save her from shame."

Clare moved restlessly then stopped in the center of the room. "It never occurred to me that Jimmy Newton might not be my father."

"Would it make a difference?"

"Emotionally, no," Clare said. "On the positive side I wouldn't have to live with the fact that my father had murdered my mother."

"If you go back to the letter Jimmy left you, it's obvious that he thought of you as his child. It was obvious that he loved you."

"Then why did he kill my mother?"

The words burst out of Clare and she slapped the palm of her hand onto the counter. Nate pushed away from the refrigerator where he was leaning and put his arms around her.

"That's something you might never know," he said.

Nate held her close, feeling the tension in her body ease. He could not imagine the kind of emotional turmoil she must be going through. He was trying to restrain his own physical involvement with her, knowing that she was in such a vulnerable state. For the moment, all he could do was be there for her. A support at least, although he would prefer to be more.

"Is dinner ready yet?"

Nate jumped at Erika's voice in the doorway. Clare pushed away from him and moved across to open the oven door. Watching the blank expression on his daughter's face, he wondered how long she'd been standing there and what she might have heard.

"I'm sure it's hot enough," Clare said. "Pot holders?"

"The drawer on your left," Nate said. "If you'd get the salad out of the refrigerator, Erika, I'll get the salad bowls."

Nate kept Erika busy trying to give Clare a chance to recover.

He was so intent on watching his daughter that he overpoured a glass of milk and watched in annoyance as it dribbled down the front of the cabinet. The accident seemed to cut through the tension, and soon both Erika and Clare were warning about spilling other things.

Once they were served, he asked Erika about the movie she'd seen while they were at the farm show. He pretended he didn't understand the plot and that led to additional teasing.

"You missed the smashing display of tractors," Clare said. "Your father was drooling over several of the old ones and I wouldn't be surprised if he bought one. He could drive you to school on the back of a lovely red tractor."

"He dragged me to the show last year. How lame could it be?" Erika grimaced.

"Some people think tractors are sexy," Nate said. "In fact there used to be a hot country song about that. Maybe I can get Debbie and Margaret to work up a clogging routine for that song."

"Very funny. Did you remember I have practice tomorrow?" Erika said.

"I thought you had your writing class tomorrow and clogging on Wednesday?" Nate said.

"I have writing in the morning, but I have clogging right after that, Dad. The rehearsal schedule was changed because we have the show on Friday afternoon at the Itasca Nursing Home. Thursday we're going to Bemidji to see Aunt Susie."

"No wonder I can't keep your schedule straight. In any case, I've got to go to Duluth tomorrow."

"Dad!! You said you'd take me to practice and then we'd go to Bovey for pizza." Erika flung herself against the back of her chair and folded her arms over her chest.

"I'm sorry, Erika, but I got my days mixed up. I was going to ask Cindy's mom if she could pick you up after your writing class and I'd stop for you on my way back from Duluth."

"Cindy's leaving the writing class early tomorrow. She's got an orthodontist appointment. I told you that already, but you never listen to me," Erika whined.

"We'll talk about this later," Nate said.

"If it would help, I could take you to the class," Clare said. "I've been really looking forward to seeing you clogging . . ."

"Clog. See me clog," Erika interrupted ill-humoredly. Nate cleared his throat and her face reddened. "Sorry for being crabby, Clare. I was just so looking forward to going for pizza."

"I could take you for pizza too. Is it the thin crust or pan pizza?"

Nate was pleased that Clare had offered and was anxious to see if his daughter would accept. It would be a major breakthrough if she did.

"It's thin crust," Erika said after a momentary pause.

"They don't put pineapple on it, do they? I hate that." Clare's mouth puckered to show her disgust.

Erika's eyes widened at the funny face and she giggled. "I hate pineapple too."

"Then it's a date," Nate said, before either of them could reconsider.

The rest of the meal went off peacefully. Although Erika didn't chatter as much as usual, he could see that she was getting a little more comfortable around Clare. His daughter warmed up considerably when dessert was served. He was glad that he'd told Clare that Erika's favorite treat was chocolate éclairs. When Erika excused herself, Nate sighed, relieved that the evening had gone so well. He and Clare were clearing the table when he heard Erika's shout.

"Come look, Dad."

Nate and Clare hurried to the family room where Erika was watching television.

"Someone got killed at the Farm Show," Erika said. She turned up the volume on the TV.

". . . was found earlier today but the information was not released until the body was identified. Heavy rains during the evening delayed the clean up after the Farm Show. Andrea Solderitch, supervisor of the county park crew, made the sad discovery at one thirty Monday afternoon."

The camera panned across the fairgrounds, showing footage of the Farm Show. Suddenly a photograph appeared on the screen.

"The victim was identified as Margaret Robinson, a resident of Deer River, fifteen miles west of Grand Rapids."

Nate heard Clare gasp, then felt her hands grasp his arm.

"It's her, Nate. It's Margee."

Chapter Fifteen

"It's Margee. Rose's friend," Clare said, her voice barely above a whisper.

Clare couldn't take her eyes off the picture of the woman she had seen once in the grocery store and once at the Farm Show. Even after the screen shifted to a reporter in Grand Rapids, she could still see the woman's face.

"According to the sheriff's office it was a freak accident. Miss Robinson appears to have tripped while entering a storeroom at the exhibit hall and hit her head against a concrete wall. The blow must have knocked her unconscious. The cut was deep and she bled to death. The coroner's office announced that the death occurred sometime Sunday, either in the afternoon or early evening."

Behind the reporter, Clare could see a cement block structure with several police cars and an ambulance beside it.

"That building is right next to where the main tent was," Nate said, putting his arm around Clare for support. "She was in the main tent when you saw her."

"You knew her?" Erika asked, jerking around to stare at Clare. "You saw her that day?"

"Hush, Erika, we need to hear this."

Erika opened her mouth to argue then pressed it shut in a thin line of anger. Without a word, she stormed out of the room.

"A resident of Deer Lake, Minnesota, Miss Robinson had volunteered to help out at the Farm Show. She was born in Grand

Rapids, and lived there for almost thirty years and still felt a part of the community according to her sister-in-law."

The newscast ended and Nate turned to Clare.

"You're sure that was the woman?"

"Positive." She began to shake and Nate pushed her down on the sofa. "So that's why she didn't meet me."

"It sounds like she might have been on her way to meet you. She would have passed the storage building if she was heading for the beer tent."

"I should have waited until she was free to leave, but she acted like she didn't want to be seen talking to me."

"Did she say that?" Nate asked.

"No, she said something like 'talking about the murder wasn't popular.' Then the Egners and Ed Wiklander came up and she made it sound like I was just asking about the different jams."

"That's strange. I know this is bothering you, Clare. Before I leave for Duluth, I'll give the chief of police a call. Jon Fogt and I went to school together and he trained under my father. I'll see if I can get the details on what happened."

"Would you? I'd really appreciate it."

Clare looked up at Nate who was hovering protectively over her. She wondered how she could have become so involved with him after only a few days. No matter how it had happened it was clearly a godsend.

"I'll call you tomorrow and let you know what I hear." Nate pulled her to her feet. "I think you've had enough excitement for the day. Time for you to go home."

Although Nate wanted to follow Clare home in his car, she convinced him that she was perfectly fine on her own. They made arrangements for her to pick up Erika at her school and take her to the clogging class. Music was blaring upstairs, so Clare suggested he just tell the girl good night.

Clare had left plenty of lights on when she left the cottage. There was a message from Ruth on her answering machine. There were lights on in Ruth's place, so she called her back.

"I have a half day off tomorrow and wondered if you'd like to go over to the Itasca Cemetery in the morning."

"Usually I don't get such tempting offers," Clare said. "I'd like to go. If you have time for lunch after, I can fill you in on what's been going on."

"How's ten o'clock sound?"

"See you then." Clare hung up and got ready for bed.

She made the rounds of the doors and windows, making sure everything was locked up. She left the window in the bedroom partially open. She didn't feel unsafe, but she also felt she needed to be careful. Too many things had happened to make her wary of letting down her guard. Not only the note under the door, but the possibility that someone had been outside the cottage the night before.

It was just a week ago tomorrow that she had arrived in Grand Rapids. At that time she was hopeful that she could learn who she was. In six days, she had found her parents and lost them all at the same time. So many questions had been answered and there were still so many more that had been raised.

The latest of these was whether Jimmy Newton was really her father.

She had to think about it. It was entirely possible that he had married Lily despite the fact she was carrying another man's child. The age difference made that scenario possible. However, the letter in the jewelry box and the pictures argued against that.

Bruce Young, Cindy's father, was a possible candidate. He mentioned that he had dated Lily. According to Ruth he had married late in life. Could he have been holding a torch for Lily? Even if he was her father, how could she ever prove it. She could hardly ask him for a DNA sample. Based on what? A hunch?

Ed Wiklander's father sounded more likely the kind of man who loved the chase but lost interest once he'd scored. Again, she had no basis to suspect he might have fathered her. It did strike her as strange that Ed was so wary about any investigation into the murder. If the reason for the fight the night of the dance had been jealousy, it made Lily's pregnancy a little more suspect.

If Jimmy discovered that he was not Abby's father, could that be the catalyst for the murder?

Olli was the only other person she'd met who was the right age and might have been involved with Lily. He was living in Minneapolis and Duluth in those days so she didn't know how often he came back to Grand Rapids. Somehow she couldn't see Olli as a roaming ladies' man. He had a massive ego, but his attitude toward women was old-fashioned, almost chauvinistic.

Just thinking about the possibilities made her aware of the fact that there were hundreds of men in Grand Rapids who might have fathered a child twenty-five years ago. And that didn't take into account the number of men who had moved away from Grand Rapids. The more she looked at it, the more she realized that, if Jimmy Newton wasn't her father, her ability to discover the truth might prove hopeless.

True to his word, Nate called first thing in the morning.

"Did I wake you?" he asked.

"No, I'm just out of the shower and having my breakfast."

"Ahh."

"How can you make one syllable sound so sexy?" Clare chuckled. "I was feeling down this morning and that just picked up my spirits."

"It picked up more than my spirits but we'll talk more about that the next time I see you. I'm on my way to Duluth. I'm speaking at a luncheon given by the Chamber of Commerce then I've got a meeting at the library. I'm on the board of directors. It's a long meeting so I don't think I'll get back until close to nine."

"Don't worry. I'll stay at the house with Erika until you get home. Do you want us to bring you some pizza?"

"No. I'll grab something before I leave. I talked to the chief of police about Rose's friend."

"What did he say?" Clare's fingers tightened around the phone as she pressed it against her ear.

"Pretty much what we heard on the TV last night. He talked to Margee's sister-in-law in Deer River. It seems she was having a lot of knee trouble and wasn't very steady on her feet. It appears that she tripped on the steps going down into the storage room. She fell forward and hit her head on the cement block wall."

"Why didn't they find her right away?"

"Because of the storm last night the ground was too wet to begin taking down the tents. They didn't start the cleanup until around ten o'clock and that's when they found her. She didn't have any identification on her so they didn't know who she was immediately."

"No purse? No wallet?" Clare asked in surprise.

"Apparently not. The sister-in-law lives in the same condo building and they go shopping every Monday morning. When she got to Margee's place, the newspaper was still at the front door and her cat hadn't been fed, so she got worried. She checked with the garage man and he said she never came home Sunday night. Convinced Margee'd been in an auto accident, she called the police."

"Did they find her car or her purse?"

"Yes and no," Nate said. "They found her car parked on one of the side streets near the fairgrounds. Her purse hasn't turned up. Most of the women put their purses beneath the tables in the booths. Someone might have taken it at the end of the evening. Either they were planning to hold it for her or they planned to steal it."

"The chief of police is convinced her death was an accident?"

Nate didn't speak immediately, and when he did, his voice was hesitant. "Is there any reason you think it could have been anything else?"

"Not really," Clare said. "It's strange that she didn't have a purse with her. Women always carry their purses, if for no other reason than to hold their car keys and lipstick. Besides, the timing of her death seems too coincidental to my meeting with her. She seemed almost frightened when I talked to her. She definitely wanted to tell me something. Now I'll never know what it was."

"So much has happened to you in this last week that I'm sure you're looking at everything as if it's all part of some conspiracy. Nothing seems to be real anymore. However, think about this. If it wasn't an accident, what was it? Do you think someone tried to stop Margee from talking to you?"

Clare shook her head.

"Are you still there?" Nate asked.

"Yes, I'm here. I don't know what I think. Forget I said anything."

"I have the feeling you're not telling me something. I hate talking on the phone. Let me get through this meeting and when I get home tonight we'll talk about it. Okay?"

"Okay. I'm sorry I sound so psychotic. It's been a very long week."

"Take it easy today and have fun tonight. Maybe just having some one-on-one time with Erika will break through the barrier she's built up. I know it's a poor time to bring this up, but I want you to be part of my life and Erika's too."

Clare was surprised at how much his words meant to her. She pressed the phone against her ear as if that brought him closer. "I would like that too."

"See you tonight," Nate said and was gone.

Clare felt warmed by the phone call. It was hard to know at this stage where their relationship was going. She had meant it when she said she wanted to be part of his life. Erika resented her as if she too realized that her father's interest was serious. Her time with Erika was important today and she'd have to make the most of it.

"I thought you might like to see where your parents are buried," Ruth said, as she drove Clare out of town. "Itasca Cemetery is a lovely place. Very restful. No pun intended."

"It's jarring hearing you call them my parents, although I'm not sure why. I've been thinking of them as Lily and Jimmy," Clare said.

"Probably a form of protection. The word 'parents' is very personal and I think you've been trying to keep them emotionally at arm's length."

Ruth slowed down as they approached the entrance. They

turned in and started up the hill ahead. Clare rolled down her window so that she could see clearly. Although the day was hot under a cloudless sky, the cemetery, shaded by so many large trees, felt about ten degrees cooler.

"Up here is a whole section that is Serbian Orthodox. A friend of mine was from Bosnia and she's buried over there. I haven't been here much. At my age, you try not to spend too much time in cemeteries." Ruth drove to the far end of the road and pulled the car over. She got out of the car and Clare joined her as she started across the grass. "Carolyn Cain, the secretary at the cemetery office, is in my garden club. She gave me some directions and a map that shows where the graves are."

"Watch your step, Ruth."

She grabbed the older woman's arm as she staggered on the uneven ground.

"Take a look at this map," she said, pulling a folded paper out of her purse. She unfolded it and held it so Clare could see it. "I'm not sure I'm holding it in the right direction. You'd think they'd put directional signs on it to help you out."

Clare held the paper out in front of her, looking back and forth between the grave markers and the map.

"There," she said, pointing, "see that clump of bushes. I think that's right here on the map. Now count over three rows."

They counted the markers and looked back at the paper.

"I think it's upside down," Ruth said. "See that fuzzy line? I think that indicates where the road turns and runs across the back. Yes, that's better. Look at that circle. I think it's that monument over there."

Clare nodded as she looked down at the map. Holding the paper in one hand, she counted out three rows. Holding Ruth's arm, she led her up the path. "There's an X on the marker at the end of this row."

They walked along the path between the granite headstones, checking the names on each. They got to the end of the row beside the drive leading back down to the other side of the cemetery.

"Mitrovic," Ruth said.

"Damn. Are we reading this map wrong?"

Clare handed the map to Ruth and began to search around the last headstone. Staying on the same line, she crossed the road to a narrow band about three feet wide that ended at the wrought iron boundary fence. Here the grass was higher, not neatly mowed as the rest of the cemetery. She brushed her foot back and forth as she walked. Two feet in from the road, she made solid contact.

"I've got something, Ruth."

She leaned over and felt beneath the grass, running her hands around the rectangular shape. Pulling out chunks of grass, she uncovered the stone. The granite marker was only raised two inches above the ground. It was slightly longer than a foot across and eight inches deep. One word was etched into the stone: NEWTON.

"How very sad," Ruth said, coming to stand beside Clare.

The single word on the granite headstone seemed almost accusatory. A lonely grave, in a lonely spot. After running away in shame, Jimmy Newton had been brought back to lie abandoned on a hilltop. Clare could feel tears well up in her eyes and she forced down the lump in her throat.

Ruth put her arm around her. "It does make him real, doesn't it?"

"Yes. I've tried to keep all thoughts of him objective, but each fact I learn about Lily and Jimmy fills in a puzzle piece in the picture of them in my mind. The other night when it was raining, I thought I remembered something about my father comforting me during a storm when I was a child. In that memory I felt safe and warm in his presence. It's hard to equate that with the idea that he's a murderer."

"Yes, I can see how that must be for you." Ruth squeezed her shoulder. "One can't change the past, you know. All you can do is learn to accept it."

"I'm trying," Clare said.

She knelt down and continued to pull the grass until she'd cleared an area several inches around the headstone. She brushed the dirt off the granite, running her fingertips across the letters. Satisfied, she sat back on her heels and stared down at the now fully visible marker. Bowing her head she said a silent prayer, then stood up and followed Ruth back to the car.

Ruth turned the corner, driving across the top edge of the cemetery, then turned again to coast down the hill to the front part of the cemetery. Once more she pulled close to the side of the road.

"Here's another map, although if we find the angel monument, we shouldn't have any trouble finding Lily's grave."

Clare noticed that this was an older part of the cemetery, the carvings on the tombstones blurred from years in the harsh Minnesota winters. Ruth led the way toward a tall monument of an angel with outspread wings. After looking at the names and dates on a long row of small markers, Clare stopped, calling softly to Ruth.

"These are all babies," she said. Looking at the next row she noticed the same thing. "And all the same year."

"It was the influenza epidemic. Babies and old people were the most susceptible. I'd forgotten about it until Carolyn reminded me. So many babies died that year that they decided to bury them all in a circle with the guardian angel to watch over them."

"What a lovely idea," Clare said.

"And here is your mother's grave," Ruth said, stopping beside a headstone at the outer edge of the circle.

The gravestone was a four inch thick slab of polished granite, three feet wide and two feet high. Across the top was the name Newton. On the left side was etched: LILLIAN. Beneath her name was a carved lily, perhaps representing her nickname. The dates: 1959–1982 were cut in below the flower.

The right side was blank as if waiting for another death, belying the fact of the solitary grave up the hill.

The contrast between the two gravesites couldn't have been more striking. While Jimmy's had been overgrown and neglected, Lily's grave was meticulously cared for. The grass was green and lush, trimmed in a perfect rectangle as if it were the framework of a bed. At the base of the marker there was a metal receptacle set in the ground below Lily's name.

In the vase was a bouquet of fresh flowers.

Chapter Sixteen

"Who do you suppose put the flowers on Lily's grave?" Clare asked Ruth as they finished ordering their lunch.

"I haven't a clue. The flowers were only a day or two old at the most."

"Someone has been taking care of the grave. Did Lily have any more family here, beside her parents and Rose?"

"Not that I'm aware of. I never heard that there were cousins or any other extended family members in Grand Rapids. It's clear that whoever it is was very fond of Lily. She's been gone for twenty-five years."

"Do you think your friend in the cemetery office would know?" Clare asked.

"I'll definitely ask her."

When their lunch came, Clare filled in Ruth on all that had transpired since she'd talked to her last. The older woman was most curious about Margee's death and very sympathetic about Clare's disappointment in not being able to find out what the woman wanted to tell her. She suggested that Clare might talk to Margee's sister-in-law.

"According to the newspaper, the funeral will be private," Clare said. "Aside from the brother and sister-in-law, she had only nieces and nephews. She never married and spent about fifteen years in China teaching school, then came back to Minnesota to be near her brother who is in poor health. I'll wait a few days, and then call the sister-in-law to see if she'll see me."

"I wonder if this woman Margee could be the one who put the flowers at Lily's grave. She could have stopped at the cemetery on the way to the Farm Show. If she put them there on Sunday, they would have stayed fresh."

"She was Rose's best friend so she probably knew Lily too." Clare smiled across the table at her friend. "I'll bet you that's exactly the answer. It makes perfect sense."

Clare felt pleased that at least one question had a reasonable answer. She'd make a note to ask Nate to call the chief of police to get the sister-in-law's phone number. Ruth asked how things were going with Nate and she explained that she would be spending the evening with Erika.

"I'm glad you're getting to know the child. Eleven's a tough age," Ruth said. "You'll have a few hours together and should eventually have a good time. After all, she can't sulk all evening."

Clare tried to remember those words after she picked up Erika at Forest Lake Elementary. The girl's expression gravitated between a blank stare and a sullen pout. Although Clare tried to engage her in conversation, her replies were monosyllablic. Totally frustrated, she drove in silence the final mile to Pastor Olli's church where the clogging was held.

Erika disappeared into the bathroom to change her clothes; Clare wandered into the rehearsal room and was surprised to find so many people there. Apparently it was a full dress rehearsal and parents and friends had come to cheer on the dancers. Clare found her way to one of the chairs on the side where she would have a good view of the girls.

She was pleasantly surprised at how many people she knew. Bruce and Sue Young were already seated while their daughter Cindy was showing her braces to several friends who were grimacing as she talked. Several women whom Clare had met at the church dinner waved to her.

Pastor Olli was making the rounds, saying hello to the gathering. Bianca was fluttering around one girl, trying to sew a tear in the girl's outfit. Just before she sat down, Ed Wiklander came over to say hello. He appeared glad to see her and she didn't detect any animosity in his manner. He introduced her to his sister, Rachel, whose twin girls, Julia and Lyla, were also in the dance group.

When the dancers came out in their costumes, the audience applauded. Clare was surprised at the number of boys who were in the class. They all looked excited and for the moment even Erika had a smile on her face. The girls' costumes were hot pink and black. The blouse had black fur trim at the neck and the edge of the sleeves and the underside of the skirt was black. They wore several crinolines beneath their skirts, which reminded Clare of square dancing costumes. The outfits were completed with hot pink socks and white clogging shoes.

The boys were wearing black pants with hot pink shirts and black suspenders. They wore black clogging shoes.

The instructors lined the group up in two rows. There were fourteen children in all, eight girls and six boys. Erika was neither the oldest nor the youngest in the group. When she spotted Clare she gave a slight wave and then leaned over to whisper in Cindy's ear. Grateful that she couldn't hear the exchange, Clare sighed and sat back to watch the entertainment.

The music started. It was a country song that she'd heard on the radio and had always liked. When the group started to dance, Clare couldn't take her eyes off them. The footwork was intricate as they tapped and glided across the floor in well-choreographed routines. It reminded her of a combination of tap dancing and Irish dancing and she found herself clapping along with the rest of the audience.

"That was fantastic, Erika," Clare said, as she approached the girl after the rehearsal was finished. "I can't imagine how you can make your feet move so quickly and not trip. Thank you so much for letting me come."

Erika's face flushed and she looked pleased but embarrassed at Clare's enthusiasm.

"I'm glad you liked it," she said. "If you'd like, I'll introduce you to my teachers."

"That would be lovely."

Clare followed Erika as she made her way through the milling crowd. She introduced Clare and then excused herself so she could change. Clare congratulated the instructors and told them how much she had enjoyed the performance. Then she said hello to Bianca and Olli and stopped by to say good-bye to Ed Wiklander and his sister. Having made the full circle of the room, she returned to her chair and picked up her purse and her jacket, then waited for Erika to return.

With her costume on a hanger and her clogging shoes in a bag over her arm, Erika skipped across the floor. She smiled at Clare and appeared for once to be in a good mood, almost hyperactive. Grateful to see the girl exhilarated, she followed Erika's dancing steps along the hall to the parking lot.

"Are you getting hungry?" Clare asked. "I think you must have worked up a big appetite. Your dad gave me directions to Good Time Pizza so we can be on our way."

Erika put her things in the backseat and then opened the door of the passenger side, hesitating before she got in. Clare looked across the top of the car at the girl.

"Problem?" she asked.

"No-o." Erika stopped, then started again. "It's still early and I thought since you're taking me out for pizza, you might like to make a stop to look at something on the way."

Clare hesitated, not quite trusting the cheery tone of Erika's voice. "Where do you want to stop?"

"There's a place called the Forest History Center on the way to Bovey. They've got a logging camp all set up and we could walk around the buildings and I could tell you what I learned on my school trip." Erika shrugged. "I'm not totally starving yet and it would be fun to show it to you."

"You say it's on the way?"

"Yes. And it won't be getting dark for ages yet."

Since it was the first time Erika had shown any interest in her company, Clare was hesitant to say no. She looked down at her sandals and her white slacks and wished she had time to go home and change. There was only about an hour of daylight left so they wouldn't have to stay long.

"Since I've never seen a logging camp, I'd hate to miss such a perfect opportunity," Clare said.

She climbed into the car, waiting as Erika got in and fastened her seat belt. It took only fifteen minutes to drive to the logging camp. They turned in at the sign and drove down a gravel driveway to the parking lot. Clare's heart sank when she realized there were no other cars in the lot and a closed sign hung on the front door of the administration building.

"I'm sorry, Erika, but the sign says it closed at five."

Erika opened her door and jumped out. "I forgot that it closed early. But as long as we're here, I can show you some things."

"I don't think so, Erika. I think that comes under the heading of trespassing."

"Please, Clare. We won't go into any of the buildings. I'll just show you a couple of things and then we'll go to dinner."

Clare sighed and turned off the motor. "All right. Let's make this quick. I'm really getting hungry now."

"Oh, thanks so much. You won't be sorry. I know lots of stuff to tell you."

Stopping occasionally to remove gravel from her sandals, Clare followed the excited child down a trail until they came to the camp reconstruction built along the river. As they walked around the area, she was pleasantly surprised at how much Erika did know.

"This is like a camp that would have been in the woods in the winter time. That's when they cut white pine. It's a real strong straight tree and they cut it for masts on sailing ships. Over there is the blacksmith's shop. The day we were here they had a real blacksmith and he let me push on the bellows thing."

"Was he making horseshoes?" Clare stared at the log building wondering what it would be like to work in a windowless building in the dead of a Minnesota winter.

"No. He was making tools. I can't remember what kind, but he heated a metal piece and then bent it into a shape. It was mega-cool."

"I'll bet. What's that?" Clare said pointing to what looked like a pontoon boat with a roof pulled up against the bank.

"That's called a wanigan."

"A wagon?"

"No, a wanigan. I think it means boat. It might be an Indian word. I'm not sure. The lumber guys lived inside there when they floated the logs down the river. It sounded pretty icky. They'd get their clothes all wet during the day and then at night they'd pull the boat over to the side and hang everything up to dry."

"I agree. It must have been rather smelly. I drove up to Lake Itasca because I figured I was never going to get another opportunity to see the source of the Mississippi. It's just a little trickle and I walked across. The water was ice cold so I can imagine how it would be to work in it all day."

Erika was walking backwards listening to Clare. She had never seen her so animated. Maybe she'd not paid enough attention to the girl. She'd have to try harder if she wanted Erika to tolerate her presence.

"Do you know how they called the men to dinner?"

"If it was like the western movies, they banged one of those triangle things." Clare illustrated waving her arms wildly.

Erika laughed. "That would be good too. What they did was blow a horn. It was called Gabriel's horn. Isn't that awesome?"

Clare agreed that it was and Erika turned around and skipped ahead.

"This is the cookhouse where the lumber men would come for their breakfast and their dinner. The bosses didn't want them to come back from the woods so they took the lunches right out to them."

"What did they eat?" The thought of food made Clare's stomach growl and she was grateful that the light was starting to fade and they could leave soon and get some dinner.

"I don't remember. Soup, I think, or maybe stew." Erika turned to look at Clare, her face screwed up in thought. "They might have had pasties. There's a place in town that makes them."

"I saw that restaurant. I was going to go in but I didn't have time."

"They're really good in the winter. It's like a meat pie. Meat and carrots and potatoes and onions stuffed inside this pie dough and then they add gravy."

"That's it, Erika, I'm starving," Clare said, laughing as she grabbed the girl's hand. "I promise I'll bring you back here when it's open. Let's go get some pizza."

They followed the trail back to the administration building. Clare cursed under her breath every time she had to stop to take a stone out of her shoe. It was darker now and she had to concentrate as she navigated over the uneven ground. She sighed in relief as she saw the car ahead, until she noticed that it was tilted to the side.

"It can't be," she said, staring at the car. Both tires on the driver's side were flat.

She turned to Erika. The girl's hands were covering her mouth and her eyes were wide with shock.

"What happened?" she said.

"I don't have a clue. I suppose there could have been some glass on the road." Clare looked around the empty parking lot. "At this rate we're never going to get to dinner."

"Can't you fix them?"

"No, Erika, I can't fix them. If it was only one flat tire I might be able to figure out how to change the tire but I can't fix two tires."

Clare spoke more sharply then she'd intended because she was hot and tired and furious that they were stuck at the logging camp until a tow truck could reach them.

"But it's getting dark. And I don't want to be out here in the dark."

The frightened voice brought Clare to the realization that she was dealing with a child.

"Don't worry, honey," she said, softening her tone. "I'll call Mrs. Grabenbauer and see if she can come get us and then we'll send the garage people out to fix the tires."

"Hurry, Clare, it's going to be dark soon."

Clare reached for her cell phone. Not finding it immediately, she set her purse on the hood of the car and looked through it. Her phone wasn't in her purse.

"My phone must have fallen out in the car." She opened the front door and searched on the floor of the front seat. "Can you look on your side, Erika?"

The girl jerked open the car door and looked on the floor and the front seat. They both looked in the back, but the phone was not in the car.

"I don't suppose you have a cell phone?" Clare asked Erika.

"Dad said I could have one when I'm twelve."

"Remind me to tell your father you need one now. You must be the only child in the entire civilized world who isn't text messaging every minute of the day."

"What are we going to do?"

Erika's voice was so high that Clare realized she was close to panic.

"We're going to walk out to the road and hitch a ride. I'm sure your father will be furious at me for my stupidity in losing the phone but that can't be helped. I know you thought we'd have an adventure, but this one is a little more than even I'd planned on."

Clare put the car keys in a pocket of her slacks. Her wallet went into the other pocket and she dumped her purse on the floor of the car. She looked over at Erika who was wearing shorts and a sleeveless jersey. Although it was still hot out, she suspected that it might get cold before they got home. Reaching into the back seat, she grabbed her jacket then closed and locked the car.

"All set, Erika. Take my hand."

The girl stood motionless, and in the fading light Clare could see the beginning of tears in her eyes. She didn't know if the emotion was fear or rebellion, but she knew it didn't matter. If she didn't get her moving now, the girl would end up in hysterics.

"Erika!" she spoke sharply and the girl blinked. "No nonsense now. It's time to go home."

At the word home, Erika reached for Clare's hand. She walked woodenly at first then after a minute or two her steps became more normal. Slowly, they made their way back down the drive to the highway. The going was rough and Clare's shoes continually picked up stones, causing a momentary stop. Eventually Erika complained of the cold and Clare gave her the jacket, buttoning it up around the girl's neck.

"Look up at the sky, Erika. The stars are beautiful. I've never seen so many in my whole life. In Chicago there are so many lights that the only stars you can see are the really bright ones." She raised her arm and pointed. "See over there. That's Orion. I have to admit that it's the only constellation I recognize."

She tried to keep up a cheerful patter as they walked, but Erika failed to respond except for an occasional grunting sound.

"My mother, Rose, bought me a first-aid kit when I bought my first car," Clare said. "It was enormous. It had everything necessary for any kind of emergency. Here I was living in Chicago, and one of the things in the kit was a packet to use in case of snakebite. Believe me, Erika, you have as much chance of being bitten by an elephant as you do by a snake in downtown Chicago."

She was encouraged when Erika gave a smothered sound that might have been a laugh.

"My favorite was an emergency hammer. It was glow-in-the-dark orange and stuck to the side of the car door with a piece of Velcro. Rose said that if my car ever went into water, I could use the hammer to cut my seat belt and break the window. All my friends thought it was funny. I actually thought it was a good idea. The only trouble was that in the summer heat the adhesive on the Velcro would loosen and the hammer would fall. If I was driving it invariably would drop on my foot and scare the life out of me. Too bad the kit's gone. It had flares and we . . ."

In the dark, Clare stepped on a rock and lost her balance. She put her hands out to save herself as she fell on the driveway.

"Are you okay?" Erika said, leaning over her.

Clare pushed herself to her feet, feeling a burning sensation on her hands where she had scuffed her palms against the gravel. Her slacks were torn and she could see there was blood on the edge of the tear. Her knee seemed to be scraped but she was, thankfully, unhurt.

"I messed up these pants but good. Lucky we're not still going out to dinner." She looked ahead, relieved to see that the highway was just a short distance away. "We're almost there. Then it will be easy walking."

"Oh, Clare, I'm so sorry." Her voice was choked and tears would soon follow.

"It wasn't your fault that I tripped, honey." Clare put a comforting arm around the girl. "Just think of how much fun you'll have telling about your adventure at the logging camp. Come on. I'd offer to race you but, as you can see, I'm not all that speedy in these sandals."

Arm around Erika, Clare moved as quickly as she could toward the highway. Her feet were bruised and she could feel a blister forming. She'd have to remember to keep a pair of sneakers in the car in case of emergency. She wished she'd thought to break the window in the administration building and call for help. It was too late to go back and, with her luck, they might not have had a working phone. When they reached the highway, she wanted to kneel down and kiss the asphalt.

"Now we should be able to make better time."

"Can't we wait here until a car comes along?" Erika's voice was a definite whine.

"It's better to keep walking if for no other reason than to stay warm."

Since Clare hadn't seen the lights of any cars on the highway as they were walking toward it, she wondered how soon someone would come along. In the moonlight, she could see that it was close to nine-thirty. She knew Nate would worry if he got home before them and then couldn't reach her by cell phone.

She remembered all the movies she'd seen where the people broke into song to keep up their spirits. She couldn't think of any songs and when she suggested it, Erika said she didn't feel like singing. She decided humming would be a good substitute, but they were going up hill and she needed all her breath. They were almost at the top of the hill where it turned and headed downhill, when suddenly lights behind them illuminated the road.

"It's a car," Erika yelled, whirling around to look back down the road. "It's a car!"

"Thank goodness," Clare said, watching in relief as the car came toward them. "Come off the road so he has room to pull over. Be careful. The ground falls away on the side."

The car was picking up speed. Erika stood on the shoulder of the road, waving wildly. As the car came closer, the girl jumped up and down in her excitement.

"It's coming. It's coming," she shouted.

The car was coming too fast. Erika was silhouetted in the headlights, but the car wasn't slowing down.

"Get back, Erika," she screamed.

Clare raced back to the girl who was frozen in place, arms held straight out, palms up as if she could physically hold off the car. Clare's feet slipped in the sandals as she stretched to reach the girl. The car picked up speed and the angle of the light changed as the car swerved directly toward Erika and Clare.

Chapter Seventeen

"Erika!" Clare screamed as the car bore down on them.

Blinded by the twin beams of the oncoming vehicle, Clare reached out to grab hold of Erika's arm. She yanked the girl back from the edge of the road, instinctively turning away from the speeding car. The girl's body catapulted into Clare, hitting her shoulder and knocking her off her feet. Clare's vision was filled with the looming shape of the car, then she hit the grassy verge with a thump and began to roll down the side of the hill. She smacked into the base of a clump of bushes with a bone-jarring jolt.

In the darkness, Clare heard the car racing away, heading down the hill toward town. Then there was silence. Her vision blurred and she could feel her body sliding into a void. She struggled to breathe but a sharp pain lanced her side.

"Clare! Clare! Where are you?"

Erika. The name came to Clare from a distance and it took her a moment before she remembered the car and the girl silhouetted in the oncoming headlights. Was Erika hurt? She tried to raise her head, but the muscles in her neck refused to respond.

Clare could hear the girl shrieking at the top of the hill, but she couldn't catch her breath. She gulped at the fresh air, her lungs burning with the pressure. She crossed her arms over her chest and fought to take in several shuddering breaths.

"Erika." The sound was a mere whisper. Clare licked her lips and tried again. "Erika."

"Clare. I heard you. Where are you?"

Mustering as much energy as she could, Clare coughed out a shout, not trying for words, only a sound. Above her, she heard scraping steps and she coughed again.

"Oh Clare," Erika cried from the top of the hill as she scrambled down the side. "Oh, please don't be dead. Oh please, Clare."

Erika half slid, half crawled to Clare's side. She lay down beside her, sobbing uncontrollably. Clare didn't have the energy to speak. She merely put her arm over the girl and made soft shushing sounds in her ear. By the time Erika's crying had reached the hiccupping stage, Clare's breathing was back to normal. Her one side was really painful, but she didn't think she'd broken any ribs. She thought she'd just had the wind knocked out of her.

"Erika, I'm all right."

"Clare, oh, thank you, God. Did the car hit you?" She squirmed around until they were facing and she could put her arms around Clare's waist.

"No, it missed me. I just fell down the hill. How about you?"

"I've got a sore knee." Erika took a great gulping breath. "The car didn't stop, Clare. It didn't stop."

The words were spoken in a shocked whisper as if it hurt her to say it.

"I know it didn't." The implications of that fact had not been lost on Clare, but she didn't want Erika to consider what that might mean. "It's all right, dear. We're both alive."

"You saved my life. You pulled me onto the grass. That's why you got hurt."

"I don't think I'm hurt, but I think we'll both be better if we get out from under these bushes."

Erika wiggled away and Clare used the branches to pull herself into a sitting position. She ran her hands over her legs and moved her feet, grateful that everything seemed to be in working order. Erika stood over her and looked almost ethereal with the blanket of stars and the moonlight above her.

"You look like an angel," Clare said, staggering to her feet. "It must be a miracle that we're both all right."

"Oh, Clare, I'm so sorry." Once more the girl put her arms

around Clare's waist and pressed her head into her chest. "This is all my fault."

"We'll call it a combination of errors," Clare said briskly. "Look around and see if you can find my shoes. I'd hate to have to walk back barefoot."

"There's one," Erika said, pointing.

She scrambled up the hill, grabbed it and brought it back down to Clare. It took longer to find the second one, but eventually she let out a cry of excitement as she found it. Clare held onto the girl's shoulder as she gingerly put the sandal on her badly bruised foot. Putting her weight on it cautiously, she found it a little more comfortable after several steps.

"Now watch your footing and let's see if we can get back up to the road without any more missteps."

Hand in hand, they climbed up the grassy bank. Clare winced as her muscles rebelled at each step. Once on the top, she surveyed herself and Erika and let out a hearty laugh.

"We look rather the worse for wear, my dear. I don't think your father is going to be well pleased with my guardianship."

Clare's white slacks were torn at the knees and had dirt streaks and patches down both legs. Her arms were covered with bloody scratches from the branches that had lashed her as she rolled down the hill. Luckily Clare's jacket had protected Erika's upper body but her knee was scraped and bleeding.

"Your knee looks swollen. How does it feel?"

"A little bit sore. And I hit my funny bone when I fell."

"Can you bend your arm?"

"Yep."

"Thank God," Clare said. She reached across and put her hands on either side of Erika's head, tilting it so that she could look down at her face. Leaning over, she kissed her on the forehead. "I couldn't bear it if you were hurt."

She found she was close to tears and as she looked at Erika she could see the girl was too.

"All right, young lady, I'm back to feeling hungry again. Let's get going."

Each step was painful. Her body was bruised and the soles of her feet burned. Teeth gritted, she limped along. After a while, her body loosened up and a numbness settled over her.

"Why didn't the car stop, Clare?"

"I don't know. Perhaps whoever was driving didn't see us."

"It was like the car was trying to hit us. It turned right toward us."

"My best guess is that the driver might have been drunk."

"Oh, I didn't think of that," Erika said. "I'll bet that's it, Clare. I'll bet you're right."

Clare was relieved when she heard the lightness in the girl's voice. It was better for the girl's peace of mind if she believed such a rationale. She would have loved to have been able to accept such an explanation, but her thoughts had followed a much darker scenario. In Clare's mind, the car had intentionally targeted them.

"A car is coming."

There was enough fear in Erika's tone to make Clare wonder if she too doubted.

"Come over to the side, Erika. Stand by that tree."

The car coming toward them was not moving as quickly as the first one. Watching to make sure Erika was well protected, Clare stepped out in the road and waved as the headlights illuminated the road. She held her position until the driver shifted to high beams, then she stepped closer to the side of the road.

"Don't come out until I tell you to," she called to Erika.

The car was definitely slowing, but Clare was taking no chances. She moved closer to the drop-off and prayed she wouldn't have to go over the side again. The car crept closer and once more Clare waved. As a pickup truck rolled to a stop, Erika scurried over to stand beside Clare. The passenger-side window rolled down.

Clare leaned over until she could see the young girl driving the car. Afraid of frightening her, she didn't approach the car, only shouted. "My car's broken down and my friend and I need a ride. Can you help us?"

"Sure. No problem." She put the car in park and turned the lights on inside the car. "Hop in."

Clare opened the front door and boosted Erika into the front seat, then climbed in. Erika grabbed the edge of her pant leg as she slid onto the seat and closed the door.

"Is that blood?" the driver asked in concern. "Did you have an accident?"

"No. I tripped and fell down." Clare was unprepared to give any more of an explanation. "I'm Clare by the way and this is Erika."

"I'm Sheila Grange. Are you going to Grand Rapids?"

"Yes. The house is along this road, just before you get into town."

"Super. It's right on my way. I was in Coleraine bowling with some friends. I was later getting away than usual, so I'm grateful for the company. There's not much traffic on this road at night. You're lucky I decided to take the back way home."

"I can't tell you how glad we were to see you."

"There's construction as you come out of Coleraine, so most of the people are sticking to the main route."

"Ah," Clare said, not trusting her voice.

She was so relieved that they were safe that she felt close to tears. Erika was silent, her small body pressed against Clare as if she was afraid to lose contact. It took only fifteen minutes to get to Nate's house. After thanking the woman profusely, Clare and Erika hurried inside.

The answering machine was blinking. The first message was from Nate, saying he was running late and wouldn't be home until after ten.

"Thank heavens, we'll have some time to get cleaned up," Clare said, "although I don't know what I can do to salvage these pants."

The second message was from Ruth, letting Clare know that someone had found her cell phone. She asked Clare to call when she got the message even if it was late. Sending Erika upstairs to change, she dialed Heart's Content.

"I was so worried that you might need the phone," Ruth said.

Not up to a full explanation, Clare asked, "Where did you find it?"

"I didn't. One of the instructors from Erika's rehearsal found it. When she discovered the phone was registered in Chicago, she remembered talking to you. Someone told her you were my renter and she called me."

"It must have fallen out of my purse," Clare said.

"She said it was on the floor and one of the girls brought it up to her. She dropped it off on her way home and I put it down in the cottage."

"Thanks I appreciate it. I'm sorry for being so careless." Clare sighed. "I don't know when I'll be back so don't worry about me. Nate's going to be later than he thought so I'll be here with Erika until he gets home. I'll talk to you tomorrow."

"Before you ring off I have some information for you. I called my friend at the cemetery office and she looked up the records. An anonymous donor paid your father's burial arrangements. Your father paid for all the arrangements for your mother. He bought the plot in Itasca Cemetery. He asked specifically if she could be buried near the influenza babies so that she wouldn't miss her own child."

Tears filled Clare's eyes at the words. What an extraordinarily lovely gesture.

"Are you still there, Clare?" Ruth asked

Clare swallowed several times before she could speak. "Yes, I'm here. Was there anything else?"

"Yes. My friend didn't know anything about the maintenance on the graves but she checked with the groundskeeper. He said that he'd never seen anyone doing it, but ever since Lily's death someone had been taking care of the grave site."

"For twenty-five years?"

"Yes and whoever it is puts flowers in the vase at the grave site."

"That's really interesting. Thanks, Ruth, for following up on that. I better run. I'll talk to you tomorrow."

She hated to be abrupt, but she was afraid Ruth would ask her how her time with Erika had gone. She didn't want to talk about the evening until she'd had time to analyze all that had happened.

After hanging up, Clare used the downstairs bathroom. She washed her hands, wincing as the soap burned the abrasions on her hands. Once she'd washed off the dirt, she could see that none of the cuts on her arms were deep. Her knee was badly scraped. She picked out several small pieces of gravel, then covered it with a wet washcloth until the stinging eased.

After one look at her feet, she decided to wait until she got back to the cottage before she dealt with them. They were covered with little cuts and blisters and generally felt bruised. Since none of the cuts looked deep and most of them weren't actively bleeding, she decided she'd leave them alone until she could soak them.

"I brought some stuff for your cuts," Erika called as Clare returned to the kitchen. "I'm sorry but there's a rip in your jacket."

Erika held out the corduroy jacket pointing to a gash on the sleeve. Clare transferred her wallet and her car keys to the jacket, setting it on a chair by the door to the garage.

"Let me check your knee," she said, looking over the supplies Erika had brought down.

The girl had changed to a sweat suit and had washed her face and combed her hair. She rolled up her pants and Clare inspected her knee. Setting Erika on one of the kitchen stools, Clare washed the scrapes again.

"Sorry, I know this stings," she said as the girl sucked in her breath. "I'm going to put some antiseptic cream on it. It should feel better in a minute."

She slathered on the cream then covered it with a gauze bandage.

"Roll up your sleeves and let me make sure you don't have any other cuts or gouges. Where did that sleeve get torn?"

She found another long scratch on Erika's arm and covered that with the cream.

"I don't think you need a bandage, but have your dad look at it tomorrow."

Clare rubbed some of the cream on the palms of her hands. After the initial sting, the lubrication felt soothing.

"You should put some of that goo on your knee too," Erika said. "Here you sit here and I can do it."

Clare changed seats and pulled up her pant leg so that the girl could see her knee.

"Oh ick, Clare. That looks awful. Does it hurt a lot?"

"It's sort of numb now. I don't think it's very deep. It just looks messy."

Her face puckered in concentration, Erika rubbed cream on the gashes.

"Where did you get that?" she said, pointing to a jagged scar on Clare's knee.

"I don't know. I've had it ever since I was a little girl. I dreamt once that I cut my knee when I fell down in the woods during a thunderstorm. I don't know if it really happened or if it was a nightmare."

After putting away the first aid supplies, Clare made omelets and they sat on the stools in the kitchen to eat them. It was close to ten when they finished cleaning up. Leaving just the light over the stove on, they went into the family room and turned on the television. Erika pulled the ottoman over to the couch so Clare could put up her feet.

"Thank you for taking such good care of me," she said as the girl came to sit next to her. "Put that pillow on my lap and you can curl up."

Clare had noticed the child was dragging by the end of dinner and suspected that reaction to the night's adventures was setting in. Once Erika was snuggled up on the couch, Clare put an afghan over her. She stroked her head and soon the steady breathing indicated she'd fallen asleep. Clare lay her own head against the back of the couch and dozed as she watched the news.

She came awake when she heard the electric garage door opener. Moving cautiously, she eased out from under the pillow on her lap but Erika didn't wake up. She stood up, grimacing as she put weight on her bruised feet. Walking gingerly, she went out to the kitchen and was standing behind the counter when Nate came in from the garage.

"Clare," he said, looking surprised. "I saw the lights were on but didn't think you were here because your car's not outside."

"It's not here. I had car trouble and Erika and I got a ride to the house."

"What kind of trouble?" Nate said, reaching for the overhead light. When the lights came on, he looked shocked. "Judas Priest. Were you in an accident? Is Erika all right?"

Before Clare could answer, he was across the room, gripping her shoulders.

"Erika is fine. She's asleep on the couch," Clare said.

"Thank God," he said. "But how did you get hurt?"

Clare had been so caught up in the ominous questions in her own mind that the fact that Nate was holding her, his face tight with concern, tore down the wall of control she'd built up. Silent tears rolled down her cheeks and she pressed one hand against her mouth to keep from sobbing. He pulled her against his body and wrapped his arms around her.

"I need to know what's happened, Clare."

His voice was soft and he lay his head on top of hers, rocking her in place. Relief at his presence helped her gain back control of her emotions. She sniffed and pulled away.

"You must think I'm a chronic crybaby. That's all I've done since I met you."

"You do have an air of dampness around you." Although he was trying for a light tone, his face was still lined with concern. Reaching in the pocket of his sports jacket, he pulled out a handkerchief. "I'll buy you a dozen tomorrow."

Clare blew her nose and smiled weakly. "Let's go get Erika so that you can see she's all right. Then we'll talk about what happened."

In the family room, Nate leaned over his daughter, smoothing the hair off her forehead.

"Erika, it's me," he said.

He had to shake her shoulder before she woke up. For a moment she smiled up at him, then caught sight of Clare and came more fully awake.

"Oh, Daddy, it was all my fault," she wailed.

"It wasn't your fault, honey," Clare said. "I'll explain it to your father. Let him help you up to your room."

"Okay. Will you still be here in the morning?"

Nate's eyes widened at Erika's change of attitude toward Clare.

"You'll definitely see her tomorrow," he said, as he helped her to her feet. "Let's get you upstairs."

Downstairs, Clare spent the time running through a list of questions and possible answers that covered the week she'd been in Grand Rapids. Maybe talking to Nate would help clarify some of the confusion in her mind. One look at his grim expression as he returned didn't necessarily reassure her.

"I think we both need a drink before we talk," he said, jerking his head toward the kitchen.

He poured Clare a white wine and a Scotch for himself. He winced when he handed her the glass and spotted the reddened abrasions on the palms of her hands. He took a healthy sip as he eyed her over the rim of his glass. She stood quiet beneath his searching gaze as he appeared to catalogue every bump and bruise on her body.

"Erika said you were walking along the road after you left the car with the flat tires. She said she was almost hit by a drunk driver, but you saved her life." The muscles in his jaw rippled as he appeared to struggle with his emotions. "She said that's how you got hurt. Is any of that true?"

"First of all, I don't think the driver was drunk." Clare took a sip of her wine then set the glass on the counter as her hands began to shake. "And second, I don't think it was an accident."

"What do you mean it wasn't an accident?"

"I think the driver of the car was deliberately trying to hit me."

Chapter Eighteen

"Whoever was driving the car intended to hit me." Clare repeated the words over in her mind, watching Nate's face for his reaction.

"You've got to be kidding."

She shook her head. "The driver turned the wheel in our direction, then accelerated."

Nate stood motionless, just staring at her. The expression on his face was a mixture of anger and fear. Thankfully, he didn't look as if he thought she was crazy.

"I think you need to start from the beginning."

When she shifted uncomfortably, his gaze dropped to her feet, taking in the visible scrapes and bruises and the bandage he could see through the tear on her bloodied slacks. "Let's get your feet up first."

She grabbed her wine and limped back to the family room. She put her feet up on the ottoman and Nate leaned over to remove her shoes. He swore when he saw the state of her feet. He went back to the kitchen, returning with a basin of water and a soft cloth. Very gently he bathed her feet, stopping occasionally to examine a cut more thoroughly. Finished, he went in search of the same first aid supplies that she and Erika had used earlier.

"You'll have to stay here tonight," he said as he put the last Band-Aid onto a blister on her heel. "You need to stay off your feet for a while."

Clare was too tired and sore to argue. She let him refill her glass and his own, then he pulled a chair up facing the couch. He sat down, put his feet up and took another long pull on his drink, then nodded at her.

"From the beginning, please," he said.

Clare described what had happened from the time she picked up Erika until they arrived back at the house. He remained passive throughout the narrative, only occasionally interrupting to ask a question. When she described the car careening toward them, he put his hand comfortingly on her feet on the ottoman beside his chair. There was silence after she'd finished talking as if he were sorting through all he'd heard.

"You didn't see anyone else while you were in the logging camp?"

"No. I suppose someone could have been in one of the buildings, but we didn't see them. And anyone could have come into the parking lot or the administrative building while we were down by the river looking at the camp."

"What are the chances that you would have had two flat tires in one night?"

"Not likely," Clare said. "My Corolla is only two years old. I don't put a lot of wear and tear on the car and I had it fully serviced before I came north."

"Did you look to see if there was any damage to the tires?"

"No. Erika was getting close to panic. I just locked the car and we started walking. If I'd been smart, I would have tried to break a window to see if there was a phone in the office. Frankly, I was surprised there wasn't some kind of security guard around."

"We don't have a lot of crime in Grand Rapids," Nate said. "I doubt if there's much to steal out at the Forest History Center. They probably have someone who comes around sometime during the night to make sure everything's all right. When you came out to the highway, did you see any cars around?"

"It was nearly dark by then so, unless it had its headlights on, I doubt if I'd have seen a car." Clare's throat was dry and she took a sip of wine. "It occurred to me after it happened, that someone could have waited on the road until they saw us come out of the drive."

"How would they know where you were?"

Nate was asking the questions she'd been trying to ask herself all night. "Erika didn't ask me about the camp until we were out in the parking lot. I suppose someone could have overheard us or she could have talked about it during the rehearsal. I didn't see anyone following us, however, I'm not sure I would have thought much about it if I had."

"And you're sure that the person driving swerved toward you? Was it possible he was just pulling over?"

Nate's eyes were steady on her face as she responded.

"No. I mean, yes. Yes, I'm sure he jerked the wheel toward me. We were walking up hill and there was a drop-off on our side of the road. Whoever it was would have seen that and pulled closer to the center line rather than risk running off the road." Clare reached over and put her hand on his legs, reassuring herself of his presence. "And right after he turned the wheel, he sped up. The car practically leaped forward."

They were both silent, caught up in their own thoughts. Clare rubbed his legs as he gently massaged her feet. She had never felt so connected to anyone in her life. Much as she thought she had loved Doug, it was nothing to what she was beginning to feel about Nate. Just talking to him about what she had been churning over in her mind all evening gave her a sense of security. All she knew was that she wanted to spend as much time as possible with him. She looked up and he was smiling across at her.

"You feel it too?" he asked.

"Yes." She didn't have to define her answer. They were very much in tune with each other.

"I asked you the other day if something was bothering you. What was it?"

Clare told him about the note slipped under her door and the man she saw outside the cottage the night of the storm. She told him about finding the flowers on the grave and what Ruth had discovered from the cemetery office. If they included someone searching the cottage while Clare was out, the list of strange events was getting longer. Taken together and culminating in the loss of her phone and the car attack, it looked as if she was definitely in danger.

"Going back to tonight," Nate said, "could someone have taken the phone out of your purse?"

"I thought about that. It's entirely possible. I set my purse on the floor when I got to the rehearsal. Afterward, I went up to talk to the instructors and I didn't take my purse with me. So there was about a half hour when anyone could have taken it. " Clare shifted to a more comfortable position. "But why would they take it?"

"Just so you wouldn't be able to call anyone when you found your tires were flat."

Clare shivered at his words. Even though she had thought of the possibility, saying it out loud made the whole incident sound totally premeditated.

"What's going on, Nate?"

"I don't know, but I'm going to talk to Chief Fogt in the morning. I think you need to tell him who you are because I think it might have some bearing on what's been going on. For some reason, someone doesn't want you prying into Lily Newton's murder."

"Tonight, before you came home, I was wondering about that. Is there any possibility that Lily was killed by someone other than Jimmy?"

Nate shook his head. "I honestly don't think so. All the evidence pointed to him. Over the years no one has ever questioned it."

"I think your father did," Clare said. "I don't know if it's wishful thinking on my part, but what if Jimmy didn't commit the murder?"

Nate took his feet off the couch and leaned forward in his chair, taking hold of Clare's hands. "Look at it logically instead of with your heart. Jimmy ran away before he could be arrested and he left behind a note confessing to the crime. If he wasn't guilty, why would he do that?"

"I don't know. Maybe he was covering up for someone?"

"That doesn't make sense, Clare."

"What if he thought somehow that it was his fault that Lily was murdered? Maybe he'd done something or made someone angry and that person killed Lily by mistake." She pulled her hands away and crossed her arms over her chest, shaking her head in frustration. "Why couldn't it be something like that?"

"I suppose it could be," Nate said, although there was no conviction in his tone. "It could be any number of things, but is it likely?"

"Did you ever see Jimmy's confession?"

Nate tipped his head up, looking at the ceiling, his mouth puckered in concentration. "No, I don't think I ever did."

"Is there any way we could look at it?"

"I assume it's in the files somewhere. What are you thinking?"

"All the newspaper clippings said was that he left a confession, but what if he didn't really say he killed Lily. What if everyone just assumed it was a confession because he ran away."

When Nate didn't look convinced, Clare tried again.

"Do you remember the note he left in the jewelry box? It didn't sound like a note from a murderer. It sounded like a heartbroken father who was trying to protect his daughter. All he said was that he had to go away. He talked about how happy he and Lily were."

"I doubt if he'd tell his daughter that he was leaving because he killed her mother."

"But would a man who'd just killed his wife, write such a loving letter?"

"How can we know the mind of a killer? Maybe he was in denial. Maybe he just wanted you to think of him as a loving father not a murderer. Why are you suddenly thinking he didn't kill Lily?"

"Because it's the only reason any of the things that have happened this week make sense." Clare slapped her hands together in her agitation. "I really believe that someone is trying to stop me from digging into Lily's murder. I think the attack tonight was to keep me from looking into it any further. Someone wants to chase me out of town or, in a worst case scenario, kill me."

After she spoke, she sagged against the back of the couch, feeling drained. Nate rubbed the lines in his forehead as if he had a headache. He stared across at Clare without speaking.

"You don't think I'm nuts or paranoid, do you?" Clare asked.

"Nuts in a nice sort of way." He patted her clenched hands until she felt the tension ease and they lay loose in her lap.

"Do you suppose we could look through the files of the case?" she asked.

"Yes, I'm sure that I can get access to the files. After my father died I took all his old case files over to the police station. I'm sure they're in storage. It'd just be a matter of finding them."

"I really want to see the confession he left behind." Clare was excited at the prospect. "We can compare the writing against the letter he left me to know if it's authentic. Mostly I want to see the exact wording of the confession. That might help to answer some of our questions."

"The other thing that would help is to have a list of the people that were at the dance the night of the murder." Nate leaned on the chair back. "It seems logical that whatever happened at the dance was the catalyst for the fight and may have somehow triggered the events that led to the murder."

"Bruce Young was at the dance," Clare said.

"Cindy's dad?"

Clare nodded. "I ran into him when I was looking up my birth certificate. I asked if I could talk to him about Grand Rapids. He explained how your father ended up owning this house. At one point I asked him if he was at the dance and he was."

"I'll give him a call and see if he can remember anyone else who might have been there." Nate shrugged. "The trouble is that it's so long ago now that most people won't be able to remember anything important. If they knew anything, they would have come forward years ago."

"Maybe that's what happened with Margee. Maybe when she saw me it jarred some memory long buried about the murder. That would make sense then why she seemed frightened and wanted to talk to me. It's such a shame we never got together."

"We'll talk to the chief about all this tomorrow."

Clare nodded and yawned.

"For now," he said, "I think you should get some sleep. Stay right where you are for the moment. Let me get the guest room ready, and then I'll help you upstairs."

Clare was too tired to argue. She lay back against the pillows running all that they'd talked about back and forth in her mind. So many questions and each time she thought they had an answer something else cropped up. Round and round she went, but she always came back to the same question.

Why was she a danger to anyone?

What would be gained if she were injured or killed? The investigation into the murder would stop. Who would gain by that? Lily's murderer. In the midst of all the other crazy theories they had come up with, there was one that neither of them had thought of.

"What are you thinking now?" Nate said, coming back into the family room. "You look like you've seen a ghost."

"I have in a way," she said. "Something we didn't think about that would turn everything upside down. Assume that Jimmy did commit the murder. And that he ran away at the time of the investigation. What if the body found at the train accident wasn't Jimmy? What if Jimmy Newton is still alive?"

Chapter Nineteen

"What if Jimmy Newton is still alive?" Clare asked.

"Now that's something to consider. It makes a certain amount of sense." Nate set a pile of clothes on the end of the couch, then rubbed the back of his neck. "Of course it doesn't account for the identification of his body after the train accident."

This new theory energized Clare and dissipated some of the exhaustion she'd been feeling.

"The body was hit by a train and it most probably was beyond recognition. Remember this all happened twenty-five years ago," Clare said. "Forensic identification was fairly simplistic in those days. Now we have all the technological wizardry to make identifications. DNA, fingerprints, and so forth."

"If we assume that his identification was based solely on the items that were found on his body, then it might be feasible."

"Maybe Jimmy deliberately changed identities with someone. Maybe someone he met on his travels. He changes identities in case he's picked up for some reason. With the new name and a decent cover story he wouldn't have to worry so much about being found."

Nate sighed. "It's too far-fetched. Somehow he discovers you're investigating the murder and comes back to Grand Rapids to kill off anyone who might have information? It doesn't make sense."

"Not when you put it that way," Clare snapped. "Jimmy would be in his late sixties, so he would look a lot different than he did when he left. He could have come back to Grand Rapids just recently too."

"Okay for the moment let's say you're right. If you think your father is trying to kill you, why didn't he do it years ago? He knew where you were and he had to assume that at some point Rose would tell you about your adoption and the reasons behind it. And, at that point, you would come to Grand Rapids."

"Oh, Nate, why is this so complicated?" Clare said. She could hear the tremor in her voice and was annoyed at her own weakness.

"Do you really believe it's your father who is trying to kill you?"

Clare squeezed her eyes shut as if she could block out everything that had happened in the past week. She took a deep breath. Opening her eyes, she looked up at Nate.

"No," she said. "The man who wrote me that letter would never try to kill me."

A smile broke out on Nate's face. "That's what I think too."

He picked up the pile of clothes he'd set on the couch and rummaged through them until he found a pair of thick socks. Pulling the tube of antiseptic cream from his shirt pocket, he sat down in the chair beside the ottoman.

"I'm going to put some more cream on and then the socks. You can walk upstairs without slip sliding around. Look in there and see if you can find something you'd like to wear. Or if you're the hardy type, you can go buck naked."

Heat burned her cheeks and she busied herself looking through the clothes. She settled for a long sleeved jersey and a pair of flannel drawstring trousers.

"This probably gives you some clue as to the state of my love life that I don't have a closet full of slinky nightgowns."

His head was bent as he worked on her feet, but she could hear the humor in his tone. When he finished with the cream, he carefully slipped the socks onto her feet and helped her up off the couch. She'd been sitting so long that her muscles were stiff when she started to move. With one hand on the banister and Nate's arm around her waist, she managed the stairs with a minimum of pain.

The guest room bed was turned down. She was too tired to look around. She hobbled into the bathroom and stripped off her bloody clothes. In the mirror over the sink, she caught a glimpse of the black-and-blue spots blossoming on her torso and a particularly nasty bruise along her ribs on the right side. She sucked in her breath at the pain when she raised her arms to pull on the jersey. The flannel pants were enormous but she could keep them up by pulling on the drawstrings.

She washed her hands and face, leaving the rest for the next day. After undoing the braid of hair, she combed it back with her fingers and returned to the bedroom where Nate was waiting. Seeing the concern etched in his face, she did her best not to limp.

"You Chicago gals sure know how to dress in the latest fashion," he said. "Mighty sexy, Clare."

"I suspect we'll be seeing this style on all the runways this year."

She pushed the sleeves of the jersey up past her elbows, but still felt as if she was swallowed up in all the material.

"I don't know if I thanked you for taking such good care of Erika. It was very clear when I tucked her in that you've made great inroads in your relationship."

He put his hands on her shoulders and smiled down at her.

"She's a lovely child, Nate. I'm only sorry that I managed to put her in danger," Clare said. "You would have been very proud of her. It was a scary night for her and she handled herself very well."

He reached up and stroked her cheek with the side of his thumb. She closed her eyes and leaned in to the caress.

"I'm not sure our relationship is going the way I'd like it to," he said. "As you may have gathered, I'm extremely attracted to you and I'd like nothing better than to take you to bed. Tame kisses aren't satisfying when I'd like to rip all your clothes off and make wild, savage love to you."

Clare's breath caught in her throat at his words. She felt it too. A desire to throw caution to the wind. A tingling along every nerve in her body. She raised her arms to put them around his neck, wincing at the pain in her side at the movement. He saw her discomfort and caught her wrists in his hands, bringing her arms down.

"It'll wait," he said. "I want you writhing beneath me, not crying out in pain."

He gave her a hard kiss on the lips, then pulled away and pushed her down on the edge of the bed.

"Don't look at me that way or it'll ruin my resolve. I'll see you in the morning."

Turning on his heels, he left the room, closing the door quietly behind him. Clare's breathing was ragged as she sat on the edge of the bed. She slid under the covers and turned out the light. Smiling, she lay back on the pillows, savoring the taste of him on her lips.

Clare woke to a sunlit bedroom and for a moment didn't know where she was. She stretched and felt the twinges in her body that reminded her of what had transpired the day before. Looking at the clock, she was jolted when she realized it was already nine o'clock. She threw back the covers and swung her legs over the side of the bed.

On the chair beside the door was a pile of clothes neatly folded and a plastic bag filled with toiletries. Clare recognized her own peach-colored blouse and the sneakers on the floor. Nate must have gone over to the cottage to get her fresh clothes. Her cell phone was on top of the pile. She smiled at the thought that he'd not only picked out a shirt and slacks but clean underwear as well. She must have been sleeping soundly if he was able to slip in and out of the room without her waking.

In the bathroom, she peeled off the socks she'd worn to bed, relieved to see that none of the cuts on her feet appeared inflamed. Her body was covered with a colorful array of black-and-blue marks from her plunge down the hill. The shower stung when she first got in but as she stood under the stream of warm water some of the soreness oozed out of her body. She washed her hair, letting the lather slide down her body in soothing waves.

Once showered and dressed in clean clothes, Clare felt almost totally recovered from her ordeal of the day before. Socks and sneakers protected her feet and she walked down stairs with very little discomfort.

"Clare's awake, Daddy," Erika called as she raced across the floor from the family room. "I thought you'd never get up."

"Morning, Erika." Clare leaned over and kissed the girl's cheek. "Are you all slept out?"

"I've been up for ages," the girl said.

Clare put her arm around Erika's shoulder and walked along the hallway toward the kitchen. "No need to sound so smug, young lady. You went to bed way earlier than I did."

"You look much better today," Nate said, as they came into the kitchen. "A little less like roadkill."

Clare laughed. "I can't begin to tell you how much better I feel. Sorry I slept so late. And thanks for the clothes. You must have been out and about early."

"Erika and I ate first thing this morning so I could pick up some clothes for you. I ran into Ruth and told her I'd kidnapped you, but would bring you back some time today."

He pulled out a stool for her to sit at the counter. Erika sat down next to her.

"Guess who Daddy found waiting on your doorstep this morning?" Erika asked. When Clare shook her head, she laughed. "Waldo."

"According to Ruth," Nate said, "he was there the better part of yesterday and back again this morning when she went out to get the newspaper. The dog seems to be missing you."

A car horn sounded at the front of the house. Erika jumped up.

"That's Mrs. Wolfram," she said to Clare. "She's taking Kaya and me to Cass Lake for the day. Will you still be here when I get home?"

"I don't think so." Seeing the look of disappointment on Erika's face, she said, "Why don't we see if we can convince your father to take us out Thursday for that pizza we missed."

"Can we, Dad?" Erika asked.

"We're going to Bemidji to see your cousins on Thursday."

"Dad?" Erika whined.

"We should be back in the afternoon so we'd have plenty of time to go for pizza."

"Awesome, Dad. Thanks."

The car horn sounded again.

"Make sure you've got everything in your beach bag," Nate said. "I'll be right back, Clare. I want to thank Sophia for taking Erika with her."

Erika's shoes pounded up the stairs and then she came racing back down, beach bag in one hand and a Styrofoam "Noodle" in the other. She cut through the kitchen to give Clare a hug and then she went sprinting along the hall and out through the screened porch.

"Ah, youth," Nate said when he returned to the kitchen. "I don't think I had that much energy when I was Erika's age."

"I'm glad she seems recovered from yesterday," Clare said. "I was afraid there would be some aftereffects."

"I gather you told her that the driver was drunk when he tried to run you off the road. A rationale to keep her from thinking it was anything worse?"

"Yes. I didn't want to scare her."

Nate put on a kettle of water for tea and when it was ready, put bread in the toaster and scrambled some eggs. Under his steady gaze, Clare ate everything with gusto.

"I hoped that after your solitary night, with no lusty exercise, you'd be picking at your food."

"I have a healthy appetite."

"For everything, I hope," he said. "We have the house to ourselves until at least five."

"What about your plans to talk to the chief?" she said, raising an eyebrow as he leered across the counter.

"Reality rears its ugly head. You're right. Business first." Nate sighed. "I called the Forest History Center and told them we'd send a truck out to get the car. I found your car keys in your jacket and, after I picked up your clothes this morning, I dropped the keys off at my garage. They'll pick up the car and let me know what they find."

"I'm exhausted just listening to you. Thanks for doing all this."

"Just part of my plan to make myself indispensable to you." He leaned over and kissed her on the nose. "By the way, I had a long talk with Erika. I asked her all about the rehearsal yesterday and how she'd gotten the idea to stop at the logging camp. She said a couple of girls were talking about it and someone suggested you'd like to see it."

"I figured it was something like that."

"I don't know. She was holding something back, but I don't know what it was. I think it's because she's feeling guilty that she took you there. She thinks it's her fault that you got hurt."

"Remind her that I agreed to go because I thought it would be fun. And it was."

"I'll tell her. Something else is on her mind. She'll eventually tell me. By the way, she was the one who told everyone that you were investigating the murder."

"I don't suppose that really matters," Clare said.

"She said she told her friends because she thought it was cool." Nate shook his head. "I didn't push it because she's still upset about last night."

"I feel terrible about last night. She was in danger because of me. I don't want that to happen again."

"We're going to get to the bottom of this, Clare. And in the meantime I'm going to keep an eye on you."

They cleaned up the kitchen and then wandered out to the patio. It was hot but there was a steady breeze off the lake.

"Now that you've had a chance to think about last night, do you still think that car was trying to hit you?"

"Yes," Clare said without hesitation. "I'm not paranoid, Nate. The driver turned the wheel directly toward me."

"I'm not doubting you. I just wanted to make sure it wasn't just a combination of events that made you jumpy." Nate sat down on the stone wall and faced Clare. "The one thing I wondered was the purpose behind the attack. Was it intended to be lethal or was it intended to frighten you?"

"All I know is that if Erika and I hadn't gotten out of the way, the car would have hit us. That would have been more than a scare." Her tone was defensive and she took a deep breath before she continued. "I know what you're saying, Nate, and I don't know the answer."

"If it was meant to scare you, the driver might have lost control of the car and then it would have been lethal." Nate shook his head. "What I'm trying to figure out is how high the threat level is to you. I don't feel you're safe. The break in, the note under the door, the man outside during the storm. I feel you're in danger even if someone just wants to frighten you away."

"To what purpose?" Clare asked, pacing across the flagstones.

"At one point we talked about the possibility that Jimmy might not have been your father. If that's true there might be someone in town who is threatened by either exposure or some sort of financial blackmail."

"I don't follow that."

"Suppose it's Big Red. When he died he left a sizable fortune to Ed Wiklander. Ed adored his father and he wouldn't want any scandal attached to his name. When his father died, he inherited the estate. Maybe he's afraid you'd have some inheritance rights."

"Even if that was true, I'd never contest the will, for God's sake." Clare felt hurt that Nate would even bring it up.

"Steady, Clare. I'm on your side. The thing is when money is involved, people do strange things. Ed doesn't know anything about you, so he might think you'd want a piece of the pie. Bruce Young is in the same situation. He said he dated Lily. He's the right age and he's got plenty of money."

"I could be Cindy's older sister?" Clare laughed.

Nate laughed too but his face was serious. "It sounds funny but you can see why either of those men might want you to stop digging in the past and get out of town."

"What about Pastor Olli?" Clare said. "It's about as likely to be him. He was at the dance the night of the murder too."

"I suspect Bianca would have something to say about that. She keeps a pretty close eye on him."

The telephone rang and Nate hurried inside to answer it. Clare stared out over the lake trying to get back to the feeling of well-being she'd had when she woke up. How could there be talk of murder in such a beautiful setting? She turned when she heard Nate's footsteps behind her.

"That was Anderson's Garage. Your car will be ready in another hour. Jeanne said that Andy had to put on two new tires."

"Couldn't they repair the old ones?"

"No. The tires had been slashed."

Chapter Twenty

"The tires were slashed. There was no way to patch them." Nate spoke harshly.

Clare felt a sinking sensation in the pit of her stomach. She sat down on the stone wall, afraid that her legs wouldn't hold her.

"Having it confirmed makes it worse," she said.

"It still doesn't prove anything. It could be two separate incidents."

"I know you're trying to keep me from freaking out, but I don't see how it could be two incidents."

"What if someone wanted to get you to go back to Chicago? They might slash your tires just to force you to walk back to town. It might scare you enough that you'd give it up and go home." Nate grimaced. "I know this sounds pretty thin, but it's possible."

"What about the car?"

"It could very well have been a drunk driver. Maybe he saw you on the side of the road and intended to stop for you but lost control of the car."

"Do you not believe me or do you just not want to believe me?"

Nate crossed to her and pulled her up and into his embrace. "I believe everything you've told me, but I'm hoping that your perception of the details is wrong. The thought that someone in Grand Rapids is trying to kill you is something that I find almost impossible to accept."

Clare lay her forehead against his chest. "I know what you

mean. Murder isn't something that's within the realm of my understanding either."

"While I was inside, I called Chief Fogt and asked if we could drop by to see him. He said to come now because he's got a meeting after lunch."

"Maybe he can look at all this objectively and come up with some theory that we haven't thought of."

Nate squeezed Clare's shoulders and then released her. "I think the only thing we haven't thought of is: famine and pestilence."

Clare pulled into the parking space above the cottage and waited for Nate who had followed her from the garage. She transferred Erika's clogging costume and shoebag to the back seat of Nate's car.

"Tell Erika to hang her costume up and the wrinkles should come out of the skirt," Clare said.

"You may not believe it to look at me, but, for an author, I'm a wizard with a steam iron."

"I'm very impressed. No wonder you always look so well turned out," she said, eyeing his rumpled khaki shorts and short-sleeved, button-down shirt. "A trendy contrast in fashion."

"I'll have you know I have my own special iron. A Rowenta Advancer. Considered by aficionados to be the Cadillac of steam irons."

"You're kidding," Clare said.

"A man never mocks his iron." Although he tried to keep a straight face, Clare's giggle dissolved his control and he laughed out loud. "Next time you're at the house, I'll show it to you."

"I'll hold you to that," Clare said, then pointed to the cardboard box in the back seat. "Do you want to look at the files now?"

Nate looked at his watch. "It's two o'clock. I want to get back to the house around four in case Erika comes home early. I don't think that gives us enough time. I'll look through it tonight and see if there's anything new and different in it."

"I forgot to ask why you brought this box. There was a whole shelfful of boxes that held files on the murder investigation."

"This was the box that had my father's personal files on the case. After he died, I took it over to the station and added it to what they already had. I don't think they would have let me take any of the other files, but this one technically belonged to me."

"I liked Chief Fogt. He listened to all my conspiracy theories and didn't seem to think I was crazy."

"He's a good guy. We don't have a lot of crime in Grand Rapids, so when something comes up, he'll give it his full attention. He's going to check the Forest History Center to see if they have any security cameras. If they do we might get some idea of what happened to your tires."

"He said it was a long shot but at least he's willing to look into it. I do feel better after he went over the reports about Margee's death. I've been so worried that somehow I caused her death."

"I know you mentioned that," Nate said, "but it appears to have had nothing to do with you. Someone saw her go into the storage room carrying some empty cardboard boxes. She might not have seen the step and that's what caused the fall."

"By the way, thanks for the lunch. Erika and I were just talking about pasties."

"You didn't say whether you liked them or not. I noticed you skipped the ones with rutabaga."

"A useless vegetable at best. The pasties were good but I think it was too hot today to really enjoy them. I can imagine on a cold day you could eat a half dozen."

"How do you think we tolerate the winter up here?"

"Do you have time for a cold drink?"

"That I do. Don't tell me you have beer." Nate closed the car door and followed Clare to the path. "Looks like you've already got company."

Waldo was sprawled on the front porch. He let out a soft woofing sound at their approach. His bushy tail swished across the floorboards by way of greeting, but he didn't get up.

"What a patient friend you are," Clare said. "Have you been waiting for me to come home?"

She leaned over to pet the dog. His fur was soft to the touch. She sniffed the air, grateful for the normal doggy smell.

"What? No fish today?" She rubbed his head but when she touched his ear, he jerked away and let out a sharp yelp. "What's up, old boy? Nate, something's wrong."

Kneeling down beside the dog, she gently lifted his ear. There was a bloody bruise on the side of his head just below his ear. Although his sides heaved as he panted, Waldo remained quiet while they examined his wound.

"That looks nasty," Nate said. "I don't have Jake's phone number so it'll be just as fast to take him over there. I think Waldo needs to see the vet, but we'll let him decide."

"Let me get some towels."

Clare unlocked the front door and hurried inside. She grabbed some bath towels from the linen closet and returned to the dog's side.

"Come on, Waldo. Let's go get Jake."

The dog struggled to roll over on his stomach and it was only then they realized that his leg was injured. His left front paw shook as he tried to keep it from pressing on the floor.

"It's okay. It's okay." Nate spoke softly as he ran his hands over the rest of the dog's body. "It looks like just his front leg. I don't know if it's broken so I better carry him."

"Give me your keys," she said. "I'll open the back of the SUV and then come back to help. Just keep him quiet."

Nate dug out his keys and handed them to Clare. She ran up the flagstone path and got in the driver's seat. Starting the car, she turned the SUV around so that the back was at the top of the path. She unlocked the back door, grateful that the RAV4 door opened to the side rather than laying down flat. She spread the bath towels on the carpet in the back then hurried back down the path.

"It's going to be okay, Waldo," she said, stroking the top of the panting dog's head. Nate squatted beside the dog preparing to lift him. "Don't pick him up yet. Let me get one more thing."

She ran into the house checking the linen closet and finally pulled her pashmina scarf from the dresser in her room. Back outside she knelt down beside Waldo. "I'm going to wrap the scarf around his muzzle. I don't think he'll bite but if he's in pain it might just be an automatic reaction."

Careful not to knock against his sore paw, she wrapped the scarf around his jaws, keeping it away from the cut on his head. She kept up a steady patter of soft shushing noises as she tied the soft material in a loose knot.

"Easy, Waldo," Nate said as he put his arms around the dog's middle.

With a mighty effort he raised the dog until he was standing on his back legs. Although Waldo's panting increased, he made no aggressive moves, only emitted soft cries. Keeping the injured leg to the front, Nate shifted his grip and lifted the dog off the ground. Leaning back, he bent his legs, bracing to support the dog's deadweight. With the dog in his arms, he started slowly up the path.

Clare raced ahead smoothing the towels in the back of the SUV, just as Nate got to the top. She could see his arms quiver with the strain of setting the dog down slowly, turning his body so the injured leg didn't touch the floor.

"Good dog. Good boy," Nate gasped, panting in his turn. "Next time you decide to rescue a dog, Clare, make sure it's a cockapoo instead of a woolly mammoth?"

"I'll definitely keep that in mind. " she said. "Do you want me to sit back here?"

"No. I think he'll be all right. It's just a short ride."

It took only ten minutes to get to Jake's house. Nate drove slowly up a rutted drive to a secluded cabin on the edge of the lake. Jake must have heard them coming, because the door opened and he came down the stairs to the drive. His face was less than welcoming as the car came to a stop. Nate ran down the window on Clare's side and leaned over.

"We've got Waldo in the back, Jake. He's been hurt."

Without comment, Jake moved to the back of the car and

jerked open the door. Nate put the car in park and got out. Clare stayed in her seat, watching the two men in the rear doorway.

"It's the side of his head and his left paw," Nate said.

"Steady there, Waldo," Jake said as he leaned over the dog. "It's just me."

Clare could hear the slow thump of the dog's tail.

"Any idea what happened?"

"No. Clare and I found him on her front porch after lunch today. He was just lying there. If you want to climb in back, we'll make a run over to the vet."

"Thanks, Nate. Much appreciated."

With another soft pat, Jake closed the back door and came around to get in the backseat. All the way to the vet, he hung over the seat, one hand firmly anchored in the dog's fur.

"You go with Jake," Clare said to Nate when they arrived. "I'll take care of the car."

She waited as the two men carried Waldo inside, then parked the SUV and walked into the empty waiting room. Sitting down, she picked up a magazine, but just sat with it in her lap. It wasn't long before Nate joined her. He handed her the neatly folded pashmina wrap.

"There's a little blood on the scarf. Jake said he'd have it cleaned, but I figured you'd know what to do with it. He said thanks for sacrificing it for the dog."

"How's Waldo doing?"

"The wound on the side of his head needed some stitches, so Dr. Watson had to give him an anesthetic. They're currently checking out his paw."

"Poor Waldo." Tears came to her eyes and she blinked them back. "A week ago I didn't even know the dog and now it's breaking my heart to think he's in pain."

Nate put his arm around her. She rested her head on his shoulder and stared at the clock on the wall as the second hand clicked its way around the circular face. It was forty-five minutes before Jake returned.

His face was drawn and his white hair stood on end as if he'd been running his hands through it. He walked slowly, his shoulders slumped over his tall, gaunt body.

"They're going to hold Waldo overnight," Jake said. "Margaret wants to keep an eye on him until the anesthetic wears off. Luckily there are no broken bones. Just a bad bruise. She gave him a painkiller, but she wants to make sure he rests his foot tonight and tomorrow morning at least. A couple days and he'll be walking okay. He might have a bit of a limp but that'll ease up by next week."

"That's great news," Nate said. He stood up and put his hand on Jake's shoulder. "He's a tough old boy."

"Does it look like he was hit by a car?" Clare asked.

Jake turned to her and the muscles of his jaw rippled. "Not a car. Someone beat him with a tree branch."

"You can't be serious," Clare said, grabbing Nate's arm in her distress. "Someone deliberately hurt Waldo?"

" 'Fraid so. The doc found pieces of bark embedded in the wound on his face. She thinks he was hit a second time to try to break the leg."

Despite Jake's tan, the skin on his face appeared pale. His whole body slumped and he looked all of his seventy plus years.

"I need a drink," Nate said.

He pulled Clare to her feet and led the way out to the SUV. No one spoke until they arrived back at Jake's place.

Jake didn't make a move to get out. His head was down and he seemed to hesitate before he spoke.

"I've got some real cold beer, if you want to come in."

For answer, Nate opened his car door. Jake opened Clare's door and helped her down. She followed as he led the way into the house.

"All I've got is Leinenkugel," he said to Clare, by way of apology. "I'm partial to it because it's a Wisconsin brew. I spent the better part of my youth drinking it. I think I've got a couple of light beers, if that's what you'd prefer."

"I'll take one of those."

"Nate? Leinie Creamy Dark?"

"You betchem."

While the men were getting the beer, Clare looked around. She realized that it was a duplicate layout to that of the cottage. One main room and a bedroom and bath off to the left. The similarity ended there. Aside from a sofa and a TV on the right side of the fireplace, the room was devoid of usable furniture. Book shelves on the left of the fireplace held an array of fishing equipment, an odd assortment of books, and other items, including a batch of dog bones and chew toys. The rest of the space was arranged as an artist's studio.

Along the right side was a slotted framework that held canvasses of all sizes. Some were painted, others blank. There was an easel beside the back window and on various tables and chairs there were palettes, jars with brushes, tubes of paint, and other miscellaneous items. Painting supplies covered every surface.

"The cleaning lady resigned," Jake said as he handed her a frosted glass and poured half a bottle of beer into it.

Clare chuckled as she took a sip of the beer. The first swallow was so cold that she didn't quite catch the taste. She sighed at the second. "It's got a nice crisp bite."

"Isn't that better than wine?" Nate asked with a teasing look.

"When it's cold like this, it's really good."

"Thanks for taking such good care of Waldo," Jake said, raising his glass in a salute. "I've never known him to take to anyone quite like he has to you."

"I understand how he feels," Nate said. He winked at her and Clare caught the surprise on Jake's face.

"May I look at some of your paintings?" Clare asked.

"Sure. Help yourself."

While Jake told Nate about a new fishing spot that he'd just discovered, Clare wandered over to the line of canvases. She could see many of the paintings without pulling them out of their slots. The bottom row held most of the larger pieces. Most of those were landscapes of the lake or deep woods. The care in the details indicated how comfortable Jake was in the outdoors and how much he loved the subject. Each picture appeared as real as a photo.

It appeared as if early evening was his favorite time. The pictures glowed in the changing light. She was almost at the end of the line when she saw the painting she had seen at the art show. It was tucked back into the corner on the second tier of paintings. She reached in and pulled it out, leaning it against one of the struts.

It was small and very intense. It showed a heavy rainstorm on the lake. At the edge of the picture, shrouded among the trees was an old boarded-up boathouse. Once again the painting held her in its grip. She could almost feel the rain beating down and breathe the heavy wet air.

"It's not my best," Jake said at her shoulder.

"Is it a real place?" she asked.

"Just someplace on the lake."

"I know where that is," Nate said, coming to join them. "That's part of Pastor Olli's youth camp. His property borders mine. I know the place well and can quite literally find it in the dark. It's the old boathouse."

"I suppose it is," Jake said.

"That really brings back my youth. It was the only place I knew of that you could take a girl, other than the woods, where you could have a little privacy." Nate took a long pull on his beer. "Many a Grand Rapids girl lost her innocence in the boathouse. A number of babies owed their very existence to that place. Some of the guys called it the 'bedhouse.' There were other names for it but they were even less polite."

"Wasn't it kept locked?" Clare asked.

"Sure but someone made a copy of the key. The threshold board was loose. You just pulled it out and the key was underneath. Sometimes a bunch of us guys would just sneak over with a six-pack of stolen beer. We'd sit in the dark and drink and tell lies to each other about the gals we used to bring there."

"I didn't realize I was painting a national landmark," Jake said. He picked the canvas up and slipped it back into the shelf unit. "I paint so much I forget where I've been. A lot of the time I see something and when I'm back home and I paint it, it turns out to look unrecognizable from the original. There's one I'm working on that I think is going well."

He led them over to the easel. At the base, leaning against one of the wooden legs was a rectangular canvas about eighteen inches across. He picked it up and set it on the easel so they could see it better.

Like most of his paintings, it was a scene of the lake. The viewpoint was from the water toward the shore. The trees and sky and much of the lakeshore had been filled in. On the left side of the foreground was an old wooden dock. Sitting on the edge of the dock, was a young girl, one leg dangling over the edge above the water and the other leg bent, her bare foot flat beside her hip. Her body was turned so that her back rested against the side of a large, hairy dog.

"It's Waldo," Clare said, smiling broadly as she recognized the familiar figure.

Leaning closer, she examined the details. Jake had caught the tensed body language of the dog as if he were on guard, watching over the girl. Her red-brown pigtails blended into the dog's brown fur as if the two figures were connected. Although the features of the girl were only sketched in, the feeling of companionship between the pair was apparent in the lines of the bodies.

"Oh, it's going to be wonderful when it's done," Clare said.

She could almost feel a lump in her throat as she stared at the warm rendering of the dog. Nate didn't comment, but she could tell that he too found an emotional impact in the painting. She reached out and touched Jake lightly on the arm. He jumped slightly at the familiar contact, but didn't move away.

"I hope I'll still be here when you finish the picture. I'd very much like to see it again."

Jake ducked his head as if embarrassed by her reaction and muttered what sounded like an affirmative response. He set the painting back on the floor, turning it so that the light from the window wouldn't shine on the surface.

"I hate to leave when you've still got beer in the fridge, but

Erika will be getting back from Cass Lake shortly," Nate said.

Jake walked them back outside to the car.

"Thanks again for watching out for Waldo," he said, as he held the car door for Clare.

"Let me know how he's doing," she replied. She waved as they pulled out of the driveway.

"Want to come over for dinner?" Nate said, as they arrived back at the cottage.

"I can't. Ruth and I are going out to dinner and maybe to a movie. She was going to check what's playing."

"Will you be all right here? You could stay over at my place where I can keep an eye on you."

"Nice try, Hanssen." She grinned at the look on his face. "Shame on you for suggesting such a thing with a child in the house."

"What if I convinced Cindy's mom into taking Erika overnight?"

"I thought you and Erika were going to Bemidji tomorrow."

Nate smacked his forehead with the palm of his hand. "I forgot all about it."

"Go home and take a nice long shower," Clare said as she opened the door of the car. "I'll see you tomorrow night for pizza."

"You're way too old-fashioned, Clare. Why couldn't you be a little more slutty?" He leaned over and gave her a quick kiss on the mouth. "I'll pick you up around six tomorrow."

"That'll work," she said.

Back in the cottage, Clare called Ruth to coordinate their times. She washed the blood spots on the pashmina wrap and blocked it out on a towel on the kitchen counter. Quickly showering, she put on a floral print voile skirt and a white jersey, grabbing a sweater at the last minute in case it got chilly later. Leaving lights on in the cottage, she locked up and met Ruth at her car.

They went to the Forest Lake restaurant for dinner. It took so long for Clare to fill Ruth in on everything that had happened that they decided to skip the movie all together. After dinner they splurged on dessert, splitting a chocolate brownie with ice cream and chocolate sauce.

"Downright decadent," Ruth said as she licked the last of the sauce off her spoon.

"Good choice. I think I needed a sugar high."

Ruth took a sip of her tea and looked across the table at Clare. "After everything that's happened since you came to Grand Rapids, you actually look less stressed than the day you arrived. Despite all you've learned, are you glad you came?"

"Yes. All my life I felt I didn't fit in. There always seemed to be some part of me that was out of tune with the rest of the world. I feel like Rose thought my mother didn't live up to her high moral standards. When I was a child, she was constantly telling me that I had the potential to lead a bad life."

"Do you think your mother was a bad person? That she brought on her own death?"

Clare picked up the spoon beside her cup and ran it back and forth between her fingers. "It's funny, but for years I've had flashes of pictures in my mind of a woman that I think is my mother. Her face isn't clear but in my mind, she's always smiling and sometimes I can almost hear her laughter in my head."

"What a lovely thought. I'd hold on to that idea that she's your mother." Ruth finished the last of her tea. "And Nate? Where does he fit into your life?"

"I'm almost afraid to guess. Today is Wednesday. Eight days ago I'd never seen the man. Is it possible that someone I've only known for such a short time could be so important to me?"

"Are you afraid to trust your instincts?"

"Yes. My whole life turned out to be a conspiracy of lies. I'm not sure I know what's real. Ever since I arrived my emotions have been in turmoil. I'm afraid that I may be reaching out to Nate because I have such a need for security and grounding."

"Listening to you talk about your relationship, I don't get the idea that it's born of desperation. He's a good man and I think you two have an excellent chance of making each other very happy."

Ruth smiled across the table. "And it looks as if you're making great progress with Erika. She's a very sweet child, just a bit spoiled. I suspect your nighttime adventure has made a solid foundation to build on."

They talked for a while about Erika and then after they paid the bill, drove back to Heart's Content. Clare waited until Ruth went inside before she started down the path to the cottage. She stood on the porch, looking out over the lake. The moon was high in the sky, painting a swath of white light across the surface. A loon called, the haunting sound echoing in the quiet of the night. She thought back to the question Ruth had asked. Yes, she was very happy that she'd come to Grand Rapids.

Clare woke at seven in the morning with a throbbing headache. She lay quietly on her back, waiting for the waves of nausea to lessen. Outside the window the sky was a metallic gray blue. It had rained during the night. She remembered waking to thunder and faint flashes of lightning. Sitting up slowly, she swung her legs over the side of the bed and stood up. Pain hammered at her senses.

Barefoot, she padded out to the kitchen. She took out a plastic bag, put a handful of ice in it and wrapped it in a dish towel. Reaching in her purse, she pulled out a packet of Pain-Aid and took two tablets. Moving slowly so as not to jar her head, she went back to the bedroom. She lay on her back with the towel-wrapped ice at the base of her skull. Closing her eyes, she tried to concentrate on her breathing instead of the pounding in her head.

She dozed and when she woke, the pain had subsided and she no longer felt sick to her stomach. She felt less than rested and knew it was because she had slept so poorly.

She'd had the woods dream again.

This time the nightmare was different. It started as it had the last time with the squeaking screen door. She was a child again, lost and running through the woods. This time she had a baby in her arms. She came to a building and ran inside. The pirate was waiting for her inside the house. She could see oars for a rowboat and a steel license plate. There was rain all around her and flickering light. Lightning illuminated the sky and then she woke at the sound of thunder.

Just remembering the dream in the safety of the cottage, Clare's body tensed and sweat broke out all over it. There was some important difference in the dream but she couldn't place it. Closing her eyes, she tried to bring back the dream sequence in her mind.

Then she saw it.

She realized why Jake's rainstorm picture had frightened her. In the corner of the canvas, he had painted the boathouse at Pastor Olli's youth camp. In her dream she had been running to a building. She recognized the building for the first time. It was the boathouse.

Chapter Twenty-One

The building in her recurring nightmare was the boathouse. She had always thought the dream was just some figment of her imagination, pieced together randomly. Now that she could see the building clearly, she was convinced that she'd actually been in the boathouse.

Each time she had the dream, she seemed able to recall more of the details. If she could ever remember the entire dream when she was awake, she was convinced her lost memories would return. She had the nagging feeling that there was a major portion of the dream that was missing. It was as if she were looking at a jigsaw puzzle and trying to fit in pieces that belonged to another puzzle. She was on the brink of some kind of discovery if only she could find the key.

Nate said the boathouse was along a path beside his property. Too bad he wasn't around to go exploring with her.

Getting out of bed, she was grateful that her headache had almost disappeared. She stood under the shower for a long time, breathing in the warm steam. She could feel her sinuses clear and the last remnants of her headache vanished. Although she had started the day in a state of depression, her gloom had been replaced by a shiver of excitement at the possibility of getting some answers. The day was chilly so she wore jeans, a T-shirt and sneakers. She had just finished a breakfast of scrambled eggs and toast when the phone rang.

"Morning to you," Nate said. "Are you missing me?"

"I refuse to answer that loaded question. Are you in Bemidji?"

"Yes. We stopped off to see the sights before we go to my sister-in-law's house."

"What kind of sights does Bemidji have to offer?"

"Now you're really going to be jealous that you weren't invited to come along. For a starter there's an eighteen-foot-tall statue of Paul Bunyan. I've just taken Erika's picture with him. I hope that, even in the cosmopolitan atmosphere of Chicago, you've heard of Mr. Bunyan, the greatest woodsman who ever lived."

Clare laughed. "You'll find this hard to believe, Nate, but his fame has actually gotten as far as the shores of Lake Michigan. Eighteen feet, you say. That would be something to see."

"And I haven't even mentioned Babe, the Blue Ox. According to the brochure I'm holding in my hands, he weighs five tons. It's the horns that are impressive. They're fourteen feet across," Nate said. "I just wanted to let you know we'll be back in plenty of time for the pizza."

"I've got some things I need to do today," Clare said. "I hope you're having a grand time with Erika."

"We have a packed program today. Susie and Greg have four children and best of all, a pool. I'll be totally exhausted when I get back but I'm looking forward to seeing you at six."

"Just give me a call if you're running late," Clare said. "Don't forget to take lots of pictures. I can't wait to see you standing next to the Blue Ox."

"I almost forgot the other reason I called," Nate said. "I looked through Dad's files last night and I found a copy of Jimmy's confession."

Clare's breath caught in her throat and she swallowed several times before she could speak. "What did it say?"

"I'm sorry, Clare, but it definitely says he shot Lily. I know you were hoping for some vague language but he was very clear in his statement." He paused but she made no comment. "Are you still there?"

"Yes, I'm here." She sighed. "It was wishful thinking on my

part. No one wants to have to admit their father killed their mother. It's not unexpected news. Even so, I would like to see the confession sometime. Did you find anything else of interest in the box?"

"I just had time to look through it for the confession. You could come back to the house after dinner and go through it with me."

"Sounds like the old etchings ploy."

Nate laughed. "A guy's got to do what he can. Besides, after a day with five children, I'll be looking for some adult entertainment. Stay out of trouble today and I'll see you later."

"Drive carefully," Clare said.

Nate disconnected, but, not wanting to give up the tenuous contact with him, she held the receiver in her hand for a moment longer. Finally she sighed and hung up the phone. After cleaning up the cottage, she got into the car and drove around the lake to the Egner's place.

She stopped in front of the house and, even before she got out, she could tell that no one was home. She rang the bell several times but no one answered. Back in the car, she debated driving to Olli's church to see if he or Bianca was there. As she drove out to the main highway, she passed another drive that had a sign indicating the entrance to the youth camp. She turned in and headed down the winding hill toward the lake.

She parked in the gravel parking lot, next to a small log building. Leaving her purse inside, she locked the car and put the keys in the pocket of her jeans. She walked around the log house, guessing it was the office when the camp was in session. There were shutters on the windows and the door was locked with a padlock. On the side wall of the office was a chart that showed the layout of the camp.

There were four buildings on four sides of a baseball field. The largest building was marked: meeting/dining hall. Two smaller buildings were marked as bunkhouses. One labeled Beavers; the other Badgers. The last building was designated the bathhouse. Nowhere on the diagram did she see anything marked as the boathouse. However behind the bunkhouse marked Beavers was a broken line indicating the trail down to the beach.

She walked along the trail of the deserted camp, admiring the simple design of the log cabin buildings. There were wooden bleachers along two sides of the baseball diamond and a scoreboard at the far end of the field. At the side of the meeting hall there was a group of picnic tables lying sideways so that rainwater wouldn't collect on the flat surfaces. As she approached the first of the bunkhouses, she saw a trail leading over the hill. It had been freshly covered with red bark mulch.

Walking around, she could see that a great deal of work had been put into making it a pleasant environment. Now it had the air of a ghost town. When she'd had lunch with Olli and Bianca she remembered that he'd had to leave early to help the volunteers who were winterizing the camp.

She paused at the head of the trail to the beach, wondering if this was the way to the boathouse. Looking through the branches of the trees, she could see a building at the edge of the lake. She started down the trail, taking her time on the wet surface. The rain the night before had made the bark slippery.

As she got closer to the shoreline, she got a better look at the building. It wasn't the boathouse she had seen in Jake's picture or the one she remembered from her dream. It was a newer building, a small log cabin similar to the buildings in the main camp. Disappointed, she tried to remember what Nate had said about the boathouse.

He said he was familiar with it because it was close to his property. Getting her bearings, Clare walked along the shoreline, heading in the general direction of Nate's house on the east end of the camp. The woods jutted out and she rounded a corner and spotted the boathouse ahead. Bushes and small trees grew thickly on the side of the building facing the camp to make it almost invisible to a casual observer.

Cutting into the woods on the side away from the lake, she stumbled across fallen branches and high grass until she came out into a clearing and got a full view of the boathouse.

Weather-beaten boards made up the side of the building. High up at the roofline was a small window, which was boarded up. On the far side of the structure was an old wooden walkway that ran along the lakeside of the building.

She stood motionless as she stared at the boathouse. Although in her dreams the building was new, with unshuttered windows, she recognized it immediately.

There was no doubt in Clare's mind. It was so familiar that she suspected she had been in it several times. Since she had once lived in Nate's house, it would have been logical that she would follow the same path that Nate had mentioned. She looked around, but she couldn't see anything that looked like a path. In twenty-five years, the woods had reclaimed it.

She closed her eyes and tried to remember. She could picture the woods and the rainstorm. She could see the boathouse clearly. Beyond that her mind refused to go.

The walkway was old and she walked carefully, testing each board before she stepped on it. Several boards were missing and she stepped over the gaps until she reached the door. The door was locked with an old rusted padlock and the window beside it was boarded up.

She pulled on the boards across the window. The one at the bottom gave a little and she applied enough pressure to pull it away from one side. She grabbed the end of the board and wiggled it back and forth but it was firmly attached at the far end. Giving one more downward pull she managed to loosen it enough that about an inch of glass showed between the boards. She pressed her head against the side of the window and peered into the boathouse.

With a sliver of light illuminating the inside, she could only see a small portion of the floor. Odd shapes of objects indicated that it was probably used as a storeroom. One of the small panes of glass was broken and as she breathed in, she caught the musty smell of the stagnant air.

Her heart beat erratically and her body broke out in a cold sweat. She pushed away from the window and fought to control her breathing. It was almost as if she were having a panic attack. She staggered across the old dock until she was back on solid ground again.

In the midst of her fear, one thought came to her. This was the place where her mother had died.

Clare had no idea how she knew that fact, but she did. None of the clippings had ever mentioned where Lily was killed. All that was said was that Lily had been shot somewhere else and that her body had been left on the shore of the lake. Many had suspected she was shot in the house where Nate lived. Clare didn't believe it. Without knowing why, she was convinced that Lily had been killed in the boathouse.

Clare staggered over to a fallen tree and dropped down on the rough surface. That was the meaning of the dream. That was the reason her memories were blank. She had been in the boathouse and seen her mother killed.

It made perfect sense. She shivered at the thought, unwilling to push her memories further. There were some things she didn't want to discover.

Anxious to get as far away as possible from the boathouse, she cut back downhill, crashing through the underbrush until she broke through at the shoreline of the lake. Standing at the water's edge, her chest heaved with the exertion of her panicky flight. She stared out at the sparkling water and let the peace of the scene calm her. Slowly her breathing returned to normal.

She didn't want to think about the frightening conclusions she had arrived at. She only wanted to get away and not have to think about Lily's death. She would push everything to the back of her mind again and think about it later.

"I've become Scarlett O'Hara," she muttered. Just saying the words aloud, Clare felt as if she'd returned to a more rational state and was ready to go home.

She walked along the edge of the beach until she reached the trail she'd followed down from the camp. She was halfway up the hill when she heard a shout.

"Clare? Is that you?"

Looking up she could see Bianca standing at the top of the hill, peering down the bank. Embarrassed to be caught snooping, she hoped she didn't look as guilty as she felt.

"Hello, Bianca. I'm on my way up," she called as she continued up the trail.

"What on earth are you doing down there?" Bianca's normally cheerful face was set in disapproval.

"I'm afraid I've been trespassing," Clare admitted. "I stopped at your house but no one answered the bell. I was so interested in the camp after talking to Olli that I wanted to see it for myself."

"Just look at your clothes, Clare. Did you fall?"

Bianca hurried over as Clare reached the top and brushed at the twigs and leaves that were caught on her T-shirt. There was a long smudge of dirt on her shirt and her socks were covered with flat burrs.

"I took what I thought was a shortcut to get back to the trail," Clare said, hoping her explanation would suffice. She leaned over to pull some of the burrs off her socks. "Ouch."

"You must have run into a patch of Swamp Beggar's Ticks. The seedpods are called stick-tights because they have two barbs that stick to anything they come in contact with. It's the same premise as Velcro. Fascinating but such a nuisance. "

"I give up. I've got them all over my pants legs too."

Clare stood up, hoping that Bianca would assume her red face was from bending over.

"Just soak your things overnight and they'll come right out in the washing machine."

"Thanks, Bianca. I'll try that."

"I saw a car in the parking lot when I came home and came over to find out who was here. We normally have a chain across the entrance, but we had a plumber here yesterday to fix a leak in the bathhouse. Olli must have forgotten to put the chain back up. He's going to get a piece of my mind for that. No telling who could have driven down here."

"I can't tell you how impressed I am with the camp, Bianca. It must be a great source of pride for both you and Olli."

"I wish you could see it when the boys are here. Shouting and laughter all day long." She took Clare's arm and led her back toward the parking lot. "You shouldn't be walking in the woods alone, dear. You might have fallen and no one would have known you were here."

"It was silly of me. I'm used to the parks in Chicago where there is always someone walking or bike riding. My apologies."

"I just don't want to worry about you," Bianca said. "It was good to see you at Erika's rehearsal on Tuesday. Olli was sorry he didn't have a chance to say hello to you. He's so busy. He just had time to pop in to see them dance. Aren't the children talented?"

"I loved it. It was the first time I'd ever seen clogging."

"Will you be going to the performance on Friday?"

"Yes. I'm looking forward to it," Clare said.

Bianca's car was parked beside Clare's in the parking lot. Clare took out her keys and pressed the button to unlock her doors. Bianca did the same.

"I noticed you've been seeing quite a bit of Nate Hanssen. He is such a charming man. It would be wonderful if he could find someone special in his life. Will you be staying much longer in Grand Rapids?"

Clare refused to take the bait thrown out by the gossipy older woman. Opening the car door, she started the car. "I don't know how long I'll stay. I've got some more research to do before I can complete my assignments."

"I forgot about your story on our murder. In case you didn't find it in your research, we had another murder you know. Much more recent. I believe it was in 1997. It was in the performers' building down by the Melodie Showboat."

"Yes, I read about that. I may include some details of that when I do my article," Clare said. "Thanks for checking on me, Bianca. I didn't mean to trespass. I was just curious."

"That's the mark of a good reporter," the older woman said, wagging her finger at Clare. "You go ahead, dear. I'll put the chain up when I leave."

Waving her hand, Clare drove out of the parking lot. In her

rearview mirror she could see Bianca standing beside her car, watching. The muscles in Clare's body were tight with tension. She left the car window down, letting the fresh air wash over her. She was almost back at the cottage before she felt relaxed.

Inside the house, she stripped off her dirty clothes and carefully peeled off her burr-covered socks. She put them in the bathroom sink and filled the basin with water. She changed into a striped jersey, white slacks, and sandals. Back in the main room she checked the answering machine, but there were no messages.

She felt at loose ends with Nate gone for the day. It was surprising how quickly she had become so dependent on his company. Opening the backdoor, she stepped out on the porch. For a while she sat on the porch and stared at the lake, still feeling the aftereffects of her visit to the youth camp. The view did much to calm her.

For lunch she made a sandwich and took it and a glass of milk back out to the porch. She read the newspaper that she'd skipped at breakfast. Finished, she picked up her lunch dishes and went inside. She opened the dishwasher and put the sandwich plate on the lower rack. Picking up her milk glass, she rinsed it under cold water. Turning to put it in the dishwasher, she clipped the edge of the counter and the glass flew out of her hand. It hit the tile floor, shattering, the explosion of glass sounding like a gunshot.

At the sound, her knees buckled and she grabbed the counter to keep from falling, sliding slowly down to the floor. Her vision blurred and she was catapulted into the middle of her dream.

She was running through the woods in the middle of a rainstorm. Branches slashed at her face and arms. She could see the object in her hand. It was a gun. Suddenly she was inside the boathouse. She could smell the damp musty odor in the stuffy room. Lightning flashed and she saw the gun again. Thunder crashed overhead and her fingers tightened.

There was an explosion, a flash of lightning, and everything went black.

Clare never lost consciousness although the darkness threatened to overcome her. She sat on the floor, surrounded by broken glass, staring at her hands. Her fingers shook as if she had palsy. She laced them together, squeezing as hard as she could until she could actually feel the pain in her hands.

Knowledge crashed through all the barriers she had built up over the years. Scenes flashed in her mind. She was a child again. She could actually see Lily's face. She could hear Jimmy's voice. Even Rose appeared in her waking nightmare. And through all the scenes, there was one that was burned into her memory. She was holding the gun in her hands and on the floor in front of her was her mother.

"I shot Lily. Oh God! I killed my mother."

Chapter Twenty-two

"I shot Lily."

Clare spoke the words softly. It was a statement not a question.

"It was an accident," she said. "I shot my mother."

That was why the dream recurred over the years. Coming back stronger each time. All along her mind was trying to come to terms with what she had done. First it buried the knowledge so deep she couldn't remember it. Over the years her dreams combined with reality, forcing its way into a portion of her consciousness. Coming to Grand Rapids had ripped away the barrier between the two worlds until finally she could discover the truth.

She could put whole portions of the dream together. She remembered being frightened for her mother. Her mother was going to the boathouse and she had followed, caught in the woods when it started to rain. She didn't know where she got it but she was holding a gun. The storm had frightened her and she'd squeezed the trigger and the gun went off.

Clare bent her legs, resting her forehead on her knees. Arms around her legs, she pulled herself into a tight ball and rocked slowly back and forth. The knowledge of the accident was too much to tolerate.

"Clare. Are you home?"

A shouted greeting at the front door brought her back to the present.

"Clare?"

She shivered when she heard Waldo bark. She tried to get up but she didn't have the strength to move. Suddenly Jake Jorgensen's face appeared in the front window and he saw her on the floor.

"Are you all right?"

He didn't wait for her response. With a jerk he opened the unlocked door.

"Don't let Waldo in," Clare said. "There's glass all over the floor."

Jake turned toward the porch. "Sit, Waldo. Stay."

Clare heard the thud as the dog dropped to the porch floor. Jake walked inside and closed the door. She could hear Waldo whining outside.

"I dropped a glass," she said by way of explanation.

"Stay right where you are until I get a broom." He disappeared into the hallway and returned in a moment with a dustpan and broom. "I don't know if you realize my house and this cottage were built by the same man. It helps knowing the layout."

While Clare remained seated on the floor, Jake swept up the glass. He moved efficiently back and forth, staring down at the floor to catch any glint from a missed sliver. He refrained from looking directly at Clare until he finished, then he came over and knelt down in front of her.

"Are you cut?"

She shook her head.

"Can you get up?"

Clare nodded, still too caught up in her emotions to talk. He helped her up, not intruding into her personal space. His tanned face was expressionless as he led her over to the couch, standing beside her until she sat down.

The whining outside increased in volume and pitch.

"I brought Waldo over so you could see he was all right," Jake said, walking over to open the back door.

Waldo sat on the porch, his whole body wriggling as his tail pounded the floor. His tongue hung out as he panted, making him look almost clownish.

"All right," Jake said. "You can come in and say hello."

Clare was surprised that he didn't bound to his feet, but rose slowly and limped into the room. She'd forgotten about his foot.

"Poor Waldo. How are you doing, boy?"

He hobbled over to stand in front of her, then lay his head in her lap, big eyes staring up at her. The side of his head had been shaved below his ear and Clare could see the sutures crisscrossing the pink skin.

"Oh, Jake, who could have hurt him like this?"

"Dunno," came the curt reply. "Not sure we'll ever know."

Clare leaned over until her head was touching the top of the dog's. She stroked the uninjured side of his head with one hand and buried the other in the soft fur on his back. Suddenly she started to cry, quietly at first and then sobs that seemed to well up from deep inside. She held onto the dog, who waited patiently, letting her hold him for strength.

The sound of the kettle whistling broke through her emotional meltdown. She raised her head to see Jake pouring boiling water into two mugs. Tucking a box of Kleenex under his arm, he carried the tea across to the table in front of the sofa. Setting down the mugs, he handed her the box of tissues, then sat down in the chair beside the couch.

Clare gave Waldo a final pat on his back and the dog took his head out of her lap and curled up at her feet. Taking a tissue, she blew her nose and wiped her eyes. She peeked through her lashes at Jake. Although he lounged back in his chair, one long leg casually crossed, ankle on knee, his body language was anything but relaxed. She could imagine he must be mystified by her fit of hysterics, debating what to say.

"I need to tell you who I am," she said, "and what I've done."

His body tensed, startled by the abruptness of her words. Before she could speak again, he raised his hand, palm toward her.

"I already know who you are. You're Abby Newton. Daughter of Jimmy and Lily Newton."

A shiver ran down Clare's back at the confirmation that other people besides Ruth and Nate knew her identity.

"How do you know that?" she asked, more out of curiosity than for any other reason.

"Bruce Young told me at the art show," Jake said. "He was annoyed that you were digging around in what he called 'old, sad memories.' I had the feeling he'd been crazy about Lily before she was married. Maybe he thought your story would mention him and he didn't want that chapter of his life reopened."

Clare shook her head. "I interviewed him when I was first here in Grand Rapids. He told me that he'd dated Lily, but I didn't think he was particularly obsessed with her." She shrugged. "It doesn't matter, I guess. At least now that you know who I am it will be easier for you to understand what I've done."

Again Jake raised his hand to stop her. "You don't have to tell me anything, Clare. I know you're upset but you don't owe me any explanation." He paused then said, " 'Course you can tell Waldo if you want."

At the mention of his name, the dog let out a woofing sigh and Jake smiled across at her.

It was the first time she'd seen him smile. His eyes crinkled at the corners and for the first time she could imagine how good looking he would have been in his younger days. There was something solid about him that made her comfortable in his presence.

"I'd like to tell you both," she said. Her throat was dry and she swallowed several times and then continued. "I've just discovered I've done a terrible thing."

Hearing her own words, Clare felt a wave of peace wash over her. She'd bottled up so much emotion that it would be a pleasure to find a release. Slowly she began to tell Jake the trail that had led her to Grand Rapids, and the discovery of who she was. When her voice grew hoarse, she took a sip of tea. She found it easy to talk to him because he had no knowledge of her history or the history of her parents. And, as she spoke, she was finally able to speak about the terrible night in the woods and the awful consequences of her actions.

Other than drinking his tea, Jake sat perfectly still while she spoke. She didn't know how much he knew about the murder. She did her best to fill in the gaps, and although she could see when a question seemed to form on his lips, he didn't speak.

"When I broke the glass it sounded just like a gunshot," Clare said. "I think that was what triggered the final memory and I realized that I was the one who shot Lily."

"It's quite a story, Clare. I can see you've had a long journey of discovery." He ran a gnarled hand up through his white hair, his mouth puckered in a frown. "The only question in my mind is how much is real and how much is just a dream. It doesn't make sense. Where would you get a gun?"

"My father had a gun. I could have taken it."

"For what purpose, Clare? You were only four."

"I don't know. I was frightened. Maybe I thought my mother was in danger. It could have been any number of reasons."

"It would help if you could remember why you took the gun."

"I know it would, but that piece of the memory hasn't come to me."

Clare stopped, hearing the shrill pitch to her voice. Waldo moved restlessly on the floor as if he sensed the tension in the room

"Sorry, Clare. I have no right to push you," Jake said.

"That's all right. I'm glad I have someone objective to talk to. It's hard enough making sense of any of this. I know there are parts of my memory that haven't returned. Maybe they will or maybe I'll never know. However, the one thing I do know is that my father didn't kill my mother. I did."

Her voice shook on the last words. The words seemed to echo in the silent room. Jake's shoulders were slumped and he stared down at the floor. He cleared his throat several times, then lifted his head.

"Knowing that, what do you intend to do with this knowledge?"

"I'll have to go to the police. I realize it was a tragic accident and there may be no penalty but I need to explain what actually happened."

"All of this took place twenty-five years ago. Even if you're right, there's nothing to be gained by coming forward at this time."

"I can clear my father's name."

Jake nodded his head as if satisfied with the answer. "From all you've told me about your father, I can't believe he would want you to do that. He sacrificed everything to protect you from this knowledge. He wanted to keep you safe."

"I am safe. The truth can't hurt me now."

Jake cocked his head, as if listening to her words replay in his mind. Abruptly, he went out to the kitchen and heated more water. Clare watched him in a daze, not offering to help in any way. She was emotionally drained.

Jake brought her more tea. When she didn't move to take it, he folded the mug in her hands.

"Drink that while I take Waldo out. I need to clear my mind and then we'll talk again."

At the mention of his name, Waldo scrambled to his feet, his back end wiggling as Jake opened the door. The two figures trudged across the porch, one limping, the other stiff legged. Clare wondered if she should have confided in the older man. He moved as if he'd aged just listening to her story. She raised the mug to her lips, breathing in the slight lemony scent of the tea. She took several sips, letting the warmth creep through her body. Her muscles began to relax, but her mind whirled with questions.

The door opened and Waldo limped across to Clare. He let her inspect his ear and rub his head, then raised his head to indicate he'd had enough. Once more he flopped down on the floor.

She was pleased to see that the fresh air had rejuvenated Jake. His movements were more relaxed and less rigid. The lines on his face were softer and his eyes sparkled with warmth. He didn't sit down, wandering the living room area, touching objects on the shelves as if too restless to remain still. When he spoke, his voice was strong and steady.

"Tell me one more time about the gun," he said. "It was on the floor in the boathouse?"

"Yes." Clare nodded. "I came in and the gun was on the floor."

"I thought you said you had it in your hand when you were running in the woods."

"I did. I must have brought it into the boathouse." Clare looked over at Jake who was watching her intently. "I've seen so many versions of this event that it's hard to remember. I do remember that I fell, so maybe I dropped the gun on the floor at that point."

Jake stood up and walked over to the fireplace. He stared at the logs in the basket on the floor. He raised his head and turned to face Clare.

"How did you see the gun? Wasn't it dark?"

"Y-yes. But there was some light." She squeezed her eyes shut, trying to remember. Opening them, she said, "It was in a circle of light."

"Then what happened?"

Clare felt rattled by the intensity of Jake's stare. His eyebrows were bunched over his eyes, deepening the lines in his forehead.

"I picked up the gun," she said.

"Did the gun frighten you?"

"No. I think I was curious. My father never let me touch his gun. I remember running my fingers over the metal."

"And then?"

"The door slammed against the wall of the boathouse. It frightened me and my fingers tightened around the gun." She licked her dry lips before she could continue. "The gun fired. It was so loud in the room. I dropped the gun to cover my ears. I lost my balance and I fell down."

Clare crossed her arms over her chest, chilled by the memory. Jake looked stunned by the recital. He turned away from her and put his hand on the mantel as if he were meditating. When he turned around again he stared at her, his eyes dark with feeling.

"You shot the gun and then dropped it? Is that how you remember it, Clare?" he asked.

"Yes. "

"How many times did you shoot the gun?"

"Just once."

"You're sure?"

"I'm absolutely positive, Jake. Why do you keep asking me?"

He crossed the room and sat down on the couch beside her. He picked up her hands which were clenched into tight fists.

"I needed to be sure," he said. He stared directly into her eyes and tightened his hold on her hands. "You've forgotten one salient fact about your mother's murder, Clare. Lily wasn't shot once. She was shot three times."

Clare's whole body jerked at his words. She struggled to pull her hands away but he held them tight.

"Do you understand what I'm saying? Lily Newton was shot three times, not once. You did not kill your mother."

She was afraid to believe him. She tried to remember the clippings she'd read. Ruth had told her the main story and she'd skimmed the clippings. She had a vague recollection of reading the details of the crime but all she had focused on was the fact that Lily had been shot. Apparently she had glossed over the details or if she'd read them they never penetrated.

"I suspect you're trying to fit all your nightmares into a new scenario but I truly don't believe you fired the gun three times. You would remember that. Do you understand what I've told you, Clare?" he asked.

"I understand but I'm almost afraid to accept it. I know I should be thrilled but I still have so many questions. I thought I understood why Jimmy sent me away. I was sure it was to keep me from knowing who I was and what I had done. It made perfect sense. What does it mean, Jake? If I didn't shoot her, who did?"

"At the moment that seems to be the most important question."

With a final squeeze of her hands, Jake got to his feet and paced back to the fireplace. He turned to lean his back against the mantel, his eyes deeply shadowed.

"Did Jimmy kill Lily after all?" she asked.

"One would assume so. Do you think he did?"

Clare shook her head. "No. I know everything pointed to him, but from everything else I've learned, he doesn't seem like a murderer. He loved Lily. I truly believe he wouldn't have hurt her. Do you think he killed her?"

"Up until now I had no reason to doubt." Jake cleared his throat. "Thinking back over your story there's something that makes me suspect someone else might have killed Lily. Since you arrived in Grand Rapids, someone has been trying to prevent you from investigating Lily's death. Too many things have happened that don't make any sense. The sudden death of Rose's friend. The slashed tires, the break-in here, the runaway car. Even the attack on Waldo might be connected."

Clare sat up straight. "You think Waldo was hurt because of me?"

"I don't know, but it's possible that someone tried to come back into the house here and Waldo prevented it. For some reason he's bonded to you. He's always hanging around as if he were protecting you."

"I feel like a Jonah," Clare said. "Erika was in danger because of me and now Waldo. Maybe even Margee."

"It's always dangerous when you dig into the past."

"Do you think that all of this is just to make me drop the investigation and go home?"

After a pause, Jake said, "I think it's more serious than that. If Jimmy Newton didn't kill Lily then I think the murderer is trying to keep anyone from uncovering the truth. What does Nate have to say about it?"

"Nate thought it was someone trying to prevent me from uncovering a secret. Something unconnected with the actual murder that could be discovered during an investigation," Clare said. "We even went to talk to Chief Fogt. He said he'd look into some of the things, but I don't think he was convinced that I wasn't just a little paranoid. He said it could all be unrelated. Coincidences."

"I don't believe that," Jake said, shaking his head.

The phone rang, sounding shrill in the room. Clare got up and answered it.

"It's me," Nate said. "I'm still in Bemidji. We'll have to postpone the pizza. Erika's sick. She was all right this morning but in the afternoon she got sick to her stomach. My sister-in-law thinks we should just stay here overnight. Erika's pretty miserable right now."

"Poor baby. Don't worry about it, Nate. Do you think it's just a twenty-four hour bug?"

"I think so. Now that she hasn't got anything in her stomach she might start to feel better. When I mentioned she should skip the clogging show tomorrow, she got mildly hysterical. I said we'd decide in the morning."

"It might just be a reaction to the other night at the logging camp. Hopefully she'll be okay. I know she's been counting on clogging," Clare said. "Give me a call tomorrow and let me know how she's doing. You'll want to keep her quiet once you get back, so why don't I just figure to meet you at the nursing home tomorrow. The show is at three, isn't it?"

"Yes. I'm sorry, Clare. I was really looking forward to seeing you."

Despite her own emotional turmoil, Nate sounded so forlorn that Clare had to smile. "I was too, but Erika comes first. Give her my love and hopefully I'll see you both tomorrow."

Clare hung up and turned back to Jake. "Erika's sick, so Nate's staying up in Bemidji for the night."

"I gathered as much. Why didn't you tell him what's been going on?"

"I didn't want to worry him." She shrugged. "It would have been too much to explain over the phone. Besides, there's nothing he can do in Bemidji, and he's already concerned about Erika."

Waldo raised his head as she returned to the couch, then flopped back down on the floor.

"I'm sorry you can't talk to Nate tonight. Although you seem to be a lot calmer than when I got here. Do you think you can hold it together until tomorrow?"

Clare had to smile at his question. "Strangely enough, on some level, I feel as if a huge weight has been lifted off my shoulders. I know I should be frightened at the possibility that Lily's murderer is still alive. However it far outweighs the pain of believing that my father is a murderer."

At the mention of her father, a cloud of despair washed over her.

"If my father didn't kill my mother, why did he confess to the crime and run away?"

"I don't know, Clare."

"What if he found me with the gun and believed I'd shot Lily? The same reasons would apply as when I thought I had actually killed her. He was trying to protect a four-year-old from having her life scarred if she knew what she had done."

Jake shrugged his shoulders.

"The worst part of all this is that if we're right my father literally gave up his life for me. How can I ever forgive myself for being the instrument that led to my father's death?"

"Now why on earth are you piling on more guilt? Give it a rest, girl," Jake said.

"Do you think Jimmy committed suicide?" She whispered the question, almost afraid of asking it. "Do you think he thought his sacrifice was too great and got more and more depressed after he left Grand Rapids?"

Jake's voice was gruff. "If it were me, I would think no sacrifice would be too great to keep my child safe."

"Thank you, Jake."

She blinked away a film of tears and gave the old man a watery smile.

"Try to avoid blaming yourself for any of this or you'll go nuts. I'm going to take Waldo home and feed him and then I'm going to bring him back here for the night. I don't want to spook you, but I don't like you being here all alone."

Clare was touched by the gesture.

"I feel perfectly safe here."

"I'm sure you do, but I'm not taking any chances. Until you've had a chance to talk to Nate, I'd feel a lot better having Waldo here."

He left with the dog, telling her they'd return after dinner. When Clare got hungry, she heated up soup and watched television until Jake returned.

"Waldo can stay with you tomorrow until Nate gets back," Jake said.

"Is it all right for him to be walking around outside with the sore paw?"

"The vet said he'll be protective about it for a while, but the exercise will keep him from stiffening up." Jake scratched Waldo's head and the dog pressed his body against the older man's side.

"How about his face?" Clare asked.

Jake reached in his pocket and pulled out a small bottle of pills and two plastic bags. "She gave me some antibiotics. Give him one of these capsules tonight around nine and the other one in the morning. Here's a bag of dried food you can give him in the morning. The other bag has some liverwurst in it. Tuck the pill inside a chunk of it and he'll wolf it down without even noticing."

He handed Clare the pills and the bags, holding them well above Waldo who was sniffing and wiggling as if he could coax Jake into giving it to him now. Not wanting to tease the dog, Clare put everything in the refrigerator.

"So far he's left the stitches alone," Jake said, pointing to the side of Waldo's face. "The vet said if he starts to scratch them, she'll put one of those large plastic collars on him. I'd hate to resort to such an indignity, but let me know if he starts to worry at them."

Clare smiled at Jake's defense of the dog's pride, although since he didn't object to rolling in every odorous pile, she didn't think he'd be particularly sensitive about wearing the collar. After a final rub of the dog's head, Jake left.

Most of the evening was spent watching television with Waldo curled up on the floor beside the couch. Emotionally she was drained and tried to avoid thinking about all that she had learned. She knew she'd eventually have to confront the ghosts of her past, but for the moment preferred to hold her thoughts at bay. Before she went to bed, she took Waldo outside. Back inside, she locked the doors and got ready for bed. Waldo roamed around the cottage before he finally settled on the braided rug beside the bed.

Clare lay for a long time in the dark, willing herself to fall asleep. When she finally dozed her sleep was troubled by a series of flashbacks, recollections from her childhood that she was only now remembering. She caught flashes of her mother and her father, reinforcing the feeling that they were loving people who cared deeply for her. At times she woke to find tears on her cheeks. Other times Waldo woke her and she suspected she was tossing in her sleep.

She got up once during the night when she heard the dog, whining at the back door. Tiptoeing out to the main room in the dark, she found Waldo sprawled by the back door. His big head rested on his paws and his tail swished back and forth on the floor. Moving to the side of the window, she peeked outside. She covered her mouth to hold back a scream when she saw someone on the porch. She understood Waldo's complacence when she recognized Jake in the chaise lounge.

Creeping back to the bedroom, she crawled under the covers, shivering at the realization that the old man thought she needed protecting. Hearing Waldo's nails clicking on the wooden floor as he came back into the room, she sighed. Between Jake and Waldo, she was perfectly safe.

During the night, thunder rumbled over the lake but the rain held off. Morning brought a pileup of storm clouds overhead and air that was thick with humidity.

She'd gone to bed at ten thirty and slept on and off until seven o'clock. Eight and a half hours. She felt more tired than she had the night before. She sat on the side of the bed and stared down at the floor. Waldo lumbered to his feet and headed toward the back door. Snatching up her mandarin bathrobe, Clare slipped on her sandals and opened the back door half expecting to see Jake asleep on the porch. The chaise lounge was empty.

"Don't go far, Waldo," she said, as she stood on the porch overlooking the lake.

The water was gunmetal gray and the wind whipped the surface into a heavy chop. It might not be raining now, but she smelled the imminence in the thickness of the air. As if she'd conjured up the storm, a jagged bolt of lightning flashed across the sky, accompanied by a sharp crack of thunder. Raindrops plopped down on the steps to the porch.

"Come on, Waldo," she called.

The dog raised its head as if deciding whether to obey the command. The rain was getting heavier and another crash of thunder brought him hobbling up to the porch. Back inside, Clare rubbed his back with a dishtowel before he could shake himself dry.

"Such a good dog," she said.

Lifting his ear, she surveyed the sutures and was pleased that they looked pink and dry. He began to wriggle the moment she opened the refrigerator and took out the plastic bags and the pill bottle. She wedged the second capsule in the last piece of liverwurst and tossed it to the dog. He caught it in midair and swallowed it before Clare could put the empty bag in the trashcan.

"Haven't you ever learned to savor your treats?" she asked.

Waldo's tail thumped the floor in response and Clare grinned down at him. She poured the dry dog food into a bowl and set it on the floor just as the phone rang.

"Morning," Nate said. "I hope I didn't wake you."

"I was up. I had an overnight guest and I was just making his breakfast." She paused for effect then continued. "Waldo came for a sleepover."

"You had me worried for minute, Clare. Although I have to admit, he's stiff competition. How is he doing?"

The rainstorm hit and she pressed the phone to her ear in order to hear him clearly.

"He's limping a bit but I think he'll be fine in a couple days. How's your patient?"

"I checked on her about an hour ago. She was sleeping. I felt her forehead and I don't think she's running a fever. Her stomach had settled down by the time she went to bed so I'm thinking we'll leave Bemidji when she wakes up. If she feels good the rest of the day, I'll let her participate in the clogging show."

"Oh, I'm glad. She's practiced so hard, I'd hate to see her miss it."

"Wait a second. What you said just registered. Why is Waldo there?" Nate asked, abruptly.

"Jake was here yesterday and we had a long talk. He wasn't comfortable with me staying here alone."

"What's happened, Clare?" Nate's voice was sharp. "What were you talking to Jake about?"

"Nothing has happened. It's just that some of my memories are beginning to come back. I'm getting flashes of scenes, almost like I'm being transported back in time." Hearing the silence on the line, she hurried to explain. "I know it sounds as if I'm losing my mind, but I can't define it any other way. It's sort of like I'm having a series of short daydreams."

"How does Jake enter into this?"

Clare laughed. "The poor man was unlucky enough to stop by yesterday when I was in the midst of a meltdown. You know how weepy I've been lately. Jake must have been horrified having an emotional woman on his hands. I think he figured Waldo would make a good substitute until you got back and could listen to my whining."

"Damn it, Clare, I wish I were there. Are you upset about anything in particular?"

Clare hesitated, unsure how to explain. "I found out something yesterday that might be key to the investigation," Clare said. "It's a long story and one that I'd prefer to tell you when you're here."

"I can leave anytime now."

"It'll wait, Nate. We'll have all evening to talk. I better go. It's raining like crazy here so it's hard to hear."

Thunder crashed overhead.

"Wow, I can hear the storm now. Sounds nasty," Nate said. "Stay inside with Waldo until I get back."

Before Clare could respond the phone went dead.

* * *

"Damn," Nate said, hearing the disconnect sound in his ear.

He debated calling Clare back on his cell phone but didn't really have anything more to say. He slammed the receiver down in annoyance.

"Trouble?" Susie DeFisher asked as she poured more coffee in his cup.

"The storm knocked the phone out."

"Don't glare at me, Nate. It's not my fault."

Nate gave his sister-in-law a grim smile. "Sorry. I'm out of sorts because I can't be in two places at once."

"I was just upstairs, and Erika is definitely alive and well. She was in with my girls and the three of them were on the computer. Erika was IMing someone named Cindy."

"Sounds cured to me." He sighed in relief. "Thank Greg for taking us in last night. Hope it wasn't too much trouble."

"I'm just sorry Erika was sick. The kids love it when she comes to visit. Besides, then we get a chance to see you too."

After Rebecca died Nate had made a special effort to make sure Erika saw her cousins frequently. Initially, Nate's relationship with Greg, his brother-in-law, had been strained, but eventually they'd established a real friendship. Over the years, Nate had gotten a steady stream of advice from Susie when he needed help with Erika. Nowadays she treated him like a brother and he confided in her more and more. He had talked a little bit about Clare while they watched the kids in the pool.

Nate finished his coffee and set the mug on the kitchen table. "I better get Erika moving."

"Relax. I shooed her into the shower and fixed her up with one of Megan's outfits to go home in. She threw up on hers."

"I remember. Sorry about your rug."

Susie waved her hand in dismissal. "I'm far more interested in hearing more about the new woman in your life. Erika said Clare saved her life. From what little I heard of the phone call, it sounds like you're worried about her."

"I am. That's why I need to get home. She didn't sound all

right on the phone. She was upset about something but said it could wait until I got home."

Although he was tempted to tell Susie the whole story about Clare, Erika and the other children swarmed into the kitchen at that moment, precluding any serious discussion.

"You look much better this morning," Nate said as he gave Erika a hug. "You even smell better."

"Oh gross! Don't remind me," she said as she flopped into a chair next to her cousins. "I'm starving."

Nate helped Susie get breakfast on the table, watching Erika for any lingering signs of illness. He was pleased when she ate jellied toast and scrambled eggs without any hesitation. His cell phone rang and after checking the display, he stepped out on the patio to take the call.

"Hi, Jon, what's up?"

"Glad I caught you." The police chief's voice was all business. "You remember the woman who died at the Farm Show? Robinson?"

"Yes." Nate's pulse quickened at the name.

"Well I just got a call from Carl Phelps, the chief over in Deer Lake. There was a fire in her condo this morning."

"Why'd he call to tell you that?"

"Because it was arson."

Chapter Twenty-Three

"Arson? Are you kidding me?" The news hit Nate like he'd been broadsided.

"I wish. The place was totally gutted. Luckily it was an end unit so it didn't spread to the rest of the building and no one was hurt. A neighbor called in the fire at three o'clock this morning."

"No chance it could have been an accident?"

"No chance in hell," Jon said. "Whoever did it broke in during the night and spread gasoline around the apartment. It was a very thorough job. Every room had been targeted."

"Do they have any idea who did it?"

"Not a clue. The brother and sister-in-law are totally devastated. The funeral was yesterday." After a pause, Jon continued. "This makes it a whole new ball game. I went over everything we talked about when you brought Clare in and I think we've got something bad going on here. It sounds as if this Robinson woman had some kind of information someone didn't want her to share with your friend. I can't think of any other reason that someone would torch her condo."

"I can't either, Jon. Can you look again at the circumstances of her death?" Nate began to pace.

"That's where I'm heading, old buddy. The coroner and I went over all the reports when she died and didn't pick up any signs of foul play. I went back over all the paperwork when you and Clare came in and I still didn't find any evidence."

"Say that again, Jon, I lost you for a minute."

"Where are you? We're having a storm here. Trees down all over and half the phones are out."

"I'm in Bemidji. It's not raining here."

"It will be soon. It's heading your way. What was I saying?"

"You said you looked over the reports after we came in to see you." Nate moved farther into the backyard where the cell signal was stronger.

"Oh, yeah. I didn't see anything. We had a witness who saw her carrying some boxes into the storeroom. The coroner said the injuries were consistent with a fall."

"Who was the witness?"

"Bianca called in after she heard it on the news."

"Even so, I don't like it."

"Me neither," Jon said. "Does Clare have any clue about what the woman wanted to talk to her about?"

"She says not. She thinks Margee was a friend of her adoptive mother. Lily Newton's sister."

"When are you coming back?"

Nate looked at his watch. "I can leave in about fifteen minutes."

"Something definitely is not right here. It all seems to center around the Newton murder. I remember your dad talking about the case. He always seemed troubled about it, even though, as far as I could see, it was a slam dunk."

"I agree. My guess is that something else was going on that's connected to the murder. The general feeling was that Jimmy followed Lily because he suspected she was meeting someone. Nobody ever looked into whom it was she was meeting. Maybe whoever it was doesn't want that fact uncovered. All this started when Clare started digging into the background of the case." The muscles in Nate's back tightened as he thought about Clare. "If only she'd been able to talk to that Robinson woman."

"I'll go back through the files and see if I can find any mention of who she was meeting." Jon paused. "You're driving right past Deer River on your way home. How would you like to stop and talk to the brother and sister-in-law?"

Grateful for any chance to be proactive, Nate jumped at the chance. Jon gave him the names and address and said he'd call them to alert them to Nate's arrival. He hung up and tried calling Clare at the cottage. He swore when he got a busy signal. He tried her cell phone, but was bumped over to voice mail. He snapped his cell phone closed without leaving a message.

After hugging Susie and the kids, he and Erika got on their way back to Grand Rapids. They were almost to Deer River when he decided he'd better explain a few things to Erika.

"I need to tell you something about Clare," he said.

"You don't have to, Dad," Erika said, a slight tremor in her voice. "I already know who she is."

Nate's hands tightened on the steering wheel as he turned his head to stare at Erika. She was slumped in her seat, head down, her bottom lip caught between her teeth.

"And how do you know that?"

"It was that first day when she was at the house. I heard you talking."

"So when you said you told your friends that Clare was investigating the murder, you actually told them who she was?"

"No, I only told Cindy that part. I said it was a secret and she couldn't tell anyone, but I think she did," she paused for a beat, then continued. "Are you mad at me, Dad?"

Considering the repercussions of her actions, he should be. However, he felt guilty that he'd been so absorbed with Clare, he'd neglected his own daughter.

"Why didn't you say something to me about it?"

"I didn't know Clare was nice," she said.

Nate couldn't help smiling at the childish outburst. He would have liked to pursue it, but they were almost at Deer River, and he needed to explain why they were stopping to talk to Miss Robinson's brother and his wife. He didn't want to frighten her so he glossed over the possibility that Margee's death might not have been an accident. It was awkward having Erika along, but he felt an urgency to talk to the Robinsons. The rain started just as they arrived. He asked Erika if she would prefer to wait in the car.

"No. I want to stay with you," she said.

Her voice was subdued and she clung to his hand as they waited at the front door. A sprightly white-haired woman let them in. "I'm Posey Robinson. Chief Fogt said you'd be coming. Come in before you get wet."

Nate introduced Erika and followed her out to the family room where her husband was seated. His outstretched leg was encased in a cast that rested on an upholstered bench.

"Tripped on the damn cat," he said, by way of explanation.

While his wife fussed over Erika, getting her a soft drink and finding her a comfortable chair, Bill Robinson told Nate about the fire. In his turn, Nate described Clare's meeting with Margee and the reason behind his visit.

"Clare gathered that Margee was in touch with her mother, Rose Prentice. I wondered if she ever mentioned her."

"Can't say I recall the name," Bill said, "and I knew all her friends. Dated most of them."

"Prentice might have been her married name," Nate said.

"You must mean Rose Gundersen," Posey said. "Margee mentioned that she'd changed her name after the murder. Rose never married. Neither did Margee. I think that's why they remained such good friends all those years when Margee was in China. They went to school together, you know. It's funny you should mention her. Margee mentioned her a week or so ago. Seemed stunned that she'd run into Rose's daughter."

The old man picked up a ruler from the table beside his chair. Sticking it inside the cast, he rubbed it back and forth.

"Damn cast itches like a bad case of the chiggers." He withdrew the ruler and leaned back in his chair. Suddenly his face lit up.

"Rose Gundersen. She was the sister of the woman who was killed in Grand Rapids. I told Margee time and again that she ought to stay away from her. She was too wild. Easy, if you know what I mean," he said, with an apologetic nod of his head toward Erika.

"You're too hard on her," Posey said. "I think she fell into a bad crowd when she was in high school."

"Rumors swirled around that girl." Robinson waved the ruler to emphasize his words. "Her family said she was going away to a fancy school but everyone said she'd gotten . . ."

"In the family way," Posey interjected, with another nod toward Erika. "Whether it was true or not there was no evidence of any—um, progeny. Besides, look how well she turned out. According to Margee she'd found religion and had totally turned her life around."

"Wait." It was Nate's turn to interrupt. "I'm a little confused here as to which sister you're talking about. Lily was the wild one who was sent away?"

"No. Not Lily." Posey shook her head, her mouth in a frown. "Rose was the wild one. She was the one there were all the rumors about."

"Girl had heels rounder than ball bearings."

"Bill!" Posey cried. "Remember the child."

Erika looked totally confused, her head swinging back and forth between the Robinsons as if she were watching a tennis match. Nate wondered what kind of questions she'd have on the ride home.

"Let me see if I have this straight," he said. "Rose was Margee's friend and she was the wild sister?"

"That's right," Posey said, beaming at him as if he were an extraordinarily bright child. "That's why it came as such a shock to all of us when it was Lily who was murdered. After all, the boys at the dance got into a fight over Rose."

Nate felt like he'd been sucker punched. "The fight was about Rose? Are you sure?"

"Positive. I was waiting up for Margee when she got home that night." Bill scratched his bare toes with the ruler. "I was madder than—um, all get out because she took my car after I told her not to. Her car was in the body shop because she'd had an accident. I didn't want her tearing up my car. Speaking of wild. That girl was long on attitude in those days."

Nate tried to get back on track. "All the newspaper reports

said that Jimmy had gotten into the fight because he was jealous that some guy was hitting on Lily."

"Newspapers never get things right," Robinson said dismissively. "All I can tell you is what Margee said. She said Rose's old boyfriend was making a play for her again and Jimmy Newton took a swing at him."

All through the rainstorm, Clare had flashes of memory. Each time she touched something, she would get a picture of another time and place when she had a similar object in her hand. The only time she was free of the mind pictures was when she was stroking Waldo's fur. Eventually she curled up on the couch, keeping one hand on the dog, and went to sleep.

When she woke up, the rain was gone and the sun was shining in the front window. She opened the front door and walked outside. Waldo followed her, limping down the stairs. He sniffed his way around the yard as she breathed in the air, thick with the smell of rain.

Waldo barked and she saw Jake's gaunt figure coming through the line of trees along the shore. The dog hobbled over, greeting the old man with a wriggling body and a slobbering kiss. Jake leaned over and inspected the side of his face, then patted his side and strolled across the grass to the porch.

"I'd have called, but your phone's still out," Jake said. "I came by earlier. I looked in the window and saw you were sleeping so I figured I'd just let you be for a while."

Waldo padded up the stairs, brushing Jake's side.

"Go lie down, Waldo. You're all wet."

Before they could move, the dog shook his whole body, spraying both Clare and Jake with water.

"I'll get a towel," Clare said, laughing at the annoyance on Jake's face.

She brought out a bath towel and, after drying himself off, Jake rubbed down the dog. "Hope he hasn't been any trouble."

"He was nice to have around. I'm not sure he's much of a

watchdog since he didn't bark when you took up your post outside last night."

Jake ducked his head, avoiding any comment. "I just stopped at Nate's place and he's still not home. It's only an hour and a half from Bemidji, so he should be home by now."

Clare looked at her watch. "He said he was going to see how Erika was doing before he left. I'm meeting them over at the Itasca Nursing Home. Let me check my phone. He said he'd call if she wasn't well enough to clog."

Reaching in her purse, she pulled out her cell phone. She checked for voice mail. "That's good. There's no message so that means Erika is over her stomach flu."

"Then I'll take the dog off your hands. I'm having an early dinner at Ruth's today. She doesn't let Waldo in the house under the best of circumstances. Just imagine her expression if she found a wet, smelly dog on her doorstep. I've got plenty of time to run him home."

"Thanks for everything, Jake."

She leaned over and kissed his cheek. She wondered if he was offended by the personal gesture because he jerked away as if he'd been hit with an electric prod. He lifted a hand and waved it as he headed along the shoreline with the dog.

Looking down at her water-spattered clothes, she went into the bedroom to change. She pulled out a maroon, teal, and black striped dress that Nate hadn't seen before. She slipped it on. It was empire-waisted with a smocked tube top that accentuated her breasts without being overly sexy. The flared skirt was finished off with a ruffled hem. Feminine and flirty, she decided as she checked her reflection in the mirror.

She checked out the window, spotting the puddles left behind after the rain. Putting away her sandals, she slipped on black ballet flats with soft rubber soles. She took off the chain she'd been wearing and hunted through her jewelry box. She pulled out a silver replica of a Hershey's kiss on a delicate chain. Hooking on the matching earrings, she took one last look in the mirror.

Staring at the silver kiss, she could feel her consciousness sliding back in time. She was back in the boathouse, her mind flooded with memories. There was a rubber raft that stood in the corner and piles of beach towels. A set of oars was propped up against a canoe. She remembered that she wasn't supposed to be near the boathouse but she'd snuck in whenever she got the chance. She remembered one time peeking in the window and seeing a boy and a girl kissing.

Another time she'd almost been caught. She'd actually been inside and hid behind the raft when she heard someone coming. She remembered it was Rose. She came into the boathouse and put something into a metal box underneath the floor boards. After Rose left, she crept out and pulled up the box. She could remember the disappointment she'd felt when she discovered a letter. Since she couldn't read, she'd jammed it back into the box and put it back in the floor.

The vision faded and Clare stood holding the top of the dresser. She was shaken by this latest vision. It was much more real than the others had been. The memories were returning strongly now. Eventually she'd be able to look at each scene and not be so frightened of the past.

She wondered if the box was still in the boathouse. After all this time, would the letter still be in the box?

Checking the time, she realized that Jake had only been gone fifteen minutes and she still had an hour before she had to be at the nursing home. She picked up the phone on the counter to call Nate, but the line was still dead. Since she was all ready, she might as well go over to Nate's and they could go together. Grabbing her purse, she locked up the house and ran up the path.

She was almost at the top when she caught the toe of her shoe on the edge of one of the flagstones. Sprawling forward, she went down hard, landing on her hands and knees.

Taking a moment to assess her injuries, she was relieved that she hadn't broken any bones or twisted an ankle. Her knee was cut. Blood ran down her leg as she stood up. Reaching into her purse she brought out some tissues and pressed them on the cut.

She sucked in her breath at the burning sensation. Gritting

her teeth, she waited a minute and then pulled the tissue away. It was just a surface cut, bleeding profusely but not very serious. She shook her head as she accepted the fact she would be adding another scar to the knee.

It was the same knee she'd injured the night she fell in the boathouse, and it was the same knee she'd cut when she fell at the logging camp. It was definitely a bad omen for the rest of the evening.

Chapter Twenty-Four

"Can you make us some sandwiches, Erika?" Nate asked, as they arrived back at the house. "I need clean clothes and then I've got to check on a couple things. It won't take long and we'll take off for the nursing home."

"Do you care if it's peanut butter and jelly?"

"I don't care if it's liver and onions," he said, cutting through the kitchen. "I'm starving and we won't get anything to eat until after your show."

Upstairs he put on a fresh knit shirt and a clean pair of khakis. Grabbing a light sports jacket, he hurried back downstairs. Once in the office, he picked up the phone and cursed when he found it dead. Even though the rain had stopped, the storm must have brought down several phone lines. He wondered if the service was out all around the lake. Using his cell phone, he tried to reach Clare's cell, but it automatically jumped to voice mail. He didn't want to leave a message. He wanted to talk to Clare.

He cleared off his desk, then picked up the box of old files he'd brought from the police station and set it on his desk chair. He draped his sports jacket over the back of the chair and opened the flaps on the box, just as Erika entered with lunch.

"Thanks, honey," he said, taking the plate from her hand.

"I brought you a cold beer too."

"What a good daughter you are." He grinned as she set the bottle down on the corner of his desk. "I suspect child welfare might consider me a bad father because you know I prefer beer over milk."

"Well, duh!" she said. "Do I have enough time to IM Cindy?"

"Yes, but you can't tell her anything that you heard today. First we have to talk to Clare. Understood?"

"If Clare says it's okay, then can I tell Cindy?"

"We'll see."

"Oh, Dad. That almost always means no."

"Get your costume on and then you can go online. I'll give a holler when I'm ready to leave."

After Erika left, Nate took a long swallow of the beer, sighing in pleasure. He munched the sandwich as he began removing each item from the box. He perused it to get a general sense of what it was, then set it in the pile on his desk.

He'd called the police station after his interview with the Robinsons. Jon stated that he'd reopened the investigation on Margee's death in light of the arson. In his turn, Nate promised to skim through the contents of the files to see if he could spot anything unusual. Since he didn't know what he should be looking for, he thought it was a time waster. However, since he had some time, it would be the perfect project to keep him from worrying about Clare.

It was a slow process and he wasn't even a third of the way into the box when he picked up a newspaper clipping from the Prairie du Chien, Wisconsin newspaper. It was the article written after the train had killed Jimmy Newton. The names of the men who witnessed the accident or suicide were circled at the bottom of the page.

Fred Rea and J. Jorgenson.

Nate crumpled the paper in his hand.

J. Jorgenson. Jake Jorgenson?

Was it possible that Jake was the same man who had witnessed Jimmy Newton's death?

Jamming the clipping in his shirt pocket, he grabbed his jacket and tore out of the office to the bottom of the stairs.

"Erika, we have to leave now."

"But, Dad, we're way early," came her shouted reply.

"We have to make a stop on the way. Don't forget your shoes."

He paced the kitchen until Erika came clattering down the stairs. Remembering to tell her how cute she looked, he hustled her out the door and back into the car. She was barely buckled into her seat when he swung the car around in a spray of gravel and drove to Jake's house. Not finding him at home, he became concerned about Clare.

"Is something wrong, Daddy?"

Realizing she only called him Daddy when she was upset, Nate smiled to reassure her.

"We'll go and pick up Clare," he said. "We've still got plenty of time."

He tried to keep to the speed limit as he raced toward Heart's Content. He pulled into the driveway and swore when he saw that Clare's car was gone. In the spot closer to Ruth's house, was Jake Jorgenson's old Honda.

"We're going to see Ruth," Nate said, shutting off the engine and jerking open the car door.

With Erika behind him, he hurried across to Ruth's door and rang the bell. When she opened it, he brushed past her, stalking into the living room to confront Jake. Without a word, he reached into his shirt pocket and handed the older man the clipping.

"Ah," Jake said with a shuddering breath.

"What in the name of all that's holy is going on, Nate?" Ruth said, coming into the living room with Erika behind her.

"Jake has some explaining to do," Nate said.

He watched myriad expressions cross the older man's face and for a moment felt sorry for him. He turned his head and spotted the painting on the mantel. He recognized it immediately. It was the picture of the girl and the dog on the dock. Nate walked over to get a closer look.

"Jake brought that for Clare." The tone of Ruth's voice was a reflection of her confusion. "Is that what you want him to explain?"

Nate peered at the completed painting. It was definitely Jake's best. The colors glowed and breathed life into the subjects. At any minute the dog would move or the girl would laugh. Nate caught his breath as he studied the features of the child. It was Clare.

It was Clare as a child of four. Painted with the loving hand of a father. In a flash everything became clear. Nate turned. Jake had a curious smile on his face. He straightened his shoulders and nodded.

"Yes. I'm Jimmy Newton."

Chapter Twenty-Five

Clare's heart sank when she pulled in the driveway and realized that Nate and Erika hadn't returned. They must have gotten a later start and planned to go directly to the nursing home. She smacked the steering wheel with her open hand in annoyance.

She pulled out her cell phone only to discover her battery was dead. For one moment, she wanted to throw it out the window but after a steadying breath, she plugged it into the charger and waited. This wasn't a good start to the evening, she thought, looking down at her knee. At least the bleeding had stopped.

She stared at the house. There wasn't much left of the original house except the screened porch. She closed her eyes and tried to picture the house when she was living in it. In a flash an old memory clicked in, everything crystal clear as if she were reliving it.

It was the creak of the floorboards that woke her. She lay still on the couch in the living room, listening to the tap of footsteps crossing the screened porch beyond the open window. She scrambled upright until she could peer over the back of the couch. She recognized her mother just as she heard the unmistakable click of the screen door latch.

Where's Mommy going?

She didn't have a stomachache anymore and she didn't want to stay alone in the dark. She jumped off the couch and slipped her feet into the pink fuzzy slippers that matched her bathrobe. In the moonlight, she spotted her doll at the end of the couch, her blonde curls sticking out above the afghan. She took a grip on her hair and pulled the doll into her arms and headed for the door.

"Matilda, wake up. We have to go with Mommy," she said, whispering into the doll's ear. "We have to be quiet."

Tiptoeing across to the door, she turned the handle. The hinges squeaked and she slipped through the opening, pulling the door closed behind her. Her slippers made soft, shushing sounds as she crossed to the steps. She squinted in the darkness. A flash of lightning cut across the sky and she saw her mother's white dress as she started down the path into the woods. She opened her mouth to call out.

"No, Matilda. We can't wake Daddy."

She ran across the grass to the tree line. The reddish wood chips made the path easy to find. She'd helped Daddy put the new mulch down. It had taken a long time to spread it all the way to the boathouse. The pine bark was soft underfoot. Moonlight filtered through the cover of trees and she quickened her pace.

"We have to catch Mommy."

She skipped along, but when she didn't see anyone ahead she paused. Branches waved above her, scraping against each other in the rising wind. She jumped at the loud snap of a breaking limb. The sky lit up with another flicker of lightning and it started to rain. She hurried along the trail, hugging the soft body of the doll against her chest.

"Don't be a baby, Matilda," she whispered. "You're a big girl now. Big like me. I'm not scared."

The sleeve of her bathrobe snagged on the branch of a bush. She snatched her arm away and folded both arms over the doll, holding her tight against her body. Her breath made short hissing sounds as she pressed her face into Matilda's hair. Her heart beat loudly in her ears.

"Oh, Mommy. Where are you?"

Ahead the trees began to thin out. She ran to the end of the path, stopping at the edge of the clearing. She looked through the rain at the dark outline of the boathouse. She released her breath in a whoosh of air as she saw the patch of flickering light in the window.

"See, Matilda. Mommy's in the boathouse."

She stepped into the clearing. A loud pop split the silence of the night. Two sharp cracks followed. She turned to run back to the house, but the trees had closed in behind her. She squinted in the rain, but couldn't see the path.

"Mommy," she cried as she whirled around and ran toward the boathouse.

She clutched Matilda, pressing her against the place where her heart was hammering. A rowboat was tied up to the wooden walkway. Her slippers slid on the wet decking that surrounded the boathouse. She fell, cutting her knee. Whimpering, she limped along the decking. She could see a patch of light inside the door.

"Mommy!" She cried out, hurling herself into the room.

Thunder crashed overhead. She screamed. In the flickering light of a candle, images stood out starkly. The pirate face. Red spots on the white dress. Aunt Rose's letter box.

Within the circle of light, halfway between the candle and her slippers, lay a gun.

Tucking Matilda securely under her arm, she leaned over and picked up the gun. She used both hands to hold it. It was heavy, the metal cold against her fingers. She held it sideways, staring down at it. She knew the gun. It was Daddy's.

The door behind her slammed against the wall. The wind snuffed the candle and the room plunged into darkness. Her fingers tightened on the gun.

The explosion startled her and the flash of light and the darkness that followed blinded her. Her ears rang with the closeness of the gunshot and for a moment she was deaf. She staggered backward and dropped the gun. Matilda slipped from her grasp.

A beam of light shot through the doorway, pinning her to the floor. Ears still ringing she heard a voice from a long way off.

"Abby? Abby? What have you done?"

Clare sat motionless in the car, the voice still echoing in her head. Her hands gripped the steering wheel as if it was her lifeline to reality.

After all these years, she had seen the night of the murder

played out from start to finish. She had no doubt that what she had witnessed had wiped out her memory. She replayed the scene in the boathouse over and over in her head to be absolutely certain of what she had seen. There was no mistake.

In the fluttering light of the candle, she had seen Lily lying on the floor of the boathouse. The front of her dress was covered in blood. The gun was lying beside her mother. There was blood on her nightie, but she thought that was from her fall outside on the decking. No wonder she couldn't remember where she got that scar. It all went back to the night of the murder.

Jake was right. Her mother was already dead when she fired the gun.

Was the voice she heard calling her Rose's?

If so, it was the scenario she'd described to Jake.

Rose must have found her missing from the house and gone searching for her. When she found her in the boathouse with the gun beside her and Lily Newton's body on the floor, she would have assumed that she shot her mother. Like falling dominos, each event after that would have precipitated the next.

If Rose thought she killed Lily, she would have told Jimmy. Jimmy would have tried to protect her by sending her away and confessing to the murder. Each subsequent action the result of normal human reaction.

There were two questions in her mind. The first was, could she trust her memory?

She'd had so many versions of the boathouse dream. Each time a vital element changed or was added. This time the metal letterbox was added. Were the box and the pirate just part of her fantasy or were they real? She needed to know if what she had witnessed was the truth.

The second question was more frightening. Did Jimmy Newton kill her mother after all?

Someone had been in the boathouse before she arrived. She had heard the three shots when she was outside. Was it possible that her father believed that Lily was having an affair and came to confront the lovers? He might have brought the gun to scare them, but a struggle ensued and Lily was shot.

It was obvious she didn't want her father to be guilty of murder. She wanted to believe that someone else had killed her mother.

Too agitated to remain cooped up in the car, Clare got out and paced around Nate's gravel driveway. Suddenly it occurred to her. In the newspaper articles she had read, the boathouse was never mentioned. No crime scene was ever indicated. If there was any evidence to prove her father's guilt or innocence, it might still be in the deserted building.

Clare glanced at her watch. It was two thirty. So deep in her own thoughts, she had completely forgotten about Erika's show. If she went to the boathouse, she'd never get back to the nursing home in time. Nate would be worried when she didn't show up.

Opening the car door, she leaned in and picked up her cell phone. She punched in Nate's number but there was no answer. He must have turned his off.

"Hi, Nate. Tell Erika I'm sorry I'm going to miss her performance. I'm at your place. There's something I have to check on. I'll meet you here after the show."

She dropped the phone on the front seat and put her car keys in the ashtray. She popped the trunk. After the tire-slashing incident, she'd put a few things in the trunk in case of another emergency. She pulled up the carpet covering the spare tire, and grabbed the flashlight and a screwdriver from the wheel well. At least she'd be able to pry the boards off the door. Too bad she hadn't put a pair of sneakers in the car, but at least she didn't have sandals on this time.

Slamming the trunk of the car, she headed for the woods.

Chapter Twenty-Six

"Yes. I'm Jimmy Newton," Jake repeated, his voice loud in the silent room.

Erika hurried over to Nate. He put his arm around her, but he didn't take his attention off Jake. Ruth staggered to a chair and sat down.

"Are you all right?" Jake asked. He smiled at her when she appeared startled by the question. "I'm still the same person you knew a few minutes ago. It's just a name change."

"Did you kill Lily Newton?" Nate asked, locking gazes with Jake.

Erika's arms tightened around his waist and he squeezed her shoulder to reassure her.

"No."

It was just one word spoken without a hint of reservation. Jake didn't move, waiting for a sign from Nate. He noticed that the older man stood taller and seemed to have shed the air of shyness that had been a part of his persona ever since Nate met him. There was even a hint of a smile in his eyes that indicated his awareness that he was being judged.

"Does Clare know?" Nate asked.

Jake shook his head, running a hand up through his white hair. "I wanted to tell her yesterday, but she was already upset and I didn't want to send her into another emotional guilt trip."

Nate shifted restlessly. He had so many questions that he didn't know where to begin. Jake seemed to sense his dilemma.

"I think it might help if I told you about the night of the murder. My question for you, Nate, is whether you want Erika hearing all this."

Nate's arm tightened around Erika. He could see the curiosity written so clearly on her upturned face. He'd like to protect her from all the ugliness in the world, but it wasn't possible. He led Erika over to the couch and sat down next to her.

"She'll hear it via the grapevine so I'd rather she hear it with me."

Jake nodded his head. He walked to the mantel, staring for a moment at the painting of Clare. Then he turned and Nate could see the pain carved in the lines of his face. No matter what the man had done, he'd suffered for it.

"It was the Fourth of July. It was a hot and muggy Saturday. Lily's sister Rose had come up from Minneapolis for the weekend. The three of us were going to a dance over in Bovey. I wasn't keen on leaving Abby with a babysitter."

"You mean Clare?" Erika asked.

Jake chuckled. "Sometimes it's hard for me to remember her name is Clare. In my heart, she'll always be Abby."

He swallowed several times and cleared his throat before he could continue.

"I wasn't happy taking Rose with us. I wasn't all that fond of her. She'd been very popular in high school and college. She ran with a very fast crowd and ended up getting pregnant in her twenties. She was living in Minneapolis at the time. I don't know any of the details but, according to Lily, Rose miscarried and had to have a hysterectomy."

"What a shame at such a young age," Ruth said. "Had she wanted children?"

"Yes. It was her one saving grace. Wild as she was, she loved children and adored Abby." He smiled. "We piled in the car and drove to Bovey. It was a wonderful evening. Lily loved to dance. If I'd known it was our last evening together I would have danced every dance with her."

His voice broke and Nate could almost sense the pain at

reliving Lily's last hours. He felt a lump in his own throat and drew Erika closer to his side.

"There was a makeshift bar outside the hall and I drank a good bit that night. It was getting late when Lily came to get me. She said she wanted to go home. Rose's friend had overheard Rose making plans to meet her old boyfriend. She was worried about Rose getting back into that relationship again."

"Was Rose's friend Margee Robinson?" Nate asked.

"Yes. I didn't recognize the name when I heard that she had died at the Farm Show. I didn't make the connection until Clare and I were talking yesterday."

Nate thought Jake might say more, but one glance at Erika and he shook his head, returning to the story.

"In my drunken state, I went in search of Rose. I found her outside. She was in a heavy clinch with a man I assumed was her old boyfriend. I pulled them apart and then the fight started. It was Big Red Wiklander. We were both pretty drunk and threw a lot of wild punches, occasionally connecting, until we were pulled apart.

"Lily drove home. I sat in the front seat nursing a nosebleed. Rose sat in back crying. When we got home, Abby was on the couch in the living room sleeping. The babysitter had taken her to see the fireworks and apparently let her eat a lot of junk. She'd been sick to her stomach, but wasn't running a fever. She was all tucked up with her blanket and her doll."

"I was sick yesterday," Erika said, "but I'm all better now."

It surprised Nate that Erika seemed so at ease in a situation where the adults in the room were practically vibrating with tension. His gaze crossed Jake's and he could see that the man had sensed the same thing.

"I'm glad you are." Jake continued, "I went to bed after checking on Abby. What I didn't know until later, when Rose told me, was that Lily was furious with her. Lily accused Rose of making arrangements to meet her old boyfriend in the Egner's boathouse. That's over at the youth camp. It's the place we talked about when you and Clare were looking at the paintings. Right along the edge of Nate's property, Ruth," he said by way of explanation.

"I've seen the boathouse," Erika said. "It's all boarded up and really spooky now."

Jake began to walk around as if he were too restless to stay in one place.

"Lily told Rose she couldn't go. Rose said, no matter what had happened before she still loved him and couldn't stay away. Lily was furious and slapped her. According to Rose, Lily went to the linen closet and took down the box with my gun in it. She told Rose to go to bed because she intended to put a scare into 'that man.' Rose was so frightened, she agreed. That was the last time Rose saw Lily alive.

"At one in the morning, Rose woke me. She was sobbing, unable to speak. Abby was standing in the bedroom doorway, blood on her nightgown and her hands. I examined her and found a nasty cut on her knee but that didn't account for the amount of blood. When Rose was able to talk, she said it was Lily's blood. Lily had been shot."

Jake put his hand on the mantel, his distress readily apparent in his bowed head and slumped shoulders. No one spoke. After a minute or two, he began to pace again.

"The storm woke Rose and she got up to close the window behind the couch in the living room where Abby was sleeping. She was worried that the child might get wet. When she discovered both Abby and Lily missing, she got a flashlight and started down the trail. She ran into Bianca bringing Abby back to the house. Bianca was distraught. She'd heard gunshots in the direction of the boathouse. She'd rowed there and found Abby beside Lily. When she asked her what happened, she kept repeating, 'I shot the gun. It went boom. It went boom.' "

"Oh, dear God! Clare shot her mother." Ruth covered her mouth with her hand.

"Poor Clare," Erika cried, burying her head against Nate's chest. He tightened his grip on her, patting her back as he stared at Jake.

"No wonder she lost her memory," Nate said.

"I'll tell you more later, but for the moment you just need to know Clare did not shoot her mother. She thought she did, but her memories turned out to be faulty. I repeat. Clare did not shoot Lily."

Erika clapped her hands. Ruth smiled across at Nate and even Jake looked amused at her childish enthusiasm. Nate suspected that Erika viewed the retelling of the murder almost as if she were listening to the plot of a book.

"Like you," Jake said, "I assumed Abby had killed Lily. I couldn't bear for her to live with that knowledge. I told Rose to clean up Abby and I raced down to the boathouse where Bianca was waiting. Lily was lying on the floor. My gun beside her."

"If I had only myself to worry about, I'd have called your dad, Nate. I couldn't risk putting Abby in the glare of the media. I knew there would be traces of evidence in the boathouse. So I wrapped Lily in beach towels and put her in Bianca's boat. I rowed across the lake. I found a grassy spot where I could leave her."

Ruth was crying softly and Erika's body shook against Nate. He couldn't conceive the pain that Jake must have felt, leaving his wife on the shore. The return to the boathouse must have been hellish. Jake cleared his throat several times before he could continue.

"I erased my footprints and rowed across the lake. By the time I got back, Bianca had cleaned up the boathouse. She'd scrubbed the blood off the floor and scattered other things around so that you wouldn't know that anyone had been there. She said she'd thrown the gun as far out in the lake as she could. I told Bianca that I planned to send Abby away and she agreed it was the only thing to do. I added the floor rags to the bundle of beach towels. Outside she put the padlock back on the door and I helped her into the rowboat. Then I went home."

"So Bianca's known all along about Clare," Nate said.

"She's known about Clare's involvement in Lily's death," Jake said. "I don't think she knows that Clare and Abby are the same person."

"She does too," Erika said.

"You told her?" Nate asked.

"No, it happened by accident. She was snooping. I was telling Cindy about Clare. Miss Egner's always listening to us when we're at rehearsal. And then she tells Pastor Olli and he gives you one of those looks. You know what I mean, Dad."

"Having been on the receiving end of his famous disapproving looks, I know exactly what you mean." Looking up at Jake, he said, "I remember reading that you'd burned something in the fireplace. The newspapers mentioned how suspicious it was on such a hot night. Did you burn the towels?"

"The towels and rags used to clean up. My clothes had blood on them from holding Lily. And Abby's nightgown, robe, and slippers. It was three o'clock in the morning by the time the fire was out." He looked at Nate. "I called your father at home and told him Lily was missing. It was agony knowing where she was and not being able to tell them where to look. Luckily she was found quickly. During the night, Rose and I had worked out a reasonable plan. She was to take Abby to Minneapolis. She wouldn't go back to her place, but go to Ruth's brother, Owen, instead."

"I gathered from Clare that he was involved," Ruth said. "Now I understand why."

"We were good friends. I'd known him in Minneapolis, and I knew he was moving to Chicago. I called him and he agreed to help Rose and Abby disappear. He handled all of the paper work —property sales and adoption papers. Thank God, Rose owned the house here, since I wouldn't have been able to sell it. Owen did everything he could to help. As soon as I was convinced Abby was safe, physically and financially, I left Grand Rapids."

A heavy silence filled the room. Questions flitted through Nate's mind but he knew most of them would be answered eventually. For the moment, Clare was uppermost in his thoughts.

"What convinced you that Clare didn't shoot Lily?"

"You know that dream she's been having?"

"The one where she's running through the woods?"

"Yes. It's what I think is called a recovered memory or something similar. Her memory was coming back. She remembered picking up and firing the gun. She remembered the sound of the gun going off and her falling down. When I pressed her, she said she'd fired the gun once. Just once."

"Ah," Nate said.

Ruth and Erika looked at him in confusion.

"Lily Newton was shot three times," he explained. "I'm curious as to how you became Jorgenson and why you came back to Grand Rapids."

"I'd gone to Wisconsin after I left Grand Rapids. I lived mostly on the fringes of big cities or in small towns. I tried to bury myself in work. Physical labor so I'd be tired at night and could sleep. I had no plan. I just moved from place to place when life got unbearable. Actually, the day I died was a good one. I'd been ice fishing."

Nate grinned, reminded of how Jake had tried to introduce him to the joys of ice fishing. The only part of it he'd enjoyed was standing on the ice with other men, talking and drinking coffee, laced heavily with whiskey.

"A fella I'd met on the ice that day and I were walking back to town. We were crossing over some railroad tracks when we saw a man either slide off or jump off an embankment and get hit by a train. We raced down to see if we could help him. He was a goner. The other man was younger and said he'd go to the police if I'd stay with the body."

Jake scratched his head. "I'm not sure when the idea came to me. I took out his wallet, grateful to see his identification since no one would recognize him after the train hit him. He looked like he'd been on the road for a while. No one would know he'd even died. It occurred to me that if I died that would effectively close the murder case. There'd be no reason for anyone to look into it and Clare would be safe forever.

"I put my wallet in his pocket and took his. I took off my neck chain. I busted the clasp trying to get the medal that Lily had given me off." He reached inside the collar of his shirt and pulled out a gold medal on a chain. "I couldn't bear to leave this behind. I hooked the chain on him somehow, figuring they'd put the broken links down to the train accident. I spent the rest of the time waiting for the cops memorizing the details on his driver's license. When the cops came, Jimmy Newton was officially dead."

"Did you pay for your own grave site?" Ruth asked. "I assume that's the remains of the real Jake Jorgenson."

"Yes. I thought it was the least I could do for the man who'd given me a new life. I arranged for the funeral home here to retrieve the ashes and have him buried. Wired them the money. In his wallet, there was an obituary from the newspaper. His wife had died a year earlier in Trego, Wisconsin. I called the funeral home and the woman I talked to remembered him. It was only the wife and Jake. No kids. No other family."

"Are you also the one who's been taking care of Lily's grave?" Ruth asked. "I took Clare over to the Itasca Cemetery to see it. It pleased her."

"I never got too far away from Grand Rapids. Lily was here and I wanted to be near her. I had eventually settled in Duluth, working as a graphic designer. Three years ago I figured twenty-two years of exile was enough. It was time to come home."

"Weren't you worried that someone would recognize you?" Nate asked.

"No. According to my new ID I was six years older than Jimmy. My physical appearance was totally different. Jimmy was a hefty man with dark red hair and a beard. Pale skin from spending too much time indoors. I'd aged considerably since I left Grand Rapids. I'd lost a lot of weight and shaved off my beard. With my white hair and tanned leather skin, I was fairly certain no one would recognize me. Besides, everyone believed that Jimmy Newton was dead, so they'd never think to make the connection."

"You knew Abby was Clare," Erika said. "Does she look like her mom?"

"No. If anything she looks a little like me. I knew it was Clare at the art show because she was wearing the quartz heart necklace I'd given her mother."

"So that's why you fell out of your chair," Ruth said. "I

thought it was strange at the time because you're never that clumsy. And all the time we were in the booth you couldn't take your eyes off her. You seemed fascinated by her."

"I was. She was all grown up and so beautiful. I was stunned that she was in Grand Rapids, since we'd tried to erase the city from her memory. And she was investigating the murder. I was frightened that it would bring it all back to her. And, eventually, it did."

"Why are you telling us who you are now?" Nate asked.

"Because I'm convinced Clare is in danger. Too many strange things have happened that indicate someone is trying to stop Clare from continuing the investigation. It all started when she came to Grand Rapids. Since Clare didn't kill her mother, someone else did. I think that person is behind the attacks on Clare."

Nate stood up and confronted Jake. "What proof do we have that you didn't kill Lily? You and Bianca effectively destroyed any evidence that might establish either your guilt or your innocence. How do we know that you didn't get to the boathouse ahead of Clare and shoot Lily?"

Jake faced him unflinchingly. "If I had killed Lily, no one would be trying to hurt Clare."

Nate knew Jake was right. He too was convinced that Clare was in danger. He suspected that Margee Robinson had been murdered to keep her from talking to Clare. Even though he had found it hard to accept at the time, he believed Clare was right when she said the mystery car had tried to run her down.

"It started with Rose," Nate said. "It all started with the class ring. Everything else is distracting us from the one salient fact. Rose was meeting someone in the boathouse the night of the murder. Who was she meeting? Who was the old boyfriend?"

"I don't know," Jake said, shaking his head. "Lily knew I didn't approve of Rose so she tried to keep most of her sister's indiscretions from me. However, everyone talked about her. The names that came up most often were Big Red Wiklander, Bruce Young, and Olli Egner."

"Pastor Olli?" Nate's eyebrows rose in question.

"There were always rumors about him being a womanizer. Especially in his younger days," Jake said. "I think that's why Bianca keeps such a close eye on him. I doubt if much goes on with Olli that she doesn't know about."

"Neither Big Red nor Bruce graduated in 1962," Ruth said. "I ran off the class list. They were not in that class. Actually, Pastor Olli is the right age but he moved to Minneapolis at the end of his junior year. He didn't graduate with his class so it couldn't be his class ring."

"Dad?"

Nate had been so concentrated on Jake, he'd almost forgotten that Erika was in the room. She was shifting from foot to foot in excitement.

"What is it, honey?"

"Cindy's brother got his class ring this year and he's only a junior."

Chapter Twenty-Seven

Walking over to the door to the screened porch, Clare turned her back so that she was facing the woods and thought back to her dream to get her bearings. She walked to the edge of the woods looking for any evidence of the trail she had followed twenty-five years earlier. She wasn't surprised not to find one, but as her eyes became more adjusted to the tangle of underbrush she was able to discern a game trail. She hoped whatever animals were using the track were searching for water. Since it was heading in the general direction of the lake, she followed it.

It was rough going. She was dressed inappropriately for a woodland adventure. The straggly trees and bushes scratched her bare arms and shoulders. Elbows bent, she held her arms out, crossing them in front of her face. Flashlight it one hand and the screwdriver in the other, she took the brunt of the slashing branches on her lower arms.

The path intersected with another wider trail and walking became easier. She could sense she was going downhill, but was so busy watching her footing to make sure she didn't trip that she didn't have time to look around. The track ended at a small clearing.

Looking up, she could see a small patch of interwoven bushes. Past that was a portion of wood siding and the lake beyond. She had found the boathouse.

Once more she navigated across the rotten planks until she reached the boarded up door. She was panting in the heat and a film of sweat covered her body. She brushed the leaves and twigs off her dress and muttered at a piece of torn ruffle that hung down from the hem. Her arms and legs were covered with scratches and red welts and the cut on her knee had reopened.

Ignoring her discomfort, she drove the blade of the screwdriver under one of the boards covering the door. For leverage, she wedged the flashlight between the door and the screwdriver and pressed on the handle. Rocking the screwdriver back and forth, she heard the squeal of the rusted nails as they came away from the wood. Pulling at one end of the board, she pried it away from the frame.

Working steadily she removed the three wooden slats that had blocked access to the door. The wooden hasp holding the padlock was next.

She tried to unscrew the hasp but the screw heads were so corroded she couldn't make any progress. Once more she tried to use the screwdriver as a lever, this time with little success. She set the tools down on the deck and surveyed the building. Eyeing the boarded-up window, she shivered at the thought of having to climb through the narrow opening.

Reaching for the screwdriver lying next to the threshold, she remembered Nate's comments when he was talking about getting into the boathouse. She nudged the threshold board with the blade of the screwdriver. The board moved slightly.

She knelt down and jammed the screwdriver blade under the door at the far corner of the threshold. Shoving against the handle, she felt the threshold shift and the end slid several inches forward. Using her fingers, she pulled the entire board out from under the door. In the gap, originally covered by the threshold, lay a key.

Picking up the key, she scratched the accumulated dirt off with her fingernails. She used the hem of her dress to rub it clean. Heart pounding in anticipation, she stood up and reached for the padlock.

She swung the lock upward to expose the keyhole on the bottom. Her fingers shook as she inserted the key. It went in a quarter inch then stopped. Pressing and wiggling it, she coaxed it into the slot until it was deep in the shaft.

Taking a deep breath, she gripped the key and turned. The key was immobile.

She bent over and picked up the screwdriver. Holding it by the blade end, she hit the top of the key with the handle, driving it deeper into the slot. She cracked it several more times in frustration, missing once and hitting her thumb instead.

"Open," she shouted. "Please, God, let it open."

She smashed it two more times for good measure. She was panting with the exertion and close to tears. Once more she gripped the padlock and turned the key.

It moved.

Only a slight movement, but it had definitely moved. Her hand was sweaty and she wrapped a corner of her skirt around the key to give her better leverage. She wiggled the key in the slot, twisting it back and forth. Each turn seemed to twist the key farther in the lock. Shifting her grip on the key, she tried again.

The key turned. The body of the lock dropped, turning to the side as the bottom of the U-shaped shackle swung free.

Clare let out a half sob, half laugh as the padlock fell to the deck. She swung back the hasp and pulled on the door. It opened with a loud squeal of protest from the hinges. Picking up the flashlight, she shined it inside the boathouse.

Despite the layer of dust, the contents were the same jumble of random items that she could remember from her dream. The raft, long deflated, was a pile of cracked yellow rubber. The oars were still leaning against the wall. An old Minnesota license plate leaned against a wooden trunk. Cans and cardboard boxes, fishing tackle and rods littered the room.

Straight ahead was an old metal sign, hanging crookedly from a chain on the wall. Although covered with dust, the white skull and crossbones were still visible on the black background. A pirate scarf was tied around the head and there was a knife caught between the teeth. Above and below the pirate skull were the words: SURRENDER THE BOOTY. It was the pirate from her dreams.

"Where do I even begin?"

The words seemed to echo in the empty room. Clare stood in the doorway, her gaze running over the contents as she debated what to do next. For a starter, she could see if the metal box was still under the floor boards.

The boathouse was stifling hot. With the windows boarded up, even with the door open, there was no cross ventilation to offer any respite from the heat. She brushed away the sweat that rolled down her forehead and ran into her eyes.

She moved to the back corner of the boathouse, shining the flashlight beam along the floor. She stepped on each board, watching for any shift. Finally, the end of one board gave under the weight of her foot.

Kneeling on what was left of the rubber raft, she shined the flashlight on the floor and lifted up the loose board. In the hole between the floor joists she caught a glint of metal. Her fingers scraped against the next board, pulling it toward her until it too slid out. She reached into the hole and grabbed the edge of the metal box, turning it until she could pull it out by its short end.

She set it on the floor in front of her knees. The box was badly rusted, the remnants of orange paint in patches on the side. It was a foot long, six inches wide and four deep. The corners were rounded and a collapsible handle was on the top. It was the box that Rose had put the letter in and it was the box she had seen on the floor the night of the murder.

Fingers shaking, she reached for the latch.

Heavy footsteps tapped across the deck. A shadowy figure was silhouetted against the sunlight outside the door.

"What are you doing here?"

Chapter Twenty-Eight

"Dad! Look what time it is." Erika pulled on Nate's belt to get his attention. "I'm going to be late for the clogging show."

Nate looked at his watch. It was ten minutes to three. He'd have to leave immediately if he were to get her there on time. Clare was probably worried since they hadn't arrived. He turned to Jake.

"I need to go. We need to get Clare in on this discussion and then I think we ought to go to the police. As far as I'm concerned, you're still Jake Jorgenson. At this point I don't see that Jon Fogt needs to know any different."

He put out his hand. Jake placed one hand on his shoulder and gripped the outstretched hand with his own. The gaze they exchanged was one of mutual approval.

"The show is in about an hour. Erika and I will bring Clare back to my place. Why don't you meet us there and we'll see if we come up with some plan before we go to the police?"

In the car, Nate explained to Erika that she couldn't tell anyone about Jake's identity.

"I've been very impressed at how well you've handled yourself today. Some of what you've heard may be frightening or confusing so I hope you'll ask me questions if you're upset at all. I realize at times you think I treat you like a baby. It's only because I forget how grown up you are. Your mother would be as proud of you as I am."

"Thanks, Dad," Erika said, her voice muffled by emotion.

"And don't worry. I won't tell anyone anything that I heard. Especially about Clare. I think it was my fault that someone knew we were going to the logging camp. Miss Egner told everyone."

"Was that when Bianca overheard you telling Cindy who Clare was?"

Erika fidgeted in her seat. "Yes. I was mad about you being so nice to Clare. I said I'd like to take her some place and ditch her. I asked Cindy to think of a place we could go. Miss Egner thought I was talking about some place I thought Clare would like to go. She said I should take her to the Forest History Center. Pastor Olli said it would be closed when we got there, but Miss Egner said we could still walk around the logging village 'cause it wouldn't be dark yet."

"So Pastor Olli knew about the logging camp. Anyone else?"

"When we got out in the main room, Cindy asked her dad if she could go with us if Clare said it was okay. He said no because she hadn't practiced her scales when he told her to."

"So anyone could have heard you?"

Nate kept his eyes on the road but his mind was busy with the question of who else might have known that Clare would be going to the logging camp. And who might have waited for her on the road.

"I'm sorry about that, Dad. I won't say anything around that old snoop Miss Egner."

Nate pulled the car into the nursing home parking lot. He was amused by Erika's antipathy to Bianca.

"I should give you a fatherly warning that you shouldn't call Miss Egner an old snoop. She does so much to help Pastor Olli. She might be a bit of a gossip, but she's a nice lady."

Erika shook her head and looked over at Nate. "She's not a nice lady. I saw her kissing Pastor Olli."

Nate tried to keep from smiling at his daughter's prudish streak.

"Pastor Olli is her brother. Of course she loves him."

"It wasn't that kind of a kiss. It was like on TV. One day after school I got to clogging practice early and they were in the church office. I needed the key to the bathroom. I was outside the door and they were talking. It wasn't the kind of talk like Cindy does with her brother."

"How do you mean?" Nate was troubled by what he was hearing.

Erika folded her arms across her chest and stared at her lap. "It was like talking about bodies. Their bodies. And when I peeked through the crack in the door, Miss Egner was sitting on Pastor Olli's lap and they were kissing. Just gross!"

"I agree," Nate said quietly.

He was alarmed by this additional piece of information about the Egners. Putting it together with what they had just been talking about it made for a very troubling picture. He needed to find Clare.

"We'll talk about this later, Erika. You're going to be late."

He opened his door and looked around the parking lot. He didn't see Clare's car. Had she gotten tired of waiting? He reached in his pocket for his cell phone.

"Give me a kiss for good luck." He leaned over and gave her a hug. "Run in and get ready. I'll be right behind you."

He watched her skip along the walkway, her dance skirt bobbing up and down. Opening his phone he realized that he'd turned it off earlier. Switching over to his voice mail he listened to Clare's message.

"Hi, Nate. Tell Erika I'm sorry I'm going to miss her performance. I'm at your place. There's something I have to check on. I'll meet you here after the show."

With a curse he dialed Clare's cell phone. No answer. He didn't like the fact she had gone off on her own. He felt the danger to her was credible. Snapping his phone shut, he hurried into the nursing home. He managed to catch Erika just before the show started.

"I have to go pick up Clare, honey. I'm sorry I'm going to miss your show, but I know you'll be great. I'm going to have Mrs. Grabenbauer come to pick you up. Then we'll all go for pizza."

Even though he'd tried to keep his voice casual, Erika's eyes were wide with concern. "Is everything all right?"

"Everything's fine. Break a leg," he said, forcing a smile as he pulled on her ponytail. "I'll see you shortly."

Knowing that she was watching, he walked slowly toward the exit. Once outside he quickened his pace, crossed the parking lot, and got in the car. He called Ruth's house as he drove out of the lot. Ruth said she would leave immediately to get Erika at the nursing home, then handed the phone to Jake. After hearing that Clare was at his place, Jake agreed to meet Nate there.

By the time he reached his driveway, Nate was in a cold sweat, relaxing only when he saw both Jake's car and Clare's. It was only when he got out that he realized Clare was not there.

"Where is she?" Nate asked.

"I don't know," Jake said. "The car was empty when I got here. It's not locked. The keys are in the ashtray and the phone and her purse are inside. Everything looks all right except I found this on the floor of the car."

Jake held up a handful of bloody tissues.

"I think she's gone to the boathouse," Nate said, "but we don't know if she's alone or if she's with someone."

Nate could see the muscles in Jake's cheeks ripple with suppressed anger. The old man shoved a hand in his pocket and pulled out his car keys. Opening the trunk of his car, he reached inside and pulled out a long leather gun case. He closed the trunk and set the gun case on it, unzipping it to expose a rifle. He opened the box of ammunition and took out a handful of bullets. While he loaded the gun, Nate quickly explained.

"I think Olli killed Lily," Nate said. "Erika told me that Olli knew who Clare was and he was the one who suggested taking Clare to the logging camp. He could have slashed her tires and then waited for her to come out to the highway and tried to run her down. I think he also killed Rose's friend at the Farm Show."

"How do you figure that?"

"Jon Fogt said Bianca called in to say that she had seen

Margee go into the storeroom. I suspect she was covering for Olli."

Nate then described the kissing scene that Erika had witnessed. Jake pushed the last bullet into the chamber and snapped the bolt closed.

"If Olli's hurt her, I'll kill him," Jake said. "Can you find your way to the boathouse?"

Chapter Twenty-Nine

"What are you doing here, Clare," Bianca said.

Clare blew out her breath in relief as the older woman entered the boathouse. "You scared the life out of me. And, of course, once again you've found me trespassing."

"I thought you were going to the clogging show at the nursing home today."

"I was," Clare said, "but I wanted to check on something."

"In this old place?" Bianca set the red plastic container she was carrying down on the floor. She looked around the room, as if seeing it for the first time. "Lordy, there's a lot of junk in here."

Clare's breathing returned to normal and she tried not to look as embarrassed as she felt. "I have to apologize for breaking into the boathouse. I was looking for something. I actually do have a valid reason for coming here, but that really doesn't excuse the fact that I've entered illegally."

"Don't worry, dear. You saved me some trouble by opening up the place. I was coming down here anyway. Did you find what you were looking for?"

Bianca's voice was high-pitched as if she were excited at the possibility of a discovery. Clare was grateful that Bianca wasn't angry with her.

"Yes, I did find it." She leaned over and picked up the metal box and set it on top of a dusty spindle-legged table. The table lurched to the side and she had to grab the handle of the box to keep it from falling.

"That table used to be in my mother's sewing room. One of the legs is missing," Bianca said.

She shoved a stack of square boat cushions under the edge to steady the table. A cloud of dust swirled around and she wiped her hands on the front of her dress.

"Have you opened it?" she asked, pointing to the box.

Clare shook her head. She could feel the anticipation build as she reached for the latch. Holding the handle on the top of the box, she pressed the latch and it opened with a rusty creak. She lifted the top of the box and looked inside.

A ceramic doll in a long nightdress lay on the top.

"It's Matilda," Clare whispered.

With shaking fingers she reached in and picked up the doll. She turned it over so that she could look down at the frozen expression on the doll face. The blonde curls were tinged with brown, some of them breaking as she stroked them with her finger. The pink nightgown and bathrobe were faded and the material was splitting and fraying at the edges. There were dark brown splotches on the front of the nightgown. Stiffened blood from the night of the murder.

Clare looked up and Bianca was staring at her, her forehead puckered in question. She pressed the doll against her heart wanting to clarify everything.

"I have so much explaining to do. But first I need to tell you who I am, Bianca. I'm Lily Newton's daughter."

Bianca nodded. She pushed back the hair at her temples, leaving a streak of dust on her face. "I know who you are. I overheard Erika telling her little friend Cindy."

Although surprised that the woman had never said anything to her, she hurried to explain what she was doing. "This is where my mother was killed. Finding the doll proves it. I remember being here that night and I had Matilda in my arms."

"You came to find a doll?" Bianca said.

"No. I came to see if I could find any evidence that my father didn't kill my mother."

"Ah," Bianca said, leaning forward to look more carefully at the doll. "What kind of evidence do you think you can find after all this time?"

"I don't really know. I remembered seeing my adoptive mother, Rose, put a letter in this box and hide it under the floor. That was the first thing I was hoping to find. I still can't believe it's still here after all this time."

"It was a mail box in the old days. I found it too."

Clare held the doll tight against her and stepped around the clutter until she stood in the doorway.

"It was storming outside and I came in. My mother was lying on the floor. The gun was right there and I picked it up and it fired. If I was holding it sideways the bullet would have gone into that wall."

She ran back to the cubbyhole in the floor and picked up the flashlight. Putting the doll down, she flicked on the light. She swung it back and forth across the wall as she moved closer.

"The bullet could still be in the wall," she said.

"I doubt if you'll find it, Clare. There's really no point you know."

"What?"

Clare turned around, the beam of the flashlight angling across the floor. Bianca was standing in front of the metal box. She reached inside and pulled out a gun. Clare recognized it immediately. It was the gun that had killed Lily.

"You should have let it alone, Clare." Bianca raised the gun and pointed it directly at her. "It was so long ago. Everyone had forgotten."

"It was you?" Clare said, her fingers tightening around the flashlight. "You shot Lily?"

"Yes. I knew Rose was going to meet Olli here. This was where he always met the women who were after him. He was drinking at the dance and making a fool of himself over Rose. I gave him a sleeping pill when we got home. I came to tell her to leave him alone. It started to rain and I lit a candle. I knew the metal box was in the floor. I'd seen Rose putting love letters in it. I got the box out so I could show her that she had no secrets from me. I waited for a long time that night. Finally your mother arrived."

Clare's legs were shaking so hard that she thought she might fall down. She dropped down on an old wooden trunk, the flashlight still on, the beam a cone of light that stretched across to Bianca's feet.

"It's my father's gun, isn't it?" she asked.

"Yes. Lily brought it with her. Maybe she was planning to shoot Olli. I don't know. You're like your mother. Can't keep your nose out of other people's business. I would have made sure that Olli didn't see Rose any more. But your mother said she was going to contact the church board about Olli. I couldn't have that."

Clare was stunned that this soft-spoken woman was really a murderer. She had an aura of icy calm about her that was truly frightening.

"I tried to reason with her, but she wouldn't have any part of it. Finally I got so angry that I grabbed the gun out of her hand. She came at me then. She slapped me across the face. I was so shocked that I pointed the gun at her and pulled the trigger. I shot her twice more and she fell on the floor."

Clare covered her mouth with her hand. She wanted to cry out, but she couldn't find the strength.

"Then you came running along the deck outside," Bianca continued. "I dropped the gun on the floor. You ran in and stopped. You reached down and picked up the gun and when the wind blew the candle out you must have squeezed the trigger. You almost shot me. I was just over there in the corner."

Bianca pointed and Clare turned her head to look.

"And then it came to me. I could blame you for shooting Lily. You were too young to know any different. All the way back to the Gundersen house I told you that you'd shot the gun. When I met Rose on the trail, I told her you'd accidentally shot Lily. You were covered in blood. She believed me. She took you home and said she would send Jimmy down to the boathouse. I cleaned up everything while he took Lily's body to the other side of the lake. I put the gun and the doll in the box and put it back under the floor."

Clare shook her head back and forth. She was appalled that Bianca could have sacrificed a child's life to save her own.

"I spent my life protecting my brother from women who wanted to steal him away. I love him so much and some day he'll understand how much I've forfeited to be his partner and helpmate. He should be satisfied with me as his lover, but like most men he's weak. In the past, lustful women have led him into temptation. Most of the time a simple warning is enough to discourage them."

"Did you kill Margee Robinson?"

"Yes. She knew that Rose was going to meet Olli the night of the murder. She was the one who told your mother. I saw her at the Farm Show and I suspected she wanted to talk to you. I told her I was feeling faint and got her to go with me to the storeroom. She wasn't very strong. When we got inside, I grabbed her arm and threw her against the wall. She hit her head. I laid her out as if she'd tripped. Everyone believes it was an accident."

"Have you no remorse? No conscience?" Clare burst out. "Does Olli know what you've done?"

"Of course not. He would never condone such a thing." Bianca pursed her mouth in disapproval. "I don't intend for him to find out either."

"What will you do now?"

It was obvious to Clare that Bianca had no intention of letting her go. She had already killed twice and would have no compunction in doing it again. Clare would have to look for her best chance to escape.

"You never asked me what I was doing here," Bianca said.

She spoke conversationally, her mouth pressed into a thin-lipped smile. She walked over and unscrewed the cap on the red plastic container by the door. With the gun still on Clare, she tipped the container, letting some of the liquid splash onto the floor.

"When I found you at the camp the other day, I realized you might have been searching for the boathouse. I thought you'd be out of the way today, since you'd be going to the clogging show. I should have done this years ago."

Clare sucked in her breath at the smell of gasoline that permeated the room. It didn't take long to understand Bianca's plans for her. Whatever she did to save herself, she'd have to do immediately.

"You're crazy! You'll never get away with this."

"Get up," Bianca said, waving the gun at Clare. "Get over in that corner."

Clare pushed to her feet. She turned as if to follow Bianca's command. Taking a firm grip on the flashlight, she swung back and threw it as hard as she could at Bianca. The metal flashlight hit Bianca on the shoulder as she raised the gun to shoot. The shot was a huge explosion in the small room. Clare felt a burning sensation on her thigh and then a sharp pain.

"Clare!"

Nate's voice shouted her name and she heard running footsteps outside. She could feel blood running down her leg and fought the quivery sensation in her stomach, locking her knees to keep from falling.

"Bianca shot Lily!" she yelled. "She has the gun."

"Shut up," Bianca said. She charged across the floor and jammed the gun into Clare's side.

"It's all over, Bianca. Now that Nate knows, everyone will know what you've done. Even Olli will know."

Bianca's body jerked and the gun barrel pressed deeper into her side. Clare held her breath, knowing that one wrong move would end her life. Looking outside, she could see Nate standing on the deck, arms raised as a sign of surrender.

"Bianca," Nate shouted. "All I want is Clare. Give her to me and you're free to go."

Chapter Thirty

"Let Clare go, Bianca!" Nate shouted.

Blood pounded in Nate's temples. He had raced along the path toward the boathouse, stumbling to a halt when he heard the gunshot. Fear for Clare tore through him as he waited for a reply. He was stunned that it had been Bianca who was the author of so much pain and had brought such devastation to so many lives. Turning his head to look at Jake, he could see the same disbelief on the older man's face.

"Bianca! Release Clare and you're free to go," he repeated.

Jake cocked his head and sniffed the air. "I smell gas." He spoke softly so that his voice didn't carry inside the boathouse.

"I can see what looks like a gas can just inside the doorway," Nate whispered. "Bianca must be planning to burn the place down. Can you see either Clare or Bianca?"

"No. They're out of my sight line. We've got to get Clare out of there." There was urgency in Jake's voice. "In this heat, the fumes will be building up inside the boathouse. A spark could set it off."

Nate nodded and moved nearer to the door of the boathouse.

"Can you hear me, Bianca?" Nate called out.

"Yes. Don't come any closer. Are you alone?" Bianca asked.

"No. Jake Jorgenson is here with me."

Suddenly Nate spotted movement on the far side of the boathouse. The branches on the bushes shook and a furry brown head poked through the underbrush. Waldo's limp was more pronounced than before as he lumbered over to the end of the walkway. He stood motionless, panting and sniffing the air.

Jake swore under his breath, motioning with his arm for the dog to sit. Whether he understood or not, Waldo dropped down on the walkway.

"Bianca," Jake shouted. "It's all over now. Don't make it worse by hurting Clare."

"Stand where I can see you," Bianca shouted.

Jake moved next to Nate, in line with the doorway.

Mumbled voices could be heard inside the boathouse. Nate assumed that Clare was trying to convince Bianca to give herself up. There was silence for a minute or two then Clare's voice could be heard.

"She says she won't come out as long as you're holding the rifle, Jake."

The older man's resistance to obey was almost a physical presence. Nate could see his knuckles whiten as he tightened his grip on the barrel.

"Put it down on the end of the walkway or I'll shoot her again," Bianca shrieked.

"All right. All right," Jake said, teeth gritted with his anger.

Very slowly Jake moved to the end of the wooden planks and set the rifle down. As he bent over, he whispered to Nate.

"Be ready to grab Clare," he said, then aloud, "It's down. Let her go."

Nate tensed as Clare's figure appeared in the doorway. Bianca was behind her, one hand gripping Clare's hair, the other holding a gun against her side. Rivulets of blood ran down one of Clare's legs and her face was a mask of pain. He started forward, but was stopped by Bianca's harsh voice.

"Don't move, Nate, or I swear to God I'll kill her."

At the sound of her voice, Waldo sprang to his feet and a low savage growl rumbled up his throat. Bianca whirled to face the new threat, holding Clare as a shield.

Waldo lowered his body into a crouch and took a step closer as he continued to growl.

"Call your dog off," Bianca cried. "Get him away from me."

Taking advantage of the distraction, Nate slipped along the wooden planks, closing the distance between himself and the nearly hysterical Bianca. Sensing his movement, Bianca backed up toward the door of the boathouse. Waldo took another step forward, his teeth bared in a snarl.

"Get away," Bianca screamed, pulling the gun away from Clare's side and aiming it at the dog.

In an instant, Nate leaped forward and grabbed Clare's arm and pulled her away. Bianca swung the gun back toward them and pulled the trigger.

The bullet hit Nate in the shoulder, jerking him sideways against the wall of the boathouse, but he managed to keep his grip on Clare. He literally dragged her along the wooden walkway, until he reached the end, then stumbled off onto the path. Still holding Clare, he fell to his knees, rolling so that he took her weight as he landed on the ground. He shifted so that he held her cradled in his lap, his back toward the boathouse. Turning his head, he stared over his shoulder at the three figures frozen in a deadly tableau.

Bianca stood in the doorway of the boathouse, the gun pointed at Waldo who was only two feet away. The dog was motionless, the hair standing up on his back and his lips pulled back from his teeth as he continued to growl at her. Jake was at the other end of the walkway, his rifle aimed at Bianca.

"Are you all right, Clare?" Jake asked, never taking his eyes off Bianca.

"Yes." Clare tightened her arms around Nate's waist.

"Nate?"

"Just my shoulder."

Waldo growled, the sound deep in his throat.

"Get that dog away from me," Bianca screamed.

"It was you who hurt him," Jake said.

"I should have beaten him to death. Call him off or I swear I'll shoot him."

"You can't shoot him." Jake's voice was a monotone as if the effort to speak was too much for him. "You're out of bullets."

She looked down at the gun in her hand then jerked her head up and aimed it again at Waldo. "You're lying," she snapped.

"I know that gun. It holds six bullets. It's the gun you used to shoot Lily Newton. You shot her three times. Clare shot it once. You shot Clare just before we arrived and the last bullet you used to shoot Nate."

Jake spoke each word distinctly, the volume of his voice increasing until he was almost shouting. He lowered the rifle and called out to the dog.

"Come, Waldo. Come here." His tone was commanding.

The dog was motionless for a moment then shook his head as if to clear it. His limp was less pronounced as he came toward Jake who moved backward, coaxing the dog until he was beside Nate and Clare at a safe distance from the boathouse.

"Sit." Waldo flopped down beside Clare, who buried her face in his fur. "Stay."

Jake turned back to face Bianca.

"I'm telling you, Bianca, the gun is empty. It's totally useless."

"You're lying." She spat the words out but there was a quiver of doubt in her voice. "You can't know."

"Yes, I can. That's my gun."

Clare caught her breath and stared at Jake. She knew immediately what he meant. She understood why she had trusted him so easily and confided in him without reservation. Somewhere in her heart she had always known he was her father.

"It can't be," Bianca said. She pointed the gun directly at him. "If you're Jimmy Newton, the police won't believe anything you say. This time they'll have the murder weapon and there's no one alive who can prove your innocence."

"You're delusional, Bianca. The truth always comes out. What will your tombstone read when you're gone? Will Olli still love you when he knows what you've done?"

"I did it all to protect him. You should have been dead."

Bianca was defiant. She pointed the gun at Jake and pulled the trigger. There was a sharp click as the hammer fell on the empty chamber.

"I was dead." Jake's voice was toneless. "The moment you killed Lily, I had no desire to go on living. I was a walking dead man. You took away twenty-five years of my life. You stole my wife and my child. You stole Clare's childhood. May you rot in hell."

He raised the rifle to his shoulder. He peered through the scope, settling on a target. He fired and the bullet slammed into the metal letterbox inside the boathouse. The sparks were visible in the darkness of the room. The gasoline vapors ignited. A fireball billowed upward and the boathouse exploded.

Shards of wood and other scraps flew through the air. Eyes closed, Jake stood motionless on the fringe of the maelstrom. Nate did his best to protect Clare from the falling debris. She was curled up, sandwiched between his body and the dog. Her body shook with wave after wave of tremors. Nate shook his head to clear the echoes of the explosion from his ears.

The fire was still burning where the boathouse used to be. Bushes and shrubs had been singed by the blast but the clearing behind the boathouse kept the fire from spreading farther into the woods. There was no sign of Bianca and he assumed she was buried beneath the pile of smoldering rubble.

Waldo woofed hoarsely and lumbered to his feet. He nuzzled Clare then limped over to stand beside Jake. The old man's face and hands were dotted with blood and dust from the storm of wood chips that had cut his skin like a million razor blades. Jake placed a bloody hand on top of Waldo's head and the dog leaned against his leg.

"Is she gone?" Clare asked.

"Yes," Nate said. The one word said it all. "Let me see your leg."

The mention of Clare's injury brought Jake out of his state of shock. He put the rifle down on the ground and hurried over to look down at Clare, sitting on the grass.

"God, Clare, I'm sorry we didn't get here earlier," Jake said.

There was a bloody gash on the outside of her thigh where Bianca had shot her. Jake reached in his pocket for a folded handkerchief at the same time that Nate brought out his.

"Your choice, Clare," Nate said.

"I'll take them both," she said, smiling through her tears.

Nate folded the handkerchief and placed it on the wound, then tied the second one tightly around her leg to stop the bleeding. The muscles beneath her skin rippled and he leaned over and kissed her on the lips. In the distance he heard the high-pitched wail of the fire trucks, grateful that someone had heard the explosion or seen the smoke and called it in.

"The paramedics will be here soon," he said. "Stay as quiet as you can, Clare."

"How's the shoulder?" Jake asked, his voice gruff with suppressed emotion.

Nate pealed back his sports jacket to look at his shoulder. His knit shirt was soaked with blood.

"Oh God, Nate," Clare said. "How bad is it?"

Nate moved his arm gingerly. "I don't think the bullet hit anything vital."

The sirens appeared to be getting closer. It occurred to Nate that he should have called Jon Fogt. He rose to his feet and reached in his pocket for his cell phone. He was just about to punch in the code when he noticed the expression on Jake's face. The older man was staring down at Clare with such longing in his eyes that it brought home to Nate how much Jake had lost.

"Clare, I'd like to be the one to officially introduce you to your father."

Like the child she once was, Clare held her arms out. Jake knelt down beside her and folded her into his embrace. Head against his chest, she closed her eyes. Jake bent his head and spoke quietly into her ear.

For a moment Nate felt a stab of jealousy seeing the glow of pleasure on Clare's face. In such a short time she had become so much a part of his life that he wanted to be the one to bring joy into her life. As if she were privy to his thoughts, she opened her eyes. The look she gave him told him all that he needed to know about their future together. She had broken through the conspiracy of silence to find her identity. She would have the family she had always sought. He, Jimmy, and Erika would be a part of her new life.

His mouth widened in a grin as he keyed in the police chief's number. Sirens shrilled closer. Waldo lumbered to his feet, standing protectively beside the two figures on the ground as Nate raised the phone to his ear.

ACKNOWLEDGMENTS

To Bob and Pat Gussin and Sue Greger for their continued support and encouragement. It's an honor and a pleasure to be a part of the Oceanview Publishing family. Special thanks to Mary Adele Bogdon and Maryglenn McCombs for all their help with promotion and publicity. You make me look good. To Margaret Watson for veterinarian advice and a sense of humor. To Principal James T. Smokrovich and Mary Eidelbes of Grand Rapids High School for their help getting the details right. To all the people I met in Grand Rapids who were so friendly and generous in helping me learn about the area. Although I've changed some of the details of the town, I hope I've given a sense of the beauty and hospitality that I found there. And always to Bill who is responsible for so much joy in my life.